JONATHAN C. BLAZER

Billy Dan

First edition

This book was professionally typeset on Reedsy.
Find out more at reedsy.com

Also I heard the voice of the lord, saying whom shall I send, and who will go for us? Then said I, Here am I; send me. Isaiah 6:8 King James Version (KJV)

Preface

In February 2020, I underwent surgery that left me bedridden for nearly two months. I lost thirty-eight pounds and spent far too much time alone in my apartment. In March 2020, I published my second novel, *Beyond These Fences*. Back then, my mind was always focused on the next book. Pandemic or not, I was constantly looking ahead to my next story. By May 2020, I had written most of *Billy Dan*, with around 90% of the book completed.

But years of self-destructive behavior had finally caught up with me. Coupled with the surgery and the uncertainties of 2020, I crashed—hard. For the first time in my life, I found myself unable to write. It felt like a part of me had been severed, lost to time, and never to return. I spiraled for years, unable to find an outlet in writing. My sense of identity and confidence dissolved, and I turned to self-medication.

By the time I washed up on the shores of South Carolina, I was at my lowest point. I had pushed away everyone who cared about me, spent all my money, and was set on drinking myself into an early grave. But sometimes, when you're at your lowest, your heart is most open—finally asking the right questions. It was then that I found God and finally experienced peace in my life. It wasn't easy, but time does heal all wounds. Once I began to recover, I started writing again—doing the one thing I never thought I would do again.

I had convinced myself that I couldn't write, that I had forgotten how. But slowly, I began again, bit by bit. In May 2024, I rewrote *Billy Dan*, bringing with me everything I had learned over the past few years. I believe in the limitless nature of God's love, no matter what happens. *Billy Dan* is a simple story about a man trying to do the right thing—something we can all relate to these days. I hope you enjoy his story, and whenever or wherever you read this, know that I love you all. Thank you for your time.

Acknowledgments

I want to express my deep gratitude to the many people who helped me bring this book to completion over the past four years. First, to my test readers—Libby, David, Alex, Jeremy, and Elizabeth—thank you all, for everything! And a special, heartfelt thank you to Elizabeth and Mark. You both helped transform my humble story about a garbage man into so much more than I ever thought it could be. Thank you, everyone.

Chapter 1

"I think it's pronounced paraplegic," I responded, rolling the heavy nuclear death machine to a thundering stop—as a chattel of children crossed to a bus stop on the other side of the road. I shifted to neutral—the heavy garbage truck I was driving groaned in response to it. Not precisely an atomic rolling death machine, but ever been around the back end of a garbage truck on a long summer day, trust me—you would wish a bomb had fallen from the sky.

"Anyways, kid—I am an amputee, not paralyzed," I muttered to the kid stuffing his face with toast in the passenger seat adjacent to me. He chomped a piece of crust into his mouth, smacking his lips loudly inside the space garbage truck. That's saying something—enough room for an adult male to lie flat and take a quick nap while cleaning the city streets.

Jacob turned in his seat, bread falling from his face as he wiped the crumbs away with the back of his hand. I sighed, "Use a napkin, man, come on," I muttered, offering him a napkin from my lunch box. He took the napkin gingerly, wiping his face.

"Okay, but if you're missing part of your left hand and right leg—how can you ever become a detective?" the kid asked inquisitively. I sat up straighter, pumping out my chest, "Same way I do things now, just less driving, I suppose," I proclaimed as the last child crossed the road and the chaperon waved. I waved back, starting the massive truck, rolling forward, and crossing onto the next street. The kid looked unconvinced, "I don't know Billy Dan, I've seen you struggle to open the lid of some of the garbage cans,"

I grumbled, "First of all—those lids are seriously heavy by yourself. Secondly, for some reason, I keep finding a ten-year-old eating toast inside them, and thus, I try to be cautious. Thirdly, shut up, kid!"

The kid laughed, "I'm just joking, old man. I'm also eleven. Just for your information," he stated matter-of-factly.

"Yeah, well, if you want to live to see twelve, stop digging through the garbage; come on, man. You will get sick—plus it worries your mother," I responded, slowly easing down a suburban road. "How come I must stop if you do it every morning, Billy Dan?" he asked.

I sighed, "Because I get paid to do it because I am the adult. So there," I shot back. "Yeah, but you could pay me, then it wouldn't matter," I looked at the kid, exasperated, as he finished eating his toast in one giant bite. "Do you even taste that when you eat?"

He rolled his eyes, "That's an absurd question. You can't taste toast," he responded.

"I don't think it works like that," I muttered.

He shrugged, "Why not? The world is a weird place. You're missing two limbs and driving a dump truck. I am a kid eating toast after scoring a cool bubble head," he produced a round-headed figure from his filthy backpack. Half of its face is melted off, but I can still make out the round face of one of the teenage ninja turtle guys. I can't remember which one had the brown bandanna, though. The kid was always finding weird stuff—I had to give him props, though; I didn't know many who were willing to dive into the dumpster for almost any reason. The kid called it treasure hunting. I called it the little weirdo that would cause me to have a heart attack one of these days.

"You risked getting sick for a toy? And you call me absurd?" I shouted to him. He shrugged again. "Billy Dan, you must live your life sometimes for stupid reasons. Don't think, just do," he replied.

"What—the—I'm not taking life advice from a kid! That's just ridiculous!" I responded angrily.

The kid smiled, "See—is life just absurd. Rolling down the streets in a tank—worried about the semantics and ethics of pursuing one's dreams.

They don't have to make sense; they just have to give you something to do," he stated.

I blinked at that one as I reached the driveway to his mother's house. "You're a weird kid, you know that?" I stated.

"You're a good man, Billy Dan," he stated as the door to his suburban home flew open. Even in the early morning light, his mom was beautiful. At best, she came up to the truck door—even with a slender frame, she held herself strongly. Round brown eyes framing a button nose and soft chin. Her dark skin shined as her shoulders relaxed, and the worry fell from her eyes. She was used to me dropping off Jacob while he was out on one of his hunts. The small, pleasant bun she wore bounced lightly as she approached the garbage truck. It always warmed me to see her; I felt a big grin stretch across my face at the sight of her.

"Seriously though, kid, stop picking through the garbage. You're going to give your mother a stroke," I stated.

That caused the kid's smile to dip into a frown as his mother scolded him with an intensity that would make a grown man cower. Officer Genesis Martinez was all of five feet nothing, but don't tell her that—she always carried herself with a grace that only a mother could, yet with a square of her shoulders like she was about to check someone into the ground. Jacob looked like Gen, along with all her other many kids.

In response to seeing her, he slid down the seat, "Oh no, she's mad," he muttered.

"Good luck, kid," I said as the tiny woman's hands flew open the passenger door of the heavy garbage truck.

"What is the matter with you—Jacob!" his mother scolded as she pulled the boy into a deep hug. She closed her eyes, and I looked away. I never felt right watching people have their moments together. It was not that it was some repressed childhood emotion about love and affection; it just felt weird spying on people's moments. We don't get enough of those in life—so I won't watch it like an episode on Animal Planet with morbid fascination. When they were done hugging, Jacob exited the truck and sauntered up the walkway leading into the small but cozy house. "Wipe your feet off before entering the house, son. Don't you dare even think about sitting on a couch, young man?" Genesis shouted to her son. The boy bowed his head and muttered, "Yes, ma'am," as he reached the door, taking off his shoes.

She sighed, noticing me for the first time. Her lips moved slowly, dancing before me. "Thank you, Billy Dan. I know—I know he's a bit weird, but," she sighed heavily. I don't know what to do with him. That was what, the fifth time this week? I don't know how to convince him to stay inside, and I am worried one day he might—" she flushed, looking down.

"He's a weird kid; he's smart, though. Don't worry about it," I beamed until her frown turned into a smile.

She snorted, "Leave it to you, Billy Dan, always staying positive—I don't know how you do it," she said softly, reaching out her hand. I took it, kissing it softly. "I make great morning coffee and drink lots of juice," I stated.

Genesis laughed again as the radio on her chest sparked to life. She pulled her hand back, clicking the radio on as a fury of codes exchanged between her and the dispatcher. I let her focus as I looked up the long streets. I patrolled twelve blocks, taking out the trash and carrying it to our town's landfills and processing centers.

This is my home. I thought as the summer leaves slowly started to change into the onset of reds, yellows, and browns. Leaves from the vines, whose roots extended far past the simple nature of summer and fall—here before us, here forever more after we are gone.

She turned back, her face a panel of worry as she closed her eyes, gathering her thoughts for a moment. "Guess we have to cut this short—still on for tonight?" she beamed. I smirked at her. "Are you kidding? A chance to see you in a cute dress; I may take out your trash, but I'm not stupid, I know when I've found a treasure." I stated as she smiled.

"Thanks for always being you, Billy Dan," she stated, returning to her house. "Catch you later, alligator," she smiled once more before walking away.

I called back, "See you around, crocodile," as I put the garbage truck into drive rolling down the streets.

4

Chapter 2

I was parked on the curve waiting for Larry to move his butt already. We were behind schedule—and Larry was trying to flirt with one of the girls as he stood next to a pile of trash. I didn't bother watching what happened next. I heard a slap and a shout of the words, "Pig!". A few moments later, the mechanism for the automatic crusher went forward as Larry slapped the side of the truck, signaling that it was time to go to the next stop.

The passenger door swung open. Larry slung into the seat, slamming the door. I waited, staring at my coworker until he sighed, turning his hat backward and ballooning his hair out at the front. He needed a haircut; I would cut the kid some slack. His cheeks were blistering red from where he was hit.

"Larry," I stated.

He muttered, "Fine," buckling in his seatbelt as I put the truck in gear and started on the winding road to our next stop. "How did it go, big guy?" I asked him as he lit a cigarette. "I just don't get it, man—here you are with a beautiful woman like Genesis, and you can't even run on two legs. What am I doing wrong?" he stated.

I chuckled, "I would say—probably stop hitting on people at work. No one wants to hear a pickup line from a grown man while he is holding bags of trash with baseball cap-backwords on his head," I replied. I added, "Maybe get some rest. You look like a basement-dwelling troglodyte," I jabbed. Plus, women can sense when you're trying too hard. It's just a talent they have," I said.

He leered at me, and I glanced at him from the corner of my eye. I was being

5

too hard on the kid. "Start by saying hello. Maybe notice your surroundings more, and I don't know. Be slightly more complimentary without coming off like a starving tiger," I stated.

"Hey now, I wasn't looking that much—I wasn't that hungry," he replied gloomily.

I rolled my eyes, "Quit messing around; write down this block stats already," I directed as Larry opened the glove department, mumbling while he took out a clipboard containing the time between each stop and an estimate of what we threw into the back of the truck.

I thought Larry grumbled, writing something on the clipboard—he was a jerk, but he was my jerk. Everyone must have someone to support them somehow; life isn't as bright without that. However, he wouldn't have been my first pick for a partner.

We reached the end of the block. I put the truck into neutral and pulled us to a stop. "How about you stay in the truck? Let me get this one," I stated, opening the driver's door. I secured a pair of working gloves to my hands from my belt. Carefully pulling the left glove over my prosthetic fingers. Larry watched me do this without saying anything and muttered, "Yeah, okay, it stinks in here anyways," he joked, pulling out his phone—his fingers blurring away as he pecked at his keyboard. He lived on his phone—and couldn't show up on time to save his life. But able to send a text faster and quicker than a lightning bolt.

He looked at the watch on his wrist, "Think we have time to go to the spot after this?" he asked, almost pleading like a child. I looked at the dashboard clock; it read eight am. "We don't have to be in the office until ten—I guess a few rounds wouldn't hurt anything," I stated as Larry smiled. "My guy," he cheered, turning up the radio. I closed the truck door to the booming music as I went back to the dumpster.

I breathed deeply before picking up bags and tossing them into the container.

There was a small bookshelf, and the top bowed in. Cheap plywood manufactured a few dozen an hour. I squatted down, wrapping my hands around the wood, lifting with my knees, coming up with the wood, and coming down. I did this ten times before I set it back down again. I counted to twenty and repeated it ten more times.

My legs burned, and the sun beat hot overhead as I wiped the sweat from my brow. Larry honked the horn from inside the truck cab. "Dude, what's taking you so long? I want to get my Mc-something on," he shouted as I picked the bookcase up one last time and threw it into the back of the garbage truck.

I wiped the sweat from my forehead, smiling as I did so, catching my breath before I returned to the truck. Larry glared at me before his face scrunched into a frown, "I don't get you, man; if it was too heavy or something, you could have just left it. They don't pay us enough for this crap anyways," he muttered, dashing his ashes into the floorboard again. I sighed, handing him the makeshift ashtray we had made out of an old soda can. Piles of the gray flakes swam out as he jammed the butt of the cigarette deep into the tin.

"Yeah, totally, and next, we should just quit working altogether and stack piles of trash over the mayor's lawn—what do you think?" I joked to Larry.

Larry took me in for a long moment, his brown eyes considering the possibilities. "Yeah, maybe that could work, but I don't want to get fired. I kind of need this job," he muttered.

"Totally," I agreed, starting the truck as we continued to our next stop.

Chapter 3

I tossed the golf ball into the air as Larry smacked it with the fluorescent bulb, shattering glass over the back of the empty lot of the old wood mill. I watched the glass litter the already considerable pile around our feet rather than Larry's hit. Larry hadn't missed one yet; the kid seemed to enjoy it. Which was okay for me and gave me time to eat my lunch in peace without having to constantly have a conversation with him. For a tech nerd, he was never shy about anything.

I finished my chicken, tucking the container back into my backpack. "Did you see that, Billy Dan? I am pretty sure it went over the state line!" shouted Larry, covering his eyes from the rising morning sun.

"Maybe, man; I think we are a few miles from the border, though," I stated, zipping my bag and throwing it over my shoulder as I stood slowly, extending my good leg up first, making sure to keep the weight primarily off of my bad leg. Larry looked at me, "You always think you're so smart—you and your tiny container of chicken everyday. Just plain old chicken and rice. Just like Billy Dan. Plain and old. Do you ever eat anything else?" he asked crumbling up his bag of fast food.

"Keeps me nice and lean," I replied.

"Lean is just like tits on a bull Billy Dan. You need muscles like these," Larry gestured, rolling his sleeves as he flexed.

"You sure, right," I smiled as I gestured towards the broom we kept behind the store. "Break time is over; let's get this cleaned up already."

Larry looked at me inquisitively. "Why does it matter? We're the only ones who came back here," he said.

"Because we come back here. Now, start cleaning," I handed him the dustpan, and the younger man rolled his shoulders as I swept the glass into the pan. Our day was just about over.

We both crawled back into the truck, this time Larry driving. Dropping his cigarette onto the ground we had just cleaned. I glared at him; Larry didn't notice. I shook my head and rolled down the window. It was hot in the truck, the garbage in the back worming its way into our bones. The Carolinas were funny that way; it could be freezing first thing in the morning, then back to a blistering, borderline Florida-level heat. That made the smell of trash something that seeped into your bones after a while. No matter how much I cleaned myself, I could always smell something slightly rotten.

"It's Thursday, right?" Larry asked.

"Yeah, what about it?" I responded.

"I hate Thursdays..." he trailed off as we left the old wood mill.

I knew why he had said it; Thursday meant we had to collect the trash from the Fellowship. It was never easy with those people; if we were lucky, they would be inside doing who knows what behind their twisted dark walls. Something about people dressed all in white—more jewelry than what should ever be allowed on a person—while proclaiming themselves as the only ones who could save people bothered me. It also bothered Larry—as we both knew, they didn't believe in any outright God. Just sort of some moral conviction that always seemed to stick its nose into everyone's business and declare them a sinner because they stepped on the wrong crack in the middle of the road. New age weirdos if you asked me.

Still, loud wheels that squeak get the grease—if they new age people were anything it was loud. I kept those thoughts to myself as we neared their compound.

"What do you think they actually do in there? Eat babies?" Larry asked.

"Yeah, maybe. If they do, they probably need a lot of hot sauce. Babies are floppy and smell funny," I stated.

Larry laughed dryly as we both eyed their compound. It was fenced in and surrounded by signs stating, "Private property," but on the front of their massive coned "Church," hung, "All are welcome, EXCEPT for undesirables." I wondered who the undesirables were as we pulled up next to their garbage bin. That was probably people like me, I prayed—I think a few years ago. Never got into the whole religion thing. Wasn't going to start now. I had pulled myself up by my own bootstraps. That was enough for me. Larry slid out of the driver's seat, "You stay in; you take way too long," he said, leaving the door wide open. I thought, sliding over into the driver's seat, you don't have to tell me twice. Keeping my eyes on the church. The blinds were shut tight. The painting on the outside glowed with an almost peach hue while the highlight of white crested the afternoon sun. Giving the church an appearance that it would take off at any moment.

It gave me the creeps, making my back sweat. It wasn't that it looked like a gothic cathedral that screamed something terrible was happening there. Or the signs of some kind of dark cult. It was that it was far too perfect. Every shingle was perfectly cut, molded, and fit in such a way that nothing was wasted. The tar seemed brand new, as if it had been done the day before. The gutters gleamed like pearly whites in the mouth of a great white shark.

Tall carnival glass loomed like rainbow shadows, casting thousands of lights in every direction, supposed to convey a feeling of inclusion and diversity of thoughts welcomed under a single nest egg of modern-age religiosity.

Instead, it made my spine want to run in the opposite direction of my legs as fast as possible. Record-breaking sprints to safety. I found myself sweating—even more than the hot day would call for. I was practically going to need to change my shirt at this rate.

I watched Larry disappear behind the green dumpsters, lids that also seemed out of place. Something about pristine garbage can feel unnatural to behold—like a dog that doesn't want to roll in mud. Just felt off to me.

I pulled my shirt collar, glancing through the elephant-eared mirrors on the garbage truck's side—the coast was clear. I let out a breath. I was holding—she wouldn't be here today, but it was a nice and easy end of the day. Technically, the fellowship building of Souls Salvation was supposed to be one of our first stops. But, coming out this way—it wasn't visiting a fellowship—it was visiting a compound of doom that radiated a zealous warning that never felt like anything close to salvation. I just couldn't pinpoint what always set me off about the place. It certainly was an off-putting place, more like a place where the preacher man stole from you as you put your meager pennies into the collection plate.

I slowly started to hum to take away the tension. The radio in the cab had long since gone in and out. Now was an out time, which didn't help with the situation. When you feel uneasy about a place, silence just makes you paranoid.

I glanced at the dashboard clock; the green letters read "9:57." If Larry hurried, we could be out of here in the next three minutes before anyone was the wiser, and we could take off. A light caught my eyes, so I covered them with my hand before squinting at the snake charmer that approached the driver's window.

She seemed as perfidious as pulchritudinous. The kind of body that would make any man or woman sell you their soul for pennies on the dollar just for a night of bliss and still leave you wishing you had more to trade. But, if you resisted the charm of the superficial curves that rested on her oval face under the tussle of black sea hair, you'd uncover glaring dark eyes that were closer to a reptile than that of a human. Dark and void of anything that could resemble comfort or trust. She was instantly likable and charismatic enough to make you fall in love, but love can always be an expressway paved to Hell with a gold topcoat so pristine, you couldn't imagine your destination was destruction.

That was her—a con artist of the highest accounts. An angel of light by most accounts. All of that wasn't what scared me the most about her. The world is filled with more spiders than lions. If you knew the signs, you could pick them up instantly. What made her dangerous scared me enough to honestly send my metal leg shaking. She knew I knew what she was. Instead of the blank void of nothingness, her eyes flashed at others—for me, it was pure rage—a hunger so ravenous that it could swallow planets. When you know the darkness's true face, it will never let you go, an unbreakable stranglehold shadowed by the essence of fear: you knew what it was. Therefore, you were the only prey it could not hunt. As far as a monster was concerned, that made you a glowing torch in the gloomiest of nights.

I knew I could see what she really was: fraudulent. Or just a "pain in my butt," I muttered as she came up to the driver's door, eyes wide. "Hello Billy Dan! Beautiful morning to you!" she stated casually.

"Morning Mel—" I started before she cut me off.

"I find it funny that they still let you keep your job since the trash has been here for weeks now," she gestured to a heap of metal—wheels flattened down to the rims. A canopy that looked like it had been smashed in by an elephant. The colors washed away to a dull gray, some of the former dark green remaining. An orange sign in big, bold letters pronounced, "JUNK," scribbled across the broken windshield.

I rolled my eyes so far in the back of my head that I became momentarily concerned they wouldn't return again. "Melanie, for the last time, I told you—we are not a tow truck service. We are waste disposals, and there is a difference. I'm sure even your lazy butt can afford to get up—look up a number and make a phone call," I shot back. She narrowed her eyes as Larry finished throwing the last bag of trash and became aware of her—his mouth opening up and slowly closing.

She smirked, "We shall see about that," as she walked towards Larry. A slow tilt from side to side that offered a sensual view for anyone, poor Larry never stood a chance. "Barry, you beautiful boy—be a dear and help me with something, would you," she spoke velvety. "It's— Larry—ma'am," Larry stumbled, his words out, his cheeks flushing red as he looked at the ground. I could tell he was trying hard not to stare as she leaned against the truck with one hand. Her chest is out.

"Don't trust a snake, Billy Dan," I told myself as Larry was like a lost puppy dog following her around. "That's nice, dear. Come along," Melanie stated again, walking past Larry to the front of the church. Her long legs quickly moved in the distance. Larry dropped the bags in his hands, almost at a full sprint to catch up to her before slowing down to match a few steps behind her.

I rubbed my eyes and opened the door—listening to the sound of grated wheels being drug across the road as a group of people—clothed in all white pushed what appeared to be a small old freezer. The lid showed weld marks along the top. Crude smudges of twisted metal cast lights in several directions—I squinted my eyes at the sight. The group I noticed wasn't actually pushing, save for one beast.

After a few moments, he came full into view, a man who stood taller than the others and made the others appear to be children next to him. A body thick with muscle at almost absurd levels of proportion. I made a mental note of the man, taking in his unremarkable face, covered in acne scars, dotting it like miniature graters along his tan, bronzed skin. All of them were wearing white ropes with words proclaiming that all were welcome.

The rest, by comparison, were a lot smaller—but ten in total, after a quick count, were in their twenties to mid-thirties—some looked like teenagers. Young and of various sizes and ethnicities, it could have been anyone from town. One or two, though, I had seen at some point along my routes. The outside fringe, I noted, was people who wouldn't stand out from a crowd like the big man over there. Still though, with Melanie being the closest thing to a living walking syringe of white-hot drugs and a muscled brute whose weight I swore made the truck move. Combined that with their assortments of pristine glowing clothes, they stood out like a poodle in the middle of a German Shepherd puppy sale. An interesting pair I suppose.

I tried to take in their faces and associate what I thought they would look like outside the white ropes they wore. The chains around their necks appeared to glow under the rising sun. The latches holding them hadn't been used, which made me nervous. None of these people seemed fully aware or bothered by the hot day. None looked like they could have used a torch to weld that lid down without burning off a limb, either, I thought.

On cue, a more petite man with shaky-length hair and a ruffle of blonde hair mixed in with brown came around the corner. I noted his hands were puffed out, twisted, and gnarled, covered with callous—a local down at the repair shop in town, I imagined. Black specks and a small patch of missing hair along his forearms told me there was our welder. I also had a good idea who he was.

The benefit of a small town is that everyone has met everyone. Charlie was the name, if I recall, though I had no idea why he would be joined by people like this. Charlie never spoke much whenever I brought my car in; they just asked what I wanted and told me how much. I didn't take him for the type to be with this crowd.

Melanie followed my gaze as I approached the side of the truck. A slow, liquid smile crossed her face that normally would have made anyone's heart explode with excitement. Mine just filled with dread. She stopped moving, and Larry almost ran into her because he had not looked ahead. He shook his head, flushing red for a brief moment.

"This is just far too heavy for us—going to need some help, my dear," she stated, pressing the back of her palm against her forehead.

Larry's mouth drooled so much I thought he could fill a swimming pool. I rolled my eyes, getting out of the truck. I wasn't about to lose my partner to an evil witch. Besides, we still had a few more routes left, which wasn't challenging even with two hands. The big guy eyed me with a calm gaze. I cast back my own steady look. He held himself like someone who was trained—someone dangerous. A lot of people mistake a large body for strength, and to an extent, that was true, but when it came to the art of dealing out butt kickings—experience mattered.

The way he eyed me told me he wasn't messing around. Crippled or not, he would destroy me if I miss-stepped. Hired muscle, but why did a church need muscle? I kept that thought as I approached the growing list of details that would make Sherlock Holmes blush as the day went on. I hadn't even had my lunch break yet—I was getting cranky by the minute.

I stepped in between Melanie and Larry—cutting off her trance from my partner. She frowned at me, and Larry shook his head. Visibly confused by what just happened. "Like we've told you about the car—Melanie, we are waste disposals for the city, not personal junk collectors," I gestured towards the freezer. "If you want that thing removed, call the city, make an appointment, and have a nice day," I stated, leaving before her retort as I took Larry by the elbow.

"So, the garbage man thinks he is too good for the garbage. Think he is above everyone else, huh?" she spat, her mask slipping. Melanie knew full

14

well that we weren't going to take her junk. It was a power play, plain and simple. Every time we came by the church, she would lure Larry closer and closer to the doors. To what end, I had no idea. But, nothing good could come of it. When a group of people declare themselves righteous and anyone else besides them as evil, walk away—you're playing by their terms. Their games. You have no chance at winning like that.

"I am pretty sure I pay taxes to this city. It must mean I am kind of your boss," she called out to me as we made it to the truck. I paused at that one; Larry had already turned back. "I think," Larry started before I cut him off. My shoulders rolled back. If she wanted a fight, I would give her a fight.

"Go ahead, lady, tell us what you want us to do. The nice thing about this job is I get to decide what's the trash—not some prissy woman in her bathrobe." I pointed at her, maintaining eye contact with her as she smirked.

"We will see about that—Billy Dan," she hissed, and I felt something cold trace up my back. "Such a hateful man that cares nothing about his community—his world around him. Just a few bags of waste, a crummy paycheck so you can go home and drink your $5 beer and put your endless woes into your hands?" she stated.

I glared at her; our relationship had always been like this. She wouldn't stop until she found an end. And she would. She would call my boss, complain about everything under the sun, twisting my words until nothing resembled what was said. It was her way of saying, "That's what you get for not complying." Luckily for me, my boss was a close to retirement old woman. Most days she was deaf and very nearly blind. A kind, short lady who smiled at everyone and even took the time to learn their names. Her son, though, was a different story. It was worth it, though—any chance I got to kick the creepy hippie's teeth in was worth it. Regardless, I wasn't all that worried.

I cut her yard every other weekend, and she had little patience with bossy people doing their best to get her employees fired. She knew better than to trust the words of a "good intention" stranger over her own people. I would do anything for that old gal; even Larry would. I sighed, gritting my teeth to slow down before I said too much. I couldn't win against a person like her, but that didn't make me any less angry. I hated bullies, and this one made

15

me want to kick her where the sun would never shine—all the way up her pompous jerk.

I opted to be polite. I put on my biggest smile. "Thank you for the feedback," I turned again as she shouted one last retort. "Don't forget to come out tonight, Larry—we are meeting in Central Park... Be seeing you, garbage man," she mocked as I closed the truck door, slapping the side with my metal hand, and drove the grumbling machine onto our next stop.

Chapter 4

We finished the rest of the day in silence. Larry couldn't put his finger on why I had such a problem with Melanie. We've had the talk plenty of times. He respected me enough to stop questioning me about it, though. He was just at that age—the age where no amount of talking could get a man to realize that good looks weren't the only requirement for a woman to be considered reasonable. It was just after noon as we pulled into the last stop. I finished filling out our chart as Larry exited the driver's seat.

I gave him a look, and the truck's engine was still running. "I got this one," he said before I could object, leaving the truck as I sighed, turning the truck off. Larry quickly disappeared out of sight. He never moved that fast, I thought. I looked at the driver's seat. Sweat stains drenched over the cracked leather seats. The steering wheel looked moist as well. That was weird; what was he so nervous about? I thought just as my thoughts were interrupted by Larry shouting, "damn."

My heart skipped its rhythm. The normal beats a lonely forgotten sound tossed into a new thunderous "drum." Instantaneously, the chemicals that spin a human being from a doughy sack of meat into a jet engine that could save or destroy almost anything in its path flooded every cell in my body.

Call it whatever you like, some form of post-traumatic stress, or maybe just being high-strung, but when someone I care about uses that pitch, my heart comes close to exploding out of my chest in fear. Fear was great fuel if you utilized it correctly, though; I used mine to do what needed to be done. At that moment, as I kicked open the passenger door, landing on the ground below, my metal leg shaking along the clamps that kept it tight almost gave out. I swore as I lost my balance momentarily. I was going to fix that later, I noted, as I took off running to the other side of the truck.

Instinctively, I patted down my jacket pockets—swearing again. I had no weapons. I only had my mind, as my mother would tell me when I was a little boy. The only weapon I would ever need was my mind. I couldn't use my mind to take out the bad guy, I thought. Just would have to give it a try.

Which was exactly what I did. Think Billy Dan, calm down and use your head. I hunched over and peered under the garbage truck. Its lifted height due to the big wheels made it easy to peer onto the other side. I saw only one pair of legs—the cut-off cargo shorts that Larry wore as he stood next to a garbage can.

I let out my breath, rising again to my feet. Unless it was a giant bird, it was probably Larry dropping his cell phone again into a pile of diapers. A working hazard that we've all done if we were being honest in our line of work. I came around the truck slowly, my heart coming down from its fight mode as I scanned the wood line for anything that could be off. Just another sunny day in the neighborhood. Signs for the church dotted the landscape on nearly every pole, traffic stop, and even some people's yards. Even obscuring the bright smile of our mayor—his reelection boards looking half-ass in comparison to the iconography being deployed by the church. It was all just too bright and distracting.

I looked away, coming up to Larry. He was clutching his chest, a cigarette dangling from his lips as he muttered, staring into the garbage can. Inside was Jacob, the kid, a bag strapped tight to his shoulders. A mischievous smile pulled across his young face.

I paused, looking at the boy, a banana peel tussled in his black hair, which seemed to be doing its best to eat the fruit, like a swarm of black snakes atop his head. "What's going on, Jacob? How did you make it out here?" I asked him.

Larry glared at me, sweat rolling off his face as if all the water in his body was trying to escape all at once.

The boy answered in the awkward silence between the three of us, "Oh, you know, just finding some more stuff, Billy Dan," he stated as I noticed he clutched his black backpack straps closely.

Larry next to me seemed like he was about to jump out of his skin, shifting his eyes between the boy in the dumpster and me.

"Hey Billy Dan, do you think we could not tell my mom about this? She's still kind of mad about this morning," he blurted before trailing off, avoiding my glance. I blew out my lips, rubbing my eyes. We were off shift by now, but we still had to get the truck back to the lot.

"I'm sorry, Jacob, but we have to get the truck back. I will try to explain it to you," I started before Larry cut me off with a wave.

"Just get the kid out of here, I will finish this stop. Besides, I need to pick up something back at the office," Larry stated. I eyed him; something about how he kept looking at the garbage dumpster and how his shirt looked like it was about to slide off worried me. I sighed heavily; whatever it was, I just hoped it wasn't drugs again. We had an annual drug test coming up. Though I was no saint, this was a government job. Their stance on weed would never change, and Larry's eyes looked so red they could make a tomato blush. He just forever looked like he needed about twenty more hours of sleep. It was hard to tell with some people, though.

He was my friend. Now was no time to wonder about his behavior, especially in front of the kid. I sighed, "Alright, kid, let's get going. Stop doing this, though, alright. This isn't the best part of town," I gestured to the grimy buildings, many of which their structures swayed in the light breeze as if being blasted by a tornado. Bricks of red faded to a musky brown, and yellow would rot to earth shades of dirt.

I pulled Jacob out of the dumpster as he and I approached the bus stop. I looked back to see Larry frantically dig through the dumpster.

Jacob still clutched his bag in his hands as if it were the most important thing to him. Both of those points sent every alarm off in my head. I took a few deep breaths, ignoring this feeling that ran up my back. It wasn't my place to parent the boy, and it wasn't my place with Larry either. It was probably nothing to be worried about. Just Larry being weird and Jacob being well, Jacob. Both of them were still kids. I couldn't help but wonder as I turned Jacob around and made my way to the bus stop. My truck at home; I wished then that I had taken my truck for this kind of situation. That was life, though; you never could plan for it all. As I hummed, ignoring the weirdness in my stomach, I thought about one thing—it was odd that Larry had been digging through the can.

"Hey Billy Dan, I'm starving. Do you want to go get some toast?" the boy asked as the bus rolled to a stop sign, interrupting my thoughts.

Chapter 5

Crunches came from Jacobs's mouth as we sat on the mostly empty bus. A man at the front coughing lightly into his jacket, a youth looking out the window as the world passed us by, her music blaring through the headphones. With a huge bite, he finished the toast in his hands. Amazed, I asked him, "Did you taste that, kid?"

"Mostly—it was a bit dry, figured the faster I got it down, the less bland it would be," he stated.

I considered his words, made enough sense to me as we approached the local bridge that would lead us into the neighborhood section of the town. Along the way was a countryside littered with signs for the church and more pictures of the mayor. His green eyes gleamed like the color of rare gems. A smile that was just too good to suggest something other than distrust for me. But considering this would likely be his fourth term, what did I know? Small towns were like that; some even had Golden Retrievers for their Mayors.

I turned my attention back to Jacob. "Alright, kid. I got you the toast. Now, can you tell me at least how you got out here?"

Jacob glanced my way, his hands still tight around his backpack as it lay in his lap. "I wouldn't say it was toast," he started before seeing my gaze. "Please don't get mad—but—I sort of rode in the back of the truck," he admitted. I shook my head in disbelief, "Kid—that had to be at least ten miles or so. What were you thinking? You know your mom is busy; you shouldn't do that to her," I stated.

He looked down, "I know Billy Dan. I had no choice, though," he admitted. I squinted at that, "What do you mean you had no choice?" I asked back, trying to keep the concern out of my voice. "Just something I had to do?" he said with resolve.

I glanced up at the gum on the bus's ceiling. There was a lot I did not know and wish I didn't know. Kids generally only know a little because most adults hadn't the foggiest clue beyond something that wasn't on a laugh track. Kids had one advantage: they were more willing to seek out new answers than adults. Less stuck in their ways, far less jaded. I knew what Jacob was after was probably in his bags. I wanted to give the kid respect so he could tell me independently. Figure it all out for himself.

I nodded, "Sure, kid, I know what you mean. Just keep in mind that if you spend all your time chasing after something without telling the people around you what is happening, you will lose them, plain and simple," I informed him.

Jacob cast his eyes to the dirty bus floor, "Yeah, I know," he mumbled. An awkward silence stretched out between us. I grunted, trying to clear the air after my statement, "Look—I promise not to tell your mom about this time, okay. Just that is the last time. Can you promise me that, Jacob?" I asked the boy as this time his eyes shifted to the woods passing us by—the whole world seemed to move so quickly while we frantically tried to keep up, colors blended together like someone flipping through a picture book as fast as their eyes could manage. It made me wonder how much we missed while sitting on a bus. So much in just a few seconds it made my eyes want to burst.

"I can do that," he muttered again. I blew out my breath in tension. "Cool, enough of the serious crap," I waved my hand, catching his gaze. "I'm glad you found something to do and believe in—people need goals. We need dreams. The world is such a messy place; without something to do, we will go just bonkers—I mean, look at us already; we just visited a restaurant with a clown outside. Why would anyone in their right mind use someone to represent their company who smiles that much—it's just weird; how can someone with balloon hands be the best person to sell your burgers? Or, in your case, a dry hamburger bun." I joked.

Jacob smirked. "What are your dreams, Billy Dan?" he asked me. I blew out my lips, reaching into my cargo pockets, pulling out a stack of notecards. The rubber band holding them nearly ripped apart, and the ink smudged off from my continued use.

"Simple enough for me; I wanted to be a cop—just like your mom before I lost my hand and leg," I gestured towards my left hand, the triple Electrically powered hand prosthesis gleaming under the dull light above.

"That's so cool!" Jacob exclaimed, "You're like a machine—man—cop," he stated, touching the metal on the prosthetic. I smirked. "Yeah, kind of, but not one yet," I said.

He frowned. "You said you wanted to be one? A garbage man is way cooler. You get a nice truck and first dibs on anything you find. I hate that my mom does it. She's always tired when she comes home, spends most of her time mad or just plain sad about something," he trailed off.

I picked up before he could go to a hostile place again. " Well, yeah, I wanted to be one. I had trouble with the accident, but that's life. Now, I set my sights higher. I'm going to take the detective test tomorrow; help people like your mother and you," I gestured towards him.

He smiled, "How are you going to do that, Billy Dan, without your hand?" He looked at my hand and blushed. "Sorry—I didn't," he started as I waved him off, curling in my prosthetic fingers. The bands of metal react to the movement from my wrist, causing the mechanism within my hand to move to mimic the gestures of a real hand.

"That's so cool. How does it work?" Jacob asked inquisitively. I smiled at the boy, glad the tension from earlier had left his face. It's good he might actually listen, I thought. "Easy enough. It runs with cable-operated systems, combined with positional fingers that are fitted to move a certain way, like so," I gestured, flicking my wrist, causing my four mechanical fingers to move inwards.

"I like that a lot. Wait, how come this one is a different color?" Jacob asked, pulling on my thumb.

"That one is simple because it's real," I laughed as Jacob pulled back his hand. "Oh so, you're like only part robot—is that the same with your leg? How come you don't walk like a pirate? I've seen you walk around with my mom just fine. You even lift the garbage cans like they're nothing," he stated matter-of-factly.

I smiled again, "No, my whole right foot is gone, about six inches before my knee. I walk so well because I practice it a lot, Jacob—well, added a few things," I muttered, scratching my chin and thinking about the difficulties of learning to walk when I first got the prosthetic—falling on my face nearly every day. They struggle to just use the bathroom in the middle of the night. I was pissing my bed because I couldn't get out fast enough. I flexed my fingers; I was good at fixing things, and I was good at solving things. Learning how to walk was just another thing to be solved.

Jacob regarded me with a long look, his eyes comprehensive under a tussle of black hair that fell almost to his nose. "It makes me kind of a badass," I gestured towards my leg. Jacob smirked, "You're way too nice of a guy, Billy Dan—my mom says that all the time," he stated.

I winced; nothing was worse than being called the nice guy—well, there were many worse things to be called. That one just sucked and would be hard to shake off without coming off as a jerk afterward. Once people form an image of you, that is the image you will remain in their heads. You can either annihilate it or brighten it up, but it's tough to genuinely change that image without breaking the fragile image people have of you. Combined with your image of yourself, you have the potential for conflicting ideas. Fortunately, it can be navigated by simply being the person you think you are to those around you. Just the nice guy usually meant the end of relationships—or so every online guru would tell you with the low fee of half your soul and a subscription to their pyramid schemes.

I probably am the nicest guy in her life, but I forgot to tip the hot dog stand guy once. I was a few beers in, and I just needed some food. So, they are not the nicest of guys. I went on to Jacobs's statement, "Nope—genuine badass here—and soon going to be Detective Billy Dan," I stated. The boy's eyes lit ablaze, and I knew I had won him over to relax and hopefully heed my warning about whatever he was doing.

"How do you figure that, Billy Dan?" he asked, a genuine expression on his face. Kids were easy to read; if only more adults were like that, I thought.

"I figure that by working hard—doing the right thing; you just do what needs to be done no matter how much it hurts," I stated.

I pulled out my stack of flashcards and scribbled down what could only be considered a madman's notes or a drunk alchemist's formulas. Either way, I was feeling good for tomorrow. Above Jacobs's head was another printed picture of our mayor, his green eyes gleaming. But that wasn't what caught my eyes—a newly laminated picture of a girl about Jacobs's age, smiling down with wide teeth and black hair.

I glanced back down to find Jacob talking about my metal leg more, tapping it to see what sound it produced. The whole time, I could feel the girl on the poster staring back at me; she was missing, and I was pretending I hadn't seen her poster. My heart beat faster as the bus road along—there was something inherently wrong when a child was missing, something that made every fiber of my being long to find them. It was so easy to just accept it, I thought. A child was missing—and we just went on in this world as if nothing had happened. This was the world God had made—a place where nothing happened.

Chapter 6

I dropped Jacob off at his mother's house with very little pushback. His mother was still at work, and his older sister waved at me—I waved back and then caught the next bus, returning to my meager home on the edges of the suburbs. A tall maple tree sprouted green leaves that looked like hands waving to me as I sucked in the air—it was good to be home. I forced myself to stop; my yellow work vest with the city's logo gently moved in the breeze as the wind chimes cast low hums around my street. This was the best part of my day—returning home after a day at work, I tried to take it in as often as possible.

The air stopped, fading to the memory of a happy moment in an otherwise chaotic world. I continued walking, and today's events settled into their perspective and placed inside my head. I had work to do now, no time to worry about crazy cultists and that missing girl. Just focus on what needs to be done, I told myself. Then you can help everyone.

Funny, I thought, opening the sandy-coated door, I told myself that time would tell if I was genuine. All the while, I kept thinking of Larry digging into that garbage can. The way Jacob hadn't shown me what he found. Jacob always showed off anything interesting he found while hiding in the garbage cans. That was the first time he had jumped in the back. I thought it must have been fine as I pulled from a gallon water jug.

Chapter 7

I had opened the doors in my garage, the breeze now sweeping into my office. I had moved my car, and inside, tables cluttered with my tools—mostly just workout junk at this point—cluttered my empty garage. I was taking a break, huddled to a small part of my desk studying my notecards, a thick bead of sweat rolling off me. I detached my fingers from my hand during my workout. A metal bar hung eight feet above my head.

An off-white alarm clock sounded, interrupting my concentration and signaling it was time to switch again. I sucked in a breath, setting down my notecards as I flicked the one-minute timer on the clock again.

I lowered my weight on my knees, pushed my butt nearly down to the floor, and jumped to the bar above my head. My right hand gripped the bar, and with a grunt, I lowered myself and kept the stub of my left-hand fingers over my right elbow. After a few reps, I lowered myself and returned to studying my flashcards. I was going to become a detective.

My alarm rang again. I grunted, jumped to the bar overhead, and repeated this for an hour. When I was done, I was drenched in sweat, my right forearm on fire. I went to my desk; a hook was attached to a long harness that fit over my shoulders and waist as I slid the straps tight.

"Time for the left side," I mumbled, resetting the alarm clock for another minute before jumping to the bar above me. This was how I spent my days—a far cry from my old life—but I was past that. I needed to focus on the future. The future was now. I was going to become a detective. This is what I did, I pulled myself up by the strength of my back. I was going to have a great future.

Chapter 8

Gen sat across from me in a red dress; the night was loud and full of flavors. The kind that makes you sit back and smile, an invisible play of your favorite song, comes alive in many sounds, movements, and joyful moments. My own personal concert, every time she smiled. I was thankful for that. My life wouldn't have been what most people would call cheery. I would call those people negative Nancy's, but Nancy was a good person. Asshole was the correct moniker for people like that, I thought as I shot my wine glass back. I just needed to enjoy the moment. Think about how good Gen looked in that red dress.

"You know you're supposed to sip wine, right?" Gen asked as her face flushed red. A contrast to the bright lights coming from the glowing flames that kept us warm on the cold rooftop.

I snickered, "All comes out the same way anyways."

She laughed at that one, and a silence settled between us. It was not the awkward silence of two people frantically afraid that if they didn't speak, the other would be discomforted, but the silence of two people completely at peace.

I leaned back in my chair. Most of our small-town cheering and dancing were ahead of us at the center of the dance floor. Rhythmic melodies from a jazz band and off-beat dancers clapping to the music. That was an actual test of a musician. The ability to keep playing the tune while everyone around you was drunk, destroying the concept of music theory.

I smiled until I saw, out of the corner of my eyes, the large man from the church earlier today. A flash of the people cowering away from his almost comical amount of muscle is what caught my eye. His suit was tailored, had to be by someone that regularly suited football players—his biceps were bigger than my head, and he lumbered like a moving statue through the crowd towards a table-centered smack dab in the middle of the room. His presence caused people to back away in worry from his thick gaze.

This wasn't a high-end restaurant; an excellent $20 greased the receptionist's pockets enough to let Gen and I skip a few spots ahead in the line. But what made me pay attention to the big man was how sharp the suit was and how defined the lines were. When he reached the table, I immediately understood why. The Mayor was in the middle of the room; his sharp eyes glowed green like a lime. He sat in a sharp gray suit, his blazer hanging lazily open, but even the buttons cost more than I made in one year. He must be his bodyguard.

His comb-over highlighted his salt and pepper hair, making it almost seem blue, juxtaposed with his gray suit. A sharp smile hid his all-white and perfect teeth; it was a face I knew all too well. The Mayor. I was so tired of seeing his posters and commercials. In a small town like this, there needed to be a limit to how many times you could see someone's face in one day. The big man is definitely his muscle. A hired goon gets around a lot. Though, I wouldn't hire anyone associated with that creepy church. They were just way too happy and dazed. Even the big man looked like the lights were on, but nobody was there.

I glanced to the right of The Mayor. An attractive, real woman spoke to a tall, red-headed man with a furry beard that was as unkempt as his overalls. That stood out to me; his hands were puffed up, and he showed many scars. Not the thick knots of a fighter, though. The way his skin seemed to almost swallow the silver ring on his right hand told me he wasn't a boxer. He was probably a mechanic—and in a small town, he wasn't that unusually dressed, even in a lower-end restaurant. There were some dress codes, though. I shook it off. It was a small town, nothing to fuss over. Nothing unusual.

The ring was strange, though; my eyes lingered as I saw a red moon on the silver metal. Even from a distance, I could see the gleam. The man caught me looking and flinched his hand back, which caught the gaze of The

Mayor. His smile towards me made me feel like I had just stared down a lion. Only it was a lion that had already had his fill. Not the look of a meager, humble, small-town Mayor. Odd, it was my first time seeing him in person; I didn't expect him to be that obvious. Who knows, politicians must all be part animals to want to do their jobs. I matched his green-eyed gaze for a moment longer. They never changed, just looking hungry, like a predator that was always on the hunt. The hunger told me he was not to be messed with, and here was me, surrounded by dozens of people. I was not safe. I held his gaze, though. In the animal kingdom, like in human life, don't ever show fear around a predator. The moment I looked away, I was a dead man.

I had to find a way to survive if he decided to attack. The only way of getting out of this is with a mark. That didn't matter—I just had to let the lion know I wasn't afraid.

The Mayor broke the stare down first with a slight smirk and a slow look towards his muscled bond tank.

"Earth to Billy Dan, come in, Billy Dan. An attractive woman who's interested in you trying to pour her heart and soul. But hey, good looks can only take me so far," Gen joked as I shook my head, turning back towards her.

"Yeah, sorry about that; I was just—thinking about this wonderful song playing right now," I stated.

Gen grinned, "the band is on break, there's no music playing, Billy Dan,"

I stood up, offering my right hand, "The song you and I are about to start playing, baby," I replied.

"Smooth,"

"You've seen nothing yet—wait until I start telling jokes," I said. I wrote off my stare-down with the Mayor as drinking too much. I wasn't the type that went out often. And I was hoping Gen couldn't tell—large crowds like this always made me uncomfortable, and I would never relax—just keep looking for anything amiss in the animal kingdom. I tried to relax, an overwhelming feeling of something bad on the hunt near me. Like a sense left over from our ancestors.

We danced, enthralled in each other's embraces. Others soon joined us, and then music started playing again. While I danced with Gen, I couldn't help but stare at The Mayor and his goons. They just seemed so out of place. One was big enough to make a mountain guerrilla jealous, and the other looked too much like myself to be around that much money and power.

Gen caught me staring and turned my face back to hers, this time concern written on it. The song soon ended, followed by applause, and we slowly walked back to the table. "You know, for a one-legged man, you move surprisingly well—been dancing with many women?" she joked.

I grinned, "Just the ones that are into square dancing," I replied.

"Square dancing, huh—meet many people doing that?" she stated.

"Yeah, my mother, mostly. She still makes me do it with her once a month. You should come out sometime, country music night at Titos," I joked.

Gen tilted her head back and let loose a rich belly laugh.

"Knowing you, that was probably the truth just now," she said jubilantly.

I shrugged, "Probably," as I glanced at The Mayor again; something about that man always made me want to keep him within eyesight. It was hard enough not to take Gen and run out of this restaurant as fast as we could. She was tough, though, short, but knew how to handle herself. I was less concerned about her safety and more about what he was doing here. Sure, he was the town's Mayor—this was a small town in the Carolinas, but he was as close to famous as this town had. I needed to relax; we were just adults out having fun. He had weird company—I mean, I was dating a cop, and her son kept finding his way into my garbage truck. People lived strange lives. I just couldn't stop thinking about them, though, one of the cultists, with the Mayor of our small town and a car mechanic. Suppose it could have been a late-night brake pad change.

The Mayor only made public appearances if it was for a fundraiser or fun run around our town. Gen finally decided to cut me off before my staring got me into trouble, "I know what you're thinking, Billy Dan. Let it go. The department has tried going after him so many times already. He could probably throw someone off the roof—no one would say anything," she stated and gestured with her chin towards a few people eating their meals on the rooftop.

"See old big nose and long white hair there? She's the judge," she gestured towards a lady with a long nose and thin strands of white hair flaking past her shoulders.

"And over there," she continued, "That's the sheriff's deputy," she stated. I looked up to see the familiar high and tight of military or federal workers— Dwayne, a local sheriff patrol. He was a nice guy. He was always combing his hair and glancing in the mirror to ensure his perfect comb-over was still flying.

I arched an eyebrow at that. You read about criminals all the time. Some are out in the open, others you just have a good feeling they are. Most people are good, and others will take advantage of the appearance of good. The Mayor gave me the vibe of the rare few who hurt others, and he was more dangerous than the type of people out and about shouting in a bar one night after a few too many beers. No, The Mayor would smile, buy you a drink, maybe even pat you on the back—afterward, have two goons break your knees and do the same to your whole family.

How did I know? It was more than the crawl-out-of-my-skin vibe Melanie gave me. It was the fact that the whole police department in our small town took photos with him and played on his golf course. Got free donuts from the local bakeries—all at his expense. Gen had let slip once that she was looking into him for a permit violation at his country club golf course. Nothing good, but nothing that should have caused me to be this bothered by him. Maybe it was because her chief almost suspended her when she wouldn't drop the case. Perhaps I was just protecting my girlfriend. Or maybe one animal recognized another animal when he saw one.

I had once seen The Mayor beating a man outside one morning. You would be surprised at how much your garbage man can learn about you. Me, from accidentally seeing piles of bills unopened or some husband trying desperately to hide his second phone from his wife. One early morning, I got a good look at our town's Mayor. The Mayor had yet to see me. And when I went to report it, the sheriff told me to take a hike. Hearing it from Gen here now made me very angry. Scum got to walk, other times, it was wiped away, but in my opinion, it was never enough.

"You're a good guy, Billy Dan, but let it go," Gen said, lowering her eyes and clearly exasperated.

"Gen," I started.

She held up a finger, "A few years ago, trust me, I used to make that same face—I would gladly go over there right now and cuff that son-of-gun. But he's as protected as a bubble boy in a padded room. There's no going after him. Let it go. It's not worth your dreams," she stated.

I glared at her, "Your dreams are always worth it, Gen," I replied.

"Not when you have children, Billy Dan. Not when you have people to lose. You say you want to be a detective, well investigate the situation. I'm a cop. How much energy do you think I have? I'm paid as much as you, long hours, and hateful looks. We don't have the luxury of ever making a mistake. Constantly under eyes—even if I could go after him, who would back me? It's a lot easier to have dreams when you don't have kids," she matched my glare. She shook her head, "I didn't mean that; they're the best thing to ever happen to me—I just," she sighed. I kissed her hand. She smiled at me, a long and sad look.

I softened my look after a moment—from her perspective, a few failed investigations, one of which she even worked on, I couldn't blame her if she did quit.

"Well—I won't give up. Once I get my detective license, I will take him down and clean up these streets," I stated matter-of-factly.

"That's what I like about you; you still dream," she said sadly.

An air of silence stretched between us, "when is your test tomorrow?" she asked.

"Nine am," I said dryly, picking up my drink and examining nothing at the bottom of it.

"Feeling ready?" she asked.

"We will find out," I stated.

Gen frowned, "I know you well enough to know that you will pass the test. Don't mind me, Billy Dan. Doing this job, it's rough on people, you know? But you got this. Everyone believes in you."

I nodded my head back to her slowly. "I get that; I just can't—" I grunted, letting the conversation die. Silence was something I struggled with, especially after things like this. Luckily, Gen had far more emotional intelligence than I would ever have in even my most petite fingers. "Why does it mean so much to you, Billy Dan? Why do you dream so much about a job that has no pay, no thanks, and long hours of people hating you—you hating yourself?" she asked me, no malice in her question, just a friend genuinely trying to extend a hand to someone.

"Because I'm already used to all of those things," I said softly. Gen looked at me confused. Before she could say anything, a scream ripped through the dinner, causing everyone to turn towards the noise.

An older woman holding a glass of wine was standing before The Mayor. An empty glass was at her side, and a soaked mayor in a gray suit sat before her with an eerie smile. The woman took half a step back. The glass trembling in her hands. Everyone was dead silent; I could hear a mouth breather on the other side of the roof—it was that quiet. I stood up slowly. Gen's eyes went wide.

"Your drugs destroyed my boy!" she hissed, putting her glass up to throw it. I respected this frail old woman standing up to the big bad wolf. My heart was pounding fast; I had no idea what I was about to do.

She took aim when the muscled-bound human mountain moved in a flash and took hold of her hand with the glass, completely engulfing both in his one hand. I blinked at that. He was fast. This was going to be a problem.

"I think you owe me a new shirt," The Mayor said coolly, "I think you owe me some manners—teach her," he gestured to his two associates. I crossed the distance between us and kicked the knees out from under the big man, sending him to the ground. I swore I heard a small earthquake from his weight. Before I could react, a fist slammed into my jaw with enough force to almost send me falling to the ground. I could move quickly in a single direction as long as I didn't lose my balance or switch too fast—which was challenging even with two legs. Punching, though, tended to tip that in the wrong direction for me.

I sprawled to the ground, only stopping myself as I tripped forward with my good leg. I turned to the gingered man; a wide, toothy grin flayed over

34

his face as his ring caught a light from somewhere, causing him to squint his eyes. Taking advantage of that, I shot forward and kneed him in the balls. The man fell over when the muscled man shot from the ground, his eyes a fire, and I prepared myself for war.

"Alright, stop," Gen said firmly from behind me; a click of a gun being cocked made everyone pucker their anger. I glared at the big man, who only came up to his chest. He looked like he was ready to explode with fury. A small part of my mind was thankful that Gen brought her gun everywhere she went.

Skills on the ground or not, this giant ape would have destroyed me. "Everyone—calm down, now," she stated again, firmly, her voice radiating absolute authority.

"That won't be necessary, officer, but thank you for your service," replied The Mayor, coming around the table. He walked right over his companion on the ground, still clutching his private parts.

He stepped toward me, "I think boys will be boys—wouldn't you agree?" he asked towards someone. It took me a moment to realize that he was talking to me. I blinked and responded. "Sure, you could say that," I replied dryly. The Mayor glared at me. I matched his glare back. He was around my height but held himself far straighter than I could manage; I popped out my chest, trying to match his gusto. The Mayor looked past me as his men got to their feet. He was just one of those guys with unnatural posture. Made me dislike him even more.

"Like I said, officer, this isn't necessary. Lower your firearm," he stated— an authority of command. To my horror, I heard Gen breathe deeply, and I could tell she lowered her gun from the smile that appeared on the Mayor's face.

"Good girl," The Mayor spoke. He turned away from me once more and gestured to the entire area. "My apologies, good people. Tonight's meal is on me!" The Mayor gestured wide as the crowd cheered around me. As if this was no more than dinner and a show—just an average night.

I kept glaring at him. I wasn't laughing; I wasn't cheering. I saw only an overgrown man-child before me, and I hated just how much crap was coming out of him.

I stepped towards him and heard the muscled ape growl. I flicked him off but kept eye contact with the green-eyed Mayor.

The Mayor looked at me, a slight grin at the corner of his lips. "Mr. Mayor," I stated.

The Mayor looked me up and down, smiling boldly, "Aren't you—aren't you the garbage man? Yeah, I've seen you hauling bags of diapers once," he joked, his lips puckering in like he just sucked in a lemon.

"That's waste disposer, asshole,"

The Mayor rolled his eyes, "Right, you take out the trash,"

"That's right, it must be Tuesday. I only see your trash before me," I matched his eyes.

His smirk twitched ever so slightly before he spoke, "Cute," responded The Mayor.

"Your mother sure thinks I am," I stated dryly.

That got the anger to break through his facade finally; I caught his eyes glowing like gems inside an endlessly dark cave. "You seem like you have a problem—garbage man," he declared. That made my fire come out, and I found a way to stand taller.

"We just might. It's getting late, and it's past my bedtime—I wouldn't want to be on the receiving end of that," I stated, nodding toward the muscled man.

The Mayor growled, "You have a pair on you,"

"Definitely more than a man that has his goons try to beat on an old lady— no offense, ma'am," I retorted, gesturing slightly towards the woman on the ground. She was a frail mess, and my heart sank for her; I didn't dare take my eyes off the lion before me.

"Gentlemen," interjected Gen as she came between us and pulled my arm. "Let's go, Billy Dan," she whispered.

"Not a bad idea, officer, Genesis," stated The Mayor. There was a coldness in every word. Gen looked on with horror; her customary stoic bravery cracked for the briefest of moments. "Be seeing you around, garbage man," he called to us as Gen led me to the stairs leading off the roof. She pulled me away before I could get out what I hoped was a witty reply—but in real life, there's a funny line limit counter. I was way over my amount and had just dug my grave in many ways.

Chapter 9

"What the hell were you thinking back there, Billy Dan. Do you know who that man is? The things he's gotten away with," Gen trailed off, but I noticed she gripped the steering wheel so tight that her fingers were turning pale.

I glanced back at her face, searching for something under the anger—there was nothing, just fear. Which told me a few things. Namely, the situation was bigger than I realized. Secondly, it probably just ruined my chances of a good night. Lastly, Gen, the brave officer I had known for years, was legitimately scared. My own heart was beating like a racehorse, I noticed at that thought.

I was sure I had bitten off more than I could chew—that didn't change the fact that I hated bullies. Especially ones like The Mayor, who delighted in hurting old ladies. As we sped home, I tried to pick my words carefully, "I couldn't just let it happen,"

"Yes, you could have and should have. You have one leg, Billy Dan. He would have destroyed you. You have no idea what kind of things he's gotten away with. This is his town. If you really want to become a detective, you have to start acting like that's what you want," she stated, her voice shaking and on the verge of breaking. I realized that was the first time I had ever heard her talk like that.

I reached for her hand, placing the stub of my left hand near hers. She hesitated momentarily before putting her hand gently on top of my arm. There wasn't passion in her touch; there was respect, though. I responded slowly, "I couldn't let him do that to her,"

Gen nodded, "I understand, but I'm afraid all you accomplished was painting a target on yourself—and oh, you have a mark on your cheek," she stated.

I flipped on the overhead light; sure enough, a shiner formed, but below my right eye was the mark of the ring. "That looks like it stings," she said.

I frowned and leaned back in my chair, "Yeah, more than a tickle."

Chapter 10

I left Gen's house early that morning; the sun was still down. I didn't have to be at work for another hour, but I enjoyed the walk in the brisk air. The side of my face stung, and my eyes didn't want to stay open for long. I winced, but it allowed me to turn my head just in time to see Jacob crawl from his bedroom window—onto the roof and slowly scale down the vines on the side of Gen's house. I shook my head. The kid just refused to listen. I decided it wasn't my place to say anything. At least not now; I would give him one more day of whatever he was doing before I lectured him again. This time, I would have to pull out the big guns—the how to be a man speech.

When I was a boy about his age, I had no parents growing up, just my foster great-uncle and great-aunt. Many quiet Saturdays were spent working on his farm—those were long days, sweating, carrying loads of wood, and with very few breaks. But, for a young boy with no parents, there was nothing better for me. I shuddered at how I could have turned out without that time, without the talks from my uncle about what it meant to be a man nearly every day. "A man does not hurt others. He helps others," I repeated to myself. Yeah, Jacob was at the age now for that talk. I continued my walk to work, meeting Larry almost two hours later. However, I was reminded of what I was, so maybe I wasn't the best for that talk.

Larry looked disheveled and drained and smelled like he hadn't taken a shower in days. We didn't talk all morning on our first shift together. He didn't ask about my black eye, and I didn't ask about his red eyes. We worked until I dropped the truck back off and went home. My test was in three hours, I noted as I went into my garage for a small workout.

Time passed, and a phone call pulled me from my trance as I worked my way around a heavy bag on the garage floor. It was movement drill time, and somehow, I had forgotten about the rest of the world while I worked.

I pulled the talking brick from my pocket, "Billy Dan," I stated, catching my breath. "Come outside. I have the truck ready," Larry blurted out in a hurry. The line went silent, and I stared at the phone. The sun was rising soon, and my test was at nine. The time on the phone said, "6:32 am". I blew out my breath and got up, closing the garage door. I could see the lights from Larry's truck glowing in the hiring daylight.

What was going on? Larry sounded afraid. I went inside, throwing on a pair of pants and a hopefully clean shirt, and paused at my gun on my desk. You don't need it, a small voice in my head whispered. After a moment of indecision, I put on my baseball cap near the gun.

Chapter 11

Larry was driving with a purpose I hadn't seen on the man since I met him. He was speeding but cautiously looking, not wasting his time on any pretty women while we were stopped in traffic. He sat hunched forward, his hands gripping the vinyl cover on his truck steering wheel.

His work shirt was now stained yellow and brown around the pits, and his city vest that designated us as waste disposers had nearly fallen off his shoulders. His knee on the left side frantically tapped. We last talked ten minutes ago as he sped across town. Our little city is coming alive with people starting to come out for their days, families sending their children to schools, and some already starting their morning with lots of water. Heatwaves did that to people, I thought; nothing unusual there. Maybe that was why Larry was sweating so much.

I decided that Larry wasn't going to break the silence between us. I coughed into my hand, "How is it?" I asked my partner. Larry stared at the road ahead, unblinking, a deep frown forming hints of early crow's feet near his eyes.

He remained silent. I blew out my lips, "Okay, we can both just kind of drive off into the distance together, I suppose. I don't mind too much, but can we stop for something to eat at least? I mean, it has to be a good reason for all this cloak-and-dagger stuff—or there better be if I am going to miss my plans, Larry. I can start if you want. I am north of Cancer and south of Okay. How about you?" I asked, staring at the younger man.

He responded a moment later, looking out the window. "The kid said he found something in the dumpster," he muttered, moving his eyes back to the road.

"The kid, what kid?" I asked.

"Who do you think, Billy Dan," Larry stated.

"Crabapples," I muttered, rubbing my eyes a few moments later. What was wrong with that kid? No matter what happened, I wasn't taking him to get toast this time.

Chapter 12

We pulled into the parking area behind a local strip mall joint. Stores littered the fragmented paved roads like little dusky sand dunes. Larry killed the truck as we approached a large blue dumpster, Jacob sat on top of the lid, his backpack rattling in his hands like a jackhammer.

Instantly, my heart beat so fast I had to check to ensure it wasn't about to explode. He never looked like that. Jacob was a weird, toast—eating kid who went dumpster diving, but he was never without a smile. I was worried about the little guy as he stared into the dark abyss below him. I reached for Larry's door as he was, preparing to jump out.

"What?" he shouted. I stayed calm, looking at him, then at the kid. "Relax," I stated. Larry regarded me with pure detest. I gave him a long look before continuing. I could see the anger in his face flatter for a moment before he broke my gaze, taking his arm off his door handle and placing it on his right arm—his body language was clear.

I relaxed, pulling back into my seat slowly. The truck seemed a lot smaller than it had before. I paused another long moment before continuing. The kid was still gazing into whatever was in the dumpster.

"How did he even get out here? This place is ten miles from his mom's," I scanned the building, looking for a bike or something that indicated how a ten-year-old could travel so far. Larry glared forward, muttering before giving me my answer. "He was in the back of my truck—he—must have been back there while I was in town, you know, getting some stuff," Larry stated.

I fought the urge to question Larry outright for that statement; there would be time for that later. He lived clear on the other side of town. Furthermore, it still would need to explain why and how Jacob could sneak into a grown man's truck without anyone noticing, especially at six in the morning. None of it added up, but I wouldn't vocalize that thought until I had more information. The easiest way to get into trouble is to speak before you have the facts. I glanced at my watch; it was 7:20 am. Time was ticking away. This felt more important, though—there would always be more time for a test. I breathed out my lips.

I decided to look deeper into Larry but kept my other questions inside my toolbox. I noted a box growing way too full as the day continued. "Getting some stuff, huh?" I asked him skeptically. He turned towards me, confusion and bewilderment written on his face. "Yeah—what do you mean, yeah, I was getting some stuff," Larry replied, mental gymnastics playing across his brow as he thought of a reply. Most people would confess to a lie with minimal effort. Larry wouldn't take much. My more significant concern was how to get out info he wasn't willing to tell me. The stuff that made him care more about himself than that of a child.

I looked back at Jacob one more time, his face frozen. I needed to knock him out of whatever trance he was in before he developed trauma. I knew that look all too well, and I wore it every time I went to a mirror. Every time, I thought of how bad my life was—how awful I felt nearly every day for the things that I had chosen to do. I needed to play this game with Larry, though. Catching a liar was definitely helpful when you told countless lies yourself—I just needed to think like a liar again. Experience in that area—was something I regretted. However, it was useful right now. I just had to wait for the hole. Poke it just in the right way—the foundation would collapse. However, what would have saved me sooner in my life—was someone just taking a hammer to my walls of lies. I decided that might just be best right now.

I turned my head towards Larry, catching his gaze. "Larry, your story sounds about as real as an honest politician. I don't care why you were out here; I care about that kid. Wipe your face off before you scare him more— and hurry, I have things to do today," I stated before moving towards the truck's passenger door. I stepped out into the day—already a slow breeze causing the hair on my arms to stand up. I approached Jacob. I walked slowly but loudly as I approached the boy; he was scared enough that there was no use in terrifying him anymore. I was about three feet away from Jacob when I stopped. I cleared my throat.

If he heard, he did not react. I sighed, moving towards Jacob slowly when he suddenly spoke. "Don't come closer," he whispered, his voice drowned out in the wind like a songbird in a tornado—flapping helplessly, only to never be heard.

"What?" I muttered back stupidly. Jacob still faced forward, staring down into the dumpster. "I said, don't come closer, Billy Dan," he stated this time.

I breathed out my held breath; that was a good sign. He was not so far gone that he couldn't tell his surroundings. "Alright, I can stay right where I am. Do you think you can tell me what's going on, Jacob? You promised you wouldn't do this anymore," I replied.

"I never promised anything, Billy Dan," his voice cracked. His dark cheeks blushed under his long hair. I could tell he was on the verge of crying. "You have a point—you never did promise me. That does not matter right now. How about you and I go get some toast, and we can talk over whatever this is—"

"I don't want toast," he snarled, cutting me off.

That was a first. The kid loved toast more than anything else. "Alright, can you at least tell me what's going on? Look at me, kid—what is going on?" I asked him, fear slowly creeping its tiny feet up my back. I thought those little feet could become full-blown elephant-sized if you were not careful. I could make this far worse for him if I lost my cool now. He would keep it forever. I was not in the business of hurting children. Some people got off on that; others needed a lot more.

Not me, though; Jacob was family by this point. I would give him the respect he deserved and let him take his time. I waited for his response as a growing uneasiness ran up my spine. This area was remote; even the buses that came this way would have placed Jacob a few miles away. No, the answer was that Larry had taken him here, but the question that gnawed at me the most was, why? Why had Larry been out here? Why was Jacob out here now?

For the second time, I found a little boy inside a dumpster—a toast-eating little boy in less than twenty-four hours.

I shook that thought away; he was here now. I told myself to focus on the details and what really can be seen. "Jacob," I said sternly, slowly walking towards him. He never glanced up; he stared at whatever was in the dumpster.

When I got closer to the lid, in the fading darkness of the morning gave way to the light was a sack, I narrowed my eyes, trying to understand what I was looking at—bags of black and white trash all puffed out and overflowing with waste. Nothing out of the ordinary. Except for the sack—partially obscured by the garbage.

I realized it wasn't a sack. The cloth covering was soaked through, a deep brown that had mixed with something else. It was unmistakable, though crimson in the shade. It was blood. I looked closer and saw what had shaken Jacob so severely: a tiny hand sticking out of a sack abandoned in a dumpster. God—why?

Chapter 13

I sucked in my breath at the sight of the small form within the folds of the cloth—knowing full well if I did not choose my words carefully right now, I would damage Jacob for the rest of his life. He would carry post-traumatic stress disorder, possibly worse, as he replayed the images of the dead child huddled deep within the dumpster. I had to do something, though; I had to help Jacob.

"Jacob—" I started as Larry walked up beside me. "Okay, what the heck is going on—holy crap, is that a dead baby?" exclaimed Larry as he paused, his face a contortion of sickness. I shot a look at Larry that I hope conveyed just how much I wanted to kick his butt in that moment. As I turned to Larry, Jacob plunged from the dumpster lid and bolted across the lot behind the stores.

So fast for a kid who spent all his time reading and eating toast. I dove after him and landed hard as he spun out of the way and kept running. I busted my chin on the broken ground below and groaned, "Jacob, I'm sorry—slow down, buddy, come back." The kid was already taking off to the fence line. Larry stood there, his mouth hanging wide.

"Larry, get your butt after him!" I shouted at my partner, who stood dumbfounded before shaking his head yes and taking off running after the boy.

"Crap, crap, crap," I moaned, pulling myself to the truck as I slammed the door shut behind me. Running I could do, as long as the pace never went beyond a slow to brisk jog—at least not with the type of prosthetic leg I had on right now. I knew I should have saved up for the better one. I learned a lot of things, but maybe none at all. As I reached for the ignition and swore. Larry had taken the keys with him.

"Shit, shit, shit," I shouted as I opened the door of the truck and went after the pair.

Chapter 14

I caught Larry after a few minutes; he had sweated through his shirt, and as I came behind him—my prosthetic rubbing into my thigh with every step made me swear. The man looked like he was on the verge of dying after only a few minutes of running. I couldn't see the kid. I risked slowing down to match Larry's pace, frantically scanning the horizon. We were out of the shopping area and into the old suburbs of town. It was a place where people still lived, but only because no one could afford to live anywhere else. Most of the buildings were falling down, in desperate need of repair, or full of homeless people.

I knew because I lived in this neighborhood myself before landing the garbage man job. It wasn't a bad neighborhood, but it was no place for a scared boy to run through.

Catching my breath, I shouted at Larry as I ran past. "Which way, Larry?" Larry pointed with his right hand before collapsing his hands, his chest rising and falling like a jackhammer. I scanned the direction he pointed in and saw Jacob climb over a brown down steel fence and cross into the yard of an apartment complex that looked like it was the future set of a Hollywood horror film.

I took deep breaths, pounding the distance between the kid and me. Was he that quick, or was I just getting old? "Not today, Billy Dan, not today. Move your butt," I shouted, reaching the fence and doing my best to climb over it without tripping over my own limbs. I cursed myself for being useless as I lost my footing and fell on the other side.

I got up, wobbling on my two left feet, it seemed, before continuing towards the apartment building. As I reached the doors, though—I was blasted backward as a wave of force slammed into me and sent me sprawling to the ground.

It felt like someone had sucked the air from my chest as I lay staring at the sun on an otherwise beautiful day. I could smell something burning, and I squinted my eyes. No one should stare at the sun for too long, I thought. What had happened? That doesn't matter; I'll figure it out later. Now get your butt up, I told myself, crawling onto my elbows. The apartment was on fire. Smoke bellowed out as if it was racing towards the sky. How in the Hell did an apartment building catch on fire that quickly in just a few moments?

"Jacob," I shouted as people started flooding out of the building. Many were disheveled, some were chanting—and others swatted at the air as if something was attacking them. I blinked at that. What was going on here in the world? I grunted, people running past me as I stood up and hobbled towards the door. Something somewhere in my body felt battered and broken. No time to complain now, cry later, I told myself. As I reached the door entrances, I could hear yelling somewhere in the small apartment building.

Banging, cracking, and the popping of splintered wood. I had to find the kid—no matter what. I ripped off my jacket and tried to tie it around my mouth and nose. The smoke stung my eyes as I entered the building. The cheap wallpaper flowed from the walls like water in a river—the heat causing the walls to almost sweat. The whole world was burning, I thought. More people ran past me, screaming. Some screaming about things that made no sense. A woman was pulling her hair as she passed me, crying about snakes in her head. I thought about stopping, but what could I do? I needed to find Jacob.

How was this place burning so quickly? Why was it even on fire? I thought as I made my way deeper into the building, the scream of voices mixing in with the heavy gray smoke—as if the flames were licking out the sorrow before meeting the fire.

At the first staircase, I paused. What if the kid was not even in the building anymore? Had he even run into this one? How long had it been? That did not matter. I had to find him, I had to help the people in this building. I scrambled up the staircase, covering my eyes through the smoke. An old man was leaning against a wall, sliding down slowly. I caught him, pulling his shoulders and hand towards the staircase.

"Go down the stairs—now!" I shouted as he nodded back with what I hoped was approval. I directed him to the rail, placing his hands on it before letting go. I watched as he disappeared down the stairs into the gathering smoke.

No time, I thought, keep moving, find the kid. "Jacob!" I shouted into what seemed like the mouth of Hell. He had to be here somewhere, somewhere in this abyss. I heard footsteps, and a little girl with more braids than a bush stood before me.

I stopped, catching my breath. "Hi," I stuttered as the girl looked at me. Her braids fell like octopuses' arms on her head. She pointed down the hallway, her little hands shaking. I followed her finger until I saw what she was pointing at a door frame, a burning pile of wood blocking the front, save for a small part just big enough for a child to crawl through.

Through the black smoke, I understood what she meant. I nodded and took off in the direction of the room. Collapsed on the floor was an older woman with the same thick black hair—about the age to most likely be her mother.

I bent down, lowering myself to the floor; flames roared on the ceiling in the apartment—snapping and reaching towards the woman as if they were alive. "Ma'am!" I shouted over the roar of the flames. She didn't respond.

"Hell," I mumbled as I took in the situation. She was a few feet away from me, but there was no way I could get through the debris obscuring the doorway. I had to act fast; the smoke was stinging my eyes. "Hey, lady!" I screamed into the apartment as loud as possible before the woman slowly looked up. Her eyes were bloodshot shot, and I knew I had only a few moments to get her out of the room. Sweat fell from my head like a watering hose as I lay in the hallway.

The little girl gave me a long look as I rolled up my pants leg, detaching the clamps that held my leg. My leg had been rubbed raw from the running, blood spilled out, and I worried if it would somehow get infected for the briefest of breaths.

No time. I rolled towards the door frame, stretching under the burning debris as close as I could get. My leg was made of steel, reinforced, and could hold hundreds of pounds—or so the doctors told me. It was time to put that to the test, I thought as I braced the debris up with my leg. The flames licked away the sealing and plastic bits at the top of the fake leg, but otherwise, it held for now, I thought. I started to crawl through.

I was halfway through the door frame when the ceiling inside the apartment fell through. Molten wood chunks sang the air, burning holes in my long-sleeved shirt. I pressed forward, crawling on my hands until I reached hers. She didn't react as I took hold of her arm, nor when I started pulling her back towards the door frame. I grunted, straining my whole body as I jerked as quickly as I could. I saw her nose drag on the floor and felt guilty, but there was no time to worry about being gentle.

I strained a few moments longer. The dead weight of someone was a whole different thing than pulling my body up by a bar—not to mention, now that my leg was off—my entire body felt off. Luckily for us both, she seemed to be in some shape, or else this would have been impossible. I kept straining and pulling until we both came through the doorway. A blast of flames danced in the spots where we both were just moments before. With a massive heave, I pulled myself to my knees, taking her arm to the doorway.

Through clenched teeth, I grunted, "Kid, help me out here." The little girl hesitated momentarily before reacting, taking hold of her mom's arm and helping me get the woman out. I landed on my butt out in the hallways, gasping for air. Beyond me, the hallway was filled with smoke, and I could not go deeper into the apartment complex. "Jacob," I whispered, my eyes getting heavy as I shot my arms out, removing my leg from the door. With a few tucks, the prosthetic came loose, just in time for the door frame to come crashing down in timber.

The mom was starting to come to, her kid helping by carrying the woman over her shoulders as she put her weight against the hallway—though she wasn't strong enough to hold her for long.

I shuffled my leg back into place, clamping the metal straps over the scraps on my knee. One of the clamps was loosened, and the latch bent. I forced it into place—it came up again. I winched. It had hurt; I could cry about it later. With unsteady feet, I got up and took the other side of the woman. There was no way I could find Jacob and no way these two could get out without me.

I cursed under my breath and started carrying the woman. Smoke billowed above us; the heat caused my eyes to water and my hair to burn. This was it, I thought as we neared the end of the hallway. The kid was failing—she kept tripping over her feet, stumbling in the near-blinding darkness. I yelled at her, "Climb on my back, move it," she reacted about how I expected, I scooped her up with my clawed hand, and she gripped tightly onto my chest, nearly pushing the air out of my lungs. I wheezed, steadied myself after a few steps, and kept going.

Thankfully, there were only twelve stairs. I had counted on my way up—I had a tendency to count things—but each one felt like a mile as my foot searched in the darkness. Each step—my bad leg seemed to almost tease me with falling out, the straps digging deeper into my skin.

Thankfully, around the sixth or seventh step, the mom started to rouse, slowly. She panicked at first, but I shoved her with my shoulder to help bring her back to reality. She gave me a long look that, even in the darkness, I could tell meant, "Get bent." But, she got to the point and started stepping, taking some pressure off my legs—though she couldn't fully walk. Down the hallway on the first floor, I could see people outside the apartment, safe from the flames.

I grunted, pulling the two away from the heat that was growing on my backside. We were still a long way from Heaven, I thought. Each step was a deeper trepidation into Hell—causing me to sweat on the melting carpet below my feet. The strings twisted, spider webbing from some unknown force below as if fleeing the flames. I've never seen carpet do that before, I thought.

"They reach up like small fingers," I muttered, coughing as I said it; the little girl went wide-eyed, staring up at me. I grunted again, "Kid, go outside—get help now," I stated. She hesitated, and I growled, "Do as I say!" I shouted, and she jumped forward, bolting down the hallway as smoke started to make me feel like I was a ship in a bottle—the walls close behind me, an entrance way before me that I could never get through. I slumped against the wall with the mom. She was coughing, and each fit sent her leaning closer to the ground.

It was too far away, the smoke was way too thick, she was too heavy, and my leg was bleeding. I was coated in something wet, my pants sticking to the inside of my thighs. Was this really it? All my life, I have spent doing my best just for one thing, a thing that I thought would bring me a better future. When I had lost my limbs, my dreams up to that point were taken away in an instant. So, what else did I have? What else could I even care for after that? I had to fight for my dreams.

No one would have blamed me for giving up then; no one would blame me for giving up now. They would say I had done an excellent job already—I had accomplished what I wanted. It wasn't what I wanted—I wanted to stare down life, to stare down the devil and tell him to kick rocks. Because I would continue my race for all my life, I would finish this race. If anyone is listening, please help me with this. I screamed, "Not today," as I grunted, pulling the woman over my shoulders into a fireman's carry. She had blacked out again, her limp from feeling like a sack as I staggered, trying to find my footing.

Yes, I still had my dreams to live for. I was going to help this lady. Then, I would find Jacob, and I would put everything right. The carpet started to slide under my heavy footfalls. I kept going one step, two steps, three steps. I focused on my steps, focused on going forward as the black smoke obscured my footfalls. It was like stepping into a swirling ocean of darkness that refused to yield any information with each step I took.

I coughed, my eyes watering, and the weight started to make my knees pop; I felt myself nearly falling over when the weight was suddenly removed from my shoulders. I fell forward, smacking hard into what felt like a door latch before hands took hold of me and pulled me through the metal door frame.

My vision clouded. Before I passed out, I glanced behind me, peering into the cold darkness, which was flashing lights of red, hot orange, blood-red fires licking the wood away like sugar in water.

"Jacob," I whispered as a coughing fit caused me to shut my eyes.

Chapter 15

Cold water drenched my face, and I came to spitting water in a vain attempt to stop the jerk that was trying to drown me. I flicked open my eyes, and the mother and child were hunched over me, along with a broad-faced man—a slight look of fear in his eyes when I realized my prosthetic hand was digging into his wrist that held a now crushed water bottle.

I coughed again, "Thanks," I muttered as I set up before hands pushed me back down, "I think you should rest—Mister?" asked the mother, whose eyes were bloodshot red, her dark skin coated in a smoky outcry of oily black. I regarded her with a steady look, "Call me Billy Dan. But I have to go now," I stated flatly as I set up slower this time and stood on shaky legs. Before me, the apartment complex was convulsing like a flag in the wind, violently shaking before the flames caused the whole structure to come caving in one final lurch.

Around me, murmurs and moans of fleeting cries shook the otherwise lazy morning. My heart dropped at the sight of the building collapsing as I peered around at the group of people, scanning for Jacob, any sign of the small boy.

Instead of the toast-eating dumpster-diving child, I spotted Larry trotting leisurely at a pained pace his way to the crowd of people. A look of pure bewilderment played across his face until he spotted me. He ran in my direction at a snail's pace jog. I looked past him—hoping that Jacob had run to Larry somehow. My heart fell into a deeper hole—where was the boy?

Larry came up to me, hunched over, gasping for breath before speaking, "Billy Dan—holy crap, man, the whole place came down. Are you alright?

You look like awful, man," Larry stated.

I ignored him, doing my best to will Jacob into manifestation before me. That's how it worked right. If I wanted bad enough to see the boy—he would appear. That wasn't how it worked; we didn't have that control over the world. My heart knew the answer before my head did, though. That wasn't how life worked. Just because you wanted something or worked hard didn't mean you got it. We couldn't will/wish something into existence, no matter how much it hurt. That applied to people, even if your intentions were pure—you couldn't have them appear before you because you desired it.

A deep dagger slit through my heart, and I thought I was about to fall. I had failed the kid; I had let him run into a burning building—and he—he. I couldn't finish that thought. No, I wasn't going to think he was dead. Start with the basics, Billy Dan; what do you know? I asked myself. I looked around at the smoldering pile of rubble that was in the apartment complex as sirens in the distance blared through the air. Start small, build oversized, I chanted to myself.

With that, the world flooded into my mind. When I was a little boy, I would crawl out to an old, faded blue barn in my parents' backyard. On the side, obscured by pine and maple trees, laid the broken remains of an old basketball backboard and piles of collected sticks, leaves, and everything else I could get my hands on.

I would sit back there for hours, sometimes reading, sometimes just looking at the world around me. Life can be scary, and it can undoubtedly seem overwhelming, especially when you're a young boy missing any self-worth. In those days, I was quiet and aloof and desperately needed a friend.

I had none except that spot behind a little old blue barn. It was in this spot, nestled with my books and my leaves in the fall, that made me miss the summer breeze because those days seemed scary; those days, the world seemed far too large. Behind that barn, its paneling's falling off, the roof shingles falling like snowflakes—I learned how to retreat into my mind. I was safe. I could control what was around me.

That was how to make the world smaller, handle the world around me, and pull out what was needed. It was always simple; make the world smaller and recognize that the world around us was made up of an infinite number of tiny bits rolling into larger ones. Then, look at what you could actually get your hands on. Back then, there were some ruined paperbacks and mud. Now, it was sitting on the pavement outside an apartment complex with too many people jumping around and too glass-eyed to be used.

I took a few deep breaths, returning to that small blue barn inside my mind. Making the situation smaller. What I knew so far: I had seen Jacob running into the burning apartment building. I had not seen him leave—I was reasonably sure of that. He had at the most, maybe a minute on me as far as time went. Perfectly possible for him to have gotten out of the building. A minute is a long time when it needs to be. I also know that the fire engulfed the building at an alarming rate. I wasn't a firefighter; if I were to guess, I would think the fire wasn't natural. In fact, the whole building went up so fast, and this building—this building was filled to the brim with drug addicts. In all, I was inside for maybe ten minutes at the most, enough time to head up to rescue a mother and daughter on the second floor. Help one other old man.

So, that put eleven minutes of uncounted for time without seeing Jacob. I glanced at my watch. The time read "8:42 am". Including the drive out here and the time I had blacked out a little over an hour had passed since Larry called me. What did that leave me? That left me with a couple of things, I thought. Jacob had to be somewhere nearby, possibly scared. I wouldn't understand why he hadn't come out by now. Unless, of course, the part where Larry's involvement in this conundrum sprang into place. The baby in the dumpster had no doubt shaken the kid. It didn't explain how Jacob knew the baby was there or how he got there. Most importantly, how did Larry know that Jacob was there?

That meant that more than likely, the boy wasn't hiding. The boy had been running. But it wasn't from me. If it was from Larry, he would have done it sooner. Think Billy Dan, someone else who chased the boy, would explain why the building had gone up in flames. If that was the case, the building had to have been preset for such a thing. There was no way cheap plaster or dry wood that would explain how such a thing had occurred. And why they would wait until the exact moment Jacob had come in.

I had too many questions about why Jacob had been running in the first place. I knew where to start, but if someone was chasing Jacob—had they caught him? That was far more important than who I needed to question right now. The first thing first was to find the trail.

I looked around and ignored Larry. The firefighters arrived on the scene, and the police were just behind them. Shit. That meant Gen was going to be on her way soon. Small towns meant that the same police were generally dispatched to every city scene. An even colder fear crept into my mind in that instant. What would I tell his mother? I blocked it out and kept searching for Jacob; worry about the details, Billy Dan, stay focused, or you will never be able to find the boy.

I got to my feet, pushing away the concerns of the mother and daughter before speaking, "Just be safe, you too—get away from some of these weirdos," I gestured as one man was slowly licking a tree nearby. What would someone have to be on to make them do that? The mom regarded me, nodding as if this was a common thing. "Thank you," she stated calmly, coughing a little into her hand. "Sure," I answered before returning to her one last time. I reached into my pocket and produced a pen and my notepad. I wrote down my number, pulled a piece off, and handed it to the woman. She gave me a long look, and I stated, "I am looking for a boy that came into the apartment before me. If you see or hear anything—please let me know,". She nodded as if this was just another day at church. I thought That was weird, but as I watched the man licking the tree, I wouldn't be surprised if weird stuff happened around this building. I turned, leaving the pair quickly.

I slowly walked around the still-burning apartment building through the crowd of onlookers, displaced residents, and other curious people in town. None of them looked like any faces I knew in my village. None of them paid attention to me; they looked at the fire and weren't searching for a little boy. I had half hoped it would be that easy. From what I could tell, I looked at the streets next, but there was nothing to the north behind the apartment; I was just about to walk to the other side when I heard a screech.

On the far East side of the apartment complex, away from a parked truck, peeled out—the tires sending up a small smoke screen. I took off at a run after them, my rubbed raw leg slowing me down by the time I rounded the other side of the apartment building. I knew they were gone, so I went to where the truck had been. A set of tire tracks was freshly placed onto the road.

I took out my cellphone, snapping a picture of the tracks. I thought the truck had been red, perhaps even a faded brown, but it was hard to tell. My eyes still stung from my adventures inside the apartment complex.

I looked around all the while, my heartbeat inside my ears. Think Billy Dan, you need to solve this problem. I glanced next to the road where the truck had been parked—a set of matches in the damp grass. The matches were dry, the grass wet. The matches had a silhouette of a naked woman— big-breasted and wide hips with the logo, "Williams Whistlers," scribbled across. I remember correctly, a local strip club from the neighboring town of Bright Waters.

I jammed the matchbox into my pockets, my fist cracking as it came out. Hang on, Jacob. Wherever you are, I will find you and set things right.

Part of me hoped that Jacob had headed home. He was a resourceful kid; he would be long gone from the truck or the fire. I was freaking out over nothing; he would be at home, Gen would scold him, and he would ask me for some toast. Life would go on. That ended the moment I looked at the garbage can near where the truck was. On the ground were the tattered remains of Jacobs's black backpack. The straps are held up on one side with duct tape, pictures of aliens, and a yeti plastered all over the back. He always liked Yeti's. We talked a lot about their existence. I said it was just some hairy dude lost in the woods. He said that was boring. I felt a knife go into my heart at that moment—fear kicked in. Had Jacob been chased by whoever was in that truck? If so, why? Inside the bag, I also found a cellphone—cracked—the screen still locked. I flipped up the screen, and it flashed, showing a picture of Jacob, his sisters, and Gen. My heart sank.

Before I could dive into those thoughts, I heard footsteps behind me. I quickly tucked the bag back into the trash can, taking the cell phone into my pocket. I wasn't sure why I did that, but something told me I had just touched evidence, and I hope this ended up being a big nothing. The problem with bad things is that, as much as we wish them not to happen, no amount of wishing can stop them. This was starting to feel that way.

Turning around, I ran right into Gen's beautiful, arched eyebrow face, and with that, my heart fell into my stomach. She had a slight smile that was quickly hidden behind a mask of stoicism. Gen had entered work mode based on something from my face. I cursed myself and coughed into my hand.

"How's it going, Gen?" I asked lamely.

Gen looked unconvinced before responding, "You took off early this morning," she stated. I coughed again; this time wet. I could taste the smoke from the apartment building. I pictured my lungs looking like a pair of crumbled-up black garbage bags. I started to reply to something dumb and then coughed.

Gen's face wavered with concern. "Are you alright, Billy Dan? Let's go. The EMTs are over on the other side of the building. Honestly, why haven't you been seen yet? Don't be stupid, Billy Dan. There's so much that could kill you when you enter a building on fire," she stated.

I lowered my eyes. Gen wasn't stupid; a quick glance at my clothes and hand told me I was covered in a thick black plume that was unmistakably caused by the fire. She didn't know why I had been in the building—just that I was probably too close to the fire. My mind was working into overdrive to come up with an excuse. I realized Gen was waiting for a reply. She was giving me the benefit of the doubt.

Seeing if I was going to lie to her or not. Gen had kids from a previous marriage with an alcoholic partner; on top of that, she was a modern police officer in a small town. She had probably seen and heard every lie under the sun by now. The fact that she wasn't pinning me down and holding me in handcuffs spoke volumes about her trust in me.

I cleared my throat. "Yeah, I'm fine—I saw the fire go in," I said.

Gen frowned, "All the way out here, why? I thought you were done for the day—didn't know this was part of your route, "she pondered.

Damn—it was a weak deflect on my part. She was probing me for answers, which meant she was already suspecting me of lying. No surprise there; I would have questioned myself in the exact same situation. Or a small voice told me—she's just trusting you. Don't ruin it.

I need to tell her the truth. I just told her I saw Jacob sneaking out the window this morning and found him with Larry inside a dumpster—a small child buried inside the garbage. I couldn't, though—as I stared down into her dark eyes. Gen looked small for the first time I had known her. Her shoulders are a bit wiry, her stature coming up only to my chest. Though I knew better than to assume she couldn't kick my teeth in. I've seen her do it. She was a tough cookie. But there was someone who had feelings for me. She wasn't trying anything other than concern about me. To make it worse, she had no idea that her son was currently missing. A lie wouldn't help any of that.

I could tell by the sadness in her eyes that she was sure what I was about to say to her. That left me with a choice, I could either tell her the truth and risk causing her pain unnecessarily or lie to her and end what we were forming together. There was always the chance that Jacob had returned home, which was my hope. Was I only lying to her for myself? No, it's just to help her. It has to be to help her.

I was just about to speak when Gen blurted out, "Crap—Billy Dan, you missed your test!" she gestured towards a black wristwatch on her hands. Sure enough, it was after nine am now. I looked over at the smoldering remains of the apartment complex, "It's just a test," I mumbled, staring at the fire as it shirked away from the flames of the fireman's hoses. It would be some time before the cause of the fire would be known. Sometime before all the damage would be known, I hope that didn't mean the small body of a child.

In the distance, I could see the mother and daughter talking to our town's local news reporter. They were young kids with oversized equipment and even more oversized ambitions. They would want to interview me. I had no time for that, and Jacob had no time for that.

"You studied for years for that exam, Billy Dan. It's not just a test. Are you alright?" Gen asked. She stepped towards me.

I thought this was happening way too fast—as I was about to respond again, another officer shouted for Genesis. She turned back, nodded, and started walking away before turning to me. "Go get checked up, you look terrible. We can talk later tonight," she stated before walking away.

I nodded back. I hoped I was wrong, but there was a lot that did not add up already, and I feared that a little boy was missing. As Gen disappeared from my eyesight, I turned my attention back to the bag, my heart racing as I picked it up.

Chapter 16

The zipper had come off its tracks; something had caught it and pulled the small metal almost entirely away. I grunted, trying to pull the teeth free; they were dug into the bag's skin. "Hey, Billy Dan," shouted Larry from across the street. I looked up; the younger man was coming my way—his face ashen and coated in marks from where he had wiped the smoke away. I nodded back and bent down, trying to obscure what I was doing.

I had no idea why I was choosing not to trust Larry. Well, I knew why; my partner of five years now, every morning, taking out the trash, had lied to me about the kid. So, as I flattened Jacob's backpack on the ground, pulling out a long knife, I had no hard feelings about what needed to be done. My heart pounded, and I cupped the bag, feeling for something in the fabric.

Two tube shapes and something else. I cut the bottom of the bag quickly, reaching into the darkness. A full syringe inside a bag. I resisted the urge not to sling the needle. How often had I opened a dumpster and nearly caught the worst things because of my job? Wash your hands, cry about it later, I told myself and kept rummaging around. The only thing else I could feel was a wad of something. I took it, and the needle jammed into my cargo pants. The needle was sealed at least—thankfully, I thought.

Next, I rolled up the bag and jammed it under the dumpster. There might be something in there for later, as Larry came up beside me. He had a heavy frown on his face.

"You look like roadkill, man," he stated.

I stood up, brushing my pants off. "Thanks, Larry, so do you," I replied.

He frowned more profoundly, "Man, that was crazy... you didn't go in there, did you?" he asked.

I regarded him for a long moment before replying. "Yeah, I did," I said before walking past Larry.

"Can you drive me somewhere?" I asked the man as I started to use my sleeve to get rid of the smoke on my face. The last thing I needed was questions from someone passing by. I could see more reporters showing up on the scene. There were police and firefighters everywhere, the most this part of town had ever received.

The streets were empty despite an apartment building burning down. I knew why, though—these were the start of the slums in this town. Cross to the next block, and you were in the closest thing to a modern-day hell. And I wasn't talking about a furniture store.

Why wasn't I turning all of this over to the cops? I caught myself thinking as I pulled my jacket closer to hide my head. I walked in the direction that Larry and I had arrived here from. On a bus booth next to the street, I saw more little eyes and little noses, some close to being fully grown, but I saw the faces of the missing. And I knew as my footsteps pounded past, as my heartbeat—that was why I hadn't told Gen.

There was something wrong when any child was missing—that many—it made my spine tingle. His best chance to not end up as just another poster was to be found now. I had to see Jacob; I had to find him now.

Chapter 17

We reached the truck half an hour later, both of us panting from the heat, the annoyance of onlookers, and the congestion of traffic from the apartment burning down. I kept our walk back slower than needed, partly to help with my leg, which was stinging fiercely, and partly because I didn't want to attract attention. Getting away from the apartments was more arduous with an aid worker stopping us.

Larry slid into the driver's seat, wiping more sweat off his brow once we were back. I took the passenger seat, patting down my pockets to ensure the veil was still there, along with Jacobs's cell phone. I could feel its cold shape, and my heart took a little solace in that. The overwhelming guilt of lying to a loved one was sinking in. I just hoped that I was right. Lying is never right, Billy Dan. A small voice in the back of my head whispered. I shook that away—what was done is done.

I waited until Larry was on the road before I said anything, "I need you to take a look at something for me," I stated.

Larry glanced at me sideways, "Okay, man, but seriously, you're being weird—I mean, that was nuts with the fire and the smoke. Don't you think you should take a moment before doing something else..." Larry trailed off, looking out the window.

I sighed to hide my annoyance, "Life is short—Larry," I responded, digging into my pants to get the cell phone out. "Life is the longest thing we know, Billy Dan," he answered weakly. This time, I paused to glance at him sideways. Larry was sharper than I, and most anyone gave him credit. I once heard from a co-worker that he was an internet technology guy in a previous life. Real sharp, apparently, helped fix the guy's computer. I hoped it wasn't one of those things where he turned on some updates, and that person thought he was a genius for pushing a button. Either way, I looked toward his face; he was still avoiding my gaze. Given our proximity, I could tell the kid was hiding, through something told me it would be just as obvious a mile away. I wasn't going to force it yet. Forcing someone to speak up about something they clearly don't want to tell you is a fast way to end a friendship.

For Jacob, though, if I was right, then I was going to end everything if I had to. I needed to know who I could trust, and as of right now, I had concerns about who that was. You hear whispers of towns being corrupt, perpetually rotting to their very core. You always think of some bleak hellscape with high gothic churches and burned-down remains on every block.

Instead, it was places like our small town that were truly sinister—where Mayors could threaten to beat an elderly woman in public with cops all around and zero repercussions. Beautiful women charming you and telling you to join their cult. Missing children signs on every block. And places where garbage men thought the best thing to do was to hold their cards to their chests. I realized I was part of the problem—I could deal with that later.

I grunted in response to Larry while reaching into my pockets for the pack of matches. Carefully, I fished them out, pulling them wide so I could keep them out of sight from Larry. I glanced at the front and back of the matches again, desperate for something—finding just a phone number with an area code for a medium-sized city near our small town, felt like defeat.

Determined, I popped open the lips and found nothing as well. The pack was nearly empty. Which was why they had tossed it, I reasoned. I thought about the number for a few more moments, trying to rack my brain for which town had that number. After a few seconds, I gave up, turning to Larry in the driver's seat.

I set them down inside the glove department door. I had Jacobs's cell phone. To start with, I had something there. As I flipped the phone open, I saw it had a passcode. Damn it. I could look up what to do about getting into a protected phone online. I tended to avoid looking things up online. Learning things without the magic monkeys behind our glowing screens diligently connecting the world through one lousy joke and crooked politician at a time was a dying skill. And more than likely, that isn't accessible info. Larry kept talking, and I realized I still hadn't acknowledged him or his questions. Just ignore him a bit longer. Guilty people hate awkward silences.

After a couple of searches on my own phone, I came back with nothing. That left Larry or the matches as my leads. I rechecked the matches to make sure I spelled the name right. I was accurate. Next, I tried the area code. I recognized it immediately as a small town in South Carolina, our town. That made me pause—there was the possibility that the user of the matches had just taken a trip from the joint—maybe even worked there. Though, I've never heard of this place. The front picture was a lewd photo of a naked woman. This was a fairly conservative area—that stuff wasn't in our town. Or it could be some out-of-towner that dropped these. Honestly, it might be a nothing burger. Just the bigger city life landing on us, nothing crazy there.

This could all be a rabbit hole and nothing more. I swore, screaming into my thick skull before I calmed down. Think Billy Dan. Some things are obscured, just out of sight, and instead, inside the details of the pretty pictures people overlook. If I exhausted one resource, use my others. I tried to search once more and found mostly porn and other strip clubs before I closed off my phone. I slipped Jacobs's phone into my pocket. The whole point of a search engine is to make life easier, or just a means to give you the pleasure of being the god of your own tiny little kingdom. Neither of which was exclusively true; instead, you probably had a personal laser machine in your pockets burning away your retinas—or Hell, probably, as some of the guys at work put it, "Devices that turned you into a zombie," I mumbled. But hey, what does it matter what you become as long as it feels divine?

"What?" Larry asked, perplexed.

I looked at him. "Larry," I stated.

"What's up?" he responded, glancing over at me as I produced the pack of matches. I showed him the front of them slowly as I carefully studied his face. It went from confusion to knowing, back to a smidgen of fear, before settling somewhere between the three.

"Oh—you—want to get some smokes?" he asked nervously.

"Not exactly—much rather see something else," I stated.

He gulped, "Well, I mean, it's the middle of the day—I mean dang Billy Dan, didn't take you for a pole greaser. You turn red every time a pretty woman walks by," he trailed off, looking out the window.

I could tell Larry was thinking of a response, racking his brain for anything. "Do you know where this place is or not?" I did my best to beckon Larry, but what came out likened more to a growl even in my own ears. His flinch confirmed I hadn't succeeded in coming off gently, but he just kept looking out the window. "Yeah, I know where it is, but you don't want to go there, Billy Dan," he said incredulously.

I sighed; I could force Larry to tell me, I was confident in that. I wouldn't be able to find Jacob alone if he was missing. For now, I wouldn't push it unless I had to. I was hoping the sinking feeling I had in my guts toward Larry would go away soon. He will come clean and realize that the boy we came out here for in the first place isn't with us. I know he saw his mother outside of the apartment.

"Please—Larry, this is important. Can you take me there? I can't find it when I search for it," I stated.

"That's because they're masking it in the search algorithms. The people that control the inner webs control everything; that kind of stuff can be paid for or paid off once," he said dryly.

"Paid off with what—people in that line of business have enough money to stack dollar bills to the moon and back. What could they possibly want?" I asked.

"Control Billy Dan, that's something that people in power need. They can hide behind a smile and a white dress. All pretty smiles," Larry trailed off, and I was confused at how anyone could hide something from being looked up online, let alone how you could keep a business open with that kind of strategy. These days, even your bowel movements seem encouraged to have a marketing presence.

I pressed on, "Okay—fine, I will worry about the semantics of that later.

CHAPTER 17

Can you take me to this place, Larry?" I asked my partner of five years. We had taken out the trash for our city nearly every morning for five years. Larry would show up late from time to time and stink of grease and eyes redder than a tomato. But he would never question me when I would study on the job. When I would take the time to look into problems in the neighborhood. For that aspect alone, Larry was a beneficial partner. I needed him to treat this like another day—as if I wasn't thinking something other than what I was saying.

"Yeah, I can take you, Billy Dan, but I promise you won't like it. It's not just strippers there. It's the kind of place where folks that are hiding things don't like to be found. The kind of place where the police won't enter, and even the businesses on the block are in on it. Do you get what I mean?" he stated.

I looked at Larry, wondering why someone like him knew about a place like that. Through the yellow-stained pit stains and flappy skin dropping from his face due to a lack of sleep, I realized there was a lot I didn't know about my partner. For instance, how did he even know about that place? How did he even know about all that stuff about computer masking locations? If he knew that much, why was he a garbage man? I felt guilty about that one and dreamed of being a detective. Spent the last five years working my butt off in school, work, and everything else. Only to miss my exam for the second time. This time, for something that was way over my head, for a situation that I should have let the cops handle.

I shook my head slowly, "Before we get to that, take me to Gens, please," I directed. He stared ahead at me for a moment. His jaw opened then closed as he shut his mouth. Interestingly enough, he knew exactly where to go. I didn't even have to tell him. Another data point against my partner. Just what in the world was going on—just how deep did this go? Why couldn't I just have gone to take my test? It was too late now, though. I had started the car, and I was taking the interstate as far as I could see, this line of asphalt had no exits.

My eyes drifted out the window towards the road, tussles of thick bushes hugging against brown oak trees, like the bushes were worshipping a mighty

71

tower—high above the problems of the dirt.

Chapter 18

I combed my fingers through my tussle of black hair, laughing at her joke. We were in our town's local waffle house. Conversation flowed between us, and as our waitresses walked by to fill my coffee cup, small brown pools formed around my plate from the constant ripple of coffee that I spilled. I knew I was experiencing the closest thing to heaven. Outside, a crisp summer night had nestled into our small town. My dinner was greasy with heaps of salt and far too many cups of black coffee. Our waitresses had smoked no less than four cigarettes in the hour we had been there. A classic dirty American breakfast. Life was good as I smiled at the curly-haired woman sitting across from me. She was thin and had a face that wore a smile that pulled back to white teeth, round lips, and high cheekbones. She was beautiful—she was eating waffles with me in the middle of the night. Man, I am lucky.

We finished the meal; I paid a fifty percent tip. We were celebrating. I had been accepted into officers' school for the military—soon, I would be out of this dump. Well, it wasn't so much a dump. There were good people here; everyone knew everyone. The town has more dirt roads than paved ones. Churches on every block, endless green, and a thick smell of cows depending on which side you were on. I longed for something more—I think. I was going places, and I had a beautiful woman who loved me. And a fantastic job waiting for me. This pleasant little town just had no dreams. None like mine, for sure.

My dreams were enormous; I needed something more incredible than anything I had ever had to get out of this town. Get out there and make my mark on the world. This place would stay the same. That kept me smiling as we left the restaurant. She took my hand, our fingers laced together, and I kissed her hand. We had agreed to stay together even though I was going. It would work; she wouldn't move on. And at some point, down the line, I would marry her as our hands swayed and we walked under the leading street lights.

The yellow-brown of their flicker melts into a clear purple-black sky, twinkling with all the hopes and aspirations that life could give a guy like me. I had a great life ahead of me; I knew it. Things were finally going to get better. No more childhood traumas, no more abuse, no more failures. This was going to be it from this day forward. I had big dreams.

We crossed the road, following the crowds toward the bright lights. She smiled again as I leaned to kiss her. She asked why I was smiling so much. I said because of her. I got punched in the arm for that one, followed by a kiss that made me forget about our fantastic dinner. I asked her if she loved me because of my jokes or wit. She said why not both. I just smiled. We walked quickly—the main street giving way to the town center.

Overhead, the lights from the state fair shone brightly as we came to the ticket booth. I didn't want to let go of her hand. I awkwardly fished out my wallet with my left hand. I paid the cashier, and we went inside the fairgrounds. Lights shone with the festive twinkles of extraordinary miniature suns. A cosmic play of God for our own collection, our own universe right here on Earth. I was so happy to be alive as we danced through the fairground.

Sampling sugary foods, tasteful pretzels, and popping beers that were almost too good. At one point, I felt self-conscious; my stomach just kept on growing—but that would all be gone soon, I thought. Soon, I wouldn't have these problems anymore. I had a habit of never accomplishing anything. I was known for that. A lot of hot air, but nothing that would ever come from it. I could always tell that was what people thought when they talked to me—a blowhole that would never amount to anything. That was going to change; I was going to make something of myself. A little out-of-shape body is no big deal.

"Billy Dan!" she called, forcefully pulling me from my cave. Now was not the time for grand speeches to my audience of no one inside my skull. I told myself to go hang out with the pretty girl, taking off in her direction. Her name was Zodi; she loved me, and I loved her. That was good enough for me to just have fun for once. Stop thinking about the future. I caught up to her soon, hiding my lack of breath, taking her hand as she laughed at me. She never missed anything—the way only a lover could. When they noticed every minor imperfection and quality. They just cared, I thought. She just cared.

She pulled me to the Ferris wheel. I hesitated; she knew that I hated heights. Well, hate wasn't even the right word. It was more like extreme loathing, borderline irrational pants-pissing fear.

We got some funnel cake. I needed three more, and then I was good to go. Nothing like a sugar high to loosen you up. After a few deep breaths, we were locked into the cage and taken high above the fairground. I kept my stomach on the inside. We were high above our small town—in the distance, I could see the water towers dotting the landscape like the Earth was holding a giant metal balloon.

The ride was moving slowly. I avoided looking at the ground, instead opting to look off into the distance—searching like always for that great next thing. Soon, I would leave this town, and I would never have another problem again. I was genuinely happy.

But that was why I didn't hear the snap of a support cable jetting from the ground, cracking the air like a lion tamer. Only the lion was us, and that whip was not in control. It ripped before my eyes—narrowly missing us by only a few inches. I blinked. All around me, the world seemed to stop. The lights no longer burned with a brightness of hope. Instead, they looked like landing lights for us—as if we were some massive planes about to land on the ground; as another cable snapped, I realized we weren't supposed to be landing on a Ferris wheel. Below us, I could see onlookers, their faces racked with fear and trepidation. I looked around to see if they had a better view than we did.

They did. The wheel was still moving, just now out of alignment with its intended purpose. She took my hand as the world started to lurch.

You never think this can happen to you when something tragic occurs; a misunderstanding of the world is so vast that the pain of the event shears a brand into your skull. An immense understanding that our perceptions of control were never there, to begin with, our ideas of security and sincerity were a slice of a cosmic joke. A tumble into the darkness—for if we are to know the light, we must also see the darkness—we just don't get to choose how we experience both.

I gritted my teeth from the scream that was coming out of my mouth. She reached out towards me, our ascension near the apex of the wheel, but as the bars opened, that held us in place, and the wheel jostled forward, I watched her fall. I no longer thought we were at the top.

Smears of red dotted the world around me as cables snapped, steel became like twigs, and humans attempted to fly. My hands climbed out of the carriage, my way obscured by the details of mayhem that fluttered past anything that could be seen. I moved towards the center of the wheel, the noise around me deafening as I climbed down; it was all happening at a rate that I could not comprehend, a terrible speed made up of a force that was only acting to its nature regardless of who or what stood in its way.

I reached the bottom of the wheel, covered in sweat and blood as the wheel tipped over moments later, landing on its side with a slight hobble like a bicycle tire. I was sprayed with a fine mist of red—gawking at the carnage when I should have been moving. A cable snapped from a line pole, hitting me like an electric lance from an angel of death on high. I spun for ages, rocketing into a sack of garbage cans. Burning flesh kept me from feeling the pain in my wrist and leg. I just looked for her in Hell—I couldn't see her. I couldn't see her anymore. I couldn't see anyone, not even God.

Chapter 19

Remembering it all to this day still caused the blood to drain from my fingers. I felt nauseous as I recalled what the papers had written about the event. It was labeled a tragic mishap, but nothing was accidental. I had spent months during my recovery seeking answers. Clutching onto anything that had stood out to me. No stone was unturned. Eighty-three people had died that day. Eighty-three people with hopes and aspirations gone like a leaf in the wind.

As it turned out, the operator had been distracted while talking to a patron. He hadn't noticed a child tilting a can of paint left accidentally by cleaners earlier that day and rolling down a hill—lodging itself into a gearbox that caused a surge of electrical failures. A support chain had snapped from the sudden stop, and the rest of the pieces tumbled into the history books.

Officially, the investigating officials concluded that it was a freak accident. Maybe it was, perhaps it wasn't. But I also know that they still needed to figure out how cleaning could have rolled into the fuse box in the first place. To my knowledge, the authorities never checked to see who it belonged to.

I remember after the accident feeling so hopeless—so bitter. It was like trying to reach the moon with just a bottle rocket. And my anger quickly faded to sorrow and self-loathing. I spent months in the hospital, one of the only survivors from a carnival ride massacre, as the media called it. Instead of resting, I investigated the case.

I wanted so badly for the operator to be guilty. I wanted him to pay. I wanted someone to pay. I had so much hate boiling under my skin—I thought my flesh was going to melt away. Just like the cops, it all came down to a freak accident in the end. All I did was find out more of the pieces.

In the end, I had lost most of my left hand, my right foot, my woman, my future, and most of what I thought I was.

I had always been in the right area, not in time to help save those I cared about. I felt like a failure all my life because of that; that was my driving force, and that's why I did what I did. I woke up every morning and night hours before I had work to train and study. Moving towards some unknown tasks. I had thought I was great, but I was wrong. That was changing, though, day by day. I wasn't that boy anymore.

Life had such a way of humbling me, I thought. The accident had one silver lining—out of it, I decided to never give up. I had to keep going, and I must be better. Since that day, it's been a struggle—but it's given me time to hone my skills. Gone was that chubby boy who had no idea what he wanted or needed to do. From that day forward, I finished things. I was weak—I wasn't anymore.

Chapter 20

Larry had been driving for twenty minutes by this point. I was leaving my fog and setting those memories back where they belonged; in a tight box. It contained all my worse failures and Jacob had nothing to do with them. I had no choice but to finish this. We were at Gen's house. I cleared a lump in my throat as I shook off the memory of losing Zodi, of the time after the accident. It all seemed like looking at broken glass. Sure, I could tell it was once part of something. I had no idea how the infinite tiny pieces could ever go back together. I talked the big talk—I just hoped that I believed it.

Chapter 21

Gen's neighborhood was dotted with trimmed trees and clear streets. Some younger kids casually played with their parents despite it being a school day. A slow heat was setting in with clear blue skies. The thick humidity of the South, not quite fully awake yet, made a fantastic morning of 48 feel much higher. Tiny sprouts of budding leaves for the new year appeared, and the wild cats that stalked the underbushes were content with leading the flying rodents' scurry about unabated. The harshness of winter was over. Now was supposed to be the time of renewal. The sun is shining, and the world is slowly returning to the easier times of the year.

For everyone else—that was the case. For me, my thoughts stayed on a little boy named Jacob. He was trapped in winter—the harshest time of the year. In what situation, I dreaded even thinking about it for him. Jacob should have been one of these kids. Playing hooky by hiding in a garbage can.

I gripped the passenger door handle so hard that the metal door handle started to groan. I let go before I broke it. Larry, for his part, had parked the truck. He was wiping the sweat off his forehead with his hat. Both our windows were rolled down.

He parked his red truck outside of Gen's house. It was a modest manufactured home. A light blue and sported a shining metal roof. Very common in these parts of town. With a well-kept lawn and an underskirt, the home is almost mud-free. Despite having so many kids—she kept a tight ship. I hated myself even more at that moment. She was organized enough to understand the gravity of the situation. Maybe she could have helped you find him by now, Billy Dan. It's not too late. Just call her, and she will surely only be a little mad.

I hesitated, taking a deep breath. No, too many missing kids had come up. Whatever was going on, Jacobs's best shot was to be found quickly and without fail before anything got out of control. I just needed to be quick. However, it helped if I knew what I was looking for. I had yet to tell Larry too much about Jacobs's phone or why we were here now.

A couple of things didn't need to be added up. Namely, what was the kid looking for? That would also help with figuring out how he got there. Which still stung. I had been putting off talking to Larry just yet. I wanted him to come clean—to give me hope that there was a reason for the madness that was starting. It's never that easy, I thought, making my way to her big red frame door. A small welcome mat with a sketch of Gen and her four kids and a spoiled golden with a huge doggie smile greeted me.

I had been to her house countless times. I felt like a stranger now, a stranger in a land that I was feeling increasingly by the moment as if I wasn't supposed to be here. That may be the case. I cleared my throat of the lump of pain that was forming before knocking lightly on the door. It was March this time of year. Jacob is her oldest kid. The rest are all little girls. Two of them weren't old enough to be in school just yet. So, when the babysitter with a worn-out flannel and sweatpants answered the door, I wasn't surprised. She held Gen's youngest daughter, who desperately needed a nap—her curly brown hair looked like a ski mask on her face, obscuring her olive skin and brown eyes inherited from her mother.

Behind the young babysitter was Gen's second youngest daughter, her small frame clinging to the sitter's leg. She smiled at me behind a lock of thick brown hair, almost looking like a miniature Gen, save for her nose being a little longer than her siblings. Must have gotten that from her father, I thought.

"Billy Dan!" the little girl screamed, coming out from around the sitter's legs and jumping onto me. I caught her, fanning her weight as heavy. Laughing with her in response, "You've gotten strong kiddo!" I put her back down and nodded at the sitter, "Sara—doing alright this morning?

How's school?" I asked her as she smiled and sighed heavily. "I thought beauty school was supposed to be easy," she stated. I nodded along to that. "Some people take their haircuts very seriously," I said.

She laughed at that one, "Yeah—you need to be one of those people, Billy Dan, that's a mop of hair," she joked. I brushed through my hair—feeling the grease from the fire. And what felt like a few burnt tips. Who knew how it must have looked to her? Thankfully, my line of work gave me every excuse to be a little dirty. It also helped that Sara was used to seeing me come by. Partly to drop off Jacob and the other times when I was either seeing Gen or helping her out around the house. She smiled as I smiled at her, her big loop golden earrings sparkling in the early morning sunlight.

Sara's face turned concerned momentarily before she looked around, "Oh, I thought maybe Jacob was with you," she trailed off, looking nervous. "Speaking of that, why wasn't he in school today?" I asked her.

She became more severe and smiled a slight smirk, "You know how it is, Billy Dan. I sent him to the bus. Watched him come back up to the side of the house five minutes later. By the time I got the girls," she gestured to the baby she held and the miniature Gen behind her, "he was gone again. I thought he was with you..." she trailed off suddenly looking worried. I cleared my throat and smiled. "He's not with me, but I am sure he will pop up soon enough. Say, speaking of which—does he normally skip out of school this early?" I asked her, thinking about how often he had been caught leaving school. The kid was brilliant—but he just didn't care for school. A discussion that I just didn't feel I had the right to start with her for the time being. I wasn't the boy's father.

She shook her head no. "No—he normally at least goes to school. He rides his bike to and from. I did think it was weird he was taking the bus this morning, though," I nodded at that. "Say, do you know the bus route?" I asked her, stepping into the doorway. She nodded, "Yeah, let me set them down. Do you want some coffee?" she asked.

"Sure, thank you," I said, closing the door behind us before looking at Larry. I met his gaze for a moment and held up both my hands—all eight flesh fingers and two metal.

82

Chapter 22

Jacobs's room, I imagined, was like any other little boy around his age—well, maybe. His walls were littered with posters of superheroes and Albert Einstein. Not to mention other science-looking folks who I could only assume were intelligent or essential. Some of a cat inside a spacesuit, with the number "2311" written on the patch he was wearing. I was more concerned about his desk. From what I could tell, his desk was covered in trinkets and oddities. The rest of his room, sticking out like a sore thumb by comparison, was perfectly spotless. Must have been done by Gen, I thought.

I looked closer at his desk—taking in as much as possible while I was afforded the time inside the room. I had convinced Sara that I was returning one of Jacobs's "finds" this morning. That was the second lie I told, I realized. They were starting to add up fast—and I hated every word that came out of my mouth. But mostly, it was just how easy it was to tell her one. Hadn't even planned it; it came as naturally to me as a bowel movement. I didn't want to think about the implications of that. Just needed to stay focused on Jacob. He was what's at stake here. If I found him—this all would be worth it.

"Okay, kid. Help me find you," I mumbled, rubbing my face. I pulled his phone out of my pocket. I moved the touch screen to a locked photo of him and his mother. I sighed at that. I tried a random password before being met with a silent vibrate, indicating that my attempt was wrong, and I had two chances left. Okay, that made things a lot more problematic really fast. Why did I even try a random password? What random password did I even try? I realized that before shaking my head. Take a deep one, I thought, moving aside scattered books and what appeared to be half a blow horn attached to a pair of roller-blades. How did he even manage to do that?

I moved along and picked up a book. It was The Outsiders. I smiled at that, setting the book down on the table again when I noticed a piece of paper sliding out of the book slightly. I pulled the paper out, revealing a topographical map of our small town. It took me a moment to recognize it.

On the map were six circles, one with an "X" over the circle. I blinked at that—what was this kid up to? I stuffed the map into my pocket, looking around to see if anyone had caught me. I shook my head from that—I was alone, inside my girlfriend's house. However, I now felt like I didn't belong here. Like my guest's right had been revoked. I felt it somewhere deep inside. I had already lost her. I shook my head at that. I had no way of knowing that was where this was all going. I was going to find Jacob soon. Gen would understand—I was pretty sure of that.

I stood up from the desk and pulled Jacobs's phone from my pocket. I had hoped to find some sticky note with his passcode. Anything, just something that would help. Instead, all I saw was a map and even more questions. And a damn cat in a space suit staring at me.

I looked at the poster—it was the same cat in a suit I had seen on his shirt earlier. I looked at the cat's badge and swore not to see what was already in front of me. I moved Jacobs's phone to unlock it, punching in the key "2311" and praying it would work. A moment later, Jacobs's phone was completely unlocked.

Chapter 23

I spent more time drinking coffee with Sara than I had wanted to. Trying to be polite would be the death of all of us. I burned my tongue downing the coffee. I managed to leave Gen's house about a minute later. Promising the girls that I would play with them the next time I was over. That was something I really hoped I would get to deliver on. I realized Lego night with Gen and the kids was the highlight of my week. As I walked out of the house—that same feeling returned. I wasn't going to be coming back to that house again. That sting slid a natural dip into the pit of every man's stomach. Men truly wanted only a few things. Something to believe in, something to love, or at the least something to do. I was losing what I loved with every moment that went by. I just had to find Jacob. That was more important than Gen and mine's relationship.

I was back to Larry's truck with my head down as I reached it, opening the door and sliding into the passenger seat with no flare. Larry cleared his throat after a moment as I stared at Gen's house. "Hey Billy Dan—forget something inside?" he asked.

I looked at him, confused by what he said, "What?"

He shook his head, "I said, did you forget something? You're staring back at Gen's house as if you had lost a million bucks," he stated.

I replied, "Yeah, at least a few million..." I trailed off before continuing. "Say, we need to get out of this neighborhood," I stated.

He nodded, "Alright, where too?" he asked.

"Just drive. I will get the next part figured out soon enough, "I said, looking down at Jacob's phone again as I pulled open his search history and messages.

Chapter 24

Larry drove us out of the neighborhood—finding a less trafficked dirt road only a few blocks from Gen. The streets familiar in the South were like a doorway into a different world. A quiet getaway—yet so close to the hustle and bustle of suburbia. As if there was still something wild left— like something untouched by the movements of time. A simple dirt road, tiny bits of gravel—mostly just clay or mud. A simple back road—there you can escape, there on the road—you can think. Trees obscure everything but the road. Twists of overgrowth, some still carrying the tinges of crimson and brown on their leaves. The last vestiges of fall just before the thick blankets of winter set in.

Soon, his truck came to a slow stop on the side of the road. The keys are still in the ignition. A slow rumble as the truck echoed across the road. I counted the engine's idling, now becoming in rhythm of my heartbeat. After a few more moments of silence, Larry cleared his throat, "Um, Billy Dan," he almost whispered. I held up a finger, "Just a few more minutes, need to think," I stated, staring at Jacobs's phone.

I had scanned only a bit of Jacobs's phones. Going through his pictures was the standard stuff. Lots of photos of him and his dog, his mother, and even one of me with his mother. That one stung. I didn't linger as I kept looking through until I found one that gave me pause. It wasn't evident, the angle—I could make out the lime green of a dumpster. Jacob—I assumed he had taken the photos from some tree nearby. I could see a few gas pumps out of the farthest reaches of the picture. More importantly, the picture was at dusk—I couldn't tell what exactly I was looking at first, but the most crucial part was two men dumping a heavy bag of something. Their faces were turned away from the camera.

I sent the picture to my phone. There were other photos, five more to be exact. Similar situations. None had their faces, and some had a van parked in them. Based on the time stamps, most were very early or late at night, sometime between two in the morning and five. I made a mental note of that. I couldn't find the tags for the van. I could see the size of the tires. I typed out the sizes and sent them along with the rest of the messages to my phone. Next, I made note of the time frame Jacob had taken all of the photos. He had started roughly six and a half weeks ago this morning. I paused, looking up from the phone, Larry was sweating. His skin is a sickly white color.

"Are you alright, Larry?" I asked, eyeing the man, his hands gripping the steering wheel tightly. I lowered my hand with Jacobs's phone, and his eyes slowly traced it down. I waited for a breath longer before speaking. I gave him an out, "Coming down with something, man?" I asked him, trying to keep my voice as neutral as possible. Part of me still hoped that his involvement in all of this wasn't as bad as I dreaded in the pit of my stomach. Larry's eyes were glazed with lines—I recognized those, the eyes of someone strung out on who knows what. If I could get away from that life—so, could he. So, I hoped, even though I knew he was probably the most prominent piece in all of this. If I could find Jacob soon, this could be wiped away easily. That I was sure of.

After a moment of silence between us, he spoke, "Yeah, just caught a little cold, is all," he smiled and looked out the driver's window. "Say, is that the kids, phone?" he asked innocently. This was the test, I thought. I nodded slowly as he stared out the window like this was just another conversation. "It sure is. Do you want to take a look at it?" I gestured towards the phone towards him, readying if he tried to take it. To his credit, Larry never turned away. "Billy Dan, we should be calling the cops. I'm unsure what we are driving around town for—but that kid is gone. I mean, you look like roadkill," he stated.

I put the phone back down in my lap, "Yeah, you have a point there, man. But how many posters have you seen around town, Larry? How many kids?

So many that you can't go nearly ten feet without seeing one? Jacob will not become another one of those kids. So, help me here, man—please," I whispered, almost pleading with the man. He paused for a moment before turning back to me. "I will help," he said weakly. I nodded at him.

"Find anything on the kid's phone?" he asked. "More questions than answers, to be honest," I stated.

"Hand me the phone, I can find out who the kid has been texting, etc.," he stated matter-of-factly. "Wait—you know how to do that?" I asked him. He looked insulated momentarily before pushing his glasses up his dark nose. "Yeah, man—it's not that hard. Trust me, I can find where whoever was or is messaging him. Then I can find where they went off, too," he stated.

I nodded. "Guess the rumors were true. But do you think he was texting someone?" I asked him. He shrugged his shoulders as I handed him Jacob's phone. "I have no idea—he ran for some reason, did he not?" he stated. I took that in. Nor had he known why Jacob was there.

That was another data point in the seemingly never-ending list of points. My head was going to explode soon. I paused, reminding myself that most cases in the movies take months—sometimes even years or decades- to resolve. I wasn't going to let that be the case with Jacob. I decided to continue playing down my concerns about Larry. Keeping someone you didn't trust was a dangerous game—scorpions will always sting sooner or later. I thought I would have to accept that as a possibility, as I shrugged my shoulders in response. "Just trying to find the kid, man," I stated.

He barely looked up as his hands flew across the keypad. "Can you hand me my backpack?" he stated, not looking at the screen. I paused suddenly, very weary. This could be it—if I get him the bag, was I handing him my murder weapon? I suddenly felt sick and hoped my face wasn't sweating too bad—I felt more than a few beads roll down my head. I nodded in response and did my best as I reached behind my seat into the cluttered back of his truck. Energy drinks and wrappers littered the floor as I traced my hands to a small green bag I had seen Larry with plenty of times. I hesitated momentarily as Larry spoke with me; half turned in the seat.

"I know about the rumors at work—I don't do drugs. I just don't sleep much. A big gamer, to be honest—amongst other things," he muttered under his breath as I paused once I had ahold of the bag. I turned, looking at him, arching my eyebrows at him. "I moonlight from time to time doing odd jobs and such online. Alright? You aren't the only one with dreams, Billy Dan. Though I don't know how you could believe in any of them at this point," he trailed off, staying focused on the phone.

I relaxed at that; a man doesn't typically open up about their dreams before killing someone. I think. I finished pulling the bag out from the bag and handed it to Larry with no fanfare. He took it with one hand and unzipped it, quickly pulling out his laptop. I let out my breath before continuing on, "So, what? You want to work with computers and stuff?" I asked him as I wiped the gulps of sweat from my forehead. I hope he hadn't noticed that.

"Dude, you're like six years older than me, tops. Why do you always sound like a boomer? I worked as a white-hat penetration tester for a few years. Hated having a boss on my back—they were just mad they couldn't afford me," he stated firmly. I was skeptical about that. Larry was late nearly every morning. Not to mention, this job, while not as bad as many people would think pay-wise, there was a good reason Larry's truck was barely above just drivable.

When I didn't respond, Larry rolled his eyes, "I hacked people's stuff, man. From their phones to servers, some other stuff," he trailed off. I gave him a long look before he turned away, shrugging, "I sort of failed into this when it all came down. It wasn't my fault—things just—I don't know," he mumbled.

I cleared my throat, "I hear you, man—shit happens. I know," I said, gesturing towards my metal fingers. He looked at my hand for a moment before looking away. I continued, "The thing is—look, maybe I've made some mistakes not getting to know you this whole time, but I need your help," I stated, leaning back into my seat and fixing him with a long gaze.

He rolled his eyes before pulling a laptop out of his bag. The lid was covered in an endless number of stickers with odd sayings and colorful characters. I didn't recognize a single one. Maybe I was getting old.

"Stop with the dramatic speeches—I can help you with this. I will even do it for free—normally, my rates are very reasonable. So, consider yourself lucky," he stated as his keys flew across the keyboard.

I blinked at that before settling back into my seat. Part of me wondered if Larry would erase anything of him that may be on the phone. That was a risk I would have to take at this point. I closed my eyes. A splitting headache was forming at the front of my head, almost like a very angry little man trying to tell me to turn my music down. The rhythmic clatter of keys sounded off in union with my pounding head.

Chapter 25

We were pulling up to a house a few blocks away from Gen's house now. It was a small, manufactured home. It had a swing attached to a tree, a massive carport with a boat, and a newer-model truck next to the boat. Expensive toys, I thought. Yet, it was a small house. I was already hating the man inside that house as we sat there. I motioned to Larry to kill his truck. He did silently, handing me back Jacob's phone.

"Are you sure this is the place?" I asked him, eyeing the house. "Yeah, this is the place. This was the guy to whom Jacob was sending the pics," he stated. Larry had gone through Jacob's messages, finding even the deleted ones. Jacob had apparently met this man as the boy was trying to send the pics to him from the various photos near the garbage cans. It also appeared that by the time Jacob had started talking to the man, by photo four, the man had been following Jacob since photo two.

Larry had then found out about the man. However, he needed help finding what they talked about as it was most likely on the man's phone. That left us with only a few options at that point. Larry then somehow found the man's username on other sites. One stuck out like a giant red dragon in your grandmother's living room. The account belonged to a man who was active on adult hookup accounts. Not just active but had spent close to five hundred hours on one of the sites alone. What was worrying about those sites, though—it said eighteen only, but as Larry demonstrated, it is easy to get around that setting.

I asked what some adult would want with a kid pretending to be older than they were—that got a long look from Larry. I clenched my seatbelt so tight I was close to tearing it out from the seat. Thankfully, Jacob appears to have met the man on an online forum on weird dumpster finds.

That was perplexing enough—maybe I am sheltered as the only modern man who didn't get the most basic of the internet. Maybe I was just old-fashioned. Maybe I just still believed if you pulled the covers over your head—the monsters couldn't get you. However, as I got older, I realized the monsters weren't living in my open closet door. They were everywhere— the same amount there had always been. Just now, with everything being online—they could hide. In plain sight and belong to nearly every facet of life. All shapes and sizes. All types of collared workers. Even in this case, the man we had found, "William Bernard,". A man who was married for fifteen years and had two kids.

Volunteered as a firefighter and teaches softball twice a year. And occasionally in the late hours of the night when no one was awake. Talked to underage kids. My hands fumbled with the seatbelt ejector. I thought about the monster that was hiding in a small manufacturing home. Several black oaks dotting his yard.

Along with a maple—a tire swing attached to one of its long limbs. Like a dark hand coming out of the abyss rather than a swing that held many laughing children. No, I was seeing the dark facade of a monster. The mask is used to pretend to be normal—avoid suspicion. There was a monster in that house now. Larry had found him by pretending to be an eleven-year-old boy.

Had only taken us a total of thirty minutes to get William to invite us over. I had slammed Larry's truck door with enough force once I exited, and I was surprised the glass hadn't broken behind me. A monster was in that house. A monster that had been talking to Jacob. My girlfriend's son. A good, smart kid, and he was going to have a bright future ahead of him—he was going to have that. If this monster hurts him—I shuddered to think what sort of monster would come out of me.

My blood boiled, and everything tinted red.

Chapter 26

I composed myself the best I could, zipping up the orange vest I had borrowed from Larry. My company hat was relaxed on my head, and I tried to give myself an air of "just a working stiff" with nothing on my mind. I tried to do that at least. I worried that as I knocked, you would be able to feel my anger radiating off me like the leftover coals from a fire.

My first knock was polite, so I pulled out my cell phone to busy myself as if I didn't have a care in the world and was just going about my work day. I shifted my feet back and forth and tried to look as insecure as possible. A universal truth with the world is that predators relax once they only think you aren't a threat.

I was whistling Dixie, looking at my watch, and about to knock again when the blue door with chips at the edges of the lock cracked open slowly. William was an unassuming man, somewhere in his mid to late thirties. He had a truffle of hair around his ears and a shaggy beard that grew faster on his neck than the rest of his face. A few whiskers of gray dotted inside his dark hair. All that was overshadowed by the bowl cut of a balding patch he sported. At the top of his far receding hairline line, William had opted to comb his hair over in an attempt to make his hair appear thicker. It added nothing to it and, in fact, made me look longer at his head because of the thinning hair.

He had a thick neck, a barreled chest, and large arms covered in layers of hair. He wasn't a tall man, and his nose appeared to have been broken several times. On one of his biceps, above where his sleeve rolled up, was a fire department logo with our city's name tattooed onto his bumpy skin.

He regarded me with an almost bored expression, half opening the door to me, keeping most of his bulk and his other hand out of view.

I hesitated for a moment, trying to appear less confident than I normally was. I remembered that I needed to get information from this man. And a large part of me, just above the simmering rage inside my stomach, was hoping Jacob was on the other side of this door—though William had better pray that he was not.

He scuffed, taking control of the conversation, and pushed his glasses up his nose, "What do you want?" he asked. I put on my widest and what I hoped for was my most unlearning smile. I relaxed, "Mr. Bernard, right?" I asked him.

"Whose asking?" he replied quickly.

I nodded, pretending not to notice his response or body language change. As I could see, I could see his exposed arm tighten its grip on his door frame.

"Yes—yes, sir, I am with the city. We are here to do a routine checkup of your water pressure and check your gauges. It won't take but a moment," I stated flatly, trying my best to come off as forgettable.

He regarded me for a long moment before narrowing his eyes at me.

"My water pressure is fine," He stated while moving his hand. I stuck the toes of my good leg into the door ever so slightly to keep it from closing. He looked down at my foot as I took the time to ready myself with my other leg.

"Yes, sir, most of the residents are under good pressure. I just need to check; it will take a moment," I stated matter-of-factly.

He squinted his eyes at me, looking beyond me. "Where's your truck?" he barked at me. I smiled at that, "What do you mean?" I asked in response.

"Where's your truck if you're with the city?" he trailed off, narrowing his eyes to the point that I would have honestly thought he was taking a nap standing up. I let out a long breath, realizing the jig was up and in a fluid motion, and brought my other leg up hard into the door.

My prosthetic leg wasn't going to be kicking any door down without causing a lot of pain to my leg. But what it would do was knock over an out-of-shape child predator onto his fat butt easily enough. I swore as the metal clams bit into my ankle. I could feel the skin getting ragged from the abuse I had subjected it to today already. If only I had my other leg—my

Terminator leg, as I called it, that came with a crescent shape and was built for impact and sports. I have to deal with this leg for now. And it was plenty strong enough for what I needed it for anyway.

I stepped through the door quickly, looking both ways for a moment, and slammed the door shut behind me. William was in a heap on the ground, holding his nose—blood dripping out from his fingers. I was certain no one besides Larry had seen what I had just done. I was fairly certain I didn't care—a small part of myself was scared. What was I doing now?

I fumbled the lock closed on the door and kicked William in the stomach simultaneously. He yelled, and I jammed one of my hands into my vest, gripping my phone inside my pocket, hoping it would look like a gun to him. He held his nose, his eyes watering as he stared at me with a look of absolute hate.

"Think we should have a chat," I stated calmly. On the inside, though—I was fairly sure I could melt an iceberg.

Chapter 27

He landed in a heap on his office floor. Still clutching his nose as I slammed the door shut behind us. I was fairly certain the house was empty. Fairly certain, at least. William started to sit up; I pushed him down with my good leg and pointed my phone in my pocket towards him. He eyed my vest but seemed to reconsider any idiotic ideas he had harbored. William was a middle-aged man; he wasn't going to be springing towards a potentially loaded gun hidden in a stranger's pocket while he was already bleeding and lying on the ground. I hoped not, at least.

"What the—" he started, and I waved him off with my other hand as I walked around him and closed the blinds. A thick layer of dust greeted my fingers as I scuffed at it, wiping it on my pants. "Geez, Will, I need to clean your house," I stated.

"fu—"he said before I kicked him hard in the ribs. He bowled over and gave me a long look. "Couple of things—stop cussing. And now I'm the one asking all the questions here. Is that fair?" I asked, giving him a smirk.

He considered me for another long moment before nodding. "Good, as to who I am. That doesn't really matter. What does matter is a boy. Now, we can do this quickly and easily. No one has to get hurt. I ask a few questions. Then you crawl into a deep hole and pray I never see you again," I growled at him. William flinched away, which cooled the rage building with each moment I was in his office.

William was silent for another long moment before speaking, "What boy?" he asked with far too big of a smirk for my liking. I looked around his office momentarily and saw a black common office stapler. I picked it up with my free hand, undoing a switch on the side so that the bottom half was free from the top. He eyed me but didn't say anything. I laughed before responding, "You know—it's been a long day, to be honest, William. I can call you Will, right? William takes a long time to say, and I am afraid I'm running out of time. But you know who's running out of time faster—that's you if you don't start answering me. Now, I am going to ask you one more time. Where is the boy?"

"What fu—"he shouted as I brought the stapler hard onto his head. Clicking the pressure pad down in the process. He screamed. I jerked the stapler and the staple off his balding head. The stapler made a mark like an angry mosquito had bitten him.

He swapped his head, his eyes watering again as he opened his mouth again. I cautioned him with a look. Williams' lips moved, then seemed to go flat like a deflated balloon from something in my eyes. Begrudgingly, he titled his head. I could see a look of defeat in his eyes now. He knew he was caught—there was no getting out of this.

"I don't know what boy you're talking about," he gasped as I motioned to him with the stapler. He jerked up his hands in front of his face, "No, please! I don't know what boy you're talking about—I swear," he pleaded.

I just couldn't believe it. Not after Larry had shown me his search history. Not after I saw what he was downloading. I slapped his hands out of the way and then hit him with the stapler, this time on his busted nose. I felt the crunch as the stapler fell to the ground. Blood sprayed out, and I took a step back, breathing heavily.

What in the world was I doing? I felt myself shivering. An icy chill ran through me. I was hurting a man—no. No, I was hurting an animal, I reminded myself. A man didn't do the things he did. Yeah, that made more sense, as he was an animal. I was sure of that now—no doubt, I was sure.

Only animals cried—William was streaming tears now as he held his broken nose. The swelling started at the edges, and the dark circles of black eyes were already forming. Maybe he was still a man? What was I becoming? I suddenly just wanted to sit down. I felt so heavy—my stomach filled with sludge—urging its way to the top. I choked that down and steadied myself against the wall. This wasn't getting us anywhere fast, and now William was crying.

Even in the South where most folks had distance between each other's homes—including Williams, whose closet neighbor was only a few fields away. None of the noise we made could be heard by anyone. I sighed, "Look, I know you're home alone. And your wife won't be coming home for another few hours. We can do this the easy way—or we can do it the hard way," I stated, gesturing to the stapler on the ground. His eyes went wide with fear.

"Now, please—for the last time, where is the boy? Where did you take him?" I asked him feeling sick with every word. He shook his head, and I let out a long breath, expecting to have to him again. "No, look, I don't—I don't have him. Are you talking about the Mexican kid?" he asked weakly.

I kept his gaze as he averted his after a moment. "Yeah, he's not just some kid. Where is he? Where did you put him? I know that you two have been talking," I stated, and a realization appeared on his face.

"How did you know about that?" he asked weakly. "I know you use a burner phone to do all your talks. I know your real number. Keep playing stupid, and your wife is going to find out all about this,". I growled.

His face paled, and he started to whimper. That made me sick to my stomach, and I had to look at his forehead rather than his eyes.

After a few long breaths, he spoke, "Look, I don't know about the kid, alright? I'm just a spotter. All I do is find the kids. The actual dudes that take the kids I have no idea about. Honestly, they pay us under the table, and I never know who anyone is. I swear. They told me if I didn't help them, they would show—they would show my wife my collection," he trailed off to his computer.

I was sickened by it. Larry could first get his computer's information after we had located him at home. Terabytes of data—all with kids in them. What was he saying? Was he saying someone else knew what he was up to on his computer? If so, why would someone who knew what he was up to— would let him get away with it? Easy enough that one, I thought; whoever it was that was directing him used people like him. People that most people wouldn't give a second thought about throwing behind bars for a very long time.

A man with nothing to lose and already had a taste for children. The sludge was now gone—now the dragon inside me was coming back out. I clenched my throat and didn't say anything.

William blinked a few times and kept talking, "I swear, man, I don't know. I don't know who took the kid. I just reported that he was going to be at those old abandoned buildings on the far side of town. Honestly," he stuttered.

"Who did you report to?" I asked him through choked words of anger. He gulped down and shook his head, "I don't— "he muttered as I kicked him in the chest. He fell back against the wall, huffing out large puffs of his chest—gasping for air. I reared back with my leg again to kick him again, and he threw up his hands, "Okay, okay. Just promise me you won't say anything. Like if any of this gets out," he stated.

I bent down so that both our faces were leveled. "Brother, you don't have anything to bargain with. If you don't tell me what I need to know now. And I mean right now—I will kill you. You won't have anything else to worry about then," I stated coldly.

On the inside, though, monster or not. I had my doubts I would actually harm him. That bridge was too far—I was just a garbage man, not a cop. No matter how much I wanted to be one. I wasn't a judge or executioner either. I was just a man. He was just a man. Right?

William finally broke, and I could see the defeat in his eyes, "Okay, I can give you a little something, man, but I honestly don't know much. I just meet this guy once a month. He tells me what kind of kids he likes... I then find them and set up a time for the fishers, honestly," he pleaded, throwing up his hands to cover his face just in case.

I stayed with his words long before replying, "I have a few questions; just give me a name. Give me something," I demanded, moving closer to him.

Chapter 28

The door at the west hospital wing was locked for medical personnel only. I stuffed my hands in my pockets and went outside the hospital. William had given me a name before I had tied him to his chair—making sure that Larry could get whatever we needed off his computers. I called the police anonymously, pretending to be a neighbor, and as I left, I also had Larry call his wife behind me. I had promised I wouldn't tell anyone, William.

I looked at the stapler—the blooded object looked like the talons of a bizarre monster instead of a typical office worker's tool. Part of me wanted to pray in that moment glancing at the stapler—I couldn't do it though. I had my doubts God would listen after something like that. taking the stapler and wiping away any evidence of me being there. I wasn't sure if leaving him there was the right way to handle the situation, and I wasn't sure if I should have stayed much longer.

Once I had gotten to Larry and we started to drive, I opened the window and threw up until my throat was burning, and nothing came out but tears. Larry hadn't said anything while I was losing my mind out the side of his truck window. When I finally stopped wiping my mouth afterward, he asked if I had learned anything from William. I explained that William was kept in the dark—someone had a lot of dirt on him—the same stuff we had found.

His job was simple, find kids that matched specific descriptions—he wasn't ever to touch them in any way. But if needed, befriend them and set them up to be taken by men who drove a truck that matched the skid marks Jacob had taken pictures of. There wasn't much to go on, but Larry would look while I checked out the next spot to see if any vehicles in town matched the tire size.

William had been told to follow Jacob especially. He hadn't mentioned the baby Jacob had found. That had me asking more questions. The only name he could give me was of a particular doctor who worked at the local hospital. His name was Doctor Matt Alexander. Doctor Matt had apparently been the guy who would give William a file on what type of kid he needed and when he needed them, including age, gender, race, and sex. All walks of life, and William had been doing this for two years. I asked him if he knew of any other people doing the same.

He said he didn't know; he would just open his mailbox on the first of every month. There would be money. Whenever the doctor needed William, the people who blackmailed him in the first place would set up a time and meeting place for the two. He never knew much; he didn't even know the doctor was a doctor until he accidentally spotted the doctor's badge when the pair met once. William had kept his mouth shut and never questioned who the doctor was—where he worked. He never asked who the people who blackmailed him were. He knows that they promised to hurt him in ways he could only imagine when they first found him.

I wanted to hurt him in ways he could never imagine. It was wrong to leave a monster free like that. I needed to trust the law to handle him. I needed to find the doctor; I needed to find Jacob. Larry had found one doctor who was only twenty minutes away and matched the name William had given me. He worked in the west wing of the hospital and was only a few years from retiring.

I stuffed my hands into the trucker jacket I had borrowed from Larry—looking around at what I could use. When I got to the hospital, I had Larry wait in the parking lot. I could see his red truck at the edges of the lot. Around me, plenty of nurses, doctors, and other staff were moving quickly from place to place.

I spotted a badge on one of the nurses. That seemed like a good place, but how would I get into that wing? I started off momentarily when I saw my answer to the how. Kneeling down, I pretended to tie my shoes as I rubbed my face. I could still feel the slick oil and smoke from the fire.

I then quickly made my way over to an empty wheelchair that was near the passenger loading area. I plumped into the chair and wheeled myself to the side of the overhang at the front of the building. In a few moments, I pulled my prosthetic leg off and placed it behind me. Rolling up my pants leg on the side to hide my wounds—making me appear more like a wounded vet. An old woman was smoking on the bench near me. I motioned with my fingers, and she handed me a cigarette. I thanked her and wheeled myself deeper under the overhang. A young nurse came my way after a few moments with the lit cigarette as I pretended to smoke.

"Sir—sir, I'm going to have to ask you to put that out. You can't smoke under here," she motioned to a sign on the entrance door with a clear "No smoking" sign on the doors. I gestured towards my leg and gave her a look as I dragged on the cigarette.

She sighed heavily; I cleared my throat and said, "Tell you what—how about I bum one off you—and we both smoke out back?" I gestured to the side of the building. She smiled at me, and I gave her my most wolfish smile. She went behind my chair, "May I drive you?" she joked. I laughed and said, "The cutest driver I've ever had," I responded.

Chapter 29

We had burned two or three before she got called to come back in. I felt awful for what I had done. I took my lit cigarette as she was covering the flame on hers to light it. I melted the string holding her badge in her scrubs pocket and tucked it quickly into my sleeve. I pretended, having to adjust something in the wheelchair. We stayed out there for ten minutes before her beeper had gone off. She waved goodbye. I waved as well, trying my best not to hate myself even more than I already did. What was I becoming? A man that beats other men? Lies to his girlfriend and then steals from people.

Once she was out of sight, I dashed the cigarette quickly, wishing I had water to wash the taste out of my mouth. What was done was done. I rolled to the exit of the west wing building, attaching my leg quickly and pressing her badge up to the scanner. A small click told me the door was open as I stepped through.

The hospital staff was hustling as I quickly put my head down and started going through the building. It wouldn't be long before someone asked why a dirty man was inside the restricted section of the hospital. That or the young nurse noticed her badge was gone. Or the slight burn I had left on her lanyard as I burnt the string holding her badge. I felt guilty because I was. I just needed to keep my eye on the prize.

Inside my pocket, Larry's text buzzed. I pulled out my phone and quickly read his text, "Office 103, he should still be on his lunch break," it read. I closed my phone and jammed it in my pocket. Doing my best to seem like I belong in the area. Faith was on my side; a door lay open, revealing a janitorial closet. I pulled out a mop and bucket, kept my head down, and moved with purpose. No one paid me much attention. Most people overlook their janitors; the golden rule of looking confident is always best. People don't notice someone who doesn't seem lost. Why would they? Society was made up of polite regulations, but mostly, it was made up of distractions.

Everything around me was drawing attention. All I had to do was move quickly while appearing to focus on everything else but what they were doing; I had nothing to worry about. They must be good—he nodded as I passed them. That's the universal sign of being "okay". Why pay attention to anything else other than what I was focused on. We were all guilty of it, so it made sneaking into the west wing of a hospital relatively easy.

I kept my head down, accepting the opportunity to view the room numbers. I was feeling lost when I found his office, "Matt Alexander M.D." His door was closed. I left the mop and bucket next to it. I stepped through, opening and closing the door behind me, pulling down the blinds with one hand and locking the door with the other.

Whirling around, Doctor Matt set up his half-unfinished lunch lying on his desk. His hair was a delicate white, with busy eyebrows and flecks of black still holding onto their color. An unassuming mustache—long crowfeet at the edges of his eyes. "Can I help you?" he stated with a gruff voice that bordered on the line of uninterested. "A greasy man you don't know—comes into your office and locks the door. And you aren't even interested?" I asked him, using the conversation to clear the distance between us. He seemed to accept the situation and bolted for a corded phone on his desk.

I smacked his hand, causing him to push the phone off his desk. He followed the phone to the ground. I reached forward and yanked him up by his collar. The old man gripped my hands—I swung him into the wall and growled. He closed his eyes, and I waited until he opened them before talking.

"You and I are going to have a chat—doctor. I am going to be honest—I am pretty tired; my bull crap meter is low. So, why don't we both do each other a favor? You tell me what I need to know, and I break only one of your fingers—got it?" I asked him in a low tone.

His brown eyes met mine, and I could see understanding come into them.

He gulped, nodding his head slowly. "Good," I loosened my grip and let him slide to the floor. We were both breathing heavily. Prosthetic hand or not, pulling a grown man up by his collar against a wall takes a good amount of effort.

"Now, doc, I have some questions about kids," I asserted. His eyes went wide, his pale skin going a few shades paler. "How do you know about that?" he asked, shaking his whole body.

"Are you serious?" I asked, completely dumbfounded by the man. I sighed, then yanked the man forward. I stepped out, driving his right shoulder down and his face into the desk. With his arm pulled back, I twisted his hand, gripping one of his fingers. "Now, why are you taking the kids? Where is Jacob?" I demanded.

"Who is Jacob?" he puffed, and I countered by breaking his pinky finger. He pulled away in pain and cried. "Relax, you're a doctor. But listen—you have nine more fingers. To be honest, that's about five little piggies too long for me. If I have to one more, expect to lose something else," I stated.

I jerked up on his arm to make my point clear to him. If I had eaten something again, this would have been the time where I would vomit. I kept it down and let my hold of his arm go. He cradled his hand before slicking back against the wall. "Okay, you have made your point," he huffed, giving me a long look.

"Who are you? You aren't police—if you are—I want a lawyer," he stated.

I sighed and pulled out one of his office chairs, noting a family picture of his wife and two kids. He was the dream by all accounts. Yet, he still was choosing to do this—this horrible act that I was fighting to understand. Fighting to restrain from killing him—fighting to remember why I was here. I was here for Jacob. I reminded myself and steadied the feeling in my stomach; I gestured for him to sit in the seat across from me.

"Before you try something dumb like screaming out for anyone's help—I will shoot you," I gestured towards my jacket pocket. He gulped and kept his mouth shut. "Now, please," I gestured again to the chair. "I just want to find the boy, okay? Now help me do that," I stated.

The doctor shuffled to his feet, sliding into the chair opposite me. Never taking his eyes off me. I nodded at him and waited for him to answer my question. "You need to be more specific. And before you break another one of my extremities—there's a lot of boys," he stated.

What he said hit hard, but what hit harder was the casualness of what he said. As if no more than picking toilet paper off his shoes after leaving the bathroom. I was stunned into silence for a moment before picking my words carefully. "A boy that was chased this morning near the old town district. He is ten years old. Hispanic." I explained.

He shook his head no, "You mean the baby—the baby was ten weeks old," he said again with that same casualness. That sickened me the most. I felt myself almost wanting to laugh for a moment. An evil doctor—he even had a mustache. What in the world was going on? Something like this—in a small town of fifteen thousand?

"No, a ten-year-old boy your goons and William went after this morning, as well as the baby. Were you the reason the baby was placed in the dumpster?" I asked him, feeling my insides twist into a thicker knot than what was used for most bridges.

He went pale at the mention of the baby in the dumpster. That twisted the knot in my stomach into loops—I feared something was going to break inside me soon at this rate. I nodded my head. Not trusting myself to speak. "Goodness, surely they aren't just dumping them in a garbage can," he muttered.

I sat back and squeezed the bridge of my nose, trying to calm my hammering headache, which was forming at an alarming rate. After a few deep breaths, I spoke. "So, you do know about the baby," I stated.

"Well, not that baby, no. It's been a few weeks since my last baby. The last request was for a female girl, twelve to thirteen, Pacific Islander or Southeast Asian," he stated calmly like he was ordering at a fast-food restaurant.

I took that in stride, steadying myself through his words. It was like being eaten by a tiger and him explaining afterward that he didn't mean to start at the feet—it was just how it ended up—no hard feelings. I needed to stay focused on finding the kid; I was too deep in the waters to stop now. However, going back ashore seemed more and more like a more imaginative play. I didn't know why, but I felt I had jumped off my boat in the ocean, forgetting that I wasn't in a lake. The amount of people it would take to get this operation running and hidden would be almost an army. Something this big, hidden in such a small town, what was the world coming to? Or had it always been this way? I thought as I simply said, "Yeah," to the doctor. He continued without having to be prompted.

"A baby in a dumpster—I couldn't tell you what that is about. All I do is request more doses. Then I tell William who I need. I don't even know if he is the one who gets them or not," he stated, almost pleading with me with a long look.

I blinked at that one; he wasn't even at the top of the pyramid. I felt myself slumping in my chair at the weight of what his words meant. That weight was about to crash me like gravity pulling a crazy rocket that thought it could escape a massive planet. Like the planet, this was all bigger than me. I was just a garbage man. Sure, I took a few jujitsu classes and shot a lot of guns. Watched way too many movies and probably hadn't needed to read more books. I didn't think even a team of police and lawyers could stop something this big. I was only seeing the tip of the iceberg. Who knows how much bigger this all really was? My feet gave out first, and I felt myself falling forward. Thankfully, the doctor was in his own world, staring at his hand as he spoke. He ignored anything I was doing and kept talking.

"Are you with that cop? You know, what was her name, 'Officer Gen?'" he sneered, and that caused me to take hold of my body as it was slipping towards the floor. "Yeah, that must be it—you're with that cop. I told her to quit coming around here. Quit sniffing so much. I've called your department chief three times about her. All she did was keep harassing me and going by the insurance office," he stated, spitting at the end of his sentence.

I felt the knot in my stomach be pushed aside by rage. He had mentioned my Gen's name. He had mentioned her—I wasn't sure if I was the one that could solve all of this, but I wasn't going to keep letting him get away with this. I was doing this for Gen, a little baby who didn't deserve to be discarded in a dumpster like a crumbled-up piece of trash. I lurched forward and slapped the doctor with the backhand of my bad hand, the metal prosthetic digging into his nose and slinging his glasses across the room.

He started to cover his face, and I pushed his hands down, "Let me put the pieces together here, doc. You don't know what happens to these kids, nor do you know who gets them. You just know who to ask to help you find them, correct? Who do you make the request to? Is there anyone else that works for you?" I growled, my face inches away from his. I could see the sweat dripping from his nose as I glared at him with rage.

"I—I, okay. William isn't the only guy, okay? I have six other guys in the tri-state area. You can't ask for too many in one place. It would raise way too many alarms. Are you with the chief? I told him—the investor knows more than I do. He knows that" he said in that matter-of-fact tone that sent me reeling back as if he had punched me. He might as well have done that; just another rock on the dumpster that was becoming my broken back. Six other men in the tri-state area? That could be North Carolina, Georgia, and Tennessee even... That scared me to my core—this widespread darkness, this many people that were harming children? What was I going to do about it? How was I going to save Jacob?

One step at a time, just one foot in front of the other. That will get me to where I am going, I said to the darkness that was building inside me. I cleared my throat and let the doctor go, putting my hands at my side for now.

"Who is this investor? Give me a name and address." I asked, feeling the urgency of the situation growing. "You aren't with the chief, are you? Yeah, you're with that officer," he muttered.

"What is your takeaway from this situation? You stupid little man," I pulled him from the wall and pushed him to the desk. "Write down his name and location, hurry," I stated as he fumbled for his pen and scribbled out on the notepad. He handed me back the notepad. I nodded, ripping the page out and stuffing it into my pocket. "Give me your cell phone," I stated.

"What, no," he stated. I raised my hands, and he reached into his jacket, handing me his phone. I put his phone into my pocket. I must have shown him what was in my jacket pockets. "Wait, you don't have a gun?" he asked, befuddled. I sighed and gave him a long look. "That's the takeaway here.

You harm kids, and you only care about your own fat cheeks," I stated.

He looked at me with his head almost held high, "No—I don't just harm kids like a cartoon. I don't even know what the kids are used for exactly," he said.

"Then what, what do you get out of this? Is it just money?" I asked him.

He countered, "Well, yes, but we get proper treatment—a drug that could be used for so much. "he said, almost excitedly. I stepped back this time, wanting to distance myself as far as possible. "Do you have this drug here?" I asked, trying to salvage as much as possible from this situation. I took a look behind us for a moment. Wondering if anyone had heard this conversation. Now that he knew I didn't have a gun, I wasn't sure how much longer I could keep him talking.

"If I give you some—will you let me go? Let me guess, just a private cop that has a taste for TRIP—I get it. It's very addicting," he said, smiling.

"What the hell is TRIP?" I asked him, this time being the dumbfounded one.

He turned away from me and reached into a drawer, pulling out a syringe that contained a glowing liquid. Almost neon-like, like a mini–Las Vegas inside a tiny vile. "I will give you some if you kick rocks and leave me alone. Tell whoever sent you that I don't appreciate being shaken down like this," he stated.

I took the syringe from him with the tenderness of holding some kind of bomb. For all I knew, this was a bomb. What could make something like this glow in such wild colors? And did the doctor actually mean that people would use something like this? That was just insane in an already sizable heaping mountain of insanity. And all of this before I even had my lunch.

I wanted to sit down; I wanted to be done with this insanity. When I didn't react to what the doctor had said, he looked relieved and covered his face from the cut on the bridge of his nose. Behind us came a knock at his door; I tore my head back and stared at the nose, "Sir, are you okay? You've been paged twice and have no response. Is someone in there with you?" came the voice of some man. The doorknob started to jiggle.

I turned back, and the doctor shouted, "Yes, help! He is attacking me!" he screamed, charging forward. I elbowed him in the face, letting him close the distance, before twisting my hip into his and pulling his arm over my shoulder, slinging the doctor across the room.

Banging came from the door as the doctor sprawled into his other wall. Knocking awards down and leaving his face in a daze. I looked at his office window, thankful it was on the first floor and a standard office window.

I had a couple of seconds to react. I heard a kick from the door, the doctor groaning from his flip. I picked up his monitor, yanking the cords out with one hand and using the other to swing it into the window, breaking the glass easily.

I had just enough time to clean more of the small pieces of glass away when I heard the door frame start to crack. I had so many questions and doubted I had asked any of the right ones.

There was no time to wonder about that; I needed to be out quickly. I dove out of the shattered window and landed hard in the bushes, patting my jacket pockets to make sure the phones were still there.

I bolted for Larry's truck and didn't dare look behind me.

Chapter 30

Larry had punched his red truck to red as we peeled out of the parking lot. I slid into the passenger seat as the truck was still moving, my heart beating faster than I thought was possible without flying out of my chest like a bullet. Larry swerved and sped down the highway. After five minutes of reckless driving, I grunted, "Slow down, no one is coming," I said hesitantly. "Slow down? Are you crazy? How in the hell do you know that? I was listening on your phone, Billy Dan. You assaulted a doctor—that has to be, I don't know, some kind of crime that lands you in the worse kind of pound you in the butt prison," he said hysterically.

I shook my head. "No, we have time. Do that thing you do and make us vanish," I stated in an even tone, trying to calm us both down. Larry, to his credit, let off the gas and slowed to us to go under an overpass. He soon parked well under the bridge a moment later.

"Do that thing you do," he mocked, snapping off his seatbelt and reaching for his computer. "Yeah, sure, Billy Dan. Let me go out of my way to aid you while you also make me a felon. What's wrong with calling the police?" he snarled.

"Because this goes deep, and you know it. That was very clear after dealing with Doctor Matt," I stated.

If Larry disagreed, he wouldn't have shown a sign of it. Instead, he dug out his laptop and kept working, Muttering and cursing under his breath as his keys flew across the keyboard. I heard him whisper with a drip of venom, "Why do you even care this much?"

Chapter 31

"It's all just stupid," Jacob said, sliding down the bench chair and kicking a small pile of rocks at our feet. We were sitting at the edges of our nearest town lake. A crisp day in the south—a wet heat, but not so high that we were utterly drenched. Frogs croaked while fishermen in the distance raved their engines on the lake. A million and one things happening—a million and one things we could never understand. It was peaceful, the vastness of it all, the marvelous creativity of God stretching around us. I was oddly content. I wished that Jacob and I were here under different circumstances. I hoped this could be a father and son at the lake together.

Gen had asked if I could take Jacob to the lake since his own father had missed out again on taking him out on one of his weekends. It was the third miss in only a few months. Gen and I could understand that some people care more about themselves than their kids. Kids, though, couldn't see the trees from the forest. Not when it came to parents—not when it came to parents being there for their kids. That wasn't something any child should have to rationalize and internalize. At least not so early.

We had been sitting quietly on the bench for about twenty minutes, watching the sun drift lazily over the still waters. I decided the best thing to say at the moment was nothing; just let the boy talk.

Jacob kept his head down, his messy black hair thicker than a mop. That panned me—he was just a boy—but I couldn't shield him from everything. Life was bitter sometimes, not fair, and a beast with no fairness—just fangs and claws. I cleared my throat; he would learn that soon enough. No sense in hammering that to him now.

Jacob looked up after I cleared my throat. His brown eyes swam with tears, turning them the color of dark mud on the floor of a forest color. That broke my heart; the boy spoke up in my silence. "You know what bothers me the most, Billy Dan? It's not just that he didn't come again. Or how tired mom looks sometimes—she always seems like a brittle cookie dipped in milk. It could break at any moment. I guess it's just that I shouldn't be always doing his job. Why do I always have to comfort my sisters? Why do I always have to make sure Mom locks the doors before nighttime? Or pick up the poop from the dog in the middle of the night? He never took me to a fair. He never took me to the lake, and I needed him. We needed him, and he was never there," Jacob cried.

A lump formed in my throat, and I put my arm around him. Holding the small boy against me. After a few minutes, he stopped crying and sniffing occasionally, but there were no more tears. I realized then that he wasn't so little anymore. Gen and I had been dating for a little over a year now. He had grown up a lot since I found him smiling at me from inside a garbage bin.

Not sure what to say, I hugged the boy and let him cry it all out. We stayed that way for a few minutes, the sounds of insects buzzing while birds chirped around us in rhythm with Jacob's sobs. Another minute, he cried, then he sat up, wiping his face. "It's alright to cry, bud. It really is," I stated as he looked away.

"But we have to wipe our tears at some point. You're the man of the house—that's a big responsibility. That means knowing when to cry—and when to be strong. Right now, buddy, I don't blame you for crying. Your dad let you down again. My mother—she let me down countlessly as a child. Barely knew her, just that whenever she came around—she would promise the moon and back. I would be stuck wondering why she never showed—as if it was something I had done that wasn't good enough for her. Maybe if I had done better, she would have come," I stated softly in my memories.

Jacob wiped more tears from his eyes and then looked at me with a long face. "She abandoned you like my dad?" he asked.

I nodded my head. "Oh yeah, only it's worse for you. You have siblings—it was just me, my dad, and the dog," I smiled at him.

He gave a weak smile back, and I continued. "Everyone has a role to play, Jacob. Especially when it comes to family. Not everyone is going to do it. Not everyone even had a choice in the matter. You're a kid; your whole job is to be a kid and listen to your parents. The least amount of responsibility is placed on kids in the order of families. The thing is, though—you got dealt a bad hand. Now, you have to be responsible for your mom. And for your sisters. Your dad abandoned you; don't do the same to your own family. That's how it goes; we end up taking on roles. Some in the natural way—some in ways we didn't choose to have. You get what I mean?" I asked him.

Jacob pulled in his lip for a moment before nodding his head. "Yeah, I get what you mean. Still doesn't make it suck less," he stated.

I laughed at that and rubbed his shoulder. "Not in the slightest, pal, but it gets better. You have your own family—and someday, you will be a dad. Be the one that you wished your dad had been to you," I stated, stretching my hands behind my head and sagging onto the bench as the sun started to set.

Jacob sat thoughtfully again before speaking, "How did you ever get over what your mom did, Billy Dan? How did you put it behind you?" he asked me. I closed my eyes briefly before speaking, "You never really get over anything—it all becomes a memory. However, they will only grow if you don't make peace with things. That will lead you to do only bad things. The easiest way to put it, you will harm yourself and everyone else. A soul just can't move on if you don't have forgiveness," I stated, leaning forward toward the lake.

Jacob looked at me, completely confused. Yeah, that might have been above the kids' heads; it was for me when I first heard it. I smiled at that memory; thankful I finally got a chance to say it to someone else in their moment of need.

"I don't get that at all, Billy Dan," he said this time with a frown.

I shrugged, "It will make sense someday, I promise. Forgiveness is key. Forgive those who hurt us. It removes all the hurt and keeps us doing our responsibilities, get it?"

He nodded after a moment. "I think so—just what did you end up doing without your mom?" he asked again.

Without looking at Jacob, I kept staring out at the lake. "I did the same thing she did to me in a way, only I abandoned my hate toward her."

Chapter 32

We had driven on in silence for twenty minutes after Larry had scrubbed the cameras free that had seen us at the hospital. That wouldn't include anything taken on cell phones in the area, but it would slow down any cops looking our way for a while. Larry, the whole time, looked like he was moments away from jumping out of his skin. He patted the steering wheel the entire way and had globs of sweat bleeding down his head.

When we got to the storage garage area, he parked the truck, gripping the wheel tightly until his knuckles were white. I sighed as I opened the truck door, looking at the doctor's address on the piece of paper. We were at a pod storage facility—on the edges of town. Nothing remarkable. Just storage. That was the disconcerting part of all of this that was starting to make me worry even more. How deep did this go? And what would I find when I opened up one of the storage buildings? When I had already seen a baby in a dumpster.

The little hands and feet flashed in my eyes for a moment—I shook my head before throwing up again at the thought. There was no escaping, even if Larry and I didn't go to jail. This was almost too much. I dipped my head and looked at Larry as he stared dead ahead at the storage sheds.

He looked like a coke can that was about to burst from too much liquid on the inside. The pressure was getting to him—but it could just be what we've done so far this day. Hard to say if it was whatever he was hiding that was going to be something that needed to be dealt with soon. I needed his help, but exposing my questions to him now wouldn't end well.

A cloud moved over the top of the truck and cast a long shadow over us.

That caused both of us to look at the sky. He let out a long breath, and I relaxed my grip on the handle of the door.

"Look, Larry, whatever happens from here—just blame it all on me if we get caught," I instructed in a neutral tone. He laughed nervously before responding to me, "You assaulted a doctor, man... I don't know, I'm sure it's worse to hit a cop—but that's gotta be at least a few extra years," he stated.

I scratched my chin. "Think more than five?" I offered.

He laughed again, his voice sounding steadier. "Five? Shit, man, that's probably the minimum," he said.

"Well, how about I promise this was all my fault if anyone asks?" I responded.

"We keep having this conversation..." he stated.

I sighed before putting my hand on the door. "Yeah, we do. Make up your own mind, Larry. This isn't going to stop anytime soon at the rate we are going," I ordered, opening the door and stepping out into the noon heat of the day.

The locks on the storage sheds are just a simple padlock around a small ring. The doors are made of metal. It would be hard to bulldoze my way through, I thought. I turned and went to the back of Larry's truck. "Mind if I go into your tool bag?" I asked him. He laughed from inside of the cab.

"Go for it, man. Why even ask at this point?" he kept laughing, almost hysterically, in front of the truck.

I opened the toolbox and found two wrenches. I walked to the nearest shed. The doctor had written down the numbers 101-105. I shrugged, feeling like this was just going to be a dead-end. I fought that doubt. I didn't have much to go on anymore, but this was the most I had at the moment.

I walked up to the lock, put both wrenches in it, and turned in different directions. A moment later, with a little bit of force, the lock popped open. If anyone came to the shed, they would easily know we had been there.

They would know that anyway—there was no doubt that the doc had called whoever cut his paychecks. Which, in a way, was a good thing. Now that I thought about it, maybe that meant the cops wouldn't get involved yet. That gave me more time to find Jacob. If I could get something out of the sheds, I could turn that over to the cops. That would help stop whatever they were doing. Kidnapping kids—that was monstrous. That would need to be stopped. One man couldn't do it alone.

Keep focused on Jacob; don't worry about the bigger picture until you have the kid. I blew my lips up and set down the wrenches, pulling the metal door up. Light flooded the full shed quickly. But what I saw stilled me to my core—like a dagger sliding across my heart.

The last thing I expected was a pallet in the middle of the room. Neatly stacked and built as if it were a Tower of Babel, stretching towards the sky. Piles and piles of money. I paused at that one. "I almost would have preferred it to have been a dead body in here. I could handle that," I blew out my lips again and held the bridge of my nose. How much stress could one person handle before their head just exploded? I was worried mine would soon find out the exact amount at the rate I was going.

A couple of things happened a moment later, Larry started shouting behind me. "Billy Dan, there's a silent alarm!" he screamed. I looked around the shed as if I could somehow see it before I realized the operative word was "silent." Next, I noticed a fridge next to the giant stack of money. Accepting, I had a few seconds, and I picked up the case and booked it back to Larry's truck. He had the truck started and a look of terror on his face.

I threw the case inside Larry's driver-side seat. The black fake letter was tossed lightly off the seat and landed easily in the passenger seat.

"What's that? We need to go!" he yelled over the engine.

I held up a finger and went to the back of Larry's truck. Thankfully, like most garbage men, Larry had tools in the back of his car. Namely, he had a gas can. I picked up the jug and ran towards the shed. I poured the contents out of the jug—flooding the small room with a thick gas smell.

I pulled out a lighter from my pocket. Bending down, I lit a stack of money nearest to me. The bills went up fast as I turned and ran back to the truck. My prosthetic digging into my leg again, reminding me that I needed to switch to a different leg, I pushed the broken latch back—only to hear it pop a moment later. And possibly go to the hospital soon if I didn't stop. I could almost picture the skin rubbing off with each step.

I got into Larry's truck as he gunned it out of the shed area at top speed. Behind us, smoke billowed out—a moment later, dust shot up from the storage area as a black truck arrived at the shed.

Somehow, they missed us or were more concerned about the money, but we were able to pop down to the nearest overpass. "What the Hell, man? Are you insane? That fire—was that money in there? Who was that truck? Count your blessings that I had a scanner going. Someone was watching that place, man; we are so screwed," he screamed.

"Turn around; we need to see who that was," I said calmly, but I was feeling anything but calm.

Larry jerked his head around and stared blankly at me. "Are you nuts? Man, we must get in a hole and pull the ladder with us. I saw how much money that was in there—that much money, man—this kind of people could buy and kill a thousand of dudes like you and me, and they wouldn't even flinch," he gestured with his hands. I gripped the wheel while he flailed and steered us down the street.

"We need to see who they are and turn around. Just need to get close enough," I directed. Larry looked like I had just told him the world was ending. Maybe it was, I thought at that moment. As far as he and I were concerned, we were just shattering any semblance of reality. Men stealing children, a missing child, and money stacked on the top of the shed. It was either ending, or we didn't understand how the world worked.

Larry had a wide mouth until I said, "Please, Larry." He closed his mouth and looked forward before seeming to make up something in his mind. Then he turned the vehicle around, the truck groaning as we pulled off on an overpass and started going towards the storage sheds. We rolled slowly up to the lot. A billow of smoke drifted toward the sky at an alarming rate. Surely, someone was going to call the fire department soon.

I noticed on the clock that it had been about five minutes since we arrived at the shed and started the fire. At best, it would be another five or ten minutes before we would have to leave without being seen.

Larry started to park; I gestured for him to keep going up the hill. "We need to be able to see who it is," I stated. Larry just inched the truck forward a few feet. I glared at him and then opened the door. Stepping out on the path next to the truck.

I walked up the road until I was nearest the chain-link fence that separated the storage sheds. A small Sudan was parked on the nearest road. I got low and cowered behind a car until I could make out the two men who were now outside the sheds—their small black truck only meters away.

I took in a lot in just a moment. Both men were frantically trying to put out the fire with their jackets. The fire spread to the second shed. In minutes, I realized the whole place would be up in flames. A lot of people were going to lose their stuff. I hoped that it was only these awful people who were going to be counting their losses. Though, at this rate—it would be a big fire. I watched as the second shed was now engulfed. The two quit trying to put out the flames and rushed to another shed. They were both plain-clothed.

I had no choice but to get closer to figure out who they were. I stepped forward gingerly as both men were preoccupied with the fire. Keeping low, I walked around the car to the fence line and up to their vehicle. One man was now frantically scrambling for his phone out of his pocket. Jerking around too much was making the whole process harder than it needed to be.

Using that distraction, I reached their car and slid up, looking through the passenger window. The car's floor was a mess, but a golden glint of light showed into my eyes, and that drew my attention to the center console.

Next to the truck's shiftier was a golden badge of a police officer. I saw our town's name engraved into the metal across the top. That was a gut punch—I took that in stride. Private security—the police themselves. No wonder the cops hadn't shown up by now. I saw the driver's door was unlocked. Carefully, I popped the handle and opened the passenger door slowly until it was open just enough to get to the center console.

I reached in and took the badge from the console—just in time for one of the men to turn around.

I didn't dare close the door completely. I kept it partially closed and crawled back slowly until I could see that the man who turned around was back to paying attention to the shed. I kept low until I made it to the fence slowly. Once at the wall, I quickened my pace and moved towards Larry.

My heart was pounding the whole way. Now, the cops were involved—what had I stumbled into? What could I even do about all of this? When I reached Larry, he was driving before I closed the door. I told him to take the road we came from to prevent the two from seeing us. A giant smoke column reached towards the sky. Sirens blared in the distance as we drove away quickly.

Chapter 33

I had Larry working on identifying the badges as I steadied my breath—pulling out the pack of matches from my pocket. Larry eyeballed me as we sat on the side of the road. "You got that from the kid's bag?" he asked hesitantly. I stayed glued to my phone, pretending that I didn't know anything beyond just the bag. So, he did know about Jacobs's bag. Did he know about the glowing syringe in my pocket? That was hard, maybe. I still needed a ride; I just nodded my head instead of responding.

After a minute, I looked up from my phone and showed Larry the address. "Take me here, Larry," I stated.

Larry nodded back and set his computer back in the phone. "I know that street—never noticed a club like that," he said.

"Must be new," I offered, sticking the matches into my pocket.

"Must be,". He commented.

Chapter 34

In the next town over, we found the club. A slowly creeping place that felt like the larger city was moving in on our tiny town, one building at a time. One block full places like this. I never liked these places—they reeked of desperation and cigarettes. A place where you walked into a human grease trap. Paid workers looking only to make a buck from lousy customers unwilling to save money. Fake velvet walls and blinding lights made you feel like you were looking through kaleidoscopes. Stained tables and walls from countless spilled drinks and the hopeless dreams of people who should go home, watch a movie, and spend time with their spouse and kids. It's cheaper, and you stand a far better chance of getting something lasting and meaningful out of it than you do here.

But, as far as strip clubs went, I thought this one could be worse—I just wish someone would turn on the lights or bad guys to stop being so cliche and just do their shady business at a local burger joint. It would save me on my ophthalmologist visits. Larry pushed past me once we entered, "I'm going to—head that way," he stuttered towards a thin blonde working on the far side of the room. I sighed, "Sure, but be ready," I stated. Larry had protested that he was tired of sitting in the truck—fair enough. I just wished that would calm him down.

Larry glanced at me. "Ready for what, Billy Dan?" he asked over the soft music playing over us. I don't know yet—just be ready," I called as I turned in the direction of the bar. Where are you going?" he called.

I hiked a finger towards the bar and kept on walking. I waited in line; it was past noon, but a man dressed in a full black suit that cost more than my apartment in a year was ahead of me. He flirted with a heavily tattooed bartender. She had none of it but knew suckers with a big wallet like him were fair game. His smile flashed green, and his eyes said stupidity.

After a few seconds of chatting, she stared at me. Out of place in my dirty trousers, flannel shirt, bomber jacket, and a generous amount of dirt that looked like I had taken on someone in a cheap backyard wrestling fight and lost every round. Confusion flashed in her eyes, but she didn't break her concentration. The rich man smiled at her, and she kept a slow grin. All the while, her eyes looked me up and down. I think she was deciding if I was homeless or not.

I stood a little taller to project an air of, "I'm not on drugs—don't worry," though I wonder if it just made me look more out of place. This was an expensive room; I could tell—even the glasses on the bar shined with a brightness that made me feel like I had just walked into a jewelry store instead. I stuffed my hands in my pockets, hoping that would at the very least give me something to do—it was a weird situation; naked people and more money than I had stuffed under my bed every way I looked.

The man slipped away from the bar, slowly stirring a straw with a thin lemon cut on the lip. I stepped up. "Nice drink," I remarked. He ignored me and smirked, loosening his tie and wandering off to a corner of the strip club at the edges of my vision.

"You look like you've had a hard day," she stated, pulling out a glass and a rag. Crap on a toad, even the rag looked like it was made from silk. I would have preferred this to have been the typical grimy strip club. No wonder Larry said this place couldn't be found unless you know someone. This was odd, considering he first said he had never heard of it—after a few open-ended questions—it turns out he had heard of it but thought it was a joke. Yet another notch against Larry. That was one problem I dreaded having to solve. We had gotten in because of the matches. But the longer I stayed around here, the longer I got the sense that I was sticking out like a sore thumb; what was I even doing here?

I responded instead of getting lost in my thoughts: " Well, you know— hard as anyone else's day," I said. She smirked at me and kept polishing her glass. What can I do you for, rehab—perhaps soap?" she said.

"If you have any of those, that would be great. I've had this itchy spot on my back I just can't quite reach," I said, gesturing with my prosthetic hand over my back. That worked, and I could see the math running through her head at that time. Most people ignore homeless people on the best of days— but for someone with a missing limb—it makes some people downright uncomfortable. It was a good way of softening peoples' defenses. Most barkeeps are masters of stoic emotion control—they've seen and heard it all. The trick was to make them feel like they can relax around you.

I took her pause as an opportunity to speak. "I will take a drink, though— hold the soap," I stated, pulling out my wallet. It was stuffed full of business cards and overflowing pocket money. She produced a beer from nowhere. I nodded my head, took the beer, and slapped a twenty on the counter. "So, how about I ask you a few questions?"

"How about I ask you for ten more—big guy," she replied.

I looked at her momentarily before realizing she meant the beer was that expensive. I swore under my breath and produced another twenty. She looked at me, "that will get you two—Captain Jack," she declared.

I grumbled, scratching my face, "See anyone come in here—maybe looking as dirty as me?" I asked, pointing at my chest.

"We tend not to serve people like you—are you asking for hygiene tips or just looking for a friend?" she asked, glancing behind me.

I stayed focused on her, doing my best to remain casual. "Neither—just a curious fella trying to get a drink in a curious place from a pretty lady," she smirked, but I could tell she wasn't buying it. "That's one more—pirate man," she jabbed at me as I narrowed my eyes.

I scratched my chin again, tilting my head around the club. Seeing how the cloak and dagger showed when we had come in—we missed a lot. If my original thought was that the men chasing Jacob into the building had come in here, they wouldn't have come right after the fire; they would have gotten cleaned up.

My hope fluttered, but I needed to press on. Outright, asking her who the owners were would be even more of a red flag than the one we had sent up fumbling our way in with a pack of matches.

Outside was a parking garage with several layers—I couldn't access everyone to look for the truck. Who drives the truck, I thought—not specific enough—but a red pickup truck in a place like this had to stand out. Not to mention, I had no idea if they were even connected to what we had seen at the garage storage area earlier today. It could be that the men at the apartment were just random creeps trying to steal a kid. So, what did that leave me with? Trying to find two men after a fire in a classy strip club. I could find something here, just not the men I wanted. It was like looking for a handgun, but all you saw were cruise missiles.

"Who drives a red pickup truck—not too large, nothing fancy going on with it from what I could tell," I pondered, waiting for her response. She sucked in her bottom lip, taking a glass of gold liquid to her mouth.

"Small town pilgrim, a lot of people drive those around here. What's it to you?" she asked, eyeing me sheepishly over the lips of her glass. I glanced around me to see if anyone was paying attention. Aside from a couple of guerrilla muscle types hanging out by the far side of the club and Larry drooling not too far from them—they paid little attention to someone talking a little too long to the bartender. I pulled my wallet back out, producing a picture of Gen—one where she had been at the park with her many children.

Jacob was in the center next to her, with wide eyes and a gap in his teeth. Toast in his hands, a backpack almost comically too big for him—seemed to nearly devour the boy.

"That's who was driving that truck, as far as I'm concerned. I am looking for this boy," I casually pointed a finger at him, sliding the photograph across the counter to her. Her face contorted, and a flash of sadness ran across it.

"Look, Mr.?" she pondered.

I smiled, "Call me Billy Dan," I replied.

She cocked her head and nodded. "Look, Mr. Billy Dan. Two types of people show photos of little boys to complete strangers in a place like this. The kind that are into them more than they should be. Or those dumb enough to think they can save someone. I have not seen a cop with the balls come in here and do their job. There are already three uniforms in the backrooms right now at any given time. And you look like a stiff breeze could take you out, pirate man," she gestured towards my prosthetic.

I rolled with her commitment, pushing through her deflection. " You're right on one account. I am trying to find this boy and bring him home before anything happens to him- you know, anything the type that is too into kids might do to him Now, you can tell me, or I will show you pirate—sweetie," I narrowed my eyes at her, snatching the picture from her fingers.

She gave me a long look before registering; I wasn't that person. Still, she prodded, "Do you even know whose place you're in right now?" she asked—a small smile at the corner of her lips. "Some jerks with a bad taste in music. I don't care—I just want answers," I gestured slowly, sliding the picture back into my wallet.

Her smile got bigger before she sighed and set down the glass. "I think I will step outside for a smoke break, but if I were a betting girl, I would say check out the private booths. There's some strange sort of men, maybe just the type you're looking for," she stated, strolling past me, her hips moving in a rhythmic practiced waltz out the door.

The signal was loud enough for me, and I moved towards the far end of the club, below an overlooking ramp leading up to a balcony. I glanced up; a few questionable-aged girls danced in silk for a couple of men. But otherwise, no one was paying attention as I quietly made my way to the back area.

There was one empty table near a booth; the curtain was drawn, but the flashes of a hand poked out from under it occasionally. I couldn't get a good look. I sat down as the hand slid back behind the veil of the curtain. A cursory glance around the club told me I was alone on this side. The women were more interested in the looks of actual paying customers. Who all looked like they could buy the town with a snap of their fingers. Funny, I couldn't place any of them. Out-of-towners. No wonder I had never heard of this place.

Larry was still on the side with the two security guard-looking men. Their shoulders were pronounced and broad enough to get stuck in a door frame. I wish I had brought my gun. I sighed for far too many times today. What was done is done. A scrap was coming—I just had to pick when and where

I thought. So far, I had gotten lucky; my hands were still shaking after the hospital. What would I have done if Larry couldn't get into Jacobs's phone? He would be gone, that's what.

Cocktail napkins were on the table. I dug in my pants until I found a ballpoint pen. I really should just start carrying a backpack around. My pockets were filled to the brim with perceivable junk. I never saw it as junk, though. A pen could be your last line of defense in some situations.

I scribbled a message on the napkin when the seat on the far side of the small table was pulled out. I looked up to see Melanie's smiling face, and my heart skipped a beat.

"Hello darling—you look like poop," she stated, scrunching her nose behind her wide glasses that complimented her heart-shaped face unnaturally well. "Fancy seeing you in a place like this, Melanie; it's the perfect place for your kind. Though—you must explain how a vampire could walk around in broad daylight," I countered.

"Cute," she replied, and all pretense of friendliness was cut short. Her type would only be their authentic self when no one saw it. It was just the two of us in a dark corner. The snake was out of her hole.

She sat down, crossed her legs, and leaned forward. I did the same, sliding the napkin from the table as smoothly as I could. "What brings you here? No good rabbits to torture anymore?" I asked, keeping my eyes on her.

"Well, any good businesswoman should check out how her business is going occasionally. Make sure that filth doesn't make its way behind closed doors," she said, almost drilling into me with her look.

I cleared my throat. Damn, out of all the people that had to own this place. It had to be hers. I pretended to look around the room for an answer; no one had moved from their spots a few moments before.

Turning back, I found her black void of eyes still fixated on me. I gulped— she scared the crap out of me. I wasn't sure why, but maybe it was because any interaction the two of us ever had was her constantly trying to find a way to worm herself into the situation. Always had to be center, controlling, and just downright invasive. "Well, you're in luck, Melanie, I'm an expert in waste disposal. I can see a lot of dirt already that needs to go," I replied.

She smirked, "That's funny...Still, though, it is surprising to see you here. I would think a man such as you wouldn't sink so low to come into a place like this," she cut her eyes.

I blinked at her, "Aren't you the one that owns this place? What does that say about you?" Her facade shifted to that of a pure tiger, and I almost flinched from her reaction. "I am doing this town a service. I give people jobs. I help people. I keep," she gestured at the men behind her. I keep these types from going out and doing much, much worse to lord knows who," she defended.

I must have struck a nerve, but she kept going. "It's a tough job being a single woman in charge of multiple businesses and running a thriving community," she stated glumly.

"You provide an expensive showing of nothing left to the imagination. A trip to the back of a grimy old movie store would probably provide the same service with far fewer implications," I countered.

She glared at me with a look that conveyed she was wondering if it was possible to actually eat someone's soul. Instead, she shifted to resting her hands under her chin and narrowing her eyes.

"This is coming from a garbage man. Your type can't even afford a normal club. What are you doing here? We both know you shouldn't be here." She almost hissed.

I started to sweat, and the music overhead made it hard to concentrate. I realized then that I should have brought my drink from the bar to offset why I was sitting alone in this place. It probably made me stick out like a lighthouse in the middle of a field to a woman like her.

I responded, "Oh, you know, just sort of checking out the music—the beautiful dark colors—really adds to the depressing hellhole that this place is." I gestured around the club.

Her eyes narrowed. "My barkeep tells me you're looking for a boy—didn't take you for that type," she stated with a small smile. So much for having someone on the inside. She must have gone out and told Melanie someone was asking questions.

"Say—you really do look like highway road kill. Worse than usual. Skinny as a rail and covered in—I don't know, maybe apartment smoke," she trailed off, and I glared at her. Somewhat aware of the warning she had just given me.

She went on, "You know, Billy Dan. You're really the perfect man in some ways. All noble and righteous. Yet, you come in here and completely be disrespectful with your commits all the time—breaking more pure hearts. Makes me just want to put a spell on you—finally calm you down," she turned her head down and sniffled. I could hear soft crying under the loud music.

I scuffed. "Honestly, does that work on anyone?" I questioned, and Melanie snapped her head up. Her eyes were finally full of something, full of hate. "Only those that deserved to be controlled," she said, tilting her head back and laughing. My legs shook in fear. What was this woman? "Speaking of which, let's chat about a couple of things," she ordered. All evidence of her tears was gone.

Which made my back feel like someone had dropped me in the middle of the ocean covered in blood.

"You were at the apartment building, yes, of course you had to be. You aren't a good liar. Running into a burning building like that, how stupid. Must have been looking for something—or maybe someone," she trailed off, placing her palm on her forehead. I didn't react to what she said. I wanted to let her divulge what she knew and didn't know that I knew. "Someone has been running around causing all sorts of problems. Oh well, nothing that can't be handled—quickly and efficiently," she smiled, and I could have almost sworn her tongue flicked out like a snake.

I narrowed my eyes and reciprocated the warning, "If you—"

"If I what? Just pointing out some facts for you, Billy-boy. Maybe giving you something to think about. Perhaps get that through your thick skull that there are some things you can't do. Like walk properly and wipe your butt," her stare narrowed, and her eyes seemed to never blink.

I glared at her momentarily and did my best to keep my face from reacting. Never flinch in front of predators—moving too much will set them off to attack. Everything made of flesh and blood is governed by the same laws—

the laws that flesh could be punctured, cut, shredded, burned, and torn. That meant even sharks and snakes only attacked if they knew they could win. For now, not showing weakness was the only thing keeping her from attacking.

She continued, "All of the truths aside, I must ask a more important thing—maybe you found something while in that apartment. Maybe that is why you're here. And maybe you're feeling slightly less stupid than usual," she giggled, placing her face between her hands.

I wanted to punch her in the face as hard as I could at that moment. I felt a rush of blood flood into my face and hand. Just reach across the table and end her. I was tired of running around like a chicken with my head cut off—and here was another person who wasn't helping—it was making me sick. All of them, all I had to do was end her now. I could do it; no one was watching—that wasn't true, and I knew it. For Jacob's sake, I calmed myself down. At the very least, she knew I had entered the apartment—that was clear. Melanie didn't know why, though, beyond just chasing Jacob. I wondered if she knew where the boy was or, more importantly, if she was after something else. I suddenly thought of the viles in my pockets. They had a strange hew to them, now that I thought about it. A purple contrasted with a usual glow that shouldn't have been possible. I hadn't had the time to take them out and observe what it might be. I didn't want to look at them around Larry. Furthermore, what was in them any way that someone like her would even care about? Why was a crazy woman who annoys people about her new-age church so concerned about a child?

I pulled my jacket closer, touching the syringes in my pocket. If Melanie noticed, she didn't have to give a sign. Keep your cool, Billy Dan. If she knew, Melanie would have already acted. Though I wasn't sure how I could understand that at this juncture. I gave her a level look, but she kept her head between her hands, smiling at me.

Her smile was beautiful, with flashes of sunny beaches and endless good times. A pretty smile is a quick way to Hell—and in her case, it probably was. I refused to believe it—for now, at least, I had to assume that I had no idea what she was talking about and that if she had been looking for anything, it wasn't necessarily the viles. That was wishful thinking on my part. It gave me an out, though.

I shrugged, "I find all kinds of things in my work. You would be surprised at the amount of trash out there. Probably even more surprised by what doesn't get thrown away, though," I rambled, resisting the urge to dig too much into her ego. Throw her a jab and let her know you aren't prey. Her smile never wavered, and she held my gaze. Through the purple lights, we locked eyes, and I knew that I wasn't looking into the eyes of a human. She was anything but that and far from anything considered natural.

"Tell me, do you enjoy your line of work?" she asked me, piercing my soul with her gaze.

"It has its benefits, as I imagine owning a strip club probably does for you," I gestured towards her, feeling my stomach fold in half as nerves were getting me. She smiled again, keeping me locked in her sight.

"Ever read the Bible, Billy Dan?" she asked me, changing the subject. I blinked at her, "What do you mean?" I asked, not following where she was taking this. "Ever read the good book? I know reading can be hard sometimes, but have you ever read it?" she asked again.

I shrugged again, "Yeah, I've read it occasionally. What's your point?"

She continued as if I hadn't said anything, "Ask, and it shall be given you; seek, and ye shall find; knock, and it shall be opened unto you." she recited. I swore I nearly saw her eyes change colors while saying it. I responded, "For everyone that asketh receiveth; and he that seeketh findeth; and to him that knocketh it shall be opened,", keeping my eyes locked with hers. "Are we quoting Matthew for fun—or is there a point?" I challenged her.

"I think we both know the point—garbage man. You're looking for some trash. Why else would you grace us with your presence? You haven't looked at a single woman for longer than a moment—and you look like you are about to jump out of your delicious flesh," she stated, licking her lips. I blinked at that one, feeling my skin itch, shrieking back as if she were some kind of creature from the darkest of depths.

I held her gaze and stayed steady. Slowly, I reached into my jacket and pulled out my wallet, producing the photo of Jacob again. I made sure to cover Gen and the rest of his family. There was no need to show someone like her anything more. "Looking for a boy—huh? Didn't figure you out for the type," she laughed softly, and I held her gaze steely.

"Where is the boy?" I asked her calmly.

She contorted her lips for a moment, then spoke, "Where do you think the firstborn offspring were taken when the plaques were set upon Pharaoh?" she asked just as calmly, though no longer sitting on her hands.

I sighed; she was enjoying this—it was a lot like being a mouse and her a cat. The cat was just playing with her meal. Okay then, I was at the mercy of a snake—at least for a moment. It's never over until it's over. I would just have to outsmart her at her own game.

"I would say they went to Heaven," I guessed. She blew out her lips at that. "You really think that? Your God kills them, then takes them to Heaven? I doubt it. I bet they stayed drying up in that desert-like little raisins, going pop, pop, pop in the sun," she titled her head back and cackled.

I kept my face neutral, "You know, Satan spoke scripture to Jesus while he was in the garden. Real confident like—I gotta imagine similar to what you just did. Don't forget, "But whoso shall offend one of these little ones which belief in me, it were better for him that a millstone was hung about his neck, and that he was drowned in the depth of the sea," I stated calmly.

This time, the cat looked scared for a moment. I went on the attack after that, "Pick apart the whole Bible. I doubt for a moment you understand any of it. But hear me when I say this—if you know something about him—and I find out, I'm going to kick down that door of your church. Drag your fat butt outside, and punch you square in the jaw," I promised.

Melanie blinked a few moments, then stood up quickly—my back jerked from my seat in anticipation. "Yes, garbage man, some trash must be removed, including some in here. Try to enjoy your time. Get a drink—relax a little. I think you will find I can be quite generous once you get to know me," her words slithered from her mouth, and I felt my legs tremble from the subtext as she slowly walked away, disappearing into the night of the club. It was the middle of the day outside this building; you wouldn't think it was from the inside of the belly of a beast. I held my breath as I watched her go, streaming through the area like a fish in the river. Once she was out of sight, I sighed deeply and unclenched my fist, my heart pounding. That woman scared the Hell out of me.

I shook my head, looking around the room. It was the middle of the afternoon, and seeing so many people here was still surprising. Dancers rhythmically worked their routines,

No one looked my way; no one gave even a glance. People were in here to do their business—so was I. I picked up a napkin left on the table; it was nearly soaked through in some spots. I quickly wrote down something on the napkin. Had I really been that afraid of her? I gulped and ignored that feeling as I looked for the side of the curtain booth—pushing the paper deep inside.

I got up; the next part was going to hurt very badly.

Chapter 35

I stood in the center of the bathroom. The sinks were the automatic kind that worked on movement. I had unscrewed the bottom fireman's emergency valve. Hot water shot from all the sinks. I rolled up as many paper towels and stuck them in the sinks, causing them to flood.

I was sure that Melanie had been asking me about Jacob. The child—in the dumpster. The syringes inside of his backpack—the men in the truck. Maybe even the doctor, the baby, and how it all connected. I was going to find out soon. The best way to crack this nut was with a sledgehammer. If Jacob was missing in this town, I would have only so much time to find him. It was time to pick a fight.

I waited as the bathroom mirrors flooded with steam, I started to sweat, and oily black streaks dripped from my arms down to the marble tile below my feet. The door to the bathroom kicked open, and in walked three men. One looked out of place with a scraggly red beard and a big ring gleaming with a silver moon. The other two were the bouncers from earlier inside the club.

"Hello, fellas," I declared, eyeing them as the door to the bathroom shut. One of the bouncers took the garbage can inside the bathroom and placed it under the door handle. Effectively locking us in this admittedly lovely room with a toilet. Even the faucets gleamed with an almost golden look to them. That helped annoy me—good. I was going to need it for what was about to come next. I recognized the redheaded man. He had been with the mayor last night on top of that roof.

I was about to find out what his role was in all of this. I suspected that the

Mayor was on the operation's books side, leaving Melanie as the operations. Still far too many holes to finish the puzzle, though. I needed to focus on these three clowns first. I had stuffed some paper towels around the vials in my pocket. I hoped that they would remain safe. Whatever protection I could get in this place. The redheaded man held up a folded piece of paper, "This you? You write this?" he smirked.

"Well, judging by how you said that I am surprised you could read it. I think it's safe to be safe, so I dabbled a few words on that paper. You solved the case—guess what? You still look like a backwoods redneck with that neck beard of yours and stringy, greasy hair. " I rolled off as the man's smirk disappeared.

"You just drew a picture of a donkey," he stated. "An ass, to be exact," I replied.

"Cute," He crumbled the paper, balled it up, and tossed it on the ground. The two bouncers slowly started to circle me. The truth about fighting is that most people just could never fathom it. You were likely to lose if it was more than one at a time. That left me with a few options. The bathrooms were small by design. You didn't need a mansion to take a crap. So, movement was out of the picture.

I could take the three on and get one of them down on the ground before the others ganged up and got me. Biding my time was not a good option either, as Larry and I had established nothing on the way here. It wasn't until my talk with Melanie that I confirmed that my suspicions were justified. What did that leave me? It left me with a somewhere-in-the-middle approach. I had no backup, and I knew her security would find me once Melanie went. I was in a building with who knows how much security and probably zero qualms about kicking my teeth in. I needed to separate the three and take them out quickly and efficiently while still getting any information I might need. Fight dirty. That was my only option here.

This was going to hurt—I just had to suck it up. The first bouncer took a swing with his right arm, haymaker behind me, completely telegraphing his punch; I ducked, successfully side-stepping the hit. In a quick movement, I was at his side, controlling his punching arm by pulling it downwards. My other fist uppercut his shirt into his face, followed by a quick elbow to the neck.

My right foot stepped over, and I tripped his heel from under him, sending the big ox down to the ground. I pulled his controlled arm past my hips and pivoted forward while turning the joint. I heard a crunch and popping, and his screams told me that I had just broken his elbow.

I didn't have long before I was shoved against the wall, tripping over the down thug and my face hitting the tile sides. But whoever shoved me hadn't bothered to clear his wounded friend and tripped as well, sending us both sliding down. I shrugged, popping off his weak hold of me; he should have held on to my back or taken my head in better control—his mistake, not mine. His face fell forward—I gripped his head with my hand and shoved it into the urinal cake to try and soften the blow.

His head bounced, breaking the bottom lip, and he fell to the ground. I was kneeling when a punch took me in the side of the face. I hit the wall again, tucked myself into a ball, and rolled over my shoulders just as another kick struck the wall. I heard curses from the ginger man. The room was filled with steam; I could still see his expensive shoes sticking out of the bottom of the now-broken drywall. I rolled towards him, fitting in under his feet—pushing out one of his legs while I placed one of mine on the outside, circling up until I hit his waist. My other did the same, only on the inside. Clenching with both my legs, he fell forward and smacked the wall, falling in a heap.

The steam was becoming overwhelming, and I knew I had, at most, maybe a minute or two more before someone would kick the bathroom doors in. Luckily for me, these amateurs made it safer by locking the doors behind them.

The ginger man squirmed on the ground; I pivoted, rotating around his body until I had my knee in his chest. He gasped, pressing his hands against my knee; I applied pressure until he stopped fighting and stared up at me.

I smacked him hard with the back of my hand, turning his face in the opposite direction. My face still stung from where he had hit me. It might have hit him harder than I needed to at that moment. He turned his face back towards me, blood draining from his nose.

"Piss off" he shouted, both of us completely drenched in sweat. Outside, I could hear people panicking about the steam. No one had pulled a fire alarm yet. This confirmed another thing: Melanie didn't want cops or firemen here. Which was both good and bad for me. It gave me time to do what I needed to this jerk but also meant they wouldn't play fair. I hoped Larry had enough sense to leave after seeing all the steam. Or I don't know. Come back up, your partner, I grumbled.

I looked at the man, sighed, and licked one of my fingers—followed by sticking said finger in his ear. His eyes bulged and squirmed away from me. The fire in his face went from rage to confusion in a few moments. "What the heck are you doing?" he gasped.

"Wet-willy buddy. Come on, we have all been six-year-olds on the playground. Something tells me you had to get beat up a bit as a kid. Or maybe not enough. Either way, going to calm down now?" I stated casually.

He scrambled again, which only forced my knee deeper into his chest before he grunted, cursing me. I smacked him again, enough to rock his head back on the hard ground. I waited until the whites came back into his eyes; they were afraid this time. He was a low-level henchman type. Sure, he had taken a few beatings in his day, probably more than most people would think, but not enough to put up with what he was enduring now. Smacking a man in the face had a way of breaking down the toughest of tough guys—especially when they start feeling overpowered.

"What the heck do you want?" he screamed as I smacked him again. Both of his cheeks were bright red, his eyes watering.

"Oh, you know, just a couple of questions. First, I want you to stop yelling. Can you do that?" I nearly whispered, taking his collar deep into my fist.

He scrunched his nose at me—a leer of pure hatred. I paused, holding his focus. There wasn't enough time to thoroughly work him over, especially when I was still trying to figure out precisely what I could gain from him. Outside, I could hear steps running towards the door. The heavy wooden doors jostled as someone attempted to kick them. More steps shook the door, and I knew I would only have so much time now. I pulled him up with his collar until his face was inches from mine.

"I am going to ask you once—only once. If it is anything dumb, it won't be a slap next time, right?" I growled at the man. Arrogance flashed across his brow, I pulled him closer and shouted, "Do you understand me?"

He jerked away, trying to distance us. I smacked him again and moved us both closer to the wall. That did the trick; it finally sank into the man, and he couldn't escape. It also helped that the two bouncers started groaning at that moment.

"What do you want?" he spits out, fear running through his eyes. Here was the tricky part: I had to get information out of him; I would only get a few guesses about what exactly that was.

I gave him one last warning before continuing in case he needed to get the picture. "I want you to answer my questions—nothing smart," I commanded as sweat dripped down my forehead. The room was getting too steamy, and it was hard to breathe.

"Were you at the apartment complex in the old town this morning?" I asked.

"What apart—" he started before I backhanded him hard. This time, with the prosthetic hand cutting a gash across his face. His eyes begin to water and become unfocused before he spits an answer, "Yes, yes, I was."

"Why were you there? Were you looking for a boy?" I shouted, pulling his upper half off the ground. He looked on in total fear before nodding his head once more. He paused, avoiding my eye contact, almost as if searching for something on my face that he could hide from.

I started to reach back for another punch when he yelled, "Yes, okay. We were looking for the boy, but he got away once we followed him into the complex,"

I stuttered, "Why, why were you looking for him?" he glanced at me with confusion for a moment. Low-level people like him probably weren't even told why they wanted to follow Jacob, but his reactions told me everything. So, Jacob was being followed. "Were you the ones that started the fire?" I suddenly felt rage build up inside me. Something must have shown on my face; the man squirmed away from me in an attempt to put distance between us.

That pissed me off enough that I was pretty sure I would start breathing fire on the man at any moment. This time, I nodded my head and waited to use that anger. I was going to need it later.

"Where is he? Who sent you? Who do you guys work for? Why were you after a nine-year-old little boy?" I stated. "Was it for some kind of sick game?" I questioned him, barely over a whisper. He shook his head no.

I glared into his eyes, praying that he was telling the truth. I couldn't imagine something happening to Jacob or any kid, but the world wasn't friendly. He glanced away, and malice injected itself into my blood like a drug—shooting my flesh to a burning point where I thought if I opened my mouth for a moment, flames just might come out. I paused, catching my breath, "Was that what you—had—planned?" I asked through clenched teeth, my rage about to cause me to explode.

"I don't—look, the kid has something we, I mean, my..." the man trailed off, pure terror racing across his face. I started to growl through clenched teeth, my breath coming in waves through the hot mist.

"Are...you... going to kill me?" the man stuttered.

I shifted my weight and leaned back cocking my fist. The man threw up his hands, and I caught sight of his ring again. I could see the sigil of a lock and chain with a closer look. The chain looped around in such a way that it formed a pretzel. In the keyhole was a small crescent moon. I took a mental picture of that as the bathroom door bursting open. Time was up.

I growled one last time, pulling him closer, "We will talk," I stated before letting my fist find its way toward his face. His eyes rolled back; his nose busted. I gently dropped his head on the bathroom floor. I wasn't trying to kill the man. That I would not do. Though my anger was telling me, I was far too soft. I had no time for a moral debate. I glanced at the only window in the bathroom. A small carnival glassed frame—about the size of an average-sized man on the walls leading out to an alleyway. I couldn't see out, but that was my only chance. A place this obscured probably didn't want a passersby to see inside. This unnerved me to a degree I had never felt before. How long had something like this been in my town, and I had never noticed it?

I moved away from the man and bolted towards the window, my leg rubbing raw from the prosthetic. At this point, I needed to change the sock used to cover the stub of a limb before it got infected, but I would have to worry about that later. The bathroom door flew open as I popped out the glass with a few heavy kicks.

Shards cut through my pants; I moved on, jumping out the window. I fell for ten feet, landing hard on the dumpster. My shoulder struck first, and I tucked into a ball to cushion the blow. Sirens blared in the distance. Even shady places like this couldn't keep the police away forever—though I still tucked myself inside the dumpster, burying myself under piles of filth. Whoever had kicked through that door, I had no way of outrunning. I hid as I heard shouting above me.

I held my breath; footsteps thundered past me. "Where did he go?" shouted one voice, causing me to shake. I was tired, bleeding from somewhere on my back, praying that none of the trash got into the cut. What was I doing in the garbage, going up against people with security on the payroll? By one of the vilest people who ever graced the pavement of this town. They could kill me—some of them had guns. And here I was, acting like a tough guy. Could I really do this? I should go to the police now and tell Gen what happened. She could figure out a way to sort this out with the police. They could find Jacob, and I could go home. Start training for your test next year, I chided myself. You missed the date this morning—that was alright, yeah, that was all I needed to do. Just give up the life of a small child for comfort and security.

I bit my tongue until blood flowed, thrusting me back into the reality of the situation. You saw it yourself, Billy Dan. The cops in this town could only do so much with a Mayor like that. I mean, for crying out loud, the Mayor's brother is the police chief, now that I thought about it. A fire had happened at a storage facility, and the fire department never showed, just two out-of-uniform police. A cold chill in my spine met the burning fear attacking my heart, resulting in a hard crust forming in my mind. A shape that knew the moment I stopped—Jacob would be dead. I just knew it. I was in over my head. I had to do this anyway.

I took a deep breath, removed the banana peel, and crushed yogurt from my chest. Someone was after a friend of mine. A close kid who was scared and running somewhere on the streets for what reasons I had no idea. I had to find him; I had protected him. I could worry about being a scared chicken later. I peeped open the lid; two men were arguing with a police officer, only one unit. Why only one unit? Where was the fire department? That was when the crust around my heart got a little thicker. They had this much control?

That thought scared me. Jacob being hurt frightened me far worse. I popped out of the garbage bin and took off down the alley towards the parking garage, hurried my steps, and took off as the sun reached its highest point in the day. Every second counted, hold on, Jacob.

Chapter 36

Rain started falling in heavy succession as I approached the truck. I was out of breath, and the humidity from the heat and the rain made it feel like I was drinking the air. I decided to take my time getting to the truck. Someone from the club could have spotted my appearance—I needed to be careful. I had been far too active today already—someone would find me. The flashes of the money I burned came to mind; people storing that much treasure—there would be dragons.

I jammed my hat down. Pulling my jacket in tighter despite the heat. It wasn't uncommon for it to be cold in the morning and a blistering oven by noon in this state. Hopefully, I will come off as someone who hasn't gone home yet for the day. Judging by the state of my clothes after falling out the window—probably a homeless person to some.

Good. My heart was still pounding from the fight in the bathroom. Why was I acting so cocky, so tough? Sure, I had devoted myself to training the last few years, but this was different. I Paused, coming through the stairway doors leading out to the level where we had parked the truck. A man and a woman, both dressed in black, circled the floor—brandishing pistols in broad daylight.

I gulped as I ducked behind the nearest car, a green heap that was a bit underclass compared to the others here. I realized this and kept moving as I watched the pair find our truck. How could they know that was Larry's truck? Looking around, cars you only see in expensive movies and fancy hotels dotted the area. I smacked my forehead. Of course, this was their parking garage. And the two of us had parked near the red truck we had seen earlier. Both trucks were within ten spots of each other. This wasn't a good idea at all. I pulled out my phone, checking to make sure that it was on silent, and snapped pictures of them both from behind a luxury model car that I couldn't begin to pronounce the name of. The two of them circled Larry's truck, which confirmed I was right about someone in the club owning that truck. More importantly, someone from the club had been there this morning when the apartment went up in flames. My bet was on the ginger with the strange ring, I thought. He kept popping up in way too many places, but how did all of this fit together?

I needed to act quickly before one of the two got the bright idea of taking a picture of the plates. The man, his hair combed back in a no-descriptive comb-over, had just the idea as he pulled out his phone. I cursed the technology gods for making this so easy for people and got to thinking. What did I have that I could use? What could I use? I looked around and spotted the only thing I could find. A chuck of rocks had come along with the nearest car. Thank you. I thought gravel roads in tiny towns were good for something as I picked up the rock and aimed it at the man.

My throw went right on target and smacked the man hard in the back of the head. He turned around immediately, dropping his phone and flashing his gun in my direction. I had already moved on to the next row of cars, keeping low under the base so they couldn't see me.

The pair flanked the car where I had been while I quickly edged my way over to the truck. Thankfully, I had Larry's keys as I held my breath, unlocking the driver's door and sliding into it. The pair were in the expensive car in front of me. I paused, wishing I had broken into the red truck. That very quickly could have been the end to all of this nonsense. I gripped the wheel tightly—what was I about to do?

No time to think, I jammed the key into the ignition, placing my hand on the horn, and pressed in. The closed garage became a war zone of noise in a pitch. The blare was a battle cry to the two, to the whole town.

It had the desired effect and sent both the pair into covering their ears in frustration. I popped the truck into drive and sped away as one of them managed to get off a shot despite the ear-splitting noise flooding the area.

Sparks flew from somewhere in the truck, and I kept driving until I popped out of the entranceway.

On the main street, people had gathered, already glancing toward the garage noises; some had enough sense to run after the shots went off. I tore down the street, my heart beating fast—sweat falling onto my fingers.

Now I just had to find Jacob.

Chapter 37

I called Larry, he had ditched the club when he lost sight of me. This was true enough to some extent, though my mistrust of Larry was already reaching its peak. We met a couple of blocks away from the club. I threw open the door as Larry started swearing.

"Billy Dan, what the Hell did you do to my truck? Is that a gunshot?" He stammered as I floored the truck back to our work center. Shifting gears in the car while also doing my best to not come off as a madman or get pulled over was mentally exhausting enough. Part of me wanted to go home and die in the shower. Just rest for a long time—let everyone else handle the world's problems.

"Earth to Billy Dan, this is God—am I talking to myself here?" shouted Larry until I finally turned my head towards him, "What's up?" I asked, turning my head back to the road.

"What's up, the man says?" Larry scuffed. "Well, here is what's up, Billy Dan. You're driving like a madman; you've run three lights—now make that four. You're bleeding from your nose, and I don't know, it might be that big hole in the side of my truck," He screamed.

I put two fingers up to my nose and felt something warm. Sure enough, I was bleeding. I grunted, "Thanks for looking out, Larry."

Larry regarded me with a long look that shifted between nervousness and absolute anger in seconds.

"Dude, will you answer something? What the Hell are you doing?" the younger man pleaded. I regarded him for a long moment. Larry was still pale over his darker skin—his hair creased back from the day. I needed to know if I could trust him. I needed to get rid of this truck.

I grunted, "We are heading into work."

"Why would we go back to work?" he asked, perplexed.

"To get a truck," I replied.

"Yeah, a truck,"

"But we are in a truck already, Billy Dan..." Larry trailed off.

"Exactly," I stated, pushing the truck even faster. The needle was heading towards the redline, and my heart was replicating the same.

Chapter 38

We reached the city's waste processing plant—or dump if you had trouble with fancy words. I grunted as I parked the truck, killing the engine before Larry could say anything else. The truck door slammed; my breath was steady as I entered our work center. Larry followed at my feet, not saying one word.

The afternoon was approaching, and the day shift was preparing to make way for the night crew. For the most part, everything was empty as I made my way to the truck lot at the back of the massive bay attached to our building. We had a collection of key rings that stored our various vehicles.

Without looking, I knew which one would be best for anything that might happen. So far, I had been playing by these jerk's rules. It had got me into a bathroom brawl, a burning apartment building, and I am pretty sure the meanest rash in South Carolina around my thighs now. Stuff was about to get real, so it was time for "Big Booty Brenda."

She is something else, a front-loader beauty. Front-loader garbage trucks are generally used to service commercial and industrial businesses by collecting waste materials in large refuse containers known as dumpsters. Judging by today, it could be anything.

Big Brenda was equipped with a hydraulically controlled fork on the front of the vehicle, which is used by the operator to lift and dump the contents of the dumpster containers into the vehicle hopper, where it is compacted by a hydraulically actuated packer into the massive rear of the body. Most front loaders in the United States will hold up to 40 cubic yards of trash and can lift containers weighing 8,000 lbs. The addition of a Curotto Can system, which has an automated arm attachment, also allows the front loader to be used as a computerized side loader, enabling the operator to dump residential carts. It's the next best thing to a tank I could ever find. It was perfect; it even had cup holders and only a bit of graffiti written on the side.

"Wait, you need to check that out with the boss first," Larry mumbled, and I glared at him until he averted his gaze. Shifting through the lock boxes for the keys proved to be a time sink: the day crew seemed to always stick things in the right places. To be fair, though, Larry and I always managed to park the trucks on the far side of the compound. From what I've been told, change and minor annoyances suit people.

"What's going on, Billy Dan?" asked a short breath from behind me. I spun to see Marv, my donuts-shaped-haired, balding boss. His brief, flat nose is a blessing in such a career. He was a timid man, coming up to just my shoulders. Arms that seemed to be growing their own jungle, combined with beady eyes that sunk into his head behind thick-framed glasses.

Marv held a clipboard, a very used fountain pin, and a face sourer than a prune. "Yes," I replied, turning back to the key box—searching for Brenda's key. I felt heavy eyes on my back. A loud clearing of my throat almost made me gag. Marv had allergies that only seemed to exasperate anything he said.

With another gurgling clear of his throat, he spoke again, causing me to halfway turn my head towards him, "Billy Dan, you know your shift ended a couple of hours ago. You can work, but I'm not paying you. I don't know what you think you're doing, but you aren't taking a truck. We have enough problems with people crashing into things," he glared at Larry.

Larry blushed and turned away—it had taken every ounce of my goodwill to help Larry keep his job that day. Curves came out of nowhere when you drove something so big. The problem was that Larry hit a few curves, followed by the side of the actual compound.

I paused, letting his words sink in. Marv was not going to let me take one of the trucks. His pleasant smile bordered on a smirk that made the moles around his lips quiver as he had "won" the discussion. Marv had a way of doing that; for him, once he said something like that, he was A remarkably unreasonable person to most: just an asshole to all of us here at the shop.

I cleared my throat with force, beating his, and stated, "Just need to borrow Brenda for a few hours. Tell you what, I will even pay for the gas—you can take it out of my next paycheck,".

Marv's smirk disappeared, replaced with a deep frown, making him appear like a hairy potato. "Brenda. You know, we just had the cab reinforced. She's not going anywhere until the inspector signs off on her. I would think, Billy Dan, that you would know better. You are the shift lead. I thought you would come in here suggesting something like this, especially after I allowed you to go and take your silly test this morning," he informed me.

"Marv—I am taking Big Brenda; I will have her back in twenty-four hours," I stated, checking my anger. I curled my fist hard enough to pop all my knuckles. Larry sucked in his breath—Marv turned a few shades red.

"Excuse me, I allowed you to study for your test today. You missed an extra shift. I allow you to study while you are on the job. Yeah, don't think I haven't heard about you, Billy Dan," he said.

Marv's hands moved towards his hips. A smug look on his face that honestly made it seem like he had sucked on a lemon. "That's right, you know better than to bite the hand that feeds you," Marv suggested, pointing at me with one of his stubby hands. I shot mine forward, twisting his arm as I pulled him into my hip until the pudgy man was lower than me, a shock of pain and confusion written across his face.

"First of all, no one allows me to do shit, boss man. Secondly, consider this my resignation," I stated, pulling on his arm. Marv cried out, and I felt guilty for just a moment. All the late shifts, shady business cuts, and doxing of our pay made me want to twist up. It took a lot more restraint than what I wanted to admit.

I took a deep breath, steadying myself as I pulled slightly on Marv's arm. He cried out in pain, Larry stepped forward, then thought better after he saw something on my face.

"Thirdly, I am taking Brenda. I need it to save a kid. You can fire me if you want, claim it was me that had you in this lock, but I am taking the truck, a couple of lollipops—and I will even leave it with a full tank of gas when I am done. Are we clear?" I asked the man, giving him one more yank before he cried out, falling to the ground. I let go, slowly stepping away. Keeping my hands in front of me in case he decided to fight back.

Marv did not. Instead, he remained on the ground with his head bowed. I felt terrible for a moment, and then I remembered Marv had made one of the other guys come in on their child's birthday so he could go on vacation.

I turned back to the key rack, Marv still blubbering on the ground. Larry standing there slack-jawed.

"I would suggest moving your truck, Larry, to the other side of the lot. Marv, you don't mind, do you?" I asked the man; he still lay slobbering on the ground. "Sure, take whatever you need—you're fired," he sniffled.

"I understand, thank you," I stated, flipping through the clipboard. Brenda had a full tank of gas, brand-new plates, and a reinforced steel frame. No one in the city had seen her in months. She was a clean tank in a rusty town.

I debated saying something more to Marv; he wasn't bad, but maybe I was too hard on the man. This was for Jacob. How many more times today was I going to say that? An easy path to Hell: justifying your actions with good intentions.

"Worry about that later; get in the truck," I grumbled, making my way to the driver's side door. A short set of stairs leads up to the operator's seats. Brenda's new car smell was back. I took a moment to let that sink in. Some trucks were getting so old that the scent seemed to be a part of the metal by now. No matter how many times we sprayed it down. It was lovely—the moment cleared my mind as I fumbled for the ignition.

The passenger door opened, and Larry slid in, "State regulations on a vehicle this big is a class B license for anything under 10,000 pounds. But let's be real, Billy Dan, you can't possibly hope to get this out of here without me," Larry stated, clicking his seatbelt in.

Despite my increasing feelings of mistrust of Larry, he had a point. It was darn near impossible to pull out in such a massive machine. Still, I needed to address those feelings sooner rather than later.

"Shoot yourself," I stated, starting the big machine. In the rear-view mirror, Marv had gotten off the ground. The first thing he did was sprint to the phone. The shift slammed in reverse, and I used the elephant-sized mirrors on the side to pull back until I was right next to Marv. He looked dumbfounded. He would keep a telephone in the middle of the garage instead of just using his cell phone.

Over the loud engine, I shouted, "Marv, give me your phone," I held out of my hand. Marv glanced at it, glanced at me, and decided it was best not to be put on the ground again. He reluctantly placed his small device into my hand. A slight shock from my prosthetic caused the screen to flicker. I smirked, handing it back. Marv was too scared to notice the screen going crazy before stopping. I had lost two phones to my hand before realizing that something in this hand caused the devices to short out.

I waited until he handed me the phone in the receiver. With a grunt, I threw the archaic device half across the lot until it smashed into the opposite wall. Those were the only phones in the building. Marv needed to be longer-sighted to think of putting office phones anywhere else. Technology or not, be smart and keep a single point of failure. I nodded my head to Marv. "Hand me your keys," I stated flatly. He hesitated, and I held him in a long gaze. He handed me the keys through the driver's window. "Full tank of gas; you will get these back as well," I stated. "Be seeing you, Marv," I said as I took us out the open bay doors.

Taking Brenda and leaving Marv without a phone gave us at least thirty minutes. He lived on the far side of town. Marv would have to wait until the night shift came in, which was in six hours. It took ten minutes to get the license plate changed on this machine and another thirty minutes to solve the problem of what would transpire between Larry and me.

Chapter 39

We drove for ten minutes until I was sure we had put the bay behind us. I glanced in the rear-view mirror—no one was following us. That was a relief—as the day went on, I was starting to shake at the thought of what had occurred. Who the heck was driving this thing called my life? Had to be a madman. I avoided my reflection in the mirrors and looked at Larry. He sat comfortably spread out in the seat next to me. His skin was still sickly pale, his pores leaking endless sweat. While his leg tapped rhythmically on the floorboard.

Larry was easy to write off and just as quickly to be entirely flabbergasted by in the same breath. The man came off as a drugged-out pervert, but at the same time, he had completely set up our company's website, network, and security. Skills like that made me wonder why he was a garbage man. On the other hand, though, the same could be said of me. Professions are just a title at the end of the day, not a summary of a person's skills or life.

I distrusted the man after the events of this morning. Even more so when I thought of how crazy I had been today, but Larry was still sitting next to me, riding around in a stolen dump truck heading lord knows where.

That gave me pause, and I turned onto the city dump grounds. Pulling into the gate, Frank, the old security guard, waved us through; his white hair on his dark skin gleamed on what was otherwise an ordinary day. I rolled down the window when I pulled in, "Hey Frank, what's good?"

"Billy Dan! Always good to see! Oh, you know everything is good! I don't see anything on the schedule for you guys for a couple more hours—last-minute problem?" Frank asked, nodding to Larry as he folded his arms comfortably on the side of the truck.

"Something like that won't be long. Just need to take care of something, you know how it is," I stated.

Frank looked skeptical before deciding that it was good enough for him. "Sure, just don't take forever—damn buzzards are pecking around here again. I'm telling you, man—those beady little eyes of theirs. It's like they know they lost when they were dinosaurs. And now the best they could get was the leftover of the ape people's food," he said.

I nodded understanding, looking at the crows, hawks, and other birds flying around the junkyard. It was true; their dinosaurs did show—just flattened down and far less likely to spawn a creatively bankrupt movie franchise.

Smiling at Frank, I shifted us back into gear and lurched the heavy machine forward. Due to the frame having been mostly updated, the hydraulics weren't completely installed. Brenda shook enough to cause my teeth to chatter if I opened my mouth. I kept it shut for fear that Frank would notice. Frank gave nothing away if he had, but as Larry and I pulled through, Frank was on the phone tracing us with his eyes, writing something down. That made me pause; Larry and I would only be here briefly. Hopefully, we will leave together.

Chapter 40

Cars littered the junkyard—crushed steel, heaps of bags, couches, broken fans, landfills of useless junk to some, and almost anything a person would ever need, I thought. I was going to take advantage of that right now. I parked Brenda next to a pile of crushed trucks, the furthest from Franks's post at the front. I wiped the sweat from my head and crawled out of the truck's step ladder down to the ground, slamming the door shut.

The nearest car had plates on both the front and back that were in good condition. I pulled out my pocketknife, unscrewing the plates on the back of the car, when I heard Larry approach behind me.

"Don't just stand there, Larry, get the plates off of the front of this—thing. I think it used to be a Volvo. I never liked those cars; they are way too heavy," I stated in a conversational tone.

"Oh right, my bad," he trotted to the front. "Yeah, man, this was a Volvo, it has one of those old, reinforced metal frames. Basically, a slow-moving tank," Larry joked. I smirked, pulling the last screw out as I went back to Brenda and started replacing the plates on her. In a few minutes, we had both completely changed. I pulled out my drenched shirt—how could Frank stand out here every day doing this in such a tiny box? The man deserved a medal. Larry came back from behind Brenda, nodding that it was finished.

"Come help me with one final thing," I said as I walked behind the truck on the far side, keeping myself from view. Our team always kept a collection of clamps, straps, and bungee cords in a compact on the side of the truck. I opened that compartment now and pulled out a long chain, taking it to the back. When I reached the compactor, I started it up, the heavy truck started to beep, and the compactor shook like a giant hungry dog waiting to get a treat for being a good boy.

The lid opened, and Larry said, "What's up? This thing should be empty— she's been sitting on the compound for months," he said nervously, sticking his head to peer inside Brenda. Larry didn't notice my hand moving around his neck until I looped the chain around his head.

He reacted like a caged animal. Clawing at the chain with both his hands as I heard him choke. I clicked the lock close and stepped back. Larry panicked for a few moments, fiddling with a hole in the chains before resigning himself to being stuck. "Billy Dan—what the," he started before I clocked him— hard on the side of his jaw. Larry fell to one knee and gripped his face with the other. His face swelled a deep red, but otherwise, he remained standing. Good, I didn't want to knock him out during this. I raised my fist again, and he flinched. Larry wasn't stupid; he had already realized he was in trouble.

My right hand fumbled for the switch on the side of the truck that started to compactor. The truck rumbled to life. The flat jaws of the compactor began to close, crushing anything with eight thousand pounds of force. Larry eyeballed the chain and followed where it led directly in the back attached to the compactor. A slow tuck as the chain started to get caught in the mouth of the machine—unflinching and indifferent to whatever ended up in its jaws.

Larry bolted until the chain yanked, pulling him slowly up the side of the truck towards the awaiting slabs of metal that would crush him flat as a pancake. Through a constricted hold, Larry gasped, "Billy Dan."

"You're only going to get a few questions, Larry. If you lie to me—I can always find a new partner. Understand?" I asked him calmly.

I kept eye contact with Larry, my hand on the switch. Calm can sometimes make people panic, worse than anger. It plays on their insecurities and plants the seed of doubt in their mind. No one wants to ever feel like they aren't in control of a situation. We are all the kings of our mushy little bio kingdoms. We forget that that doesn't extend outside of our calcium-rich skull. Our influence on our environment is grossly overestimated by just a single person. Without a tide of others, we are very weak on our own. Larry was feeling that right now. The slow, engrossing pull of nature's futility. The chain wasn't robust; it could have been broken by someone with abnormal strength or a well-time pull as it slowly disappeared under the crushing void. Larry was alone, panicked, and stressed. He was still processing this rather than addressing me.

The compactor was on its slowest setting—if I wanted it, Larry would already be gone, eaten by Brenda's tomb. Part of me felt guilty for doing this to a friend. The rest of me was absolute in my convictions. A little boy was lost in a city that never returned the children once they were gone.

Larry squirmed one last time before glancing up at me, his face a contorted source of rage behind his thick-framed glasses. He looked on the verge of tears. Either way, I thought I was going to lose a friend. With a slow tilt of his head, Larry acknowledged what I said. I breathed a sigh of relief at that. My mind was elsewhere; that was the only explanation for this insanity. The decision has been made, Billy Dan, stick to your guns and don't look back.

"This morning, you came by my house, telling me about a boy that is very important to me. A friend of ours was even in trouble. Somehow, he had made it all the way to the far part of town, found a baby inside a dumpster, and you just happened to find him, or he stole away in the back of your truck. Seeing how you knew about a mysterious strip club in the middle of a bible-thumping, the grass is always green up our sunshine-ass neighborhood. This makes me suspect that you might know more than, "I didn't know about such and such." That may be true; a lot here, Larry, just looks like a pig. Even with all the lipstick you've tried putting on this pig—it is still a foul-smelling—pig," I stated, glaring into his eyes with all the rage I felt only millimeters below my skin.

Larry gulped his eyes a pool of sadness and fear. I pressed, "So, help me fill the gaps, Larry. Do that now, or else I will let Big Brenda crush you. And we both know they won't be able to peel you off the inside of the truck with how flat you will be. Someone will have to come and take a hose—probably high pressure and spray away the pancaked remains of your dead body. Your balls crushed to dust, nothing left of you," I let my threat sink in as I hovered my hand over the button. Larry's skin was paled to that of milk. He was the lighter of the two of us—I imagined I must have looked like some kind of demon, ablaze with fury about to smite the man. There was no joy in this; however, my anger would keep me from feeling guilty for a long time.

A few moments passed, and Larry broke eye contact and wept. I sighed, readying myself to press the button when he finally spoke. "I knew where the kid was last seen," he muttered. "what was that?" I started, killing the engine to Big Brenda, who died in a slow whisper. "I said, I knew where the kid was this morning. Or I had an idea," he cried out. I killed the engine, and a small part of my mind was thankful I didn't have to go that far. The rest of me wondered if I was really willing to kill a friend. Not just kill him, but crush him under 8,000 pounds of force? It would be a slow death, one that Larry would have time to think about as the slap of metal pushed into his skull, bones breaking, organs splattering open. It was a gruesome image that made me want to vomit. I held it in and stood above Larry.

"What do you mean you knew where he was last seen? Did you know he would be at the dumpster this morning?" I asked Larry. My hand still hovering over the startup button to the Big Brenda's heavy plow. Larry looked at my hand and seemed to swallow whatever reply he would make.

"I mean, I didn't know he was going to be in that exact dumpster—just, you know, an educated guess," he muttered.

"An educated guess," I scuffed.

"That's one Hell of a guess, Larry. Are you just going to tell me lies, or should I just press the button and get this over with? To tell you the truth, I am over both at the moment and the more time I waste dealing with you, the less time Jacob has," I stated matter-of-factly.

Larry gulped again and seemed to recognize finally that whatever he was protecting wasn't worth it. "Can you take this damn chain off my neck at least, please?" he pleaded and finally met my eye contact again. His eyes were a puffy red, but it was impossible to tell what was in them.

I glared for a few more moments before pulling the chain off his neck, not before rolling Larry out of the truck on the hard ground below.

Chapter 41

Larry and I sat on the tail of the garbage truck. He rubbed his neck while I spoke.

"Don't make me regret not killing you; now talk," I stated.

"Alright, alright," he sighed deeply.

I tapped my wrist; Larry fought the urge to roll his eyes as I saw them twitch momentarily. He coughed before speaking, "The kid found something that some—well—you have to understand, Billy Dan, I'm not with them. Just in a bad way," he trailed off, looking into the distance.

I waited for him to continue. When he didn't, I spoke, "Let me guess, is that why you always look like the backside of a meth house every time I see you? Did they have something on you?" I asked.

Larry blinked, seeming to be shocked by my statement, "What, do you think I am on drugs? Hardly any, man, just lots of energy drinks and late nights. That's not what was going on here, I swear," he defended.

"Then help me out; what is going on," I asked my friend. I tried to warm my words, but I wouldn't have accepted them after something like this. What was I doing here? Why was I trying to be the tough guy? There are people whose jobs are to do such things. Let them do their jobs. My prosthetic hand caught the light, and I examined it. My chest suddenly became tight, and the world shrunk momentarily. Because when I was going through Hell—I always hoped for a hero to come. They never did; I always had to save myself. Jacob needed that. I could get over this.

"Spill the beans, man," I stated, sitting next to Larry in the back of the truck after almost killing him. I still positioned myself to press the button at any time, though. If Larry had noticed, nothing would have shown on his face. He kept rubbing the chain around his neck. The skin was a raw red and festering already.

Larry stopped rubbing his neck before noticing my hand. He flinched before realizing the futility of the situation. "Alright—do you need context or just the get to the chase?" he asked. I glared at him momentarily and blew out my lips, exasperated.

"Holy crap, if I didn't need you to be quick, I wouldn't have tied you up and thrown you in the back of a dump truck," I stated.

Larry stared back blankly before I sighed, "Be quick," I paused before adding, "On second thought, just tell me whatever is prudent, but be quick about it," I stated, rubbing my face as the sheer absurdity of the day was running its way through my fingers. My hand was shaking, and I jammed it into my pockets before Larry noticed.

"Well, remember how I fumbled out of that tech job? Larry asked, shame written across his face. "Yeah, I remember—tough break, kid, you couldn't have—" I started before he waved me off. "No, I didn't get fired for the reasons I told you. I am the master at what I do. I just suck at everything else," Larry said, his voice laced with shame.

"I don't..."

Larry continued, "I bounced around a lot, kept looking for anything that could fill that void, modern man war—losing a job, don't be ashamed, but also try not to kill yourself. That's always what it was. A handshake and off to the next job. Over and over again. Seems like a small thing now. I remember they found me first during that time. My skills as a keyboard warrior made me cocky, and I hacked the wrong people," he trailed off, and the pieces started to fit together. Larry had shown up out of the blue for two years to work as a garbage man; no one knew why when his resume would easily place him into a field making a great deal of money. He reeked of a person running away. Most of our team was made up of runaways and dreamers. Me included.

"Who did you hack, Larry?" I asked.

He hesitated; I spoke up, "Larry, I will kill you and sleep like a baby—now tell me," I spoke. Larry's face broke out in sweat, and he nodded, "Here's the thing: they were smart enough to come to me hidden. It wasn't smart for me not to figure out who they were sooner, but these guys go deep, Billy Dan. They have hackers, thugs, judges, and even cops," Larry stated.

"Who came for you? Who are these people?" I almost pleaded.

"They work for the Mayor."

Chapter 42

That was surprising, the implications dawning on me each time my heart skipped. Someone so powerful that, at this point, it was as if the man had been born into our town's role. The wealthiest person—who felt so beyond reproach that he could beat up an old lady on top of a restaurant on Tuesday. I wasn't sure how that fit in with William and the doctor. Nor with the church or the baby. Or with the storage shed area.

I sighed heavily, "You said they, who are they?"

"I never really got that far exactly—just that within an hour after I did it, some folks showed up at my place," Larry cast his eyes down. I recalled the last several years that the two of us had together; there was the time Larry showed up after a week off. His face crusted yellow, and his eyes a swollen mirage of purple. He had told us it was a skiing accident. It seemed legit enough, though it was the middle of summer if I remember correctly. And the closest slopes would have been out of town. An outright lie. I felt guilty for not digging deeper into that sooner.

Larry took a deep breath before continuing, "But basically, by the time they were done with me, I didn't really have a choice," he spoke, ashamed.

"You always have a choice; it's just that some tend to only be bad for yourself later," I corrected him. Larry looked up as I sat on the tailgate of the truck. "So, these people, who exactly are they, and what do you do for them?" I asked, trying to pull the malice I felt growing under my skin. There would be a time and a place for my anger. Easy to have and lose myself if I just started to react to everything. Figure out what needs to be done first, Billy Dan, then you unleash whatever was tightening around your heart.

"Okay, this you won't believe," he paused before adding, "I honestly have no idea who these people are. Like I'm good—these people make me look like amateur hour. Whoever runs the show has some deep pockets. And they are buying all the drinks at the titty bar on a Saturday night if you know what I mean," he explained.

I glared at him, "So, is this the Mayor, or do you also not know the answer? Also, what have you been doing for these people?" I asked, the clock ticking in the back of my head. This was all for Jacob, and I repeated it again despite the howling force of thoughts that slammed into my skull every time Larry did not get to the point.

He paused again, unsure of my reaction, as I sighed, sliding off the truck bed, "If I didn't believe you, Larry, you and I wouldn't be having this conversation. Continue, stop worrying about it,".

He nodded once, taking a deep breath, "Honestly—a lot of low-level stuff. I changed shipping manifestos, addresses, and other stuff in the first few weeks. All the while, it ensures that certain products are never looked at the wrong way online. He had me on a short leash, and if I am honest, I don't think he is even at the top of it. I think I wasn't even supposed to know that he was running the show here." he explained.

"Do you happen to know what was being shipped?" I asked, and Larry gulped, "I'm not sure, but the things that it was being shipped in were always big, breathable, and needed to be able to dispense water while also being compact," he trailed off, his eyes cast to the ground. The answer came slamming into my head. "You were helping to ship, people?" I stammered as Larry remained silent.

Anger isn't what overtook me—I would reflect on that later—it was just the assertion of something cold—something primal. An act so terrible— being done in my town—my knuckles cracked even before I punched Larry so hard he flew out of the truck and down onto the hard ground below.

I snarled, looking at Larry, his nose bleeding and his cheek rounded from my hit. He kept his hands flat on the ground along with his eyes. He wasn't going to fight back—not after a sucker punch like that, even. Good. I took a few deep breaths, staring into the darkness of the truck. The bottom was obscured by the light, and the compressor was waiting at the end like an unmoving mountain. Unconcerned by what was happening. All it cared about was the power to do its job. Efficiently and with no remorse. Is that what it would take before all of this was done? Just do my job efficiently and with zero remorse. Just a number in the grand scheme of things, crushed under the never-ending pile of filth. I balled my fist and spit on the ground. I didn't want to believe that—not even for a moment.

Larry was starting to sit up slowly when I outstretched my hand towards him. He hesitated and took it gratefully. "Do you happen to know what they were using these people for, where they were transporting them?" I growled, yanking him to his feet. Larry looked wide-eyed before steadying himself.

"Not off the top of my head, but I could get that information back home. They were having me keep tabs on William. I didn't know his role, Billy Dan. They just wanted to know where he was at all times. I think William worked for them, but Jacob had something they wanted. I don't know who those two dudes were—I promise. It's like all these people work together but in different departments. And one is doing something shady. Honest, they always had me keep track of shipping and such. I didn't know about anything else," he mumbled as I stepped closer. "What are they missing? What could they want that bad?" I asked. He didn't respond, so I searched his face until it dawned on me. "Oh no, the kid," I stated, turning away and running towards the driver's seat. Larry called after me, "Where are you going?"

"Get in the damn truck, Larry."

Chapter 43

We took off down the urban streets in the fading morning with the afternoon sun kissing the shadow on the dashboard. Larry fiddled with the handlebar above him, gripping the hanging metal like a security blanket, hard enough to turn his knuckles a deep hue of pink.

My mind raced—keying in on the critical details that I hadn't even considered this morning before giving chase after Jacob. What else might be in the dumpster? Had Jacob gone back? Jacob clearly had found something not meant to be seen by a little boy in a dumpster. Whatever it was, it belonged to some very awful people. I was sweating, panicking about what might be happening to a scared ten-year-old wandering the streets all by himself.

I pushed the truck faster, the console line ticking closer to red. I kept my focus by replaying what had happened. My pockets held two vials in them. Whatever was in them was yet unknown, but I had a feeling that, for whatever reason, the children and people being shipped had to do with their contents.

"Do you know anything else they had your ship, Larry?" I asked my partner as the sun glassed over my skin, shadows dancing to the rhythm of my heart, the pound of the heavy tires on the road. I needed to relax—I needed to find Jacob. The only way was to ask the right questions. Any problem can be solved; the hard part is figuring out what pieces must be used to solve the problem. This was simply a problem that I wasn't seeing all the angles yet.

Larry hesitated for a moment before clearing his throat softly. "I'm not sure, to be honest—usually it was just supplies," he stated.

"What kind of supplies?"

"You know, weird stuff. I don't know; it's mostly just bottles, and there are many glasses. And oh," he paused again as if coming to the end of a good plate of food before realizing it was all gone. His face lit up with embarrassment before speaking, "A lot of chemicals..."

I glanced his way; Larry looked about to pass out. I sighed and turned my attention back to the road. "Okay, I'm assuming we probably won't be able to guess what they are between the two of us. So, could you find a manifest of those chemicals? Even criminals have to know what they're shipping. There has to be some sort of list somewhere," I stated, gunning the truck back in the direction of where this had all started earlier.

"Yeah—I think, no, I will find it. But Billy Dan—this won't be easy, and they might know it's me trying to find out what it is," He stated. I glared at Larry until he looked away, pulling out his cell phone. It was bigger than a brick and looked like something from a SC-FI movie.

"Is that what you will use to hack their systems?" I asked.

This time, it was Larry's turn to give me a patronizing look. "No—I will use it to get into their network and poke around. They will easily find it. However, it will give me time to go in and find enough—hopefully," he replied. I nodded as if to imply I somehow understood what he meant. Computers, drugs, kidnappings. What had Jacob gotten himself into?

Chapter 44

Larry fidgeted on his phone. His fingers flew at a speed I didn't believe was possible until I saw him do it with my own eyes. His eyes-only inches from the screen, a flurry of types in the shaking cabin of the truck. I sighed, gunning the truck, when I heard the sirens. The dumpster was on the next block over—I could listen to fire trucks and squad cars sounding their alarms in the afternoon sun. That could only mean that they had discovered the baby. How that was possible, I didn't know. This part of town was remote—not even the truck drivers were scheduled to come this way until tomorrow.

Most of the homeless in town hung out on the west side, near the bridge, in their tent cities. Someone could have come through here, but I had my doubts. This area was in the wrong part of town. So, assuming it was the cops—which, as I inched the garbage truck slower and slower to a complete stop, my stomach did backflips at that thought. I suddenly braked, killing the engine. Without taking my eyes off the road, I said to Larry, who hadn't even noticed we had stopped, "Larry, take the truck and head by my place. The key is inside the birdhouse—don't worry, the bottom comes off," I instructed.

"What—" he started before we both saw a patrol man stepping out at the road's end. "I think we weren't the only two looking for Jacob. Take the truck, get to my house, and keep doing what you're doing. Find out whatever you can," I continued.

He looked nervous, nodding slowly, "What will you do?" he said.

I sighed, "Someone needs to talk to them. I suspect that whoever was following Jacob could have been following us. Who knows what else might be in that dumpster? And if these people are as good as you claim them to be, we will lose any lead that might turn up, Jacob," I said, keeping my eyes on the officer who appeared, thankfully, to be more concerned with someone else than directing traffic.

"Are you sure, Billy Dan—I can help," he muttered. I smiled at him, "Larry, get this truck out of here. Park it somewhere safe, and probably not at my house in hindsight. Then, get that info before I kick you square where the sun doesn't shine," I stated before sliding the vials out of my pocket into the glove department below the steering column. I would just have to trust Larry. I opened the door and exited the truck, heading toward the officer.

Chapter 45

I heard Larry pulling away while I took as many deep breaths as possible without looking like I was a fish out of water. Nothing makes a person seem more guilty than labored breathing. Relax, I told myself. How can I relax when I am likely to get arrested? That made me pause for a moment before continuing. Even if they arrested me, I still could find out something about what was going on—I needed a lead, though it hurt to admit that. Kill the ego; this is for Jacob. Once they arrested me, though, it would slow down my chances of finding the boy, and every moment mattered. That left just winging it.

"Great," I muttered as the officer approached me. He was a younger man—younger than me, with pale skin and dower eyes as panic from the day's events had set in. The discoloration and the sweat just rolling off him made me wonder if he had seen what was in the dumpster.

"Morning, officer," I waved as he straightened up and smiled. "Good morning, sir," he started before his eyes went wide and his hand slid to the radio on his chest. It was good, at least he wasn't too green to go for his gun. I sighed, placed my hand behind my head, and dropped to the ground as he shouted into his radio, "It's him."

That answered the question of if we had been followed. But by whom and for how long? His gun was out, and I heard the pounding of several footsteps. My heartbeat is in tune with their steps. I just hope Larry can find something. Every moment lost dealing with this stuff could spell the end of Jacob. Just hold on, kid, I will find you.

Chapter 46

I sat handcuffed in the middle of a small room, obscured by a massive wall mirror, with my only company being a metal table and my thoughts. At least they didn't cuff my missing limb. Even cops get uncomfortable around an amputee. Though, they did take my prosthetic. Bright on their part, I suppose.

So far, I have been sitting here for an hour since they arrested me, and I have asked for my lawyer. Most of the cops down at the station knew me—I wish it had been for my superb detective skills, but mostly because I took their trash out on Fridays. And I had been down to the precinct a few times, training to become a detective. It was amazing how quickly your life can change and head in a direction you never saw coming. I had spent years getting my master's in criminology, studying, training, learning, and doing everything I could to finally become a detective. All that had changed this morning, and now I doubted it would ever become a reality. That was fine with me; the trade-off would be rescuing the boy.

A few more minutes passed, and I started to sigh. This was the game. Wait me out; try to cause me to freak out about the possibilities. The joke was on them; the moment I took the truck this morning was the moment I would do anything to rescue Jacob. Every minute that passed was life or death. So, I decided on the one thing that would get their attention without making this problem far worse: music.

"I know a song that gets everybody nervous," I bellowed into the empty room. I continued the line with vigor until my voice started to crack. I took a few deep breaths and prepared to swallow my spit for another round when the door flew open, slamming into the wall with the grace that only professional office types can manage without outright destroying the foundation of the door itself.

The first person to come through was aging, with shaggy skin, bottomless glasses, and a gray hue to his hair that could have been the color of the cigarettes he smoked, judging by the way he wheezed and the square shape in his coat pocket. The next made my heart sink, but I wasn't surprised. It was officer Genesis. Her eyes were a puffy red that had long since been dried out and hardened by a furious mother who had resolved whatever caused her tears in the first place. Judging by the chainsaw-like daggers she was throwing at me; I could only guess she knew about Jacob. This was going to be a long day.

The man approached the table, pulling a file from under his armpit as I hummed the song. He gave me a sharp look; I stopped, if only because my throat was getting dry, giving him a wink. A mutter escaped his lips before he spoke, "William Franklin Daniel. 5'11, Caucasian, male," he stated flatly.

I cleared my throat, "Don't forget disc-golf enthusiast," I replied.

He rolled his eyes with enough force that any rebellious teenager would be proud of the effort.

"What can I do for you, officer—"

"Detective," he cut me off, pulling out a chair on the other side of the table. His eyes were deep inside the folder, pretending he hadn't read whatever was in it twice by now. Genesis glared at me; she looked at something behind me when I tried making eye contact. That hurt but wasn't surprising. A lie is a lie—even if it was for what I thought were good reasons. I still had lied to the woman I love. The relationship was over, and it didn't need to be said. I just wish I could have told her what was really going on. However, nothing came to mind that wouldn't make me sound insane. I had no idea who I could trust, even here in this building.

Instead, I kept my mouth shut and faced forward—hoping Larry could pull through something. Though, as each minute ticked by, that absurdity was dawning on me. How rough this would be would depend entirely on what Detective Smoker had to say. So far, I haven't been formally charged;

just escorted in. No phone call, I wish that was the case; police don't have to give you a phone call while you're in the county. That meant they were still figuring out my role in all of this. A slight edge, but an edge, nonetheless. One that I would take full advantage of—I calmed myself readying for the next play. They had made me sweat it out, and now they had brought in someone on the force that I personally knew.

Handling this will be hard. They might turn around and ruin Gen's career if I say anything wrong. Her department was known for those types. There was the possibility that they did not know about our relationship—I had my doubts about that one. We've been dating for a while now, and this was a small town. In small towns, you're almost required to be married by the start of year two.

As the detective continued studying my file, I continued, "Well, this has been fun, and all detectives, I have to ask. What's the point of all of this? You could have at least brought me some water." I stated flatly.

He eyed me before rolling his eyes again; the stain of his pupils confirmed that he smoked—smoked a lot. That was something to use; I filed it away in the growing list of tools I would have to deploy today. "Well, to answer your question, Mr. Daniel,"

"Most folks call me Billy. Usually Billy Dan. Minus my mother—she just calls me dumb mostly," I replied. A slight snicker followed by a cover of her mouth from Gen saved her from the detective's gaze.

"Cute, now cut the shit. Let's start with the easy stuff—why were you on the west side of town—on abandoned property?" He asked dryly.

"Maybe I felt like going for a stroll; maybe I was doing my job. You know, waste manager, I dispose of things. Keep the city safe from the filth at all morning hours," I stated.

"You really believe that? That's why your boss informed us that you stole a working vehicle from him this morning. And oh, you're also fired. Might want to consider cleaning yourself off," he smiled.

I chewed on my tongue for a moment. Okay, so my boss had called the truck in. But no mention of the baby. If the cops knew about that, I would have been under arrest, and Detective Smokes wouldn't have been so calm about my cheeky remarks.

Oddly enough, that only gave me a moment of relief. I was still in this situation, with no sign of getting out quickly. I just shrugged in response to what the agent said. "Things happen, I suppose, a lot of trash still out—I should be fine with finding a new job,"

The agent grinned at me, his teeth stained yellow, "Ugh huh, well, that's assuming you're getting out of this—we have some questions for you," he stated, slamming his fists on the table. I followed his fists down to the table as it shook.

He continued, "Why were you on that property?" he asked sternly. I had none of his false bravado; part of me wanted to leap up from the table and smack his head against the wall. I resisted—for Jacob and just because I would most likely end up in jail once this was all over—I wasn't stupid. Anything I said or did now would be the end of any help for the boy; I just needed to play it cool long enough for Larry to come through. However, with each second, I knew my time was getting shorter.

"I want my lawyer," I stated.

"Guilty people only want a lawyer," he scuffed.

This time, I grinned back and repeated, "Lawyer."

He growled once more and made eye contact with Gen. "Can you believe this guy?" he pretended as if I wasn't in the room as he spoke. She glared hard at me, and I momentarily cast my eyes to the table before meeting her gaze. Yeah, I had lied to her—I would do it again for Jacob, for any kid. It wasn't supposed to be easy to walk away from someone you cared about.

"Yeah, I definitely can't believe him," she replied with ice in her voice. That hurt, but I caught the subtext. There would be no love here between us. "Good thing I asked for my lawyer then—lawyer, please," I replied, holding her gaze. Fire showed behind her eyes momentarily, but something else did as well—fear. What was she afraid of? Gen was the type to have met every moron out there and kicked them to the curve, but at that moment when our eyes met, she was afraid. It wasn't for me; it was for Jacob.

"Yeah, we can hold you for a while—start with that. In the meantime, sure, your lawyer will be here soon enough," The detective smiled before a bang came from the door, sending them out into the hallway. The metal door shut, and I breathed a sigh of relief. That was the easy part. The hard questions would start once they sweated me out a bit. I had no idea what I was even going to say.

No lawyer either—or at least I didn't think one would help me. I had to get out of here; maybe I could search for one good enough to get me out on bail—with what little funds I had, though. It was tough enough going to school and eating simultaneously on a garbage man's salary.

The room was walled off with no windows, and I had confidence I could get out of the cuffs based on the fact that people tend to treat amputees with far less restraint than they should. I jiggled the cuffs and felt them slide around on my wrist. Just as I thought I could pop my thumb out of place and slide them right off. The door would likely be the next problem; the table and chairs were likely bolted to the ground.

That was a last resort anyway—a building full of police officers was a certain death wish if I tried anything. What did that leave me? I blew out my breath, "A lot of nothing," I muttered, looking around the room. The clock above the mirror showed "4:23 pm". Larry and I had parted ways about four hours ago. That should have left him roughly three hours to find something.

Who was I kidding? I was basing someone's computer skills—who I had just tried to kill that person. Why would Larry help me at this point, assuming he even could? I just had to have faith in Larry for the time being. People let you down—loved ones and enemies. Trust in people will always be fickle; however, the only way to ever learn if you can trust someone is to put your trust in them. I moved my limb hand around and wondered why they hadn't cuffed that one. They really thought I wasn't a threat. Good. I smiled, thinking about how many ways I could use them. I just had to keep believing, keep moving for Jacob, and use my advantage to win. Even if that was only the foolish hope that the people holding me were full of hubris.

Chapter 47

Thirty minutes later, I had to stop looking at the clock. They were sweating me out—I needed to have my wits about me before I said something that could make Jacob's situation far worse. I was about to lecture myself for twenty minutes about ignoring the clock when the interrogation room door cracked open ever so slightly. It was enough for me to lean in my seat and see Detective Smokes arguing with someone in the distance, his hands animated and huffing enough air that I worried he might pass out at that rate. I pushed that thought aside—whoever he was talking to waved him off and headed towards the door; it was a silvery voice—full of velvet and promises of everything that could drive a man crazy.

"Crabapples, it's Satan, why is she here?" I whispered as her hands reached the edges of the door, sliding open past the uniformed officer guarding the door. She strolled in as if she owned the place—her walk sliding across the plain, tiled floor. Footsteps were light, hands swaying like a gentle unseen breeze floating in the building that only she could ride on. Her hair was pulled back in a tight bun across her brow—and her clothes were the delicate white of a woman working for a legal team. I didn't let any of that fool me, even as her dark eyes glistened after sending sparks down the officer who held the body of the door—she was a woman who inspired every sense of the word sex, but she also inspired snake, I thought. I knew better than to stare into the eyes of the abyss too long—she was one of the monsters that had crawled its way ashore, all long legs and curves.

I sucked in a big breath of air. Mostly out of fear and confusion as to why she was there. Admittedly, part of me felt the spell she had seemingly cast on the officer upon entering the room. She smiled wide once she had crossed the threshold.

"Hello—Billy Dan," she declared as if her presence alone was the birth of an angelic god. I pretended to act nonplussed by her appearance, which I was. Very soon, I would respond cunningly to her—that would wipe that smile from her face. Just after pigs could fly, said a small voice in my head. I couldn't beat her in her game.

My response was a small smile, "Hello, Melanie, what brings you here? Run out of kittens to hang at your weird little church?" I asked.

"Cute," she said sourly.

"Not the first time I've heard that today," I replied, just as sour.

"I suppose it just might be true, lover; you always had a cute face," she stated, pulling out the silver chair in front of me with ease and sitting down, crossing her legs in one smooth gesture. I rolled my eyes nearly into the back of my head.

"To what do I owe the displeasure of seeing you twice in one day, Melanie?"

"Displeasure?" she gripped her chest as if she was wounded by my words.

"Billy Dan, you act like you don't miss seeing me—we always have such fun together. I mean, first, you leave. Then come back, then I find you in one of my establishments only to end up beating up some of my folks. That's not very nice, don't you think?" she asked, rubbing her eyes as if pretending she was on the verge of crying.

I shook my head, keeping my eyes on her as my thoughts raced. Why was she here? It was a mind game. That was the strength of someone like her—it always had to be a game. Anyway, she could twist the knife; she would twist it. Deeper and deeper until I was floundering like a fish out of water.

This was a mind game with her; it always was. I just had to figure out what her game was. The first thing that came to mind was how she was here inside the police station—talking to me now.

I scuffed at her comment, "Sure do. Why are you here, Melanie?" I asked her bluntly. Her frown turned into a smile that resembled a shark's grin before she spoke. "Oh, you know, Billy Dan, just saving your never-ending lack of any intelligent moves—once again," she stated.

I paused at that, my heart beating faster. She implied at the strip club that she held power—but this was absurd, even she couldn't walk into a police station and pull me out. A corrupt one, yes, but even she couldn't do that.

"How do you plan on that? Going to pull a rabbit out of your butt and do a trick?" I jabbed. "Even your weird little church doesn't have that kind of power," I stated.

Melanie tilted her head back and laughed for a solid minute. I shivered in response to that. "I have all the power I need—except I don't have everything," she stated.

"What is it that you need?" I asked, feeling a sweat drift way down my forehead. "Oh, you know, just a thing or two. Power is only kept when you make sure you have everything you need, isn't that right, dear?" she asked, smiling that large grin again.

Unperturbed, I smiled back, "Woman—I pray for anyone that is your "dear." Now, cut the shit. What is it that you're missing?" I asked her.

Her smile was replaced by a snarl that made her soft edges turn into hard lines. "Fine, Billy Dan. I was going to say we could talk, but obviously, you've not learned a thing after all these hours. You know, I could use someone like you—what you did to my men—who would have thought," she trailed off.

Once upon a time, Melanie and I had a fling—more like a fling with a flesh-eating spider the size of a car trapped inside a tiny room. It had been a thing, however short-lived and painful. She had been at the hospital after I was injured. She had appeared like a nurse in an old black-and-white movie. Like an angel of light, shades of lust and beauty—someone so perfect that it made you wonder if the world could produce someone so beautiful. Of course, though, as recovery went on, it became clear that I wasn't interested in worshiping her like everyone else did. She left one day, and I saw her in the parking lot with the janitor. After that, I could never have unseen her for the snake that she was. A thick veil obscured her and gave her an air of mystery. It was a veil made of poison. I remembered her promises and how she would subvert and change her answers based on anything I said. There was no reason, only that she wanted something from me. Just as then, she wanted something—my gut told me it was Jacob.

Shaking my head cleared the memory—like swirling a stick in a dark creek. The memories are still there, just lost in the dark mud of moving water that will never be what I thought it was. Not exactly the same, at least—the water was disturbed, and the creek bed changed. It would never be the same creek, not for me.

I smiled, "Nope, still haven't learned a damn thing. I am still wasting time chatting with you."

Her face scrunched up into a deep frown. "I suppose you must be at least wondering why I am here," she said, staring at me like an animal in a zoo.

My hand held up, and the handcuffs jingled as a response. She stared at me for almost a full minute before I sighed, "Okay, okay, I will bite. What do you want? Or did you come all the way in here—inside a police precinct just to drive me crazy? Knowing you, that could very well be the case," I muttered, placing my hands flat. One thing I learned very early in life was not to move your hands quickly in a building full of people with guns. I had no idea who might be watching behind the two-way mirror. I kept my hands on the table and waited for her to continue.

She shark smiled again and began to speak slowly, "The boy has something we want; we need that back very much," she stated.

"And what is it that he has?" I asked, the words trailing slowly out of my mouth. I gazed at the mirrors, wondering if Gen was behind them. The cat was out of the bag—she would surely guess it was Jacob. So, did Gen know that Jacob was missing? Did the police find the baby in the dumpster? The fact that I was still speaking outside bars told me Melanie must have a pull here that was beyond imagination.

"Oh, just some stuff a compelling person would like to have very badly. And I believe all parties bigger than you garbage man—would like that back," she stated.

I scratched my chin at that, "You know you can use a different word besides very to get your point across. How about, "screw" and throw in a "you" I flicked her off, doing my best to get something out of her. Anger was a good tool for most people. Melanie was a viper, but the problem with snakes is they know when to get angry. My games did not affect her as she smiled at me and waited.

Sighing, "If you won't tell me what he has, you could at least tell me why you need me to find him," I picked my words carefully, glancing at the mirror.

"I already told—" she started before I cut her off.

"I know he has something you want, and you won't tell me what it is. Which makes me think you aren't entirely sure of yourself or it's of great importance to someone you're afraid of," I stated, letting my words hang in the silence between us. Melanie gave me a look that could shatter glass and make even the most insidious snakes recoil in fear. I shivered; the room was cold, but her eyes made me freeze. Behind the veil of bright brown—there was nothing. Not even the blackness of an animal's eyes. Just an abyss that had long since turned off the light.

Time stopped, the blackness enveloped me, and I felt my hands crawling to escape inside a circular prison with no ledges—a hungry predator chewing on the bones of the fools who had fallen inside before. I thought this was it, the pit, a place of no return, swimming my hands away from the ledge. The only thing was, I've always found a way out from beneath the monsters. The trick was realizing they had no control unless you gave it to them.

I smiled at Melanie until the dip into her darkness was done. She frowned for a hairline of a moment, then slowly nodded. A gleam of fire danced inside her coal-black eyes. She cleared her throat. "You're correct on many things, Billy Dan. I will make this easier for you. Right now—those children outside this door don't know the difference between a wet fart and a sneeze because they're paid to be that way. All it would take is me mentioning that you found a baby—you will be done. Small-town justice style. Hung up figuratively, left to dry until it's time for a sparky chair that will shock you to death on a never-ending ride," she stated coldly.

I scuffed, "No one has that kind of power—no one at all," I challenged her statement as the tension in my back turned to full-blown sweat out of fear. So, the two chasing Jacob were her men—that confirmed it. Still, it didn't solve who was at the shed or who the doctor and William worked for either.

She smirked, "Oh, you really think that? The Mayor has most of the cops and judges in this town under his fingers. No crime gets punished unless he wants it to happen. I'm sure your little broad with all her little children, even the missing ones, has said as much," she giggled.

That froze me; the threat was clear—she knew Jacob had not only found something he shouldn't have but was missing whatever he found. She also knew everything about him—which meant Gen was in danger.

The pressure of Gen behind the mirror was almost palpable by this point—she was behind the glass and had heard every word Melanie had said. That left me with only one choice: work with the devil and cross her later. I resolved myself to that, stealing away any ounce of fear before meeting her gaze. "So, what, the Mayor is corrupt. Water is wet, puppies are cute," I twirled my hand at her.

She laughed at that, and I held my breath, waiting for a response. "Thank you, I needed that. No darling—it's not the Mayor that you should fear. It is me; it is the greater good you should fear," she hissed between clenched teeth. I noted that she had power, but not as much as she liked to have.

"And what the hell is the "greater good"?" I asked her, perplexed at the statement. "Let me show you," she stated, standing up and flashing long legs as she approached the steel door. She knocked gently on the door with her middle knuckle twice. The silence after the knock was quickly followed by fumbling hands with a key ring before the interrogation room door opened to a young officer. His hair was combed back, and his tie hung loose around a sweaty face.

"Yes, ma'am," stated the officer.

"Be a dear and give me your gun, darling. I have a point to prove," she declared.

The officer nodded before dropping his hand to his gun belt, undoing the strap around his pistol, and handing it to Melanie. "For the greater good," mouthed the officer solemnly.

"For the greater good," Melanie replied, smiling at the officer.

"Thanks, love," she stated, closing the door on his face. She held the gun like a slimy dog toy, examining it and pointing in haphazard directions. Elegantly, she aimed the gun at me. "This is the greater good—Billy Dan," she stated, pointing the gun directly at my face. Even inexperienced shooters wouldn't miss from this range. I blinked, feeling sweat roll down my head.

Melanie had taken a weapon from an armed officer in one of their buildings with no force and was now pointing it at my head. No one was bursting through the doors to stop her; no one was telling her no. She was calm, smiling like a cat finally catching a mouse—with zero remorse or fear. Oh, snap.

"Feeling pretty clear on how things work around here, Billy Dan? Say one thing wrong, and my organization will bury you under enough weight of bad attention that you will never be able to recover. That's not the power of money or arms. That's the power of controlling a town's soul. The power of the mob doesn't matter if you disagree—we save your soul. If you don't want that, well—you must be a nonbeliever and will be punished as such," she giggled, her finger dancing over the trigger with far too much ease to make me comfortable.

I gulped, nodding my head slowly as the pieces tumbled into place. Her church had a place in the local newspaper every day. Now that I thought about it, most of the town's advertising had something to do with her church in one form or another. Hell, they had taken over the city, and anyone who disagreed would face the mob. Low-level stuff, just enough to leave you bloody. Small things—things that happen in every town, really. Maybe there are a few missing kids here or there. That was a bit of a stretch, but it was a working idea. The amount of power it would take to pull off what they had done—and to go unnoticed. Enough to go unnoticed by anyone not paying attention, and before you knew it, everyone was caught in the beast's jaws. Even if it seemed so pretty and promising.

That caused me to shiver—all the signs around town about missing children, all the crime—yet nothing ever got done. This many powers competing for control—the thought almost caused me to want to cover myself, get in a ball, and cry.

I did my best to stand up to it; this was life. Only, you weren't allowed to check out of life when you desired it the most—no matter how unseemly it was. I wasn't allowed; I had to find Jacob. I didn't know what the boy had, but if it was enough to cause Melanie to come down here herself—pull a gun out in a police building, it was big.

I looked at Melanie, the gun in her hand—the round open hole of the weapon leading up to the darkness of the barrel. Inside was a tiny piece of metal that could end my life faster than I could blink. Made everything seem so much smaller in hindsight.

My lips blew out, and I spit on the ground while keeping eye contact with Melanie. "Sure, I will bite—but you aren't getting the boy. I will find whatever he has; you won't get him," I stated, making a promise with my words that I knew I meant the moment they left my lips. Melanie's eyes glazed. "Good boy," she said, setting the gun on the table—within arm's reach. I noticed before she absently mildly thumbed through a stack of cards from her purse. An eggshell white card gleamed in the low light, scribbled with fine lettering and a water stamp mark of a lock and chain shaped like a pretzel. Another symbol of the church, I thought.

"Call me once you have the boy—I would hurry Billy Dan. A lot of people want that kid; you have two days to find him or well—might be best to tell these poor saps who killed that child," she sobbed into her hands, a broad smile flashing under her hands.

"You're an insane, crazy freak," I barked out at her.

Her eyes seemed to become full black pools of darkness as her head twitched. "Don't call me that—Billy Dan," she said, chilling my bones.

"Let me out already, and I will call you much, much worse," I replied, ignoring the urge to flee out of my skin.

She shook her head and pulled out a phone. Within seconds, she had someone dialed, and I couldn't make out who she was speaking to—just that I didn't like her smile. "No one calls me a freak, Billy Dan," she said as the door swung open, and a massive man stepped through along with another goon. Because when it comes to goons—they roll in pairs. I just had to do my best to figure out who they were; I had plenty of time to figure out more, I thought as he popped his knuckles. This was going to hurt.

"Don't kill him, love; just teach him a few lessons," she spoke, giggling, heading to the door. "See you around, garbage man."

Chapter 48

The door flew open to the interrogation room at about the time my face smacked against the desk again as a meaty fist hit me. Both of their punches had stopped hurting a few swings ago, partly because of the lack of feeling in my face but mostly because punching someone is a limited game. Sooner or later, the bones in your hand will give out long before the skull breaks. Then everything just hurts—only more mushy.

I glanced out of the one eye that could still be open; blood swam down from my eyelid, tricking me into almost thinking that it was worse than I thought it was. Through a blood-red haze, I could make out Gen. She was yelling at the two goons, my ears were still ringing, but I could still make out the gleam of one of their rings—that damn church symbol again. I mentally noted that, plus the heavy scaring around his hands. Weird, he punched as if he was brand new at the Gooning game. It hurt, though he wasn't punching like a professional. I would have to look that up; those scars should have meant he knew a lot about punching someone in the face.

Gen ushered both of them out the door a few long breaths later. I felt her slender hands pull on my sore wrists. A click later, and the cuffs were free. I groaned, rubbing my wrists as she hauled me to my shaky feet. "Shut up, stop being a baby," she growled.

I whizzed through heavy teeth, "Thanks." She grunted as we left the room and entered a long hallway. She held one of my arms behind my back as I staggered in the hallway—my feet dragging across the floor. Small gasps of pain escaped my lips as she pushed me forward. I staggered into the wall and empty desks.

Where were the police? I thought—shouts echoed outside the building as an officer ran past. Pushing into us. I fell onto a desk, blood coming out of my mouth. Gen grunted and pulled me off the desk. "Get the heck up—you big baby," she hissed again as I grunted in reply.

We made it to the front of the building, going through the doors, when I felt her grip come off my arm. The pressure relief was enough to almost make me cry as I staggered into the back parking lot of the police station. I squinted; the sun was coming down. I had two days to find the boy. I reminded myself as Gen turned back to deal with me.

Her frown could have scared a bull—but it was dotted with the looks of a former lover. That quickly passed as I stood shakily.

"Gen—I," I stuttered as she waved me off.

"How long have you known, Billy Dan?" she asked, cutting me off. I couldn't have missed the ice in her voice—she was only helping me because of Jacob. I sighed heavily, "This morning—before I lost him on the far side of the town."

"Was that why you were in the fire this morning?" she asked.

I remained silent as the weight of her gaze drilled into me.

She scuffed, "Yeah, I wouldn't expect you to start telling the truth now. The only reason you aren't behind bars—I didn't let those two harm you was for Jacob," she said flatly.

I nodded slowly, "Why are you letting me go now?" I asked.

She looked exasperated, and under the steel of her resolve, I could see the worry for Jacob hanging over her like a dark cloud.

"Because a high maintenance woman came into my department, took an officer's gun, and had a person of interest beat without anyone even saying a word. Because the Mayor in this town scares the hell out of me—because I know you won't give up on Jacob. This place is crooked—that weird cult scares me. Is that enough, Billy Dan? Just please—I don't care that you lied—find him—just I am trying something. Anything—just help," she sobbed. "Because I still care about you Billy Dan, I want to believe you still care about us. Please, just help." She handed me my prosthetic. I nodded attaching the device, wiping blood from my face in the process.

I gestured to reach out for comfort. I dropped my hand, though, as I turned. Now wasn't the time for comforting hugs. Besides, I had betrayed her; it didn't matter how warm my hugs were now. Trust wasn't like a sword being sheathed, well maybe to a bit it was; trust only worked as long as the sword kept its proper shape. In this case, I had taken our sword and beat it against a mountain as far as Gen was concerned. It was never going to slide back into the sheathe.

When I turned away from her, I reminded myself that nothing had changed—she was gone. Well, that wasn't the best way to put it, either. Everything had changed, and I feared this was only the lead-up. I wanted to say I love you to her, I realized then I had never said it. Not saying it was best now. I reminded myself as she held me with tears in her eyes. First time I had ever seen her cry; the first time I was walking away.

I hobbled away, hearing more yelling from the front of the police station. Whatever it was, that many voices wouldn't be good even if I wasn't a fugitive. Which now I was. This morning, I woke up prepared to take out the trash on the corner of 5th and North Carolina. Along the same route that I had been taking for years. Not getting beat up inside a police integration room, nor saving a mother and daughter from a fire. Things were sure off to a great start, I grumbled, pushing deeper into the parking lot while keeping low in case someone recognized me.

At the edge of the parking lot, more people were heading toward whatever had distracted the cops enough for me to leave. I breathed a sigh of relief but panicked, nearly hitting the ground as a blue suitor officer passed by. I wasn't entirely sure if Melanie had me taken out—or if Gen had sprung me. Neither was going to do me well, though.

"Breath, Billy boy, can't do nothing if your head is in your butt," my father's grumpily, long-drawn accent played in my head as I stood on shaky legs. I took a moment to wipe dirt off myself and took a few deep breaths.

I needed to get my head on straight. The hard part was getting out of the station; everything else would be cake—right? Somehow, that was too far-fetched for me. And I once saw someone throw away a lava lamp with Goku. That was just silly. This was just crazy.

Chapter 49

Running was never my strong suit, even when I had two functioning legs—after this morning's adventures, I had doubts that there would be any skin around my leg where the prosthetic rubbed my thigh. I found myself rubbing the area around my prosthetic, winching in pain from the simple touch.

The bus rolled its wheels forward, and I breathed a sigh of relief once the police station was far behind me. I needed to be careful—Gen had let me go—I was reasonably sure of that. There would be repercussions for that, not to mention whatever must have been big enough to wake up the whole force to get off their collective asses seemed like a tar pit I needed to avoid at all costs.

Outside, on the street, were dozens of protesters. They carried signs proclaiming such things as "Save the kids". I blinked at that; our small town had only seemed like a little slice of Heaven until just a few hours ago. What was I doing? What were any of us doing? Would protesting the streets for children really help? Or was it just stupid? People do silly things, I thought. Case and point me—I thought, fiddling with my hands as the smoke from earlier rubbed away.

I shook my head—stuff like this would never end with people until humans finally learn the truth: none of it is worth hurting someone else.

It sickened me—my hands shook, but I had a feeling in the pits of my stomach—that the worst was yet to come. No matter what, these parents would be out there until someone had a problem with it—the worse would happen.

For what reason, I didn't know. All it would lead to was violence and hatred.

I pulled my eyes from the protesters to meet the eyes of a scraggly old man from the seat across from me.

"Crazy to think what the world is coming to, crazy to think that there ever was a world," he stated as if he and I had been in a fierce debate. I paused, looking the old man up and down. His jacket had patches indicating a long time past war but could have been stolen and made up just as quickly. His hands were gnarled and faded purple under tattered gloves. A wind-blown face that raced away seemingly from the growing feet stretched from his eyes to his chin. I thought he had seen a thing or two, pale skin dotted with scars that told a story that only mattered if someone cared to ask.

"What's it to you, old man?" I replied, sighing heavily as I tried to relax in my seat. We were about fifteen to twenty minutes from my home, which was a stretch. I was surprised to find out who could be waiting for me there.

"What's it to me? Well, it's the world, son, don't you care about it?" he asked, flabbergasted.

"Sure, I care about it. I live in it," I said.

"That's good—certainly is a thing to be a part of. Was starting to wonder why someone as young as you had such a long brow," he stated.

"Lots of things to be long about these days," I replied.

The old man scratched his chin and shook his head as if to agree before speaking.

"Tell you what—you're going to need that these days. Certainly, there seem to be plenty of reasons to care," he threw it out there as if I had no choice but to listen to him. To an extent, he was right. It was an empty bus, and my heart was still beating. Might as well try and calm down. A frantic mind was a caught mind. A caught mind led to dumb mistakes—I needed to relax.

"What kind of world would we live in if all men want to do is tear down and not create?" He asked.

I slid forward in my seat until we were at eye level. "Tell you what, old man—angry churches, protests, political ramblings—I could care less about. What I do care about is a missing friend of mine. Everything else is just stupid things—religious zealots running around acting like their moral truth is superior; it's all the same. We all poop, and one day, we will be gone from this Earth. If you spend all your time fighting over the deeds of the past—you will forget the future," I replied, leaning back into my chair as the old man cracked a wide, toothy grin.

"Sounds good to me! Sounds like you're a man that cares," he exclaimed.

"I do care, far more than I ever should have, though," I said as the road drifted past me. How many times had I ridden this bus? How often had I found Jacob hiding in a garbage can eating toast while regaling some story about something he had found in a dumpster? I looked at the old man; his face was long and weathered. I had no doubt that he had seen a thing or two—I wondered how long it would be until I started to resemble him. The other day, I found the first few gray sprouts. My usual jokes, even to myself, weren't helping.

I liked old people like that man. Willing to strike up some philosophical conversation as if we were sitting in Athens about to attend Socrates' lecture. However, part of me wondered now if I had failed him on the many trips I had taken with Jacob. Had I let him down by rambling like an old man? The old man across from me had simply wanted to strike up a conversation because he saw something on my face. Or, more likely, it was because of how I looked. Glancing down, I could see trails of dust and dirt from this morning. A hole was in my pants, and I felt a light breeze on my legs. I sighed; he probably thinks I look worse than him. He's probably right.

That was the point I should have told Jacob about all those times we had spent together on this bus riding back to his home. I looked at the old man and thought more about his words, "Old man, what's worth creating in such a crazy place?" I asked him sincerely.

He smiled, "Everything,".

Chapter 50

"The goal is not to be better than your friends but to be a better friend to your friends," I told Jacob as the heavy Greyhound bus rolled to its next stop. The old bus rumbled to its next destination as I lurched forward in my seat. Jacob's face was crumbled, making me see the thick gum of yogurt still stuck in his hair. I found him again this morning digging through a pile of trash for what he claimed was a good find.

A talking bass moved and swayed based on a motion sensor in the front. The thing gave me the creeps—something about an animal singing a happy song while being attached to a wooden frame, displayed as a trophy, just hit all the wrong parts of my head. Regardless, I didn't think an excellent find was worth his mother worrying herself sick about him. I had only met Gen a few times, a beautiful woman—but a mamma bear I did not want to make mad.

I was still having nightmares about the last time I had heard her yelling— and I wasn't even the one her anger was directed at. I sighed; this was the third time I had found the kid messing around inside a dumpster. He was weird—skinny and definitely needed a shower. But he was a good kid. Not a liar or a bully—seemed to self-study, which was more than most of us could say, even as adults.

Jacob frowned at my statement before seeming to go through a library worth of responses before replying, "Why would I want to help any of the boys in school that pick on me?" he asked, perplexed as he looked down at his fish as if expecting it to come alive at that moment and give a better talk than I was.

"Because how will you ever teach them to be better people if you outsmart them all the time like you said? Your teacher already knows your smart kid; trust me, I have no doubt," I replied.

He huffed, crossing his arms, "Well, I still don't see why I should help them. About all they ever help me to is a wedgy," he gestured towards his pants.

"You got me there, kid. But listen—I mean, really listen since you won't stop digging into dumpsters. You won't find friends in there, trust me. You need people; we all need them. You have to help people, help them be better. Or, one day, you will find yourself in a situation you can't handle. No matter how smart you are, someday you will need help, and you don't want to be the one who isn't getting it. Do you understand?" I started, trying to get eye level with Jacob the best I could on the shaking old bus.

With a deep sigh, Jacob shrugged his shoulders. "I guess so, Billy Dan. Seems kind of pointless to me. How can I help them when all they do is hurt me?" he asked.

I scratched my chin at that—he wasn't wrong. People do all sorts of evil for no other reason than they can. Though, to be fair, people could also accomplish great things when they really wanted to—when they came together for a purpose bigger than just the simple things we feel. These were just kids, probably insecure that someone like Jacob was showing them up in class.

Hell, one of the men at our plant got fired by pressure from a mob calling our boss over and over because of something dumb he said while drunk at the county fair one year. People would go out of their way to hurt one another to seek their version of justice in a cruel world. However, that never set right to me—never set right even when I had the chance to get my own justice, I thought, squeezing my prosthetic hand into the flesh of my thumb. I remember that same look of anger Jacob carried now—the same pain I felt for a long time. So much hate driving me forward to a place I had no idea could ever exist within myself. Indeed, humans weren't too far off from animals. Humans do things that should never exist outside of fiction. However, we do differ from animals—outside of fangs and claws, we have something else.

As I looked at my hand and felt the hot anger of what happened that day at the fair slide away, I returned to focus.

If we could learn to be afraid of the dark because our ancestors were hunted by creatures of our wildest nightmares, it stands to reason that we could learn how to love. We could learn how to move beyond the things defining our worst traits. Maybe not all of them; jealousy, envy, lust, and ego will always be there. But earnestness, truth, humanity, and compassion can be developed further than anyone could imagine.

Clearing my throat with a loud cough, Jacob eyed me sheepishly as I spoke, "Because we must be better, Jacob. We have to be better. We are no better than them when we do things to harm each other. No matter how afraid we may feel, fear is not a right. It is only a feeling and survival trait. We must be better—understand?" I gestured towards the boy as he looked at me, completely perplexed by my statement.

"That's pretty weird, Billy Dan. You're always weird," he stated, leaning back in his chair. I could tell his mind was reflecting on what I had said. I whispered silently, praying I had said the right things to him. An angry person could quickly be born from the wrong words when dealing with others. My worries were put to rest when Jacob perked up, "Say Billy Dan, can we stop by Toaster Tims and get some toast?" he asked excitedly.

"Sure, kid—we can do that," I smiled.

Chapter 51

I exited the gray bus as it sped away—casting a deep frown at the sidewalk as I stumbled home. I knew the way—I could probably have walked the whole part with my eyes closed, but that was problematic, to say the least. It couldn't be worse than what I was facing at the moment. The old man's words left me like a speeding bullet as reality washed over me like a bucket of ice water. Outside my house was Larry's truck. Behind it was a tiny tow truck—flanked by a civic on the front. Larry's truck was pinned in—he was nowhere to be seen.

Littered on the ground by the driver's window was broken Glass; tiny traces of hair, and something brown were smeared on a few spots on the ground. Dried blood. As I dove for the bushes, I covered my swear words, my heart beating faster with every breath I took. I had almost walked right into that. I needed to keep my shit together for Jacob.

Time to curse myself later, I thought, deal with this problem. The neighborhood was quiet, save for one of my neighbors mowing a lawn. I glanced his way. It was one of my neighbors I seldom spoke with, but I couldn't have been more thankful for suburban living at that moment. Whatever prompted a grown man to mow his lawn this late afternoon was fine. The noise would help conceal me as I travel towards my home. However, a fleeting thought worried me about this—corrupt cops or not, this much blood in the middle of the day—no cops. Gulp.

Following the bush line low, I made it to the cars and trucks. Glass littered the ground with fresh blood doted in a few places. That was good, I thought; they hadn't been brazen enough to pull Larry out of the truck in broad daylight. However, that only helped my nerves with the situation so much. They weren't crazy, at least; it just meant they were brilliant. I almost wanted crazy—only that would be worse for Larry.

Clever means Larry would likely still be alive—if they had been crazy. I shook those thoughts away and focused. I needed a weapon. There would have to be at least two to three people inside. I should have brought my gun; why hadn't I done that earlier? I wanted to kick myself; these small mistakes were adding up. "But I'm still a few pennies short from getting a candy bar. Kill the ego; you have a job to do," I whispered to myself as I lowered to a crawl and moved my way to the corner of the house closest to me. My windows had the curtains drawn tightly shut. For once, I wish I wasn't such a homebody and maybe opened the blinds to the outside world. They kept me from seeing inside, but as I got closer, I could hear voices coming from the other side of the window. Muffled noise told me they weren't frantic, which was another good sign.

Drawing in my breath, I glanced around me. I had yet to learn who was in the house or how many. What did I have, though? I had the element of surprise. I had, after all, crawled all the way to the wall of my shady townhouse relativity quickly and with no immediate obstructions. So, I'm intact, I thought. Taking on roughly two to three intruders who may know I am coming based on whatever they could have gotten out of Larry in a few hours.

Big Bertha heats like a small furnace once she's been running for a while— Larry and I had gone long enough that it should have made me sweat getting close to it as I had once I started crawling towards the house. That wasn't a good sign. I had to assume that home-field advantage was still on my side.

Around me were the chunks of rocks I intended to use for a path leading to my backyard. Life had gotten away—but that laziness might be a use. Okay, that's one potential tool, Billy-boy. What else do you have? Good question. My neighbor was thankfully still mowing the lawn. The sound would provide visual and auditory cover. Sure, the noise attracted people, but the thing about people was commonly seeming noises were almost completely blocked out if someone didn't interact with those noises.

He just needs to keep doing that for a few minutes. "I hope no frogs jump into his mower again," I mumbled as I traced the fence line. Laying at the corner was a dirty tennis ball. I glanced at the closed blinds, waiting for a hair breath for any movement. I saw no shadows as I danced my way across the lawn again—hugging the bushes as I more than likely would have looked like a crazy person to anyone who would have been watching.

Reaching the ball, I quickly scooped it up and headed to the nearest vehicle pointing towards the house. This whole idea, I realized, as I came to the driver's side of the fancy car, was predicated on a couple of things I thought. Most of this would cause me to flat-line and thus be brutally caught, or worse, Larry taking the brunt of that. I gulped; what other choice did I have?

I peered into the driver's side. It was no dice. I swore and took a gamble on Larry leaving the keys inside the dump truck. Larry was the worst at doing it; his absentmindedness might save many lives. Please, just give me some luck. Sure enough, on top of the steering wheel was the key. The door was locked—I took the tennis ball out. I had no knife since I had gotten arrested; what I did have was my prosthetic. The edges of my steel fingers scrapped along the material of the ball for a few moments before pressure and tearing from the metal punctured a small hole about the size of my thumb. I looked around; the neighborhood was still quiet—as if holding its breath for some kind of bomb, except the mower. Maybe, if this works, things could get crazy fast. It would help if I could see out of both my eyes. I felt a sting on my left eye as I tried to open it. I had no time to wish for anything, even an advantage like both eyes.

It was too late to turn back now, and I had no choice but to go for it. The problem with newer cars is their lock mechanisms are more complicated than simple curves and twists. However, Bertha was a massive dump truck. Even if someone could get into the machine, I doubted they could drive it.

The ball hovered over the keyhole, and I popped the ball with all my strength. A rush of air shot from the hole in the ball and blew into the keyhole. I held my breath as the lock slid open. "Now we are cooking with gas. Hold on, Larry," I muttered as I took the two syringes out of the hiding space where I had placed them. They needed to be protected first.

Something about Melanie's words haunted me. They fit snugly enough into my pockets—please stay safe. This is for Jacob. They will be fine, I hope.

Chapter 52

If it hadn't been for Larry's driving, I thought this plan would have never worked as I waited for the moment to strike. I was sweating bullets from outside the door frame, a rock in my hand waiting—shaking. The slow hum of the engine was muffled because of the mower. I waited, any moment now.

I had placed the tennis ball inside the muffler. Pressure was building—luck seemed to be on my side. However, that was wishful thinking. For all I knew, my plan wouldn't wor—.

My thoughts were abruptly interrupted as a pop came from the truck, blasting the tennis ball forward with enough momentum to send the tiny ball smashing through my windows like a rock thrown through a poster. Half a breath later, the ball hit my living room wall.

I covered my ears and waited as the expected return fire came echoing out, shattering the peaceful isolation of the neighborhood in an instant. The firing was fierce, and I could hear the sound of the trucks and cars being peppered with bullets. Just wait! Even my thoughts seemed loud as the firing continued and stopped within a few moments of each other.

Luck had held out for a few more seconds. The damage to the big dump truck would have to remain a mystery. My focus was on the door to the house. It swung open. A scraggly-looking man came out holding a shotgun low and almost at his waist. He was rattled. Good.

I kicked forward, hitting his gun, and sent it sprawling to the ground as I came forward with my hand holding the rock.

I smacked with all my force, hearing bones break from the blow. No time to feel guilty now, I thought as I charged into the living room.

The man hit the ground—face first, and I heard one finally wet crunch from his weight pushing his destroyed nose into the ground. One more guy stood stunned in the doorway, his pistol drawn but coming up far too slow to be helpful.

Just slow enough for me to project the rock in my hands into his face. He was blinded, his gun firing into my ceiling, and one shot going wide, shattering my living room window. My hopes were that the shot hadn't hit one of my neighbors—there was no time to feel guilty about it either, though.

His face was tilted upwards, I went for an uppercut and jammed my fist into his chin. The blow caused him to stumble backward as I pushed forward, slamming him down on a hallway table. The glass top shattered, and the wooden frames supporting the small table collapsed as they bowed in. Photos of Gen, my family, and a few ones I wasn't too sad to see get broken flew into the hallway.

Blood flowed from under the man, his face flushed red as his eyes were closed. He was out cold—but would live. Good. Someone had some explaining to do once I found Larry. My house was small—perfect for a tiny family or a little old woman who gave it to a one-legged bachelor down on his luck a few years ago for much less than it was worth. I was thankful that my house was not bigger—my kitchen was empty from one quick glance. No one could hide for long here, I thought.

The man in front of me stirred, and I debated hitting him just to knock him out. I stopped myself—this wasn't the movies; knocking someone out took a lot more force than most people thought, plus there was always the chance that I could get hurt in the process. And more importantly, they would probably get brain damage. Instead, I went to the living room closet, pulling out an extension cord from the few I had hanging in there. For a moment, I was thankful I took my time finishing projects, that was a first. Had I not been lazy, I might not have had something to tie these two up. "Thanks, past me," I muttered, taking the cord to the first guy who was lying still on the ground, a pool of blood under his head. I glanced out the door; the neighborhood was deadly quiet as if it was constipated—ready to pop.

Was that much of the town at the police station today? I could only assume yes as I slammed the door shut, avoiding the warning of the dark clouds above me. I returned back to my work, flipping the man over before he choked from the blood; a small gasp barely over a whisper escaped his lips: he was not dead. I tied the cord around both of his hands and behind his back, as I propped him up against the wall so he wouldn't accidentally fall forward on his face. For good measure, I looped the cord into his belt. Satisfied with my work, I fetched another cord from the closet, all the time aware that Larry was somewhere in my house. Most likely, it would be the basement if I had to take a guess. Both men wore plain work clothes, and one wore a polo. They weren't super-professionals, which gave me hope as I finished tying up the second man. I left him in the hallway. I thought there was no sense in wasting any more effort, taking his pistol from his pockets. A standard Glock 19—this will do, I thought, pulling back the slide as I popped the magazine, checking the ammo.

About eight bullets, though I hope I had no need to use any—my hands were starting to shake just from what I had done to the two when I came in. It had been less than five minutes since I had taken both of them out—the adrenaline was causing my body to become cold—to start shaking. I stifled the feeling of uneasiness and took a few deep breaths. There would be time later to go to pieces. For now, though, I had no choice but to keep going. I held my breath and listened. The slow drip of my tap drifted from the kitchen. Groans of my old house waffled through—otherwise, nothing. I blew out my breath. Okay, so there had only been two. Now, I just needed to find Larry. I swept the kitchen; all my cabinets had been overthrown, dishes shattered, and the ground littered with pieces—one of my kitchen chairs was missing. I thought Larry would be tied up somewhere in the chair.

I glanced at my garage door coming out of the kitchen. It had remained closed, and the lock to it appeared steady still. I breathed out more nervous energy—had they gone into the garage—I would have been hopelessly outmatched. I came to the basement door, pausing to look at my bedroom. The door was ajar—shadows remained still in the dimming light. There would be no reason for them to go in there; besides, it was probably just as messed up as the kitchen. I was mad about that. I had nothing fancy, but it was still in my kitchen. What a bunch of clowns—breaking into my home and then tearing it to pieces. I raised the gun in my firing hand; the prosthetic I wore wasn't my shooting one and was more for general use. The fingers took a long time to move, and they lacked pressure. Though I had gotten used to missing half my hand, the feeling or lack of thereof strength in my dominant hand never returned. I wondered then if it ever would.

I turned the knob to the basement door slowly—ignoring the long-forgotten feel of my fingers. They were gone, and there was nothing more to say about it. I had to focus now, find Larry, and keep moving forward. I threw open the door and pointed the gun into the shadows below. Sweat rolled down my head before I realized I couldn't see anything in the dark. Keeping my gun trained, I pointed down in the gloom, my free hand searching the side until I found the light switch.

The lights snapped on with a flick, and the whole world came clear to me in a flash. Larry was tied to my kitchen chair—his mouth gagged with what looked like a sock. His nose was bleeding, and a cut above his right eyebrow flowed with blood. There was no way of knowing how bad it was until I got close. That would take a moment because, evidently, Larry had managed to free one hand and was frantically pointing at me. Seeing how I was at the top of the stairs—the hairs on the back of my neck had time to rise just before I swung behind me with my gun as a substantial, meaty fist clocked me with enough force to send me tumbling down the stairs.

I had forgotten about the third guy. I swore at myself as I fell down the stairs, hitting the bottom with a crunch and shattered glass. Something hot ran its way into my leg, and I squirmed in pain. Flashes of lights danced before my eyes, and fire ran through my leg and up my chest. My body did not like whatever was happening; this wasn't good at all.

With just enough coherence of mind, I noticed a man in the shadows descending the stairs. He took his time; he wasn't in a rush, and blood rushed out of me as if something was poisoning me. I held my breath, bringing up the gun. Letting my guard down had almost just cost my life; it almost cost Larry's. It would have cost Jacobs. I wasn't going to let that happen now. I steadied the gun and took aim at the man; he froze, forgetting that I had a gun before he punched me.

That was his mistake; I pulled back the trigger until it clicked dry. The man tumbled down the stairs, wet noises creaking the wood as he hit the ground a few inches away.

The gun suddenly felt heavy. Real heavy. I dropped the useless metal, and stars shined in my eyes. A chicken appeared at the top of the staircase. Somewhere, I had the feeling that someone was calling my name. They kept saying it. I wanted to figure out why the chicken was in my house. Why did my leg hurt so bad yet feel so good? I think I am bleeding; it sure feels like it. It may not be such a bad time for a nap.

Chapter 53

"What the heck, Billy Dan, you just shot that guy!" screamed Larry, his words jarring me from the fatigue that would have overtaken me. My vision was becoming blurry, colors saturating the corners with intense magenta. This really couldn't be good. I slapped my pockets, ignoring Larry screaming behind me. My leg was definitely soaked with something.

I pulled back my hands, and slime dripped from my fingers—glowing purple. That can't be good—also, I was pretty confident the syringes had not been glowing before I stuck them in my pocket. Whatever it was, I needed help before the dragons got me. Crazy winged monsters, I was already seeing them flying inside my small basement.

Wait, no, there were no such things as dragons. At least not in my basement. I may have read that wrong in my third-grade science math class. It might have been English class—no, they're no dragons in basements. They only live in the bathroom.

I shook my head, the color twisting into my mind rapidly like a moving eel. I needed to get Larry free. Larry was my only hope. Get your butt moving now, Billy. I shouted as the colors continued to twist my mind, knocking on my thoughts like an unwelcome guest at my doors. Words of encouragement weren't enough; I felt myself fading. I needed to fight this now—or I felt something terrible would happen.

Before I could finish my thoughts, I slapped the syringe down hard into my leg until the Glass broke into shards atop my skin. Blood poured out a deep red. It festered and pulsed like a dying animal—coughing up a river of oozy red and chunks of flesh. I flinched at the site—one thing you can never get used to with blood is the stuff that comes out with blood. There was always something floating within the murky depths of red, something that you knew belonged to a once-living thing. That once-living thing being myself. The pain gave me focus. The colors had retreated to the edges of my eyes, but they burned, and I knew soon there would be dragons.

I flipped myself onto my stomach. Something told me walking was out of the question. Glass shards cut into me as I dragged myself around Larry. He was still shouting something, his face awash with pain and confusion. I ignored him; I just needed to keep crawling.

Each step was a blast of color and pain—at some point, everything went dark before I forced myself back to reality. After an eternity, I reached for his hands. He was held by a bungee cord. It looked like the ones I kept in my tool case. Amateurs, I thought as I unwind the first cord. The cords had been so tight that blood flowed down Larry's hands. I kept at untying his knots as we both bled, pitiful things inside of my basement.

My fingers felt like frozen hot dogs rather than my appendages. For a long time after my accident, I would wake up in the middle of the night—checking for signs that my limbs were somehow back. All eight fingers, five toes, two arms, one leg, a big head atop a small neck. Yup, everything is all here; go back to sleep and try not to get too comfortable; it could all be taken away instantly. Just because I could count them didn't mean they were mine; it didn't mean I wouldn't lose them. That was one of the things I learned that day when my little world came flying towards the ground: did I ever have any control? Were my limbs ever something that belonged to me in the first place? Sure, they were attached to my body. Sure, as far as I knew, no one else controlled them. And sure, I'm positive a science nerd somewhere could explain the complex intricacies of my motor functions even if he was thinking I was stupid for asking such questions.

But if we never had control of our lives, wasn't that also true of our limbs? That was a scary thought; waking up one day and my hand would be strangling me. Those kinds of thoughts, the ones where you wake up—confused and lost, unaware of anything except for your knee bone being attached to your tibia. The only thing reassuring yourself is a feeling of minor control—most likely a control that doesn't exist. It's a self-assurance that only you can give yourself at the end of the day. An assurance that "hey, these are my limbs, I control them," all the little things we can do to take back control.

That helps, most of the time. Take note of what you can control. Sometimes, though, the virus is so deep that you can only do that. Count your hot dog fingers; count your toes. Try to bring balance back to the world one limb at a time—anyone can control the mind. It can be set free by itself, though. I just needed to start counting.

I stared at my toes, the maddening pain in my leg offset only by the spiral of colors flowing at the furthest parts of my mind. I clinched down; I would untie Larry. I had control over my life. Nothing coming from a cheap syringe was going to change that. My teeth gritted, and I pulled with everything I had. The elastic straps of the cords cut into Larry as he shook from the pain.

"That really hurts," Larry screamed, waving his one free arm. I paused, "If it hurts so much, shut the heck up and help me free your bonehead already," I shouted back as he scowled at me for taking so long. I ignored him, the dragons, the bright lights, and the sheering pain. The loss of feeling in my hands, that unrelenting, festering over a wall of hate I was building towards. Finally, after a colossal amount of effort, the cords snapped free. I fell towards darkness—a tunnel of light all around me, my head gone—my body... How did dragons get in here?

Chapter 54

Spin, spin, my head goes spinning. I thought in total darkness. Well, that was somewhat true—a deep horizon of black—moving and twisting all around me. Yet, in the distance, I could see a bright light glowing like a lighthouse in my sea of gloom. I sighed heavily—this was my final stop.

Focus on Billy Dan. None of this is real, I told myself. Looking into the darkness, it pulled me in. Now that I was here, I would not become a monster. It was never too late. I closed my eyes, more darkness. More endlessness of shadows and lord knows what else flooded in the darkness.

I wasn't afraid; I couldn't keep my emotions beyond my thoughts. I tried moving my limbs. They felt like they were moving, felt like something was moving. Though having lost a limb before, I was used to the sensation of things feeling like they were there, in reality, they were long gone. I had someone say once it was a "phantom itch." That's something old vets or amputees would say. They would talk about long nights laying in bed, sweating, swearing that their leg was still there. Or worse in the day, reaching out with a hand that no longer was attached only to have your knob of a stub hitting the cold steel of a door as if you were just trying to be politely holding it for someone. The itch would happen; I would still act like I was whole again. A feeling so intense that I would swear my eyes were deceiving me. I genuinely wasn't missing anything new, but my mind couldn't shake things that were real. Anything physical was a reality. I desperately held to that. I had just killed a man-maybe this was my punishment...the thought dug its way through me.

That's how everything felt now—I felt as if my whole body was one giant phantom itch, and I wasn't actually experiencing anything besides total blindness drifting into the night. I had just killed a man—maybe this was my punishment...A thought dug louder into my mind.

I had to find Jacob. I didn't have time to cry myself and get high in an infinite darkness. This kind of trip was designed to leave you in a different world. That was why they must call it a trip, a ride to a different place. And it was definitely not Kansas.

I needed to get up. Get up, Billy Dan. Move, move your lazy butt, and get out of this darkness. At first, nothing happened; it was just more of the darkness—more of the feeling as if I wasn't changing anything around me. This was infuriating me. I needed to be moving my lazy butt. I needed to find the boy. More than anything, I wanted to help.

A moment passed—nothing happened. My heart sank. I tried again, squeezing the muscles in my stomach, legs, arms, and anything else I thought I could get moved. Once more, it was just the endless darkness all around me. Like a living black sea, engulfing any sight, any feeling I had. I started to sweat, something slowly dripping down my head. Is it sweat, though? Could I even be sure of it in a place like this? Don't answer that, Billy Dan. Just focus on moving. I gritted my teeth once more, and nothing changed. In fact, rolling my tongue seemed impossible to do—how was I even biting down?

Had I imagined even that? Suddenly, my mind began to panic—the idea of being unable to move in a place like this—unable to fight back if something was there. Thoughts of floating creatures of impossible girth and size swimming all around me in the infinite darkness, waiting to eat me, caused my bladder to release. I had killed a man; I was being punished.

This was Hell. No, not Hell, Billy Dan. Just a place that you would rather not be. A small part of my mind pushed through the layers of panic like a chunk of metal hammered into a wood block. But, I had failed Larry—I wasn't sure if he was even okay. I think I had managed to untie him before the darkness. Maybe I had imagined that.

No, I had gotten his hand loose just before succumbing to the darkness. Yes, that was right; Larry could soon pull me out of this place. He would know what to do, and we could return to the more important task: finding Jacob.

That was a pleasant thought; it might even be true. But, I was putting a lot of faith in a man who couldn't even be counted to not fall asleep at the wheel if I took too long gathering the trash. Faith in a stranger working for the people who had helped take Jacob in the first place. That was entirely true. True as the sea all around me. I was all alone in this task. Was I all alone? I couldn't beat the world; I had killed a man. I had been worse than Larry once—I knew I had been worse than Larry. Larry hadn't killed a man. Larry hadn't failed the people he loved.

That reminded me of the last time I was alone, trapped inside a hospital bed. With no one, not a soul, besides the voices of medical personnel and the old man snoring heavily over the bed. No visitors, no one. Forced to lay in bed with nothing but my thoughts and my newly severed limbs. Struggling every moment of every day to keep fighting. Anything that I could grasp would give me just a moment of solace. A drop of water for the thirsty man in the worst place someone could imagine. Because what made it Hell was how I was still there when I closed my eyes—drifting off into an endless void. I was still in Hell. There was no escape.

Unacceptable—ending like this when I still had so much to do. Those thoughts of mine, thoughts of the worst days of my life. What could they possibly do for me? Nothing at all; I needed to find a way out of here. This could all be real—a sudden thought jolted its way into the chambers of my mind with the force of a bomb.

Right now, even in this ocean of space, I could very well somehow be here! Panic set in, my skin started to itch and crawl away from my bones, and sweat drifted off of me. My heartbeat and my chest pounded in pain—sucking everything vital into the deepest parts of my body in a desperate attempt to eradicate stave the fear that was now sprinting up my spine. This was real, and I was going to die.

Crying felt right; it felt like a good time for that. Tears drifted down my face endlessly—this was my faith stuck in a black void for the remainder of my life. Failing everyone—with no inkling of a better life, not even a bad life.

I would have nothing—just my thoughts and all my pain.

I closed my eyes and waited—nothing came. It was only a matter of time—hang on a second. Closed my eyes, huh? I had managed to close my eyes. I felt myself blink several times in rapid succession before laughter escaped my throat. I closed my eyes, and I had never been happier in my whole life to perform a bodily function. Instantly, all the thoughts of failure seemed like a joke. Because even in the darkest of pits—I was able to blink!

Laughter continued to struggle out as I remembered I had other limbs. Sure, I sometimes felt my missing legs and fingers. Often even swearing that when I threw off my covers, there would be a leg under my blankets. Something that would instantly make this awful joke go away—never coming back. It never happened, though; I would swing out of bed each morning. Picking up the folded pants, I would place them near my bed. Rubbing slave all over the stump of my leg. Taking my sock over the missing limb and jamming it into a metal coffin for the day. With a deep sigh, I would clamp the leg down and finally put on my pants. This was nothing new; I was stuck inside an endless, lousy joke that would never end—my sea of darkness.

Yet, in all those times when it seemed hopeless the most. When it seemed like all the light was gone forever—a force never let me stop. That force never abandoned me. The feeling that I had a mission every moment to pass before I could get anything done. That was the sense that I wasn't alone. It was not a lot, but those pants I would struggle to get into every morning, I gave it my best shot to accomplish. That had made all the difference—even in the darkest hours—I always had a purpose. Just stay alive.

Chapter 55

I've fallen down some deep rabbit holes in my day—places I never thought existed or just those deep places in the wilderness of my mind. Critical thinking is massively misunderstood—we are encouraged to think for ourselves but also told to follow what someone else believes if our own thinking doesn't align with society's current beliefs. I would much rather spend my time going down my own holes of thought—even if it leads to places like here—laying on a tan-colored hardwood floor. Stained black around the edges, showing signs of probably never being dusted as I pulled hair and lord knows what else from my mouth.

Staying alive and following the rabbit hole led me deeper into complete darkness, there was no doubt about that. Until only a small light showed in all that dark, in all that cold. I shielded my eyes from the light and heard a soft voice. It spoke simply, "Why do you want to save him?"

"Save—who—what?" I muttered confused to the light, " Why do you want to save the boy?" the light asked again.

"The boy?" I asked, unsure if this conversation was actually happening or just part of the drug effects.

"I gave him my word," I stated.

"There is more," the light replied.

"I'm afraid I just might be addicted to the darkness—but I can't walk that path. I have to find the light. Every morning and every evening—because I know others are trapped in someone else's darkness. That's what I have to do; it's what I've chosen to do. To fight the darkness: to save a boy trapped in Hell. For no other reason than it's the right thing to do," I replied.

Chapter 56

I blinked first, my whole body feeling like I had been shot from a cannon as the blood rushed back to every part of my body. It was like coming down from a high fall all at once, as my ears popped and heavy music played into my skull.

Larry was over me, his face wholly written with concern and a bloody nose that had two pieces of tissue jammed deep inside. I sighed; it must be that I am alive. That was good. I needed to get out of here and find Jacob. I started to shift before a tattooed hand pushed me back down. "Stop moving," a firm voice said with a hint of a Spanish accent and lingered up to a beautifully toned woman. She had thick black hair—high cheekbones, and brown eyes that danced over a square face.

However, her face was hidden behind a cake of white makeup and a shiny red nose, surrounded by a thick cotton head of Ferrari red hair. "I'm in Hell—now there are clowns," I coughed, turning my head. "Yeah, well look at yourself. Billy Dan. This really how you play things these days?" asked the clown woman. I squinted my head as my memory came back from a place that seemed like a deep ocean inside my head.

"Rose," I stated dryly.

"The one and only. Also about to be late thanks to your birdbrained behavior," she joked, concerned, looking into my face. "Well, you took the time to save this birdbrain," I coughed again as a tiny woman came into the room. She had pale white skin that gleamed almost like marble and a face with freckles. Her stature, slender but curvy, her body would make any man's jaw drop. Her hair was bright pink—comically so that it seemed to light up her head like an amble wildfire and draw all eyes in the room to her hair. That was saying a lot, considering I was in bed beside a woman dressed as a clown.

Her eyes searched me—that's when I caught the gleam in her eyes. Even though she looked young—slender at first glance, her eyes were deeper shades of green than the waters of Greece. Predator eyes—cold calculating, waiting for prey or something to test her defenses. Her pupils went wide for a moment as if she had suddenly found a shark inside the kiddy pool, before settling back to a tiny pin-sized hole.

The hair lady had found whatever she was looking for as a slow smile perched on her thick pink lips. "This is the garbage man I keep hearing about. Count yourself lucky, garbage man; you will look pretty awful for a few days—not that you looked that well to start with, but aside from that, you will live," she nodded matter-of-factly as if she was giving some invisible dissertation complete of thousands of youthful academic types.

I blinked at her comment before scuffing, "Look, who's talking? You look like your Irish Dad made love to a cotton candy machine," I rebutted.

Her smile winded, and she pretended to brush dirt off her shoulder. "All jokes aside, you are lucky garbage man—any longer with that dose, and I don't think even I could have saved you," she said.

"Well, not to sound ungrateful, but who are you?" I asked, already tired of this conversation as the blood slowly came back to my back. It itched like Hell—like thousands of tiny little bug bites racing up and down my spine.

Her eyes suddenly brightened to a deep hue of grass green as she shot her hand forward to one of mine, gently taking it into her hands. "You garbage man, you can call me Disco Balloon Girl," she proclaimed, giggling. A cold shudder ran up my spine, and I fought the urge to pool the covers closer around me.

Rose gave me an exasperated look as if to say be nice. I was being nice—I woke up to a clown and an elf.

She released my hand after that as it fell limply to the bedside. I did a quick count to one hundred to make sure that I was not still experiencing the effects of the drugs. Sure enough, I was still in reality—wonderful.

I cleared my throat. "Thank you," I said before I turned my head to Larry. "Not to sound ungrateful—but who the heck is the elf? Why is Rose here, and I don't know how you got untied, man?" I asked him.

My friend looked haggard, his face a chaotic mess of hair and worry. His face scrunched as the stress of whatever happened rolled its ugly head back to the forefront of his mind.

"Man, it sucked," he stated absolutely. Weakly, I pulled my hand out of the bed, gesturing for him to continue. The effort took more than I would have liked; it was a good sign. I could still move. Jacob still had a chance.

"Sorry—just been a hell of a day, Billy Dan,"

"Tell me about it," I sighed, waiting for Larry's tale. There was the cold reminder that Jacob was on his own out there—with only my imagination to worry about what might be happening to him. Visions of Jacob cold, alone, and in pain shot through my head, causing my already upset stomach to twist into knots. I was pretty confident I would have thrown up if the bile in my mouth hadn't told me I had been doing that for hours already. Hours— that hit like a hammer. How long was I out for? What happened to the man I shot? What happened to me? I recalled the dream of the writer and utter darkness for a moment. I was shuttering at that thought.

Calm minds make good decisions, I told myself. I was suffering so much in my imagination—when I had no idea what Jacob was going through. For all I knew, the kid was hiding in some dumpster outside of a box store. He was an intelligent kid and resilient; he would make it. I just had to trust that. Otherwise, I might have missed something that was happening then. It was all a jumbled mess, and I just wanted it to stop. Everything felt like walking in a dream—even Jacob's promise. It was a carrot at the end of a prolonged beating that I knew had only begun to hurt.

What was the point in carrying on then when it would only hurt in the end? I glanced down at my left hand—my three fingers left gripping the cotton sheets into a ball. Worse things had happened. Worse fates have haunted me to this day—being trapped, alone in a bed with nothing but my fears for the future, my insecurities of the past guiding me along. That terrified me to my core. What would happen when all the pain was finished when the deed was done if I found Jacob? All the unknowns, my imagination played out before me like an endless play personally made by everyone who ever caused me discomfort. I was the only fan in the theater as the applause was clapping for my demise full of demons.

Stick that pity party somewhere else; now is not the time—I needed to be strong for Jacob and myself. Things were in motion that could not be stopped. Even if I saw and did things that I never imagined in my wildest dreams, there was only one direction to go: forward. Still, a murderer and a liar whispered a voice in the back of my mind. I ignored that.

There was nothing to do but that; I shook my head, realizing that Larry had been speaking this whole time. The effects of the drug pulled back slightly like a wave from a long, cold shore. I just hoped it didn't come back.

"So yeah, man. You were on the ground, completely twitching out behind me right after you cut the knot. It took me a minute—I worked myself out of the knots," Larry showed the raw, puffed-up skin around his wrists. The thick rope had burned his wrists badly enough that they would scar. Those wounds would heal—in a way, it gave me more respect for Larry. He had risked hurting himself to save Jacob. Not such a stoner loser that I worked with every day, after all.

"Then what happened?" I asked, trying to sound at least grateful. Jacob was out there, Billy Dan. You're here. Focus on the now, and you will get there.

"That's when everything just got weird, man... you started drooling badly—like you could have filled up a gallon jug with how much drool came out. I called your name, but you didn't respond. Once I got both my hands free, I came up and tried to slap you awake. You were already gone, though— twitching like crazy. You were mumbling gibberish nonsense about a puppy and some crazy writer. I was just about to call the police when you woke up—punched me," Larry paused, pointing at a collection of bruises on his face. He had a vast shiner forming—a plush, broken nose that had two pieces of tissue jammed deep inside.

Larry would live; he would have a few scars judging from the size of some of his cuts. Some from the goons at his house, others from me. That was my fault—I had gotten Larry involved in all of this. I tucked the guilt, it did no good and if I thought too deeply about it I would probably start getting mad at Larry. I just nodded at Larry so that he could continue talking.

"After you sucker punched me—very nearly knocked my teeth out by the way you kept shouting Rosemary. I remembered it was the clown chick we talked to once after work—at the fair," Larry gestured sly towards Rosemary. A fierce scowl wrote over her face. Larry flinched from her look. I didn't blame him—Rosemary held herself like she was ready to fight anyone over anything.

"Carnival, jerk," she smirked, and Larry nodded slowly as if it was a significant revaluation. "Right—carnival- anyways, I got into your cell phone. By the way, you should make your password something other than your birthday," he stated.

I blushed at that—honestly, he was probably right. I just struggled to know my password in the age of applications for everything. I thought it was clever. Forget me for thinking that, I guess.

"Anyways, I called up old Rosemary. She came over fairly quick," he explained. This time, it was Rosemary's turn to blush as I turned towards her. Who would have thought that—last time I talked to Rose, she punched me in the arm and returned my wallet—there was no time to dive into that relationship at the moment. I ruined one relationship today, so I didn't need to add another.

I sighed heavily, "So, where did the pixy girl come from," I said.

"Pixy came from her fairy forest to save you. I am also pretty sure I am older than you," she stated, flicking her hair away from her ear.

Narrowing my eyes—I couldn't see it—maybe the pink was throwing me off. "I mean—pretty much what she just said, Billy Dan. Rosemary took one look at you, and we both panicked. She mentioned she knew someone," Larry trailed off, and I regarded the pink-haired woman with a closer look.

"Disco balloon girl, you said?" I asked her, perplexed but trying to make the most out of a confusing situation.

"That's right, I love balloons. I love disco," she giggled, and a chill ran down my spine. Her eyes didn't show the same laugh; they stayed a deep shade of green. Like the seaweed you find at the bottom of a lake, dead things moving in the water. Swimming all around you, that's what I felt when I stared into her eyes. She was dead.

"Forgive me, but how does a person who calls themselves that know how to treat an unknown toxicant? And to do it in such an effective manner as to not leave me bedridden for months?" I inquired.

"You should stay in bed for months—but your pal—Larry over there said you had to find a little boy. That you were not the sort to quit—if that's true garbage man, it just might be useful to help save someone like that," she suddenly stated, very seriously.

I scowled Larry for giving an unknown the details of our case. Man, this wasn't the case. I threw trash into a machine every morning and did some pull-ups. I had no idea what I was doing. For Jacobs's sake, I needed to cut that case crap now.

Instead of replying, I just nodded again. She got the point and continued. "Anyways, I agreed to help out old Rosemary because us freaks have to stick together. And because she promised to let me pet the cute tigers someday," the pink-haired woman giggled. Rosemary looked apologetic, standing in the door frame.

"Thank you—for helping," I interjected before the conversation could get any weirder. "Do you happen to know what it was that poisoned me?"

She frowned at that, "Actually, no—whatever this was, it made the stuff I use look like kitty litter by comparison. Not only does this toxin race through your body quickly, but it also causes hallucinations and is very long-lasting. I don't even know how you survived the dose you did. Not to mention the total disassociation from reality that you seemed to experience. You talked in your sleep, tried to move, and seemed to respond to almost zero stimuli outside of a few shots from the hips I tried. Basically—I am surprised I could even save you moron," she said matter-of-factly.

"How do you know so much about this stuff?" I asked her as her eyes lit up. The dead things in the water gave way to the darker things beneath the waves. "Oh, I have had my experiences with poisons. I've used them for a while now, and I've had them used on me. Strange things can be done to the body from the smallest and most natural ingredients," she said.

I arched my eyebrow at that one before she sighed heavily. "I don't dress like this just to look pretty," she gestured to her fishnet stockings and tight skirt. She was stunning in a dangerous lion kind of way. "Sure, I just assumed you liked looking like a goth Barbie doll," I shot her way.

This time, her eyes narrowed before she scuffed, rolling her eyes. "I had my own drug-fueled night. Ended worse than yours, big guy. When I came to, I decided to get my—well, vengeance like they did me. Rapped, poisoned, and left in a bottomless dark hole, but Rose took me in—kept me from losing myself to that animal," she said with cold steel that made everyone in the room shutter. Knowing Rose, that made sense enough to me—Rose had a way of finding those hurt by the world.

"That is the most cartoon thing I have ever heard—but I'm a garbage man who has tested to be a detective thrice. Life is weird," I stated.

She fluffed her hair and back, shrugging her shoulders.

"On that note, I must get work before I am late again. I'm working in Castle Pines all this week if you need me, Billy Dan," Rosemary stated awkwardly, navigating the conversation. Which I was intensely grateful for. The pink-haired girl's story—was tragic, and I honestly didn't have a polite way to respond to it.

I nodded my head slowly towards her. "Sure, Rose, that would be great. Thank you for everything; I can always count on you," I said as she smiled softly, glancing at the balloon girl. Vengeance or not, I think Rose realized she was around someone more dangerous than she could have possibly imagined.

She turned to leave when I rolled out of the bed quickly before anyone could interject. My legs felt like jelly. Everyone moved to help except for the balloon. That was fine with me. Those eyes told me exactly what I had thought when her words confirmed it. "Don't mess with me," I wasn't in the mood for that yet. There would come a day when I would have to go after her. She was a criminal—I couldn't let her get away with that. For now, though, I had a feeling I would need her at least for a little bit longer as I thought about the vial of drugs. I needed to find out what was in those drugs—and who had made them. It had to do with why Melanie wanted Jacob so severely. Though, did I know how to list people to go after?

As everyone was startled by my movement, I stepped to the door and took Rosemary's hand, pulling her into the hallway. "Billy—" she started before I cut her off. "Don't worry about it; I need one more thing from you," I lowered my voice so that only Rose could hear what I was about to say. "I need some guns—nothing too crazy, just enough to get the job done," I whispered. Rose's eyes got wide, "Billy Dan, you know I don't talk to those kinds of people anymore," she replied. I felt awful doing this, but my gut told me I would need something to defend myself with soon.

"I understand—I just—I need help," I sighed, hating having to ask. The last few hours were taking their toll on me. Crawl into a nice warm bed and die for a few days—that sounds like heaven right now. Only I knew this was only the first part of the day.

"Alright—I will see what I can do, Billy Dan," Rose sighed, gripping the hole scars around her elbow that I knew were covered by her clown custom. She had a past, we both did—that was how we had met. Not too long after the night at the carnival, let's say that graveyards are never-ending. And sometimes the living don't have to be at a funeral to find themselves in the middle of one. We both knew too well how long the past could last—an internal grave it seemed. It had been a tough road to leave—one that seemed to stay with me every time I looked in the mirror. Stay with the goal—find Jacob. The graveyard could be something to worry about another day.

"Thank you, Rose," I whispered.

"Don't mention it; I will text you once I have something," she said before turning and walking down the long wooded hallway. I watched her walk away before I turned, bracing myself on the door's wooden frame. I was feeling lightheaded. A couple of days of sleep were in order, but I had miles more to go before indulging in that kind of luxury. One beautiful step at a time, I thought, as I walked back into the room, sitting on the edge of the bare mattress. I looked at Larry. His face was a sickening ash color, but he nodded his head at me. I nodded back. I had a partner in all of this, and that took the edge of insecurity off—almost, I thought.

"Balloon girl, could you do me one more favor?" I asked her.

She crossed her arms and became utterly rigid. "Favors imply that I will do something for free, which none of what I did today was for free. Those two," she pointed at Larry. "Managed to front me a decent amount of what's owed my way. I will be open to negotiations on anything else. Be warned, mess with me, and I will be your worst nightmare," she finished with a stern look that left me with zero doubt as to the sincerity of her statement.

"Yes, ma'am," I stated before reaching into my pockets for the remains of the broken syringe. Numbness touched my fingers, and I shivered in fear that the drug could somehow go through my skin. "Don't worry, jackass, I took it out of your pockets. I had to find an antidote, which can leak through the skin and take effect in minutes. You were lucky I got to you when I did," she said matter-of-factly.

"Sure—I appreciate it being drugged—" I started before she leaned towards me; I recoiled back from her. I've had my butt kicked by muscled-bound bulls plenty of times in my life. Yet this five-foot-nothing pixie was enough to cause me to shiver. This woman reeked of death; I did my best to hide that. "You don't understand—by all accounts, you should be dead. It was hard for me even to save you. I am the best at what I do, at least in the United States. I feel confident when I say this—that stuff has effects you can't possibly understand," she explained.

"Like what?"

"Well, for starters—it's a Hallucinogenic," she said flatly.

"Yeah, so, like LSD, I take it," I responded coolly, trying to stay calm as a shiver raced up my spine.

"LSD is a joke compared to this stuff—let me be honest with you—the effects will stay with you the rest of your life. Take a little bit; this junk seems to increase focus for the user. Too much, and well, what happened to you would look nice by comparison. That much would have killed you. There have been rumors of similar stuff on the streets—it wasn't given too much attention because it mostly came from hospitals. Drugs from insurance companies and doctor smiles will never get questions," she stated coldly.

"Could have killed me, huh," I mumbled as if it was the first time I had ever heard the word in my life. A feeling in my heart caved in from the suddenness of her news, and I knew on some level that she was right without her even having to explain it. I was pushing my luck.

"Billy Dan—I-I," stuttered Larry, whose whole face was crestfallen. He gasped at me before lowering his eyes and looking into his hands.

"Even if I had gotten to you sooner, I couldn't undo what's in your blood now. I gave you some things to fight off the worst; it's completely different from what's been on the streets. TRIP is what they call it—and like I said. It might as well be legal. Cops won't ever care about this sort of drug until thousands are dead. TRIP is quicker and far more addictive. One hit and you will never get off. And it can come in the shape of pills or a liquid. This stuff, whatever it was—must have taken a lot to make. It's stronger and can last for hours. If I had to guess—it was the first generation of a new type of TRIP, like the Royal Royce of drugs. Again, I don't know the full effects of that much on you—it will take some time to find it all. If it doesn't outright kill you," she shrugged, and I nodded as if it had been my doctor telling me I had a terminal disease. And in a way it was. It wasn't the first time a doctor had causally dropped a bombshell on me—something so life-changing being uttered in just a few syllables.

In those situations, I couldn't be mad at the docs; it wasn't their fault that I had lost a limb or someone had cancer. They were just doing their jobs; someone had to be the messenger. The mind doesn't work like that, though; we are hard-wired to fight death. Even the laziest and most gluttonous have some reaction to the news of their demise. Cowards do as well; no one can fight that reaction, however weak they may appear. We don't want to die. It's how we've survived this long as a species. It's how we've made it this far in the race. For me, that hurt the most—I had wanted to run for a great deal longer; for all my life, it seemed that I just wasn't meant to run very far.

I glanced down at the floor for a long time. Before I opened my mouth, I knew what I would do. This task I was taking on would be my last one. For Jacob, that was the penance —that would be what I would do. Nothing else mattered, really. For years, I had felt some shame in the back of my mind. Here I was, a grown man rummaging through the garbage. I woke up every day to do some pull-ups to study for a test I kept failing. First, it was the writing I couldn't pass; I studied harder. Then it was the physical—I trained harder—yet it never happened. Sure, I had the grades—and my physical training scores weren't the highest, but I had made passing marks. Every time, though, I was rejected—they just couldn't risk a one-legged man in the field. I was too prideful to take that—I thought if I just trained harder, I just do a little more. That would somehow make up for losing her. That would make up for my mistakes at the fair. The sins after I got hurt. I felt the shame nearly every morning, strapping that long sock past my knee.

Those times when I fell flat in the beginning—unable to even lift myself off the ground enough not to wallow in my own urination. Crying for my own pity. Here I was now, just another weak person unable to do anything really about the circumstances I was in, and it made me want to drown in it. I dived head-first into a dark abyss full of an endless tide that dragged me deeper into the black.

Was that all I was, just another broken man beaten down by the world? Billy Dan, the crippled man who always wanted to be more than what he was, what a laugh that must have been to anyone who took the time to listen. It was funny, though, the mockery of effort, the yearning for self-actualization. Infuriating snippets of self-grandiosity—maybe that was all I ever was. Was it even right—caring about only myself?

Forget that. And forget you too for wasting your time crying, Billy Dan, I screamed. Even if that was true, all you ever had was what you could do with your time. Falling into the modern trap—or most likely the folly of mankind from our inception-would only leave you a blubbering mess on the ground. Covered in tissues and receipts from your regret. No, more than just eating mashed potatoes and kissing a pretty woman, you had to die with your principles. Because damn it, at least they were your own man. Something I had created even in my darkest of days. This was after my fall; it was always after my fall. The only thing I had was the only thing I would ever need. I would rise; that was my path. The righteous man was the one who kept trying.

And right now, a little boy needed me to be virtuous. I know that it may be pointless, but I had to try. I sniffled back some tears forming at the edges of my eyes.

I rubbed my eyes while sitting back on the bed, and the world almost seemed to come from under me. Larry looked concerned as he jumped up to steady me; even the pink-haired crazy woman looked momentary and paused. "Are you alright, Billy Dan? We should get you to a hospital, maybe—" Larry started before I shook his hands off.

"Balloon girl, find out whatever you can about that drug, I need to know. Larry, let's go, man, I need a ride," I stated before walking out of the room. The three stooges followed closely behind me.

"It's going to cost you," Balloon Girl called behind me as I walked down the hall.

"Everything costs something, sweetheart—I didn't want a free lunch anyways," I grumbled before pushing open a screen door and walking into the hot sun.

Chapter 57

My head was pounding—like a jackhammer into a piece of cement. "We need to get back to the dump truck. This thing has to be hot by now," I stated as Larry shifted uncomfortably, glancing in the mirror as if to see what I was seeing in the seats behind us, and I wouldn't stop staring. Everything just looked—off to me, as if something should be in the back. I had told Larry about the effects I was experiencing briefly as we left the safe house of Balloon Girl evidently. To Larry's credit, he was taking it in strides. However, he kept glancing into the back seat as if he could somehow catch whatever world I saw back there. I just wish he would drive. I wish those three would shut up.

"Hey man—if you need to talk—" he trailed off after seeing something in my face. "Forget it; I've known you long enough to know what you would say," he stated flatly.

"What would I say?" I replied.

"Probably quote some ancient dead man and make a metaphor about life disappointing or some pep talk," he said matter-of-factly.

I smiled at that one—people don't have to know everything about you, but sometimes someone can say something about you that makes all the sense for nearly everything you do.

"Thanks, Larry, I needed that. Put this thing into gear—we have a few stops to make," I stated flatly.

"Sure, where to first?" he asked

"We need to get rid of this car. I say we get back to the big truck."

"Yeah, but won't every police in town be looking for that thing right now?"

he asked, unsure. "Well, you're the hacker. Do some computer stuff, and let's get to the next part of our day," I stated.

"It's not, "Computer stuff." Fine, whatever," he stated, annoyed.

"It's a compliment, guy, just take it. I trust you know what's at stake if we don't find him soon,".

Larry turned his head momentarily from driving and nodded his head slowly. He knew we both knew. We had to find Jacob. With only a limited amount of time and resources, every moment counted.

Chapter 58

I waited in the back of the dump truck cab as Larry feverishly pecked away at his laptop keys. I kept asking him where the cool bars were with graphics that looked like something out of a bad movie with a surprisingly decent sequel.

He scuffed and told me to go do something else. Something else was writing down what I did know. Solving problems—it takes time. I needed to start small—much smaller than I would have liked.

One thing did keep playing in my mind. That was the ring—it had a distinct shape—one I had seen nearly every week as I took their trash out. It belonged to Melanie's church. The Church of the Greater Good. One man wearing it had been hanging out with the Mayor as well. He was someone I needed to find. I thought more about the ring, how it seemed almost stuck in the wade of thick skin that had been gathered up around it from many years of hard work. He could have been a lifter, but he wasn't so big as to suggest anything sports-related. No, judging by the slight bulge of his stomach line and gnarled fingers, he had to be either someone mechanical or a construction worker. Pretty blue-collar to be working with folks like the Mayor or Melanie.

How were they connected? That was the question; I needed to find him—I needed to find Jacob. I started to pull out my phone before remembering Larry told me to stay off any phone until he got us covered. I sighed heavily; we were in the parking lot of a gas station on the edges of town.

I looked at the faded orange logo above the gas station's name. It matched the rest of the building: faded, undergrad-while the rest of the world moved on around it. Or maybe that was how things were—some would just keep fading—while the world just spun.

Shaking my head, I looked around, trying to find the kindling for where my thoughts were going. Often—thinking was nothing more than the ability to project my mind at a particular time. So, the question was: where in time was I?

My feet landed off the tail-bed before I realized I was walking inside the gas station. Inside sat an un-seeming woman. Her expression was dull in the low lights of the store. "Do you have a phone book?" I asked.

"Who uses a phone book anymore?" she replied. I rolled my eyes and returned to Larry when he closed his laptop. "Okay, I think we should be good—I scrubbed all known images of the truck and police report. You should have seen the police report from our boss. What a blowhole. Half his report was about how we were always late and never did anything right. Outright lie, I tell you," he scuffed as he noticed me come up.

"Never mind all of that—I need you to find me all construction sites and car shops in town,"

"Sure, Billy Dan—but why?"

"Just do it—I have a lead," I stated, walking back to the truck as Larry pecked away at the keys.

I honestly had nothing to go on but a small piece of information, and I hoped I was right—at least for Jacobs's sake.

Chapter 59

A few minutes later, we were on the road. Larry had found me seventeen sites that matched the requirements. The first shop had yielded nothing—it was closed for the day already. The next three were more or less useless. I stayed patient each time we pulled up in the hulking dump truck—as I casually got out and went inside. I'd look at the mechanics' hands as quickly as possible—a glance was all I needed. Even with the efficiency, we had already burned an hour as we drove to the next spot. I was getting impatient—every moment felt like a century had passed.

Not to mention, even if we had cleared the truck from the police database, it was still a dump truck driving around town. A low profile was not in the cards. It was only a matter of time before someone started asking questions. I felt sick in my gut that this wouldn't produce anything. Those thoughts won't help Jacob, Billy Dan. Stay focused.

We pulled into the next destination. A small shop with a very Irish-sounding name written across the front of the store in bold yellow on the backdrop of red. "Need me to come in with you this time?" Larry asked as we parked at the edge of the lone mechanic station.

"Nah, this will probably end up being another dead end. Just keep her running and find the best way to the next spot," I stated, thinking about how late in the afternoon it was—there was no way we would get them all before they closed. I started scrambling my head for anything that would help. I exited the tank and opened the door to the mechanic shop on autopilot. I walked through, spotting the gleam of the man's ring in the light from the reflection. We stood eyeing each other for a moment before the man spoke,

"Welcome, what can I do for you?" he asked charmingly enough.

He was the red-headed man from the rooftop that night. He had copper red hair mixed in with bits of a delicate white that only gingers could get. Gnarled hands from years of turning wrenches and a slight belly bulge, indicating he didn't mind a few drinks tossed back every night. My heart skipped a beat as I tried to shrink into myself and become smaller at that moment. The last thing I needed was for him to recognize me. Admittedly, I was sure he saw many of the same faces around town, just like everyone else.

I nodded, "Just looking for some sockets," I replied, turning my head as if to head down the nearest aisle. "Two over to the left, mid-way—can't miss it," he called as I nodded again, walking in the direction he had indicated. I got to the sockets a few moments later—my heart beating fast. Okay, I found him—now what will you do, Billy Dan? My surroundings mainly consisted of various car parts, including sockets and wrenches. I debated picking one up—but I wouldn't need it. He was a mid-sized man. Hopefully, it wouldn't need to be anything too tricky. "Okay," I breathed out, shooting the nerves out of my body with a deep breath back in once finished.

"First thing first. Know your way out," I whispered, taking a wrench over to a window at the end of the store. Something I had learned from today's earlier events was that I needed to stop getting caught with my pants down; no room for any mistakes So, I popped the locks on the window silently and placed the metal wrench in a way that would keep the window from sliding back down. A thin breeze came through. The parking lot was empty, except for the dumpster truck at the edge of the lot. I turned around, walking back to the socket. I glanced one more time at the wrenches, shaking my head. Unlike in the movies, hitting someone in the back of the head with a piece of metal would more than likely kill them. I just needed to get behind him and use a blood choke. It will pass him out long enough for me to restrain him. I went around the corner to the next aisle—moving slowly.

Crutching forward, I made my way down the aisle before I felt the cold steel of a gun on the back of my head, followed by a click. "I told you—the wrenches were isle nine," the voice of the man in the ring said steadily.

"Actually, you said it was two over to the left. What's the big deal—need to see my hallway pass?"

He growled and shoved me forward out into the open of the store. "For a matter of fact, I do. You see, what's bothering me is how much you keep popping up over and over again, garbage man,"

"Waste disposer," I grumbled as he cocked his hand back, backhanding my head with the meat of his fingers. It hurt, but I could tell he was new at the business of hitting people with guns—his fingers were hurt just as much as I heard him grunt.

I made my move as I pushed forward on his loose grip on my shoulder. His fingers would be stinging—that meant his gun hand was free. I whirled, ducking low and pushing his hand, which had been on my shoulder, up with my right hand. At the same time, I was shooting forward and sliding my body close. My other hand gripped his gun hand, shaking it vigorously until the gun dropped to the floor below. Turning my hips and with his arms entirely held, I threw him over my hips onto the ground.

He smacked hard, groaning as I let go of his hands and reached for his gun. I noticed with a glance that it was an SIG. I pointed it at him, my heartbeat breathing heavily. "Alright, now I am going to give you some directions. Don't worry—it will be easy to follow commands, chowderhead," I growled.

Before I even had time to speak, the force of a rhino took me off from the sides, and I smacked hard on the ground below. A heavy weight was on me, and I groaned, swinging the gun back to shoot whoever was on top of me.

At a glance, I saw that it was a massive bull of a man. Whose neck looked wider than my legs. Veins and muscles that rippled with even more veins beneath those. He had a toss of black hair and a messy beard.

My hands moved automatically—getting to the inside of his armpits, buying me enough room to move my hips out and sprawl out from under him. I used my head like a pin and pivoted, getting myself free. The big man was snarling like a beast, mad that I had survived his best attack: super smash. The red-headed mechanic struggled back to his feet, and I reacted quickly.

First, I kicked the big man right in the balls before he got to his feet. Then I field goal kicked the mechanic's head while still on his knees. His head snapped back, and I charged forward as men with guns came busting into the store.

I stepped over the pair, tucked the SIG into my waistline, and scrambled to the window I left open, diving out into the dark parking lot.

Chapter 60

I hit the asphalt, my chest beating fast as I rolled to the side. One of my clamps on the side of my leg was digging into my thigh—bad. It must have broken when I was sacked. Grunting, I swung myself to my feet. A shot rang out behind me, and I ran towards the dump truck with everything I had.

My leg slowed me down—the broken clamp dug into my leg with every step. Something wet was sliding down my leg as another shot rang out. This one hit my leg, the wooden material shattered, and the force nearly caused me to trip on my way to the dump truck. I gasped in pain as I ran around the truck.

More shots came behind me, and Larry opened the passenger door. "Get in, Billy Dan," he screamed, and I nodded, jumping into the cap of the truck. Larry took off, jumping the curve of the hardware store, thick tires landing hard on the street.

A few more shots hit the truck as we speed down the street. Larry was taking so many turns as I kept glancing behind us to see if we were being followed. Nothing; the roads were empty for three blocks before we finally saw another car. That was weird. It was the middle of the week, and not late at all, I thought as I leaned back, drenched in sweat.

"Are you alright?" Larry yelled over the roar of the dump truck engine. "Slow down; we are alright," I replied, sitting back and closing my eyes.

"You've been shot, Billy Dan," he stated.

I looked down. My prosthetic had a hole the size of a quarter on the front. My pants were singed, and the wood in my leg was completely splintered. I unclaimed the locks around my leg and inspected the metal. One clamp was stuck in my leg. I winched as I pulled the metal out—along with pieces of my leg.

I was breathing hard when I sat back again. The sock around my knee was completely soaked in blood. "That looks awful," Larry stated.

I nodded, "Looks worse than it is. Keep slowing down and circle back to that shop," I replied.

"I don't think that is a good idea," he said.

"Just go slow, and we can make it behind the store," I said.

"Okay," he grumbled reluctantly, taking the nearest turn and going down the road. I wiped the sweat from my head and started re-closing my leg back on. A moment later, the broken latch popped back out as I sighed.

We stopped down the street from the store, and Larry killed the lights, but we were in a dump truck. Stealth wasn't the play here. I wasn't sure what we would do even if they did appear.

I tightened my leg down, grimacing about the pain. Once I was sure that it would hold, I opened the door. "No, man, I need to put my foot down here," Larry called out as I stepped out of the truck and glared at him. He looked me in the eyes for a moment before turning away. "Keep it running, Larry," I stated before closing the door and walking down the street. A few people were heading down the block, but otherwise, it was a quiet night.

The whole thing—it felt wrong. Like I had somehow driven past my turn for an area several times. For one, there still weren't many people on the streets. One thing about crime is that people always stand around in gawk, no matter how unseemly it is. Not to mention the big shaker: where were all the cops?

There had to be at least a dozen shots fired my way, and yet nothing.

I was still lost in my thoughts when I heaved forward, my chest feeling like a creature was trying to break free. I coughed loudly. Way too loudly to be ignored. I covered my mouth as blood spilled on my fingers. That was new—I heaved one more time, letting the drool from my mouth hit the pavement.

My chest felt like someone had hammered their way out, and I had to check my head to see if it was still there.

What was that? Does it really matter? A small thought came crawling forward from the furthest reaches of my mind. No, I guess it didn't matter, not in the end, anyway.

I tightened my coat around me and kept walking towards the shop. Stay focused, Billy Dan. I made my way to the side of the shop. Doing my best to blend in with the environment around me. However, I probably looked more like a crazy person stalking around on a city street, covered in blood and hiding in the bushes.

I am sure this was where someone would say I was going crazy. They could jump off a bridge. I found the drop-off parking lot part that gave me the most cover behind a sedan. I waited for a beat—noting the streets were completely dead. Which sent shivers up my spine.

Who were these people with all the power? I shook that thought away and pressed on before being consumed by anything else. But, soon, I knew I would have to deal with the backlog of thoughts growing inside my mind.

Just a little bit longer, I whispered to my brain—though I should have spoken instead to my heart. I could almost see my chest rise and fall through my jacket. Scanning the building, I noticed that there didn't seem to be anyone moving. It could have been a trap, but I had my doubts. Surely they thought no one in their right mind would come back to a place after being shot at. Well, they were right; no one in their right mind would. But, I was out of my mind.

The window I had left in my escape was wide open; in the dull light of the street lamp, I could make out dozens of casings littering the ground. This was a bizarro world now. There was no way the cops could have not shown up. Sure, it wasn't uncommon to find shells occasionally in any environment. However, this many after a crime scene would have been collected by forensics. There was no way. I shuddered at that thought, and this ran deep. The deeper it went, the more I remembered I was just a garbage man and was way out of my depth.

I whispered, "You were ideally suited for digging through the filth, Billy Dan." I stopped for another moment before making my way to the window. I needed to think outside of the box. From my vantage point, I couldn't tell anything inside the store. Leaving the window gave me a way back in; however, I couldn't trust it that easily. For one, no cop or anyone in the area meant total self-insurance on whoever had planted all of this. I could only assume the worst that someone was very likely inside the station now. I needed to think even more outside the box as I scanned the building, looking for the tell-tell sign of a camera.

My eyes glazed to the corner of the roof, directly pointing on a swivel, was an expensive-looking camera tilting its way through its surveillance. That was a costly camera to be used at an auto shop.

That only solidified that whatever was in the shop had to be something that would lead to Jacob. I held onto that feeling even if it felt like grasping onto heaps of sand in the water. First thing first—I needed to take out that camera. I could see the shining light from the machine as it made its way through its passes, scanning the empty parking lot. I traced the camera's path and pressed the button on my way to watch. The count left me with about eight seconds of movement where the camera would lose line of sight. They had expensive cameras, and to be truly effective, they would have needed multiple boxes. That didn't appear to be the case. Easy to sidestep if I could figure out its path. Think Billy Dan; just keep looking for the most significant thing you can find.

Often, the worst things are staring us right in the face, and we fail to even see them until the bottom has come out and we are already falling through the trap door. I glanced at the nearest set of vehicles; a blinking light was coming from the dashboard of a van—suspiciously seated at the far corner with a vantage point covering the other entrance. That was it.

I dug around in my pockets until I found my knife. It was a small blade that I kept sharp and always within reach. I crawled quickly to the van's passenger side. Shimming along the door, I made it to waist level, about the level of the door handle. I pushed my knife into the low lips of the window until I felt the lock jam.

My blade jiggled the old lock on the van until I felt a pressure click and release. The lock popped up. The camera was seated haphazardly and pointed towards the window. Someone must have set it up quickly. I hunched low, reached over the dash, turned the camera off, and placed it into my pocket. There might be something on it later that I could use.

I searched the glove compartment on my way out of the van. I felt cold steel and froze for a moment before pulling out the business end of a .357 revolver. A powerful gun to leave lying around in a run-down van. I checked the gun, adjusting and securing it. Fully loaded, with eight shots. A rubber grip—and it had been fired recently. I wondered if it was one of the ones that was shot at me earlier. No clue on that one—it wouldn't change the situation either. Still, though, it's a nice gun to have. However, keeping something that was a shred of potential evidence in a crime probably wasn't smart.

Bigger things to worry about now, Billy Dan. I closed the glove box; nothing else was in there. It was odd that a van that wasn't here and had a gun like this just sitting inside. I glanced in the back of the van. All the carpets and seats were missing. Combined with tinted windows, though they should have done the windshield as well, it must mean this was a vehicle for transporting. Something like, say, a garbage man snooping into the business of some awful people who were perfectly comfortable with chasing after children. That made me pretty mad.

I gritted my teeth and left the van as I glanced at the camera on the side of the station. Its view would now be obscured by a blind spot from a missing camera. I was lucky; these guys may have some powerful friends, but they weren't the brains of the operation. They weren't thinking I would come back.

I just needed to ensure I didn't fall into the same spectrum. Keep your head up, Billy Dan, and keep moving—just keep thinking. I timed the camera as I rushed through the open window, almost falling on the spent casings littering the ground. With a feat of athleticism that I wasn't confident on any other day I would ever have landed in one try, I dove through the window. I landed on the hard ground, more bullet casings scattered throughout the store and under my backside. I groaned from the leap before snapping up— and scanning the empty store. Nothing, absolute silence permeated the shop. I listened for a hair's breadth in the dark before shakily getting to my feet. More weirdness for the night; no one had bothered to clean or shut the door. I had no idea that my town was such a crime hole. That thought alone bothered me almost as much as the bullet casing that I was sure had made its way somewhere inside my pants and would take ages to find.

I debated closing the window—before turning away and deciding against it. When in doubt, know your way out. Worked once and might work again. However, that spine-tingling feeling of something trying to pull every bone out of my body only worsened. I had immense doubts about how I would get out of this.

My brain kicked in, and I pulled the recovered gun out from my pocket before continuing on. I held my breath for another moment, straining my ears to listen to the environment around me. Listening is a skill that most people fail to acquire in nearly every aspect of life. Ask almost any woman in my life, and they would agree that I fall into that category. But that aside— listening was more than just communication. It's an essential survival trait. We lived in a world of distractions, one flashing screen at a time. Hearing your surroundings without the signal blaring your way will give you an almost superhuman edge within moments. It's nothing particularly out of this world, though; it might save your life.

In this case, in the gloom of the station, I listened. I could only hear the early-night bugs playing their songs. My slow breathing. Nothing, just silence. I relaxed, keeping my gun out, and slowly made my way through the shop, creeping along the edge of the walls.

I wanted to keep a distance between me and whoever might have been in the store. Just because I did not hear or see anything—everything had been well, too easy during this escapade.

The shadows of the street lights cast dull yellows over the shelf nearest the windows, which seemed to be in a tug-of-war match with the darkness of the store. I made my way to the front of the store, hunching over as I crossed in front of the windows, I noticed the blinds had been closed and slammed shut.

Even these jerks protected as they were, didn't have that kind of power. Can't shoot off that many rounds and leave the windows open. That was just rude; no one would want that. And I felt this place was just a cover-up, but for what? I had no idea. I needed to find out, and I needed to find out quickly. The problem was, I couldn't see anything in the dimming light. Not enough to make out the details of anything specific.

I had to assume that somewhere in this building the people that shot at me. That meant not turning on the lights or making noises if I could help. I waited a moment longer for my eyes to somehow adjust to my surroundings. In the middle of the store was a low light coming beneath the flaps of the double doors.

That was the direction I needed to go. My shoes echoed like elephants on ice on the cheap linoleum floors. I stopped dead in my tracks and kept my eyes glued to the light from the doorway. No shadows passed before the light; I took a deep breath, wiping the sweat from my forehead. I should take off my shoes, but if I had to do any running, my feet would be destroyed by that escape. My leg was messed up, I doubted there was any escaping from anyone. I sighed heavily, wishing this was a choice where I was wearing sandals on some beach somewhere—instead of sneaking off in the early hours of the night, bleeding and coughing up anyone knows what. Sweaty palms and a heavy gun. Get to making decisions, Billy Dan. There is no time to waste.

I kept my shoes on and did my best to move slowly towards the door, not obscuring the light with my giant feet. I got to the door and pulled the gun up. I held my breath—listening. I could hear nothing behind the door. That could be either a good or a bad thing. I jiggled the handle, slowly turning it open. Ready to slam it shut if I heard anything. Nothing came out as the door opened up, showing a wider hallway. I took my chance and moved through the door as quickly as possible. Shutting it behind me, almost like I was putting a newborn baby down to sleep with the level of care. I was in a bare hallway. Symbols from the station on the walls, a bulletin board that had not been updated in months.

One end of the hallway led to a door with a vent in the top—behind it, I could hear machines churning along. Probably nothing in there, as I scanned, looking in the other direction. The hallway went for another ten feet before sharply turning to a deep shadow with a low light stretching from somewhere. The shadow was moving, though; people were at the end of the hallway. I steadied myself and crept along the walls until I came to the turn in the hallway. There was a pair of open doors that led to a loading dock inside of a garage.

Everything, for the most part, seemed normal. But, I suppose that's how most of these things go—for the most part, unless you're insane, most people tend to avoid things that outwardly look dangerous. It's the mundane that's the actual murder. The seemingly ordinary things lure you into a false sense of security. Nothing crazy here: just a plain old garage on the edges of town.

"Just keep looking," I muttered, almost regretting speaking. All this work would be for nothing if I got heard now. The end of the hallway met my trembling feet as I reached the doors. I leaned towards the doors. I could hear muffled voices—nothing tangible, though. That left me with only a few choices. Going inside waving a gun would certainly be an option. There was just the factor of how many were on the other side of the doors.

Next to the door was a fire extinguisher. That will do, I thought as I unlatched it from its holder.

I assured myself that stealth could only take someone so far. The extinguisher was just for precaution.

"Yeah—and pigs can fly... precautions, my foot," I whispered, pushing open the doors.

Chapter 61

I pushed open the door to reveal several things all at once. First, there were three people before me with masks over their faces. A collection of ski masks and one person with what looked like a half attempt to tie a rag around their mouths. Secondly, the key detail was that two of them held long baseball bats. A slender figure dressed all in black was leveling a pistol at me as I came into the room.

Taking all of this in, I threw the fire extinguisher in one movement; in the next, I aimed my own gun and fired into the metal at their stunned silence. A hole emerged in the metal, quickly followed by white smoke pouring out of the hole as if some kind of angry force of nature was unleashed upon the land. The pressure from the hole and gas escaping was so intense that it caused the container to spin in a different direction in midair.

The slender figure shot her gun haphazardly through the dense smoke, her bullets sailing into the door behind me. I pointed my weapon, taking advantage of the distraction by having time to aim. My second shot was deafening, but I hit my target. One of the men with a baseball bat went down hard—a gust of wind coming out of his mouth from the blow. I turned to fire at the quickly approaching figure with a baseball bat when the doors behind me were moved by some force, sending me off balance.

I had no time to turn, no time to think, really. I felt a blow to the back of my head—it was lights out before I even had time to realize what happened.

Chapter 62

By no stretch of the imagination am I a doctor. A slightly above-average individual with a wide array of corky skills—but most likely in way over my head. Regardless, I still could tell by the amount of blood that was flowing down my face, the lost assortment of memories before I became aware again that I needed to avoid any more head trauma for the day.

A superficial cut and a dull ache on the back of my head were the least of my concerns. I was more concerned about the cold water of the lake and the weight of an imposing rock sitting near my legs, tied with a chain that looped around my legs.

I still couldn't make out fully everything around me, but that was enough. Before me was a large man, another a slender figure who had removed her mask. She was dark in hair and olive in skin tone. Sunken eyes from years of life, she had to be around the same age as myself.

Her words sounded like jingle bells being rung right in my face. Her tone and mannerisms told me all I needed to know, though. That gave me a chance, though, because as my mind came racing back to the moments after I blacked out and was stuffed into a trunk, I recalled two crucial details. Number one, she wore more makeup than was practical or needed. She had soft curves in the right places and hard lines where you wanted them to be on a woman. Yet, her makeup was almost powdered on her face. Which helped me confirm the following details. Before I was locked into the truck, I had picked the pockets of the big man. People focus far too much on someone's face when dealing with them.

They forgot to watch my hands, forgot to monitor my every move. So, as they forced me into the truck, I pulled two items from the bigger man's pocket. He was most likely the fourth man that hit me from behind. Hard enough to daze me, not enough to kill me. That had been enough for me to pull a ring and matchbook out of his pockets.

Behind them, parked far too close to the pier, was a dead man in the back seat. The man I had shot. I took all the facts in and started racing my mind. These four clowns had kidnapped me. They weren't the same individuals that had shot at me earlier. Those had been professional and clean. The big man reeked of sweat and something nasty. Both of their skin tones appear pale under the milky-stained moonlight.

The woman's makeup had been smeared, and the general twist of her eyes between me and the big man suggested a great deal of anxiety.

More like a drug withdrawal, a small voice in the back of my mind whispered. Yeah, that's what that is. The sweating, even though it was cold enough to make a popsicle chilly out here. The quick eyes darted like a rat between anything and everyone. Sure, they were wet behind the ears, but an addict could spot another addict. About the only thing good about being a junkie was that ability—you could just tell one of your kind. No matter how much makeup they wore, no matter how hard they worked when a junkie is using again—you can tell.

These two, and I was guessing now, if these two clowns didn't get the third to a hospital, he was going to die. He was most likely already dead, and if he wasn't, none of them were going to help. I could use that to my advantage. It was a small piece of data; it was all I had. As my eyes reflected on the scene, my senses returned like a slowly moving dump truck. I saw how close the rock was to the pier's edge.

My heart threatened to kick out of my chest as I forced myself to start taking slow, deep breaths. With junkies, you knew only one thing was for sure: something stupid was going to happen.

The big man soon glanced back my way; a haggard expression soon gave way to a cruel grin that made his rough textured skin look like a raisin despite his age, barely out of his twenties. Heavy living would do that to you, I thought.

"This jerk is back to the land of the living, yeah—he's back," he spit the venom in his voice clear over the sounds of the waves below me.

I nodded my head, "Good to be back. I'm Billy Dan—I see that you guys took the time to wrap me up with a chain. Drive me down to the beach. What's your name?" I asked, smiling wide at the man.

He spits rage, causing his eyes to almost appear as if they were going to burst out from the pressure of my words. Good. I had to bide my time for what I didn't know yet. Just had to wait until something came to me.

After a moment, the man composed himself. His thick grin pulled up his loose skin. "Aren't you a tough guy—yeah, we will see who is tough soon," he snarled, pointing down at the big rock.

I followed his gaze and wiggled the binds around my hands enough to flick the man off. Another good thing, these rookies didn't tie my restraints very well. I would need every advantage that I could get. If someone goes through the trouble of putting you in this situation, you have to accept that you probably weren't going to talk your way out of it. No matter how silver-tongued, the odds are just too stacked against you. It's all about leverage. What I needed was to get more on these guys, and I needed to get more leverage before the big guy decided he was tired of my mouth.

I decided to go for it—play it calm to keep him calm about the rock, though part of my mind was acutely aware that this lake was freezing. And it was very deep. Stay focused, and get more out of them before it's too late. I was sweating somewhere under my coat despite the cold.

They called me demanding, but I needed to act like a tough guy and learn more about them.

Luckily for me, junkies have the patience of a puppy, "Where's the TRIP?" she blurted out.

"TRIP?" I replied. The big man scoffed and delivered a stiff right jab to my face. It took every ounce of willpower I had to stay on my feet. To keep out of the lake as my face tilted towards the black waves. Like hell made up of murky, deep brown aching to pull me into its cold embrace. A fire made of ice, cold until you can only feel warmth—the warmth of a dying man at the end of its embrace.

I slowly shifted uncomfortably, balancing myself before the big man. I spit, and bits of a tooth came out as blood filled my mouth. "That was my favorite filling jerk," I stated. The man swore, punching me again. I was expecting it this time and held firm as he punched my gut. I let out a breath of air. Pulling in more air to expand my lungs for what was now a sure thing.

Getting out of this mess would require more—I wasn't ready to go in yet. If this giant ape kept hitting me, I thought, glancing at the wide-eyed junkie man. He was bound to accidentally push me over at this rate. Stick to the facts. Now, I had a name for the drug that was being used. That was the confirmed street name for it. That was something. Though, my next question was probably going to be my last. Likely, they had searched me. I was thankful I had left the syringe with Larry. My only guess was Larry was out there somewhere trying to find me. It was tough to tell how long it had been without the sun. The sky was clouding up, hiding the milky moon above me. Which cast a silver light on the waves below, almost like a spotlight for my death.

"So, you guys weren't besties with the suits?" I remarked that the big man had pulled me by my collar. I held onto the rock as he pulled me forward, praying that he wouldn't accidentally show it off now. He snarled, spit hitting my face, "Look weirdo—you're with them. We came to get our supplies back, and those suit-wearing government folks weren't there. So, I will ask again—where's our trip?" he yelled.

I took a few more breaths, readying myself for what was coming, "I mean, there's this great beehive guy I know in town. He farms his honey, but you could have just asked him for some. Affordable prices, grown locally," I said firmly. He grinned madly, "Wrong answer," he swore, pulling me towards the lake. The boards of the duck creaked under our weight.

"No, really—he has very affordable rates. He's probably asleep at this hour, but I am sure the four, well probably three of you, now could get some honey from him," I pleaded as he pulled me by my collar. The woman darted her eyes back to the car as the man kept his eyes on me.

"We've already searched him," the woman said.

"Just a rabbit's foot and a cheap gun," she shrieked. "Hey now, that was my lucky rabbit's foot," I grunted, moving my neck in a way that would allow me to get in more as the big man pulled even higher.

"No..." he paused, looking at the rock at the edge. "No need for you," he muttered as he let go of my shirt in one gesture and kicked the rock off the deck. Almost immediately, I felt the tug of the rock like an anchor going down into the waves.

Both the pair grinned, assured in themselves of my demise. I was slammed hard into the deck, busting my chin on the old wood. I didn't fight the pull. Instead, I rolled with it, going off the edge into the dark below.

Chapter 63

The cold was biting every inch of my exposed skin first. The shock was like a bolt of lightning all over my body. It took every bit of my willpower to keep my mouth closed as the ice bites at me. I needed to stay calm; I was sinking fast, the light from the surface getting smaller and smaller. Flashes of creatures feasting on my frozen body in the deep filled my mind.

Stay calm; I eased my body back into a graceful dive down. I had one advantage in that it was junkies that put me in this situation. They had tied a chain around a one-legged man without accounting for a fake leg.

I instinctively dropped my hands to the latches on the side of the leg, undoing them in the darkness. The leg came loose, and I held onto it as it flooded. With one leg out, I quickly slipped the other out. I felt the chain scuff my leg in defiance as I slid it out of the chains. My passage to a murky hell was saved for now—somewhere in the dark below, something would be angry about my escape. The river shot up mud and muck in almost defiance as if some dark god was denied its meal.

That was one problem down; the next was air. The cold stung at my chest, and I was far from the surface. With my leg in one hand, I swam towards the surface. A distant part of my mind, the part that always looked ahead, worried if I would pop out and the junkies would still be there.

Thoughts like that, I realized, were a luxury. I still needed to escape the waters before I dreamed of air. I strained with all my might, the cold freezing my body until I was numb. The moonlight showed the outline of the beams of the dock. I swam towards them, breaking the surface as my lungs felt they were about to burst. I gasped in air, taking in every bit as I coughed up everything that had been building inside my body.

As I floated in the dead water, the wooden beams were my only salvation. I hugged the nearest beam when a body floated by me. In a panic, I jerked back, thinking it was a shark. Nope, just the remains of the man I had shot, now to be buried at sea. No honor among junkies, I told myself. Well, at least there were three of them now, for sure. But before I could get back on the trail for Jacob. I needed to escape these waters.

Chapter 64

"Appreciate it," I mumbled to the clerk at the checkout stand. I fumbled with the lid while walking to my beat-up truck from the grocery store. The lid of the sleep medicine was already off before the sliding doors closed behind me. The cap hit the ground, making a dull sound as a woman scuffed at me for littering. I flipped her the bird and made it to my truck.

I burped, wiping my mouth on the sleeve of my jacket. The sleep aid bottle is nearly empty. The purple liquid was as deep as the mouth of some great beast. I took another pull, draining the bottle. "fu—you, beast," I slurred, turning my truck's engine over. I lurched through the parking lot, shifting through the wrappers and bottles of my truck. I found the bottle of cheap whisky.

Flicking the lid off was hard with my bad hand. "Wiping my butt was hard with this hand," I grumbled as I took a pull from the whiskey. I burped and fumbled for the keys in the ignition for a good minute before I realized the truck had already started—slamming on my breaks at the long glances from other drivers.

"Yeah, well, up yours," I sneered and continued driving home. I already regretted not getting more whiskey while I was at the store. Maybe I could head back to the store later. I am sure I had frozen something in the cooler that I needed to get home before it went wrong. Who was I kidding, though? I had severe doubts my freezer was even working anymore. A few weeks back, it started to backtalk me when I tried to stuff more beer into it. So, I hit it with a hammer. That made the most sense—though cheap hot beer is the worst. In the end, the freezer won that exchange.

In the end, what did that matter anyway? I wasn't sure when the last time I had food was. Food made things worse for me; it always reminded me of her. She cooked better than anything I could find on an overpriced delivery service. That just ended in tears. No one likes to eat fish tacos while they're crying. Just takes the fun out of Taco Tuesday.

I belched again, the thoughts of food overtaking the thick haze the whiskey and pills had me in. That wasn't good—I needed to stay in the haze. I finished the whiskey. Thought about dumping it out the window. Most would probably say I was a disgusting pig by now. But, I wasn't a litterer. Draw the line somewhere, at least. I blew my lips out and rolled down the window, swerving as I threw the bottle onto the empty highway.

Signs on the road broke through the haze, though, long enough for me to read what was going on. Signs invite me to check out the most enormous sex toys in the state. The next one proclaims, "Jesus saves". It left me utterly confused—should I go to a strip club, or should I say ten Hail Mary's?

I was speeding—I was flying more like it. The truck was practically weightless as I zoomed across the road. A dim part of me knew this was wrong; a large part knew I did not care. What was left for me anyway? Chicken that may or may not be in the cooler in the back of the truck? An empty apartment, littered and filled with more angst than a teenage goth party with all-you-can-use razor blades and cover bands of cover bands playing in the background.

The open road seemed more appealing, more inviting—more fitting. Just the cold deep with no way out or forward—just endless. That was what I liked, endlessness without any care in the world, endlessness, not a devil in sight. I thought just before my eyes closed, and I suddenly felt weightless.

Chapter 65

Bright lights are the worst things to wake up under the best of circumstances. These, though, weren't the bright lights you would think to see at the end of a long tunnel. Just the unforgiving shine of cheap illuminations. Nothing pearly or salvation in their embrace, just a cold flicker. A long, unflinching shine that you can almost see the electricity beneath the glass like swimming eels inside a dark ocean.

I tried to turn my head from the lights. I was stuck in place. A sharp jolt of pain made me call out from the movement. That was followed by a small yelp from the pain of trying to move my neck from my nose, filling like someone had jammed a tub of playdough down each nostril. I stuck my tongue out to feel what was clogging my nose, only to find a wade of cotton-tasting bandages on my mouth.

What in the world was going on? My body reacted, shooting up fast as if in a wave—thrashing against the feeling of being pulled deep into the abyss. Only my whole body felt like I had suddenly gained a couple hundred pounds. With a great deal of grunting and pain, I managed to get myself into a seating position.

Right before feeling a firm, but gentle hand on my chest push me back down. I grumbled, looking up into the eyes of a minor, dark-skinned nurse with an angry brow and an exasperated look.

"lay back, sir," she said with a tone that radiated authority for someone who couldn't have been more than 100 pounds soaking wet. She was thin but not sickly. In fact, even in the unflattering scrubs, I could see the outline of toned muscles shifting as she moved. Her face was slender, with a broad nose, cupped by a tussle of long black hair. Her arms were littered with tattoos, and the unmistakable holes in the folds of her elbows—signs of a junkie. Dang, I had died and gone to the junkie graveyard, I thought.

"Look, lady," I started before she scribbled something into a notepad with a plump orange cat on the back staring bored at me.

"It's Nurse Rosemary, sir," she replied dryly with an equally bored tone as her cat on her notepad.

I rolled my eyes, and even that tiny movement made me wince, which caught the dark brown eyes of the nurse. I gulped, looking away from her gaze before continuing. "Look—nurse Rose—Mary," I drawled out her name as she stopped writing and fixed me with a long stare. "I'm not sure what's going on—or even if you're really a nurse. Because first of all—" I gestured with one of my hands that still could move, "you look like something I ran over one night at work. I imagine, which is probably saying a lot," I said, letting my words dig in.

She snorted at that, "speak for yourself, pal," she replied. "So, are you going to stop moving and sit back like I said—for the last time, by the way," she stated calmly, putting her cat journal into the pockets of her hoodie. She pushed her glasses up her nose until they framed her face with large square shapes.

"I think you've caused enough pain for one night. So, do us both a favor and just lay back. Gotta pump the crap out of your system and keep you hydrated," she said flatly.

Her words took a moment for it all to register with me. I had been driving down a long road—I had been drunk—well, a lot of things. With that realization, the pain came flooding back into me as if my body suddenly realized it had been in pain this whole time. I let out a small yelp of pain. The nurse's face frowned for a brief moment before becoming one of stoicism. A wall of professionalism. Hints of care laced her features. It's a job one can't do if they're entirely heartless. However, I imagined seeing someone like I was now was probably the worst thing for someone like them. That thought alone made me want to drink more. To escape to the actual junkie graveyard. The place where all the souls of the damn twirl into an endless gray of mist and nothingness.

Nothingness. There's that word again. I hated myself, truly. I swallowed hard and didn't say anything. Rosemary's frown depended. "You know, I know exactly what you're thinking right now," she said softly, placing her hands into her jacket pockets.

I scuffed, "Lady, you have no idea what I am thinking,"

She laughed at that.

"Nah, I do. Right now, you're probably thinking woe is me. How could this happen to someone like me? But that's not right. No one aggressively destroys themselves that hard if they like themselves that much. Nah, I would say you're thinking about nothing. How none of this makes sense. Heck, I bet you haven't even registered to think if you hurt someone or not," she said calmly.

That hit deep, my self-loathing was one thing—I didn't want to bring someone down with me, though. "Did anyone..." I started.

She shook her head slowly. "Nope, just your dumb self wrapped around a tree. God only knows how you managed to survive that without killing yourself in the process," she said.

"Geez, well, I sure am blessed," I muttered.

"I would say yeah. I've seen people die with a lot less in their systems. Count your stars on that one. Do something better than laying around in a hospital bed," She directed.

My head cocked at the sound of that one, ignoring the pain I felt in my jaw as I turned to glare at her. She didn't flinch at all. A dull expression was written across her face. A look that you wouldn't expect on someone the same age as me. Instead of someone much older. Like a mother speaking to a small child.

Lay on my butt; who does this broad think she is? I started to reply before she shook her head slowly.

"That wasn't to put you down, jack butt. It was to try and wake you up— get you to understand how you put yourself in this situation. You're lucky you aren't dead. You're lucky this is a small town, and the sheriff overlooked throwing your butt so far deep in a can that you will be thankful for some therapy with an annoying lab coat forcing you to reflect on something other than what's at the bottom of your beer. And let me tell you, it's nothing. Just an endless hole—leading to nowhere. Nothing—that's what you will find in darkness. You will find nothing; there will be no light," she stated.

A chill ran up my back, and a thought momentarily drilled its head through the fog. I could feel my back, at least. What would I do if I lost that as well? I shook the thought off and returned to focus on the nurse, who was now sitting on the edge of the bed. "I'm pretty sure I have to go to jail for being under the influence like that. This town isn't that corrupt, and I don't have that kind of sway," I replied.

Small lines formed at the edges of her mouth as she smiled at me. "Let's just say—the sheriff and I know each other very well. He likes to give second chances. Especially to those that need it," she said warmly.

I wanted to swat her for that. But the anger subsided just as quickly. I was stuck here; there was no getting out. I just wanted a drink. I wanted her to stop talking. I would have to play along for now if I ever stood a chance.

I sucked in my lips, "What are you suggesting?"

She smiled back, "Just that we go to a few meetings together,"

"Do I have a choice?"

She stood from the bed and pulled out a notepad from her jacket, writing something down, before taking a page out and handing it to me. It was an address and time a week from today. "Let's just say it wouldn't be in your best interests not to come," she stated.

I sighed, "sure I will be there," I said grumpily.

"Make it a promise, Mr. Daniels," she stated.

"Just call me Billy Dan," I replied.

She nodded. "Promise,".

"Why do I need to promise? I said I would be there," I shot back.

She shook her head before going on. "A promise is a little thicker than a word, is all. Need to earn that first before I believe you," she smiled, turning and walking out of the room.

The lights flickered. I sat under them, machines beeped, and I felt nothing as if my life had just stopped. Or it may have started. I'm not sure if I knew;

I just wanted a beer.

Chapter 66

"Well, that was fun, I guess," I mumbled in the truck's passenger seat while warming my hands. It had grown cold since my wreck. A few scraps scared over—still thick in pink, though. But not long enough to fade just yet. Since giving up drinking, I have become acutely aware of every minute of every day. Or at least I thought I did—I just needed to get away from this crap. Just a few more classes, and I was done. I could—.

"I wish for once, Billy Dan, you could keep your word," sighed Rosemary. I blew out my lips, "I wish for once we didn't have to listen to Frank from the circle blabber on about his hair loss and erectile dysfunction, but at last, some things never come to pass," I replied.

Rosemary stifled a giggle, the slightest trace of a smile at the corners of her lips. I appreciated her for that. I appreciated her for a lot of things. Without her, well, her father, the sheriff, I would have ended up inside a cell wishing my roommate was someone with a limp noodle. I appreciated that Rosemary drove us every Saturday for the last six months or so. It was nice not to have to drive all the time.

What I didn't appreciate—was going to the meetings. Therapy and group were part of my conditional release. So far, I understand when I will be done with them. I ignored her opinion and pretended to be busy looking out the window. She stayed silent as her old truck labored on the long dirt road. Rosemary wasn't going to crack first—it was our game now. See which of us was going to talk first.

I sighed deeply before clearing my throat. "I guess you win this round," I said.

"It's not a game, Billy Dan; it's just a fact. You can't keep your word," she stated instantly.

That made me angry, angry enough that I felt my hands flexing.

"Oh, chill out; we both know you will lose. We both know, more importantly, that you can't keep your word," she said again.

"I can, too. I went to this damn meeting, didn't I?" I challenged.

"No, you would have been late had I not considered this. Like always, week after week. Every group session, every practice. You're only ever on time because I come early," she stated.

I mauled her words over for a moment. She wasn't wrong, though. Rosemary could kick my butt easily. She was one of the local black belts at the jujitsu club. In addition to being a nurse and doing what seemed to be an endless number of other jobs, she worked with families. I scoffed but kept silent. "What does it matter anyway?" I swore under my breath as Rosemary slammed on her brakes. My head came forward, hitting the dashboard.

She stared at me—drilling holes into my skull as if she were a mad doctor bent on surgically injecting her ideas into the most bottomless pits of my mind. I had to admit; her look was convincing enough—looks and speeches couldn't sway people with an addiction. Salvation came from within. A long trip to the cells we all have within ourselves. Where no mirrors could be broken, no matter how hard we hit. What we are—what we've done. I could either face that or continue as I always have. That is, to not continue at all. Because of the thirst, it never stops. The voices will pull you down, kicking and screaming as you might. Until you overcome those voices and accept them for who they are. What you are—that was something I couldn't do just yet, though; Rosemary knew that. She had been clean for four years.

Something that is just thinking about honestly made me completely flabbergasted. What was life sober? It had to be a boring world. I had to be in a cold, cold place. Where winter never ended, where the angels never sang. I didn't want to feel anything again. She couldn't understand.

Wisely, I averted my gaze; I wasn't ready to meet her looks yet. Sheepishly, I responded, "My point still stands, Rosie. Why does it matter? So what if I miss a few classes? It's been months of the same thing. I am every day doing something. I'm starting to think you just enjoy my company.

She snorted, "Don't flatter yourself, Billy Dan. Jokes aren't going to get you out of this one. Not to mention, you know the deal was that you never missed a single session."

This time, I rolled my eyes, "Yeah, yeah, I know the deal," I muttered.

"You don't. You're lucky as Hell my pops is the sheriff. You're lucky that he is more forgiving than you deserve. If a jail is all you want, a cell. Alone and cold with all your thoughts forever—keep going the way you are," she stated.

I shrugged in my seatbelt. "Maybe that is all I deserve, Rosemary," her face contorted for the first time since I had met her. Maybe something I said had finally gotten through. She sighed deeply before turning back.

"Let me ask you this, Billy Dan—do actions have consequences? Do the things that we've done matter? The answer is yes. You're responsible for everything that has happened to you. And yet—you still act like what is done is not done instead of seeing this as a new chance to do some good. To look beyond the fences you've built for yourself, you keep on keeping inside a hole. If that is really what you want, then stop wasting my time. Tell me now, and I will drop you off at the station if it's not, if you want to leave that hole once and for all. Then, coming out of the night starts with this: keeping your word. You said you would do something, and you do it. Otherwise, you don't say you will in the first place. That's called being honest. Being honest starts with yourself. Whenever you're ready—we can go on. That won't happen until you take that first step. I'm not trying to change your mind on anything. Hell, most days, people would call me crazy for my lifestyle of getting up before the sun comes up. That doesn't matter; you will always be crazy to everyone who can't manipulate you. So, instead, I am saying this—can you keep your word?"

Chapter 67

I tore through the cold waters. My whole body stinging—that was good, I thought. Now I can feel it again. The numbness started to wear off. No time for that, I willed myself forward, my detached leg held so tight in my hands I felt my fingers desperately trying to tear through the waves. All strength zapped away as I swam towards the pillars.

Cold was an understatement. This was a frosty Hell. The kind where the idea of sunlight and warmth is but a nursery rhyme for children. A conception of heat—nothing more. That alone reached the depths of my soul, a tentacle of darkness that I knew if I stopped trying for the pillar, I was going to die. More importantly, if I stopped moving forward, if I quit now, Jacob would die.

"Not today," I gurgled water, regretting opening my mouth as the burst of air rushed down my throat. My teeth chattered and opened so much that I was sure a filling or two would have come loose. After a few more moments, I reached the pillars of the pier. My hands tenderly gripped the wood. It was soaked and slippery to the touch. Even if I planned to do this on dry land, I had doubts about pulling myself up the pole.

So, I tried anyway—with an effort, I wrapped my whole body around the pillar. My leg gripped the pole as my fingers dug in for any grove they could find. As I slowly climbed the pier, my breath rolled longer than the waves around me. I needed to get a bearing on which way the shore was. All I could make out was the pillars, the low moonlight above obscured by the abyss of the night. I paused, breathing more deeply than I ever had before.

I had been lucky; if I had continued swimming the way I had been, I would have gone out into the lake. The icy waters would have been my grave. I couldn't see the shoreline; I could make out buildings and lights in the distance. With only half my body out of the water, I let go, taking my leg and heading toward the lights. The comfort blanket was forgotten. The goal ahead. One step at a time, Billy Dan. Get to the shore.

Chapter 68

The shore felt like heaven, even if heaven had broken glass bottles and used diapers—I didn't care. I would never go into the water again as long as I live. Or at least until I bathed in bleach and the hottest temperatures I could stand.

"What a lovely dream that will be," I spit up water, shivering. My jacket was pulled so tight that my bruised fingers were ripping open. The cold steel of my prosthetic burned into my hand. I glanced down at it. The bottom finger had been bent to an extreme ankle.

"These things are expensive," grumbling as I patted myself down. In my pockets, I felt the wet matchbook. Hopefully, it hadn't been too waterlogged. I noticed the tape was gone, though I had a feeling who the first group was— and who had been on the tape. I peered ahead at the pair—time for the fun part. I needed a phone call.

My handles fumbled the keys of the dead man's phone. Thankfully, the water hadn't damaged the phone too much. A junkie with a good phone case—that was a first. Or maybe, I never could keep a phone back when I was a junkie, I thought.

The phone screen went dark as I waited for Larry to get me. I was huddled, soaked to the bone, on a bench near where I had gone in the water. My leg was reattached now, steel bite like a metal demon on the stub of my leg. The broken latch snapped open again, and I sighed. It was so hard to fight to stay awake.

I was fatigued, drifting in and out. The world seemed like I wasn't so far off from being back in the waves.

Chapter 69

Inside the dimly lit waffle house, I watched Larry's face scrunched while digging into his computer more than his classic dirty American breakfast. However, as I sat shivering, still trying to catch my breath, I didn't touch my hash browns either. My appetite wouldn't return anytime soon after drinking a gallon of water inside the freezing lake.

Luckily, the upstate of South Carolina was one of those places that only played with winter. It did not invite it over for dinner and a movie. It could be far colder in other places I had lived. I started my third cup of coffee and waited.

Larry had picked me up at the beach, bringing me a jacket as requested. He worked silently, which I sincerely appreciated. Talking felt like nothing more than moving hot air around now. I sipped my coffee, motioning the server for another. They filled up my coffee—another score for the House of Waffles. I could only imagine what I looked like now, a typical night for this shift. No one so much as raised an eyebrow.

I sipped my coffee, trying to maintain patience. I could have easily found the place alone—however, I needed to know what I was walking into first. Larry finished and pinched the bridge of his nose.

"You aren't going to like this," he said solemnly.

"Give me the veggies," I replied soberly.

"Alright, you're taking another trip back to that strip club you busted out of earlier. By the way, it's getting harder and harder to run interference for you with all the police. This is a small town. Not only that, if you're anywhere today, you know someone is filming,"

"Everyone but whoever took Jacob," I replied.

Larry nodded at that one. "Precisely," he stated before flipping his laptop around and showing me the faces of two of the people who had beat me and thrown me into the lake. I grumbled, knowing full well what this would mean.

"Look, man..." I stopped Larry before he could tell me to call the cops. "We are past that man; be with me—or hit the road," I stated glumly.

He nodded, "No—I got that. I just meant, why don't we try this a different way? You need to get a gun or something," he whispered, looking around the room.

I arched an eyebrow at that one. "Not a bad idea, but let me worry about that later. Could you do me a favor after you drop me off? Get a hold of Rosemary for me. She will have what I need," I said, getting up from the table and pulling out a fistful of water-sagged dollars before glancing at Larry.

"Don't worry about it," he muttered, reaching for his wallet.

"Thank you, Larry," I stated firmly.

He blinked, "yeah, man, no problem," he said.

He paid, and we headed to the parking lot, firing up his truck this time. "Where is the dump truck?" I asked.

He shrugged, "Off the streets—but man, no matter how good I am with computers, it's hard to hide something that big," he muttered.

I looked at Larry for a long moment as he drove down the road. "Some things paint on the brain better than we would like," I stated. "And I liked that truck,"

"What does that mean?" he asked, eyeing me nervously.

"Not a clue, man—just—I'm sorry for the toll this has taken on you. I couldn't do this without your help," I replied.

He blinked a few times. "Dude, did that dip in the lake mess with you that much? Because I am fairly sure that's the first time you've ever said thank you or I'm sorry," he replied.

I sighed heavily. "Larry, there's no escaping this life for me. This is what I will do. The curse of being a junkie—you can't stop once you start. Not really, that road you can never seem to leave. That's okay, though; that's what makes me, me—all the folds up in my crystal kingdom of a skull. I can't change that. But man, don't choose my colors if they don't suit you. I guess what I am trying to say, Larry, is I am sorry I dragged you into this," I whispered. Thinking about how likely Larry, Gen, Rosemary, that crazy disco girl, all of them would be affected by my actions today.

He shrugged again, "I don't know about all those colors; we don't choose our colors, Billy Dan. They pick us. That's who we are, and what we do with that is what matters. You didn't drag me into this, Billy Dan. I could have just walked away. Hell, should have walked away—at least before we took the big Bertha," he said.

I snorted, "Yeah, that's the parts we can't choose, I guess. The parts that could be good or bad,".

"Nah, man. We pick what we will do with our demons. That is that. My daddy, growing up, was a drinker. He liked to beat up on both my mother and me pretty well on his long nights. I got good at computers because my mother worked three jobs between the old man passing out on the couch. One was at the old hardware shop. I had nothing better to do in those backrooms with all the old tech guys than to watch and learn. I learned a lot from those guys. I probably could have done it for a big company, making big fancy bucks by smoking donuts and drinking whiskey all day. You know what, though? Even though I loved every minute of learning how to make a computer and how to fix things—I never did anything useful with it. So, yeah, my colors were working on computers. What I choose to do with it, man, that's all that matters. We pick our bullshit. We just hide behind the fact that we all love shit," he stated.

I considered his words for a long time before popping open his glove compartment. "Need something, Billy Dan?" he asked.

"Yeah, I need you to drive by my place after dropping me off. Pick up what I am writing down," I gestured towards the paper as Larry nodded and fished out a chewed cap ballpoint pen. He shrugged, "I get nervous. Some people pick their fingers, Billy Dan."

"Fair enough," I replied, writing down a quick list.

I handed the paper to Larry as we neared the club. "This is an insane amount of stuff; what is all this?" he asked incredulously.

"Don't worry about all that now, just get it," I said.

He nodded, coming to a park.

"Kill the lights before we park," I instructed.

"Wait down the block from the club. I don't know how recognizable this truck is—don't trust that we are off any radars just yet. Either way, if I am not back at this spot in one hour—take whatever you can get to Gen," I said.

"We don't have anything," he said.

"Probably not, but I promise if someone starts looking into all of this, they will find out soon enough. Anyone willing to toss a garbage man into the river, I promise, has a lot to hide," I stated.

He nodded again, "Sounds good, Billy Dan. Good luck,".

I nodded this time. "Going to use the colors on my brain, Larry,"

Chapter 70

I approached a bit slower this time, mainly because my chest was still stinging from the dip in the water. I was very thankful that South Carolina, outside of the mountains, tended to be warm. However, if I were deeper into the state, on the coast side, it wouldn't be a little cold; I would have to worry. I made my way down the block, and the club was surprisingly empty out front. Save for a few desperate types smoking and bragging about how the stripper scammed them.

"Desperation and cigarettes. Not the type that would do drugs like I had found earlier," I mumbled, stuffing my hands into my pocket. I scanned the club's side, the glowing lights burning their images into my eyes. They weren't trying to hide lighting up the whole area with such confidence.

"That's the thing, though—people like this—they aren't trying to hide. Monsters in plain sight," I grumbled, squeezing the pistol. I kept my head down and made myself look smaller as I walked past the local police, two sitting directly across from the club. The ease at which the two officers talked told me they were most likely there for the club. Not a care in the world.

That's two that I need to avoid. But not the goons that I needed to find. Larry had easily tracked down the club on the other side of town. Again, I never have noticed it before. He then went through video footage—until we found the three that had attacked me. The giant thug had given enough information without realizing it. They all seemed to meet people from Melanie's Church. I wasn't convinced they were a part of the Church; they were probably more like contractors. The first group seemed like professionals. I thought about the big thug, his hand tattoo, and a large black sun. There are not a lot of those types in this small town. Luckily, the club kept outstanding records of the people coming and going in the place.

"Ethan, six-five, and two-hundred and thirty pounds—two priors in the assault. Small-time drug connections are on someone's payroll. Old Ethan can barely read his name. Someone big was paying his way—I needed to find whom," I whispered.

"Also, to quit talking to myself—too late to change now," I muttered, coming to the backside of the club. No matter what building you're trying to get into, there will almost always be a complete lack of concern for the back door. Sure enough, the back alley was empty. Save for the plates of a black Volvo, license plates reading, "cat 467".

"Good thing for me; muscle never has to be smart," I realized my grip on my gun. I was pulling the small lock-picking set from my other pocket. I bent down, taking the tools out of the kit. Slowly I worked the small lock on the knob, jiggling the tools in the keyhole. Now that I thought about it, this was the first actual door I tried to pick. The rest had been on the lock the kit came with. Thanks, internet, for such great free things.

Just like the lock, a few attempts and shaky hands later—it clicked open. I sucked in a breath and unlocked the door, pushing it open. I walked into the back of a storage area. It was well-lit, with tables piled high with storage boxes. Big Ethan and a more petite man were at the end of the room. I calmly looked around and picked up a fire extinguisher near the door. Glancing at the side, I pulled the pin and walked behind Ethan. I smacked him hard with it in the back of the leg.

The other man turned quickly as I sprayed him in the face with a torrent of foam. I was pushing him over with a swift kick. Ethan was getting back up, so I gave him a dose of the spray. He powered through it, hands waving around until I hit him with the butt end of the fire extinguisher. He collapsed like a ton of bricks.

"I hit him too hard," I swore, turning back to the other man who was gasping for air on the ground after a cheap shot to the stomach. I kicked him again on his side as he turned over, groaning.

I placed the now empty extinguisher on the ground. He was pulling the man up by his collar. "How are you alive?" he gasped.

"Listen here, chicken shit, if you're going to kill a man—pro tip wait a few minutes before driving back. Because if that man gets free—they're bringing the Holy pain with them when they come back," I snarled, reaching up to the workbench near me, taking hold of the nearest thing I could find—a long call hammer. This needed to be quick; it was going to be messy. I would do it, though, a small voice screamed—I no longer cared. I would find Jacob.

Chapter 71

I continued wiping my hands in Larry's truck's front seat. He hadn't said anything about my appearance. I just asked for something to wipe my face and hands off with. The gore and blood were caked on, mixing into my cuts and bruises. Somehow, that wasn't the worst part of the last few hours. The men's screams still rang inside my head. Shattering any clarity as I tried to piece together what had happened upon leaving the club. Big Ethan was most likely going to have brain damage from the hit to his massive skull with the extinguisher.

The other guy was most likely already dead. The pain of harming them was settling in as we drove in a profound silence. Wipe all the blood off that I could because before the night was over—there was going to be more. I was going to Hell for this, or maybe not. At the moment, no matter what rationale I tried to form, I had most likely just killed two men. Another one earlier tonight—that was three people I had killed. This morning, I woke up at my girlfriend's house, ready to take a test and go to work.

Was it worth it? I was already going to jail for what had transpired that day. Would it help me find Jacob? Yeah, the man had given me a lot once I drove a knife into his knee. Both he, Ethan, and that woman were the drug mules. I was right; they were contractor types for the Church. They were simply in the right place at the wrong time. The pickup spot was the hardware store that night. And a series of shorts were happening. They suspected someone was stealing their products, so a constant venue change was in order. What the moron had told me was a lot more than I think he even realized during the shootout. Someone had hit the crew at the store. When I showed up, the three were fixing to start burning the evidence. The first group wasn't the only ones who came by the station. All they found was a whole lot of bullets—and a "moon" imprinted into the side of someone's cheek from what could only be a fist of a gorilla. That narrowed the list to precisely one—a particular thug at a specific church.

I tightened my hands around the dirty shirt, the blood now leaking from the shirt. If those three worked for the Mayor, what was the church's involvement? The Mayor seemed like the wild card, his men in this exchange. That left a lot of questions, and I was getting madder.

I was tired, felt sick to my stomach, and cringed every time I saw my face in the mirrors. Who was I now? A man that kills, that tortures others... This was all for Jacob.

Chapter 72

We headed down the long highway to my place to meet Rosemary. Larry, for his part, hadn't spoken a single word. I respected the silence between us. Well, that was probably more out of fear—I caught more than a few glances and nervous twitches of his fingers on the steering wheel.

Outside on one of the streets was a man about my age in a wheelchair. The low light from the street lamp illuminated his vacant face, a focus on pain written across his face. A language that all the heartbroken have—one of nothingness. He held a sign with the message, "Just tryna get $ 4 some crack, God bless!! N.E.thing HELPS". I recoiled from him this time as we parked at the light. A man who held nothing met mine, the face of a killer. The man didn't turn—I did, though. We drove on, I cried into my hands.

Chapter 73

I sighed, "if you want to say something, Larry—now is the time to do that," I stated. Exasperated and in desperate need of a shower. It wasn't going to be that kind of night. We had been driving for twenty minutes in silence—the night melting away like wax in a candle.

"It's nothing like that, Billy Dan. I understand; I can't talk you out of this, but why? Why go to these lengths? Does he mean that much to you?" he asked quietly.

I sucked in some air. Without browbeating or hammering the point, my energy was long gone. "A friend of mine once told me to keep my word, no matter what it was or what happens. You have to keep your word. I'm out of my depth here, man. But Jacob, he's a good kid. A little on the weird side, however—who isn't when they're a kid? How many times did I find him—just to bring him home again to his mother? I gave her a promise, my word" I stated.

Larry smirked at that, "The kid always wanted toast for some reason,"

I nodded, continuing, "That he does. More importantly—you've seen the signs. You've heard the news reports," I said, keeping the contempt out of my voice. "Someone is taking these kids. Someone is doing it for some reason. I don't give a hoot about weird drugs and corrupt politicians. Water is wet—politicians are full of crap. I will not sit by and watch Jacob become another kid on a poster. I won't allow that; I have to keep my word. No matter how big this is, I have to save him," I said firmly, hoping that would end the conversation.

This time, Larry nodded his head slowly, "Yeah, I hear you there—Billy

Dan. I will help you with this however that I can. Just, I think you need to see something first before we meet Rosemary. Trust me, I think you will need it," he said slyly.

"What? Honestly, can't we go back to my house? I was hoping for a nap before Rosemary showed up, but yeah, sure—I was never very good at sleep. All you have to do is close your eyes. Count to ten sheepy sheep. Easy enough—next, I will fly my way to Mars.

"Nah, you need this, Billy Dan," Larry said, whipping a U-turn and heading in the opposite direction of my house.

After several turns and a few more minutes, we pulled up to a crowd of people. Instantly, I felt uncomfortable—this wasn't a good idea, whatever Larry had planned. I started to say something when he cut me off. "See all these people, Billy Dan? Look closely at them," he stated.

I turned to the crowd, taking them all in; it had to be around a hundred-plus people. All somber, not defeated, though. Some had signs of children. Many wore shirts depicting missing kids. Looking at the shirts closely, I could see the same roundness of the face of one parent, a tussle of black hair, and a flat nose of the apparent father standing next to the woman with a kid on her shirt—the same features. She held back tears, each sliding down to the ground below—soaking up quickly, like a great maw that only knew hunger. I curled in my knuckles so hard that I tore the skin off one of them.

In the center of the crowd was an older man whose face I had seen plenty of times on my routes. Mr. Johnson was a dark-skinned man whose hair had gone almost entirely white save for a few lingering strands of black. He had thick square glasses and a tight jacket but a commanding voice.

He seemed small from a distance, but as he shouted into the microphone, the tears fell deeply from people in the crowd, and people lit candles and continued to chant. Their voices carried, their tears fell, and their children never came home.

Chapter 74

We arrived at my house fifteen minutes later to find Rosemary leaning against the stairwell leading to the side of the house. She held a water bottle out to both of us, shooting Larry a long look that he just shrugged his shoulders to in response as we walked past her into the house. Inside set the pink-haired yuppie who barely glanced my way. She slowly stirred something into her tea, the thick red water smelling far too strong to be just tea.

I sighed, "Do you have to use my favorite cup on whatever you're doing?" I gestured to her as she sat at my table, still stirring. "I don't know, do you have to be such a drooling child?" she replied.

"Don't flatter yourself, sweetheart. It doesn't matter how cute you are with pink and bells in your hair. Personality is all I care about," I replied, walking past her to the other room.

I heard her call over her shoulder, "Well, I have one to die for, sourpuss," I flicked her off, heading into my bathroom. "I left the keys on the counter," Rose called as I nodded, closing the door.

I flicked the lights on and held the sink. Lurching forward, I vomited. I kept going until I was dry heaving, my nostrils burning, my hands gripping the sides of the sink—the edges cutting into my hands. I held on tighter. I was covered in sweat, dirt, blood, and the look of a man who needed a hundred years of sleep. My eyes sunken deep. My busted lip and nose dripping what could have been my blood or anyone else's tonight.

The faces of the men I had killed flashed before my eyes. I threw up again. "Oh, God, I'm so sorry, I'm so sorry..." I whispered, fighting back tears. I looked myself in the face, growled, and smacked my head against the mirror. The glass cracked; I smashed it again. More cracks appeared; pieces fell into the sink. My blood mixed, making the glass glow like rubies. Banging came from the door, and I continued with one last smack before all the glass fell into the sink.

"Are you okay, Billy Dan?" asked Rose from the other side.

I grunted. What I could see in the shards of glass was a long gash on my forward. A monster is now on the surface, and the man is somewhere long gone. I took a deep breath, picked up a towel, wiping my face.

"Can't wipe away blood," a voice stated.

I continued wiping my face—afraid of the monster I would see.

"Sure, it doesn't hurt to try," I mumbled, looking up. It was just me in the dim light. My mirror shattered. A long pool of blood led to my drain, now a mixture of glass—colored crimson-like rubies.

"You're a killer," the voice whispered again.

I couldn't face the mirror again. The flashes of the homeless man on the side of the road crossed my mind again. Jacob is eating toast inside a dumpster. A man screaming in pain as I asked questions. My soul broke as I herded the unknown—a beast that couldn't be tamped. What was I becoming?

"A killer," repeated the voice.

I pressed the towel against my forehead, flicking the lights off as I turned the handle.

Chapter 75

Several curse words later and a long session with balloon weirdo, I had twelve new stitches in my head. Disco had been a doctor who worked with Rose once upon a time. I took that at face value—Rose had a way of finding people with odd skills.

The scar was going to be ugly. I didn't care; the pain had done the trick. I knew what would need to be done to find Jacob now. I needed to be a monster. Not a man. A man can be defeated or broken. But a monster with horns and fangs. Claws as dark as midnight and teeth as sharp as razor blades. That couldn't be stopped. That was a force of nature.

Rosemary and Larry exchanged hurried glances the whole time—their faces bordering on sheer terror. I waved them off, "It's just a scratch; I needed to clear my head, get my head in the game," I said calmly, sitting up once Balloon Girl was done.

"Sure would hate to see you out of the game," she jabbed.

"Sure, I would like you to shut up," I replied.

Rosemary cleared her throat, "Next time you need a pep talk, Billy Dan— just come find me. I can smack you myself. Mirrors aren't cheap, you know," she stated.

I nodded, "Noted—I hear you,"

Larry said, "Yeah, I'm not sure how to respond to any of this anymore. However, I found what you asked Billy Dan. And honestly, I have to say this—you're in no shape to take this on. That Church is built like a maze. Not only that, I counted close to sixty people inside that place tonight. You would be walking into a slaughterhouse," Larry pleaded.

"Well, I will need at least sixty bullets then, I guess," I said to Rosemary. She shook her head and scowled. I waved her off before she started. "I made a promise, Rosemary," I stated flatly. Her face relaxed instantly, and she said no more, only nodding as if we had an invisible conversation.

"Heck of a promise," snorted Balloon Girl. I ignored her, standing up too quickly from the chair she had me sit on while stitching my head. She pulled the gloves from her hands and dropped the leftover medical equipment into a trash can. Taking a small kit she had pulled it all from. Very methodically, she put the rest of her supplies into a bag at her feet. She was not concealing the small pistol tucked within reach of her hands.

For someone so flamboyant in her appearance, Balloon Girl had more layers than anyone I had ever met. I wasn't sure what could make someone that cold—I didn't want to know what that was. I knew her sarcasm was masking pain—just like my own. That made me relax enough around her. Pain was how I met Rose; it must have been similar to mine. I was thankful that she seemed to have her medical knowledge down to an uncomfortable level of skills. At the moment, she seemed to want to help us. That was good enough for me as she lit a cigarette with a small lighter. I shook my head and pulled it from her mouth, dashing it into my kitchen sink.

She lit another one, and as I reached for it—her free hand pulled out the pistol from her purse. Exasperated, I threw my hands in the air and walked to the archway that led to the rest of my house. "Thanks for healing me up, disco," I stated.

"You're welcome," she said flatly.

She didn't expect that kind of response, but the night had already been filled with strangeness. I needed coffee, a shower, and a long sleep. I only had time for one, I thought as I made my way to the coffee machine. I started making a cup; I could feel the other's gazes on me the whole time.

When I was finished, I turned around, "Alright—so I will need help with this," I stated. Larry blew out his lips and rubbed the sleep from his eyes. He looked probably worse than me, his eyes sunken into his head from lack of sleep, stress, and just general fear.

"Everything leads to the church. The mules, the finders, the dealers, and the other groups. It all comes back to Melanie's Church. That means there's a good chance that Jacob is there," I stated.

"Rosemary, you've done more than enough already. I know you have your responsibilities. Larry, you've also gone far enough. I can't ask for anything else from you two," I trailed, turning to Balloon Girl. "Do they pay elves, or do you work for candy?" I asked.

She flicked me off and just kept smoking her cigarette, eyeing me with a fierce glare.

I sighed, "None of you have to do this—but I can't alone. This is bigger than me. My word or not, I can't keep it without help. So, I am sorry from the bottom of my heart for asking—I have to, though. So, will you guys help me? If not, I will understand, and you will never hear a word from me about it again,". I said quietly.

I let that hang in the air as I turned around and started making coffee. My heartbeat thumped so hard into my chest that I wondered if the cup would break from the force slamming from within my body. Luckily, Larry cleared his throat first to break the silence.

"I figured you already knew I'm here with you, Billy Dan. I'm boned if I help you or not. I have your back on this one, man," he said, clearing his throat again. I turned and nodded at him. Rosemary just shrugged and said, "Your word is your word," she stated.

"Thank you," I said.

Disco regarded me for a long moment before finishing her cigarette. "My rates are very reasonable," she said flatly. I nodded, mumbling, "Good enough for me."

I drummed the counter for a moment before returning, ultimately failing to face the others. "Okay, so does anyone know how we should do this?" I asked the group as the smoke hung in the air, dancing towards the ceiling like there was a great beat high above us, playing a song that only the elements themselves could hear. A song that made smoke dance. I hoped that it was a great beat, indeed, one that would be playing for us. Playing for Jacob.

Chapter 76

The big dump truck flew down the empty streets; it was a small town, and the Church was on the south end. We were getting close, the long country roads turning into more residential streets as we got closer. However, it occurred to me that in a town like this in the south, there were always loads of churches. About the only thing you know was as consistent as water—in the south, there would always be a church when you needed one. Only this neighborhood strangle had none, the last one we passed a few moments back. It was as if the town was warning all the places of worship that there would only be darkness here—come no closer. I shuddered at that. I was about to go into a place where even the other places of worship dared not come closer. Where wicked things lay, the light of the world gone, and the walls of the dammed concealed demons reside.

I shook my head, clearing the thoughts away as Larry drove, nervously thumbing the wheel of the dump truck. I sighed, looking at him as I finished putting the strap on the shotgun Rosemary had given me.

"You know, Larry, in a couple of hours, it would be about that time we would be getting up for work anyway. This could be like just a normal day," I stated.

He snorted, "Yeah, in some ways, I suppose. Sending us out in the night to take out the trash," he replied. I grinned at that. That's what I was, a garbage man. I was here to take out the trash.

Chapter 77

By the time we arrived, my gusto was much more tempered. I was scared; I did not doubt that to my core. I wasn't going to succumb to it. I knew what needed to be done. Only, as the dark shadows of the church loomed over our parked spot on the nearest hill, looking at its flat plans, I had no idea what lurked behind its many curves. Pillars stuck out of the ground, holding huge chunks of metal and stone. Twisted, up, and at far too perfect of placements to be anything less than a modern eye sore.

Though the shadows it cast in the moonlight were daunting, the unlit windows were even more so. Only a few lights I could make out were turned on inside the church. Its massive roof seemed like a giant mouth that only allowed lights to shine so people could be lured into its gaping maw.

I swallowed at that. I was about to enter into that mouth. Maybe I would never come out again, I thought as Larry parked in the area we had decided would be least likely to draw attention. The problem with the dump truck was that Melanie had to know it was us at that hour. However, we were banking on the fact that whatever was going on in that church, they were wrapping up their actions quickly. What little I had learned from that man was that whoever stole their product was being made inside the church.

I had to think that they weren't worried about little old me. However, why Melanie had asked me to find Jacob also bothered me in the back of my mind. I wouldn't need to find out why Jacob would be here. It was a long shot at the most, and that thought gave me more concern than going into that dark church. However, the longer I sat on the outskirts of the parking lot, the harder that was starting to feel.

Larry turned in the seat next to me, adjusting his seatbelt in the dark. I could see him sweating from the light of the dashboard. Larry had already been a massive help with this; from what he could tell from scanning the local camera system outside the church, he estimated around sixty people were inside the church. Including Melanie—or at least we thought from the camera that had picked her up. He tried hacking into the building but found it locked down tight. Loads of closed circuits and networks. In fact, most of the prepared time for this mission was spent trying to find the one line that would cut the power to the church if we needed to do so.

That brought Rosemary, who was making her way up the power line pole with her rifle and a device Disco had given her that could short anything electronic once powered in. Which was something, at least, a point in our favor. We needed all the help that we could get. Indeed, in a world gone this mad—we needed help. That was gripping me with fear as I tested the walkie. I pressed the button that opened the channel for everyone to hear, "Can everyone hear me?" I stated.

"I hear ya," chimed Rosemary, the sound of rushing wind coming through with static on her end. The power line pole she was on overlooked the church by a few hundred yards. I just hoped that her cop father had taught her how to use that rifle to astonishing levels for this to succeed.

"All good," said Larry next to me, his voice coming in clear through the earpiece. I waited for Disco to say something. After a moment, I called out, "Disco". I heard nothing but a slap from the back cab of the dumpster.

"Good enough," I stated.

"I'm not good enough; I'm great enough," she said cheerily. I smiled at that, un-pressing the earpiece. "You two are killing me," mumbled Larry. I smirked at him, "Honestly, she should be thankful this truck has never been on the road. I would not be sitting back there if I were her, otherwise," I stated.

He nodded slowly. "Yeah, no doubt about that. I just hope we don't have to use her," he said.

"Honestly, Larry—if it gets that bad, we need her. We will be thankful that we had her. As crazy as her hair is, I haven't paid her yet. And when crap gets real, Larry—someone with killer eyes is who you want on your side," I stated matter-of-factly. He considered that for a long moment, only sighing.

"Well, ready whenever you're ready to go, man," he said quietly, and the situation became very real at that moment. I looked at the dash clock, the glowing orange letters stating that it was half past midnight. Where had all the time today gone? I wanted nothing more than this to be another morning of picking up the city's trash. I needed something to see through this, so I silently prayed and closed my eyes, "When darkness rises—this is why we do what we do. When the right thing needs to be done. Always and forever—amen," I stated, opening my eyes and sliding out of the truck.

I hooked the shotgun strap around my shoulders and racked the chamber back. I heard the comforting slide move forward while I pushed another into the tube. I had thirty shotgun shells. And three magazines of the 9mm. That would just have to do, I thought. Any more ammo and I would be out of my damn mind if I felt I needed to fire that many rounds and walk out of anywhere.

"What were all those hours at the range for Billy-boy?" I mumbled as Larry gave me a look. "It's my process, man,"

He nodded at that, "I usually just splash water in my face, but hey, do you, man," he stated. I laughed a nervous laugh at that. "Thank you, Larry," I said, closing the truck door as I heard him whisper, "Be careful."

Chapter 78

I jogged briskly towards the side parking lot of the church. It was filled with cars that covered me, but I was becoming way too aware that I was running around a church with a shotgun. This would be a big one to explain to someone someday—but hopefully, it will be all worth it.

It would be if I found Jacob, I thought, as the window leading to the basement came into view. Strangely enough, it was one of the only ones in this building. The whole thing seemed like a sprawling fortress with the way it expanded in all directions with only two discernible entries. I was sure that was a fire hazard. That gave me a rough feeling in the pit of my stomach.

I was just passing a small car, its windows tinted, when I heard the sound of screeching tires. I looked up to see two vans coming from the opposite side of the church jetting to the entranceway with the blinding speed of a bull rushing a matador. I gulped at that and doubled my pace to the window.

I replaced my damaged hand appendage once I had returned to my place. Disco had helped the best she could. Warning: if I rubbed any more skin off, there would be a good chance of an infection coming into my leg at the rate I was going. That was a given after spending an extended period in the depths of a dirty lake. Still, though, I just hoped this old leg would hold out. My spare hand part, though, was the good one. I had been saving it for a long time. Its metal fingers were tight, and it moved with the flexing of my wrist and other remaining fingers. The cold slide of metal on metal came from my fist as I moved. I thought there was no stealth right now as I kept my eyes on the window. Gunfire erupted, causing the still night to suddenly take on all sorts of forms. The shadows became alive, the building seeming like a tomb as the world exploded around me.

Looking around seemed like a bad idea, as I heard glass shattering, magazines being dropped, and fresh ones being loaded.

My walkie-talkies came to life; I could just make out Larry yelling if I was all right. I steadied my voice as much as possible before briefly pressing the button and simply stating, "Yes." As the window came into view. I was supposed to hit the glass with a glass hammer. Breaking it into a clean piece, making it easier to move through. But as I thought about reaching for a hammer, I heard the loud boom of Rosemary's .308. The crack overshadows the small arms fire.

I doubted I had time to get the hammer. Whoever it was, I wasn't sure if they were shooting at me—or at the church, just that it was two black vans. I aimed the shotgun, taking the longest of moments to shoot the window out before resuming my run. Ten yards, more bullets. Five feet—and I was sliding into a lit hallway in the basement of a building that I prayed wouldn't be my resting place.

Chapter 79

Sliding face first is only a good idea during baseball. Going through a window at the bottom of a creepy building—face first—was probably the dumbest idea I had today. I groaned, picking myself up, and the shards of glass that had scrapped my cheeks and a piece stuck in my ear. I wiped the glass off from me carefully as I sighed.

Even with the gunshots, that was louder than I should have gone through with. I grimaced, mumbling, "Yeah, the day has just started, bud." I was in a hallway, and I realized the situation as I came to understand it. I was in a long hallway; closed doors littered the hallway on each side, stretching to a sharp turn at the end.

Larry had shown me what he thought was the rough blueprint of the building. Though that was utterly useless, we had decided. There were multiple layouts and years of several contract purchases. The people running this ship wanted whatever was here to stay hidden. I hoped that whatever it was would be enough to get the police here. Get enough evidence and leave, I thought.

Only, the shooting outside made this whole thing seem even dumber than it had before I had entered a building that was currently being shot up. "Stick to what you can control; go from there, Billy Dan," I whispered. "Okay," I mumbled.

"Where do I start?" I looked around me and started on the first door. The knob was locked. I tried the one adjacent. The same thing; the simple round knobs stayed firm. The one on the exact opposite side did as well. The whole time I checked the doors, more gunfire poured out. I had to be quick;

whoever was shooting had inadvertently bought me some time. May have even made this possible. I tried another door. It remained closed.

Chapter:

Halfway through the next hallway—I realized I was getting nowhere fast. The shooting outside became louder each moment. I figured I had maybe been inside five minutes at the most. Five minutes in a gunfight was a lifetime. Police would be swarming this area soon. That made the time frame even shorter.

"What's worse is not one door has been unlocked," I mumbled again as another remained closed. I made my third turn down another hallway before another thought wormed its way through the ever-increasing panic that was building in my mind.

How many turns had I already made? Each hallway looked the same, lights adorning the sides of every door. Solid red-brown frames with a deep chestnut color for the doors. Simple knobs with more of that symbol. Blood red carpet, though. That was making the whole experience even more off-putting. "Yeah, that is the end of the discussion. Only villains and gingers have this much red," I stated, trying another door.

"Focus and stop making jokes, Billy Dan. This is serious," I stated, closing my eyes briefly. I turned to another hallway. How many turns have I made? Was I still at the bottom of the church? Where was everybody? Larry estimated that around sixty people were located in this building. Maybe all the shooting outside had caused them to panic.

Though, that made little sense to me—wouldn't they all have gone to the basement? Perhaps I had already found a bunch of them, and they were just behind one of the many locked doors. Another turn and the thought slowly creeping into the deepest parts of my skull was becoming more apparent. I was lost. Turn after turn, hallway after hallway.

I hadn't realized it, but I had picked up the pace to a near jog at some point. My breathing was becoming quick and fast. "Where was everybody?" I asked no one, but that forced me to stop long enough to start forming a plan. "Stay focused, form a plan one piece at a time," I stated. In a group meeting with Rosemary once, a person in the circle indicated that the mind was easy. It liked to take the path of least resistance. You could be homeless and have only just a few bites to take the edge off—some rainwater in a cup. As far as your head was concerned, that was technically good enough. The other thoughts pushed me in a negative direction.

The thoughts that we couldn't master the storm around us. The sea is too strong, and the waves are too massive for any man. To me, though, that never made any sense. At the end of the day, it was out of our hands. So, I wasn't going to be afraid now. All I had to do was force my mind to view the problem as essential. I was equipped with the bare essentials at all times that I would ever need. I had what I needed; I had the ferocity.

I was lost, yes—there were still options, though. I thought as I pressed my earpiece. "Larry, are you there?" I asked, feeling silly standing in an empty hallway talking to someone over a device—though for a split second, concern filled me again with the thought that maybe the reception would be too bad or worse. Before I could launch into egocentric dread, Larry chimed in.

"Billy Dan! Are you alright? Rosemary lost sight of you. Things are nuts up here. You need to hurry it up and get out," he shouted, the line cracking up. I took that in for a moment. They had been talking—I hadn't heard a thing. Meant communications weren't the best—I would just have to make do. However, at what point do the waves get too big? When you can't talk your way out of them? A small thought spoke into the darkest corners of my mind.

"Yeah, I'm fine—listen—I don't know where to go. Haven't seen a single person since coming in here. I need some help," I stated.

I waited a bit, and Larry replied, "There's not much we can do here. Move quick, Billy Dan, whoever these shooters are, they're moving quick—and they mean business. They're breaching the church doors now," Larry shouted as I could hear gunshots firing in the background. Down here, I realized I wasn't hearing the firing anymore. I wasn't hearing anything beyond the static coming from the walkies.

Rosemary had said that the walkies were police-issue. Capable of working over a mile with no sight line. Even thick steel and concrete shouldn't have been able to block it. I tried to call Larry again, but only static once more. So, this place was built to cancel sound and communication. That gave me a feeling of pure despair at the bottom of my stomach. It also gave me an idea, though—if the shooting Larry mentioned was getting intense, I needed to start finding evidence now. I looked at the nearest door. Aimed my foot a few inches from the knob and planted my good leg with full force. The lock gave way, and the door flung open.

I rushed in with the shotgun, sweeping left and right. The room was empty save a collection of folding chairs. I sighed heavily and went to the next door. This was going to take a while, there were a lot of doors.

Chapter 80

I was in a dark room, the only light dull from the hallway as I entered an expansive room with other doors. I reached the wall until I found a light switch and immediately regretted my decision. Two things were answered once the light was turned on. Number one was the baby from the dumpster that Jacob had found—well, the men chasing him were most likely at the church, seeing how the baby was on a golden altar. The altar is adorned with gibberish symbols and various other cult icons. The baby was covered in a plastic bag and left like garbage.

Two, as I closed the door just as quickly—leaving the room, I vomited into the hallway floor. These people were monsters. I was losing my grip with every moment like a broken clock whose hands kept trying to turn, even while the time was an afterthought. Because what was time anymore? Time was meaningless when we harmed our children. There was no future if these were the things that happened.

I wiped my mouth and carried on despite it. I was sorry, baby; I don't know what happened or how you ended up in such a place. I will come back for you. But first, I had to keep going—because time may have been broken for us, but it was always a matter of time before the light overtook the dark—and it always starts with light shining on the bad. Maybe then, time would work again. Despite all the gloom, the fire will go on.

Chapter 81

I was drenched in sweat when I got to the tenth door. The doors were taking more than one kick now. I also had started to move to different hallways. Frantically moving and kicking quickly. The door didn't give on the kick, and I hit the door knob. I groaned in pain and stopped for a moment. "Catch your breath—dig deep and kick where you're supposed to kick," I muttered and kicked into the door a few inches away from the knob. The door flew open, and I charged into another empty room. This one was different, though. At the center was a table with a massive pile of clothes. That took me a moment to take in, catching my breath by bending over my knees.

Small clothes and shoes no bigger than some of my fingers, only a handful the size of my hand. Shirts that were only meant for one size—pants that couldn't be mistaken for anything else. A heavy rock fell into the pit of my stomach. I knew what this was; I knew what it could only mean. The children's clothes are in a neat stack, folded nicely as if on display at a store. Rage boiled up, pushing that heavy stone slowly up from deep inside my stomach.

There were so many clothes, all different sizes. None that were close to even teenager-sized. I realized an endless amount, almost reaching the top of the ceiling in some stacks. That made me stop and gasp, my anger deflating as it dawned on me the sheer magnitude of children it would take to create that high of a stack.

I leaned over and vomited until my breath came in ragged waves. This was disgusting; that wasn't even a word vile enough to describe what had happened in this building. I stood up, wiping my mouth. "Pull yourself together, Billy Dan. This isn't proof of anything, and you aren't here to solve the mystery of whatever or whoever these belonged to," I muttered, pointing lamely to the stacks of clothes. "It could just be a donation," I whispered, hoping this place had some moral and logical reason for having all these clothes. I had a sinking feeling that wouldn't be the case. That was an outright lie, and I knew it. I just couldn't vomit anymore.

How many pictures of children had I seen around town? How many times had I seen the round and innocent faces staring at me, plastered with smiles—baby teeth in most and some with big pearly whites? How often had I walked past the missing signs and hurried on my day? Yeah, it was tragic, but was it my problem? What could I do to help find those kids—when it was so many? So many—so many that couldn't possibly all be from our small town. That would indicate that nearly every kid in the surrounding cities and counties needs to fill this up. No, not even a government this corrupt could hide this—could they? My head spun, and I held my hands on the wall to steady myself.

These people were monsters—they were the deepest creatures that lurk in the shadows of civilization. Working with their horns and fangs, biting and clawing at the corners of our world slash by bite.

What was the purpose of this nonsense? Of the worst things that humanity could offer? What was the reason? I shook my head slowly and stared at the red-carpeted floor beneath me. I couldn't assume the worst for the children. I couldn't assume the worst for Jacob. I needed to stay focused. Giving up now wouldn't solve any issue. I slowly turned away from the piles of clothes before my resolve cracked. I suddenly felt very old. I am very old and want to close my eyes for a long time. I readied my shotgun and went to the brown door behind me. My resolve built as I casually opened the door to see three roped figures in red. One of them is the better part of some kind of cross between an ape and a ginger.

My mind barely had time to register the danger, let alone react, as his meaty fist stroked me in the face. I rocketed back into the room, hitting the clothes table. The tiny shoes fell on top of me as I blacked out, a demon of a man growling—moving closer.

Chapter 82

The white mask shifted as if it were a skin, concealing her features behind an inhuman smile. I could tell it was Melanie from the shape, but as she spoke, it came out robotic. I was tied down in a chair. Just her face directly in front of me. A glowing set of screens showing images of war, sex, and drugs danced behind her. She spoke, "Need a God—no problem, we have a pill for that. Feeling down like there are demons all around—look no more, for we have only smiles,". The woman shifted in her vibrant-colored suit. Her face was a never-ending museum of emotions, flexing as if they were trying desperately to become real—like they weren't sure what they were supposed to be. She turned to me, her black hole of eyes glittering as if full of stars trying to escape their demise.

I clenched, every fiber of my being seeking to pull away—any distance, even if it was just inches. She spun around me, my wrists constrained. The clamps on my eyes tightened. I was unable to blink—I couldn't swallow— hooks digging into my gums. The woman clasped her hands on mine softly as if I were her tender lover. There was no love, only choking of my blood. She went on, his voice crackling like an electric eel, "Need love, well we have that too, any way you like. It doesn't matter—what's love when you can have it all?" she tilted her head back and let loose a wild laugh. I screamed along— the hooks biting deeper into my gums. The metal taste of blood seemed to be the only real thing in this twisted nightmare. "Need Hell, well," she pushed before smiling an endless void, "well, we are already here."

She was nearly straddling me after her statements. I chewed the hooks and spit them out at her. One staying lodged, pulling deeper into my gums.

"Have something to say?" she purred. "Yeah, lady—when I get out of here, I will send you to the real one," I snarled.

This time, she laughed before backhanding me. The stuck hook went through my gums and cheeks. I could feel the cold air on the wound and knew it had gone through my mouth.

I spat at her and stayed defiant. She reared to slap again when an urgent knock came from the door obscured behind her. She flung herself off, and I breathed a sigh of relief. Wincing from the pain. I couldn't make out the conversation; Melanie hurriedly left the room as a big man entered the room.

He smiled at me before punching me again—I was going to have brain damage at this rate.

Chapter 83

Cold water shocked me awake as I came to—blinking in the light as I entered the room I was hanging in. My hands were tied above me; what I could tell with my fingers as I was bound with bungee cords—crud, but probably all they had on hand. Even though the tightness of the cords was already cutting deep into my wrist, I knew the hold was weak at best. Tying something so elastic and tight is easier to escape than people think. Mainly when, thankfully, like continuously—no one ever checks if a half-handed individual might have something up his sleeves—especially if that half-hand had recently undergone a few changes—particularly sharp ones.

Next, I could tell my earbud was still securely in my ear. It was starting to get that dull, heavy feeling that buds get after spending too much time in your ear. Why they haven't even removed that blew my mind. It must have been quick after Melanie and her fun factory freak show. At the thought, my mouth stunk, the hook still in my cheek as I felt with my tongue. This all meant I had time; I had only one chance to do what needed to be done, I thought as a man with a distracting gap in his teeth and a yellowed smile as bright as his hair lowered the bucket he had just dosed me with.

His smile and hands told me in a second what I needed to know; he was a heavy smoker, out of shape, and too old to be in this line of work. He would be easy once this started—the ginger ape grinned as he flicked his thumb lightly on what could only be a knife designed by an infant or a madman. Probably both. But a tale of signs of arrogance next to him. My shotgun and pistol rested comfortably like a table magazine on a coffee table. From what I could see on the gun, a round was still in the chamber. I averted my eyes before they saw what I was looking at, trying to appear as if I wasn't focusing on any one thing.

My eyes flew past him, though—to the pot that was boiling behind him. The lid was ajar, almost on purpose—the sides coated in a thick brown of chemicals, and I was afraid to think what else.

They had taken me inside the kitchen. From what I could tell, pots and pans littered a dirty cabinet, and food stains pooled down the cabinets. Where in the church this room was, I could only guess. I kept looking, trying to appear scared. Next to my guns, something caught my eyes fast, a set of neatly folded pairs of clothes. With a shirt on top—the clear emblem of a cat in a space suit, torn away at the head portion, but unmistakable the shirt that Jacob had worn. A lot of things happened at once. My ears started to ring as my fist tightened against the hold I was in. The giant ape spoke, and the more diminutive guy with the bucket just laughed. The kitchen that I was in became apparent as the worst place to keep someone held—because when I got free, I was going to use the knife on the counter to carve both their hearts out. I steadied my breathing, loosening my hands so that the sharp edge of my prosthetic was pressed against the cord. I had only one chance to do this—they would die. As the lights shut off a moment later, my ears filled with flame.

Chapter 84

The cord shredded away on the knife end of my hand like tissue paper, rage fueling my cut. Somewhere behind my eyes, the blood rushing through my ears, a small part of me knew I had only a few moves to put myself into the best position. I had surprise; I had rage. I fell to the ground, unable to see anything except a small light from the boiling pot at the end of the room. The light was enough to show the outline of the two soon-to-be-dead men inside the room with me. I surged forward, kicking the bucket that had held the water thrown on me. The ginger ape snarl went wide into the room, but I could hear it. The more petite man's sudden yelp confirmed he was in front of me. I hit him first with a fast jab. My wrists got blood flow back in record time as my anger carried me across the room. I stepped back instantly as the more petite man swung wildly.

The wind from his blade and wild strikes told me he was swinging with everything he had. Usually, a knife fight was going to end in a hospital trip at best for both. But I had darkness on my side; I had a clear goal: their deaths.

My feet carried me to the cabinet. The room was loud, with the knife man swinging around and bumping into things in the dark. Not loud enough — where was the ginger —.

I thought before I felt his meaty fist cold clock me in the side. I spiraled onto the counter, my face on fire. I turned back to see the big man closing the distance to me. He was using the same light I was to navigate the room. He had kept his cool when the power went out. I spit at that, and blood came out of my mouth. I turned to face the man, inching closer to the pot. The big man swung again; I had enough light this time to see the meaty fist fly into the cabinet behind me. The wood splintering into tiny shards behind me. Fragments feel like minor little bugs biting my neck. He swung wildly as I stumbled along the counter—I reached the stove, the blade of my prosthetic coming into contact with the hot flame. While my other hand swooped up and cranked the temperature gauge to what I hoped was the highest setting. Flames responded instantly; I left the part of my prosthetic closest to the fire a few breaths longer before gripping the pot in both my hands and throwing it behind me.

Right away, one of the two men screamed, slashing out with his arms widely. In the dim light, I realized that the small man had taken the brunt of the steaming liquid. The smell of burnt pork permeates the small room. In a flash, the bigger man seized me, using the light from the roaring stove. He lifted me off my feet into the air—big mistake, don't hold go for a throw.

He found out why, my scorching hot prosthetic jammed into his neck, once, twice, three times, until I lost count. He savagely threw me into the counter, my back and shoulder catching the light from the flames of the old stove. I kept stabbing, blood spraying everywhere—heat on my shoulders. I was in Hell, I thought. This was Hell.

The giant ape released me once his head was nearly sawed off. The other more petite man fell to the ground in a tearful mess. My jacket burned, and I flung it to the ground—stomping on the remains of the coat. I patted my pockets, thankful that the two morons didn't even bother to take the ammo out of my pants. They must have thought this was going to be quick.

It wasn't—there would be nothing quick in Hell; the night was far from over. And all I could see was Jacob's shirt—illuminated by the heat of the flames. Glowing by the force of my malice. I shoved the remainder of the ammo into my pockets. Picking up my shotgun and my pistol. I tucked the gun into my belt.

I racked the shotgun; they had the sense to at least unload it. I loaded the weapon quickly—my prosthetic hand melted off as I tossed the remains of the part to the ground. That left just eight fingers, I thought. More than enough for what was coming.

The more petite man whimpered on the ground—I put my jacket back in the flames. It caught fire—I threw it on the man; this wasn't Hell—it soon would be.

Chapter 85

The rest was a blur of sounds and movement. It does not really sound as much as the music of rage. The dragon gave form, and sadness turned to flames spewing in multiple directions as my weapons fired. I reloaded, fired, dodged, swung, snarled, bit, torn, murdered until the ground was soaking wet—the carpet slouching under my feet as I walked through the building. Some fought back—most didn't as I walked through the darkness. I was a far better shooter than any of them were prepared for. My fingers singed their skin off as I loaded and reloaded at lightning speeds.

Bullets would fly above me in the darkness, my feet moving with a rhythm I didn't know was possible. It was as if they no longer belonged to me; they belonged to a different Billy Dan. One that was far from who he was before and could never go back. I was lost in the blood—awakened to the gore. What more could I do now? What else was there for me besides this? A vague part of me knew I was supposed to be looking for the boy—only he was gone now.

Jacob was gone. All I had now was the blood. Rage isn't ever given the credit it's deserved. We are constantly told not to be angry or act in anger. Genuine rage, though—that was the stuff of animals—of demons. One step, one shot. Another step, another one dead. The rage built. My eyes are heavy. My lungs choking.

My shotgun clicked empty. I reached for the last extended tube of shells and racked the chamber. I was all out. I came in with forty-five shells—I think. Five tubes of nine shells. My shotgun smoked as I dropped it to the ground, the forgotten sword of an angry angel.

Drywall felt as flimsy as tissue paper as my body collapsed to the ground. How many people had I killed? I looked at my hands, the darkness keeping me from seeing a slight glow from my metal prosthetic—hot to the touch. I hadn't killed enough; the rage spit flames like a raging volcano. "It's not right—it's not right," I muttered. Hot tears streamed down my cheeks. These people were monsters. They're monsters; they deserve to be slaughtered like monsters. "They deserved it..." I cried, weeping openly into the darkness. "They deserved to go to trial—face justice behind bars," I gulped out, thankful the lights were still off, I knew that was right. I had crossed the line from good man into the realm of monster. Was this what it took? All this blood—all these things that couldn't be washed away? It was like I had branded murder across my soul. Shackled by my own weakness. I wanted none of this; I just wanted to find the boy. I rubbed my face. It was smeared in smoke, doused in grease, drenched in blood.

I was off the floor, stumbling through to a room. A small outline of "Men's" edged into a sign. I went to the sink. I turned both handles on. Water flowed. My tears did not. I was now only a husk. There would be no more tears—how could I ever do something like crying again? That was a human emotion; I wasn't a man anymore. I was just a demon, lost to my ways, and there was never going to be a way of changing that. I angled a small pen flashlight from my pocket, the mirror reflecting at me. My skin was now the color of blood. At some point, the hook had come out. The wound is already festering and swollen. My hair was shooting at all ends, all my lines reflecting a man of eighty, not a thirty-something. It was the eyes, though; they were no longer blue. They were just empty. Like a grizzly bear, black jewels with no light. The face scared me—not because it was a monster, just that it was my own. I could handle horns and fangs. Dead eyes—instead with a brown now as deep as the murkiest of lakes.

I think I dropped my gun, the loud clunk of metal ringing like a thunderstorm all around me in the cold dead lands of the bathroom. Whatever, what was the point? Why even bother anymore? Would I fail when all I did was fail?

Laughter soon boiled up my throat. A painful retort, a stretched and ragged thing that came from deep within. Full of acid and gas, the worst things that were inside of me—coming to the surface. I did nothing to stop it, though. Just let my head back as the laughter rolled out. Each chuckle was more painful than the last until I cracked, and laughter turned into tears. And I started to sob, A never-ending wail of a broken man. What was left for me? The boy was gone. I had failed him. I couldn't even do that one thing—all I had done was flounder around—and forget the people who needed me the most. I was worthless.

I yanked the facet on with both knobs, and water started to spill from the sink. I lurched forward and spit at the reflection in the bathroom mirror before slamming my head into the glass as hard as I could. I felt something hot run down my head. I slammed my head again. This time, I could hear cracks of glass as well as see a few fall down in the small amount of light from my flashlight. The bandages from before taring uselessly off into the gloom.

My next head-butt against the glass stopped hurting. I tried once more with all my might, but my eyes blurred, and I sank to the ground, defeated. I was still crying by the time the blood and my tears flowed together, forming a long line down my cheeks. "What's the point when all I do is keep failing? What's the point?" I asked the darkness. Is this all I can do? Just fail in the end, I have no faith. I have no strength left in my bones. I can't go on like this anymore—I can't. "Please, just help me,".

Chapter 86

Cold water hit my face, and I was plunged back into some semblance of reality. What that was, I wasn't too interested in. Not when it was this cold and this rude, I thought, swearing and shaking the water off myself, "What the Hell, Rose..." I muttered before being slapped. "No, you what the Hell me, Billy Dan. What the heck is wrong with you? Why do you act this way?" she asked, sitting down the pitcher of water and knocking over the cans of beer that littered my coffee table. I grimaced at that. "Hey, that may be cheap beer—but you never pour out a beer," I started before she slapped me again. This time, with enough force to make me angry. "Stop slapping me!" I yelled as she reared back for another.

"I will stop slapping you when you pull your head out of your rear end!" she challenged with a look that dared me to try to say something. I relented under her gaze and muttered, "I am pretty sure today's not group, so calm your —"I started before she smacked me again. My head cracked back against the couch I was draped over. My legs came off the ground in protest but relented, which caused me to fall back down to the ground.

I drilled holes into my floor before talking or looking up at Rose. I was pretty sure today wasn't group... Though I wasn't a hundred percent sure what day of the week it was. "What's the big deal, Rose?" I finally asked after the sting on my face had gone down. I could already feel the redness of a bruise working its way to the top of my face.

"The big deal is, I don't know Billy Dan—I had to come drive you to the emergency room on Christmas day," she stated matter-of-factly.

"That was today? I'm sorry, Rose, honestly," I muttered. I could hear her roll her eyes as she cleared more trash off my coffee table and slid down on top of the table. I watched the crash land on the filthy floor; a small part of me was annoyed she had added more to the mess that was my living room.

She peered at a cup on the table and picked it up, grimacing at the smell. "Cheap whiskey from a red solo cup, huh," she paused, looking at more stuff in the room, never minding my silent protest at the alarm of her looking through my home like she had unfettered access to my life. In a way, she did; I had lost that right to privacy once I was placed on probation. She sighed heavily and continued, "You drown your sorrows till you can't stand up, Billy Dan. Look at you; your hands are shaking while your body sweats. Your fingers are so yellow—you live in one giant ashtray. I don't know why I bother so much with you, Billy Dan. All you do is drink whiskey, cheap beer, and cough syrup—just look at yourself. You laid on your arm for hours. Your arm is almost purple, Billy Dan," she sobbed, putting her head in her hands.

I looked down, sure enough—it was swollen and bruised. She was also right about the hospital trip—was that today? It felt like a lifetime ago. I was still hazy after we had gotten home. I looked around my apartment; it was disgusting. I felt guilty about that. I always felt guilty these days. Nothing I did was ever right; I always failed.

More seriously, this time, I said, "I'm sorry, Rose. I didn't mean for all of this to happen," I whispered. She remained with her head in her hands for a few moments before looking towards me. "Yeah, that's the thing, Billy Dan, you never mean for anything bad to happen. And it always comes back to this, right back to this moment. Me picking your butt up from your latest mess up,". I gulped at that; she had me dead to rights.

She sighed heavily, eyeing the cigarettes on my coffee table. I caught her eye and shrugged my shoulders. She shook her head and stood up. "Can't do that, Billy Dan. That's just one bad choice that will lead to another," she muttered.

I was quiet for a long moment before speaking up, "Why does it matter if it's a bad choice? It's not hurting anyone other than myself? While you're more important than me for the world—I don't see the problem,".

Rose frowned deeply, her brow moving together like paper being jammed against a wall. "It matters because we aren't supposed to do things like that to ourselves," she replied.

"Aren't supposed to? What does that even mean? We aren't owned by anyone—I," I started before she cut me off.

"We belong to God, Billy Dan. Even if we don't think it. Even if we choose to worship the devil. We belong to God," she replied soberly. I snorted, not knowing why she was taking the conversation in this direction. I half expected she would have done her usual tactic and quoted some vague philosophy. Tell me some story from her life. Tell me that it was for the good of the community that I kept it together. I forgot about her and moved on with my life. But, going on nearly two years since the accident, that just seemed stupid. There was nothing I could do to bring her back. I had severed my time for community service. I didn't owe anyone anything.

I just needed to forget; I was in pain. Rose couldn't understand that. She wouldn't be saying what she said now. Indeed, she had to realize that God was just punishing me for what was happening and what had happened in my life.

Clearing my throat loudly, I looked away from Rose, pretending to be distracted by something else in the room. "I mean—yeah, sure, whatever, Rose. But I'm not hurting anyone—I've served my time. God saw fit to dump on me; what have I ever done for anyone? I'm just here trying to live my life. That's all," I stated.

This time, she snorted, "Yeah, getting high and sleeping with anything that has a pulse," she stated this time.

"Hey, I have some standards—paying for it isn't that low. It cost a lot," I replied.

She just stared at me, now emotion on her face. "Is this really what you think God wants for you?" she asked softly.

I got mad at that, "Who gives a flying freak what he wants? Look at what has happened. I am missing my leg. My girlfriend was sawed in half by a wire at a county circus. I can't even wipe my butt Rose without taking off a metal claw. So yeah, tell me what God wants again for me. Tell me again how I belong to someone who doesn't care about me. Let me tell you this, sister, I would rather belong to the devil if he's even real. At least then I can see her again. I can be whole again," I snarled. Not realizing that I was now standing far closer to Rose than I had tended to be.

Rose, for her part, remained exactly where she was, never moving an inch during all that had happened. Save for a deeper frown and longer lines near her eyes—she didn't seem at all phased by anything I had said. That bothered me a lot. Part of what I said, I, of course, didn't mean. I was just hurt. She couldn't understand that.

"You don't mean that," she stated flatly, challenging my anger as if it were no more than a light breeze on a rainy day. I doubled down, trying to sit up from the couch, but fell back. My shirt rose, exposing my ever-growing belly. I quickly creased it down, hoping she didn't notice. I had gained a lot of weight—a lot. Where had it come from? Amazing how when the body is sad, all it can think to do is either shrink like a raisin or blow up quicker than a balloon at a child's birthday party. I decided to stay on the couch, the cushions well-worn down from my girth over the last few months.

"I do mean it, Rose. I would rather be in Hell and be with her, rather than stay here. At least then, I have someone who will accept me," I said, avoiding her gaze. She didn't reply; she didn't say anything. She simply looked ahead—past me to the wall behind me for a long moment as if she could see some world behind the cheap drywall.

I cleared my throat loudly after she drifted too much into crazy town for my liking. She shook her head slowly as a small smile appeared on her face. "You know Billy Dan, the devil will try and trick you. Appear as an angel of light. Whisper sweet nothings into your ear as you do everything you want. You may think you aren't harming anything. Hell, you may even justify its meaning. One way or another, you're hurting God. Because you're turning your back on the Lord at the end of the day. If you don't care about God—all you're doing is worshiping the devil. Regardless of subjective intent—our objective reality is simple—worship of self—is an abomination," she replied soberly.

Once more I cleared my throat, she cut me off with her hand, "What you're really doing—all of this," she gestured with her hands to the room and myself, "All of it is because you're afraid God is mad at you. You're nothing more than a scared child," she trailed off before speaking again, "You will say in that day: "I will give thanks to you, O LORD, for though you were angry with me, your anger turned away, that you might comfort me. That is Isaiah 12:1. Our ability to understand God is so limited. We only have the Bible, signs, and wonders. But, we can be rest assured that God's love is limitless. I don't know the ends and outs of what's going on inside you, Billy Dan. Only God knows that. Let me tell you, though, he's not angry with you. His grace is eternal, and his yolk is easy. You ask a lot of questions, why this, why that? Have you ever asked what can I learn from all of this? What can I do now to serve? You survived a horrific accident. You clawed your way to walking again and came out the other side when most men would give up. Most people, if they were too weak as you were to even go to the bathroom without pooping your bed, would have thrown in the towel. You haven't though—do you know why? Because your soul belongs to God. You know that deep down, he has something planned for everything. If you really want to know—then just take my hand, and we will pray together," she said, offering her hand to me.

I gazed up at her eyes. Looking for the sign of anything that might have been a joke in them. All I saw was smiles reflected in her windows. Only hope reflected in her sights. She meant every word of what she was saying. The hair on my back started going up, and I felt weird. Every part of me tingling. Like I was standing on top of the world I had just been pushed off— instead of falling, I was floating, drifting down as if being gently guided across the universe by some unseen force. It wasn't bad in any way, shape, or form. It was absolute safety. Something I had never felt. Something I wasn't accustomed to.

I was scared in that moment. More frightened than that first night in the hospital. All alone with nothing but low lights. Heavy breathing from the guard gently dosing off in the hallway. Rhythmic beats, a calling card of an uncaring metal god. Absolutely on my own, afraid in Hell and with no one there. All that pain, no way to let it out. I just ached so, so much. I longed to be with anyone. I needed—I needed help. I was so afraid. Abandoned, butchered like a piece of meat flayed open for the whole world. I wept at that memory—I wept now in front of her, tears rolling down my dirty cheeks. "Only you can make the choice Billy Dan, just come with me sometime. Come with me to church," she said gently. I wiped my tears before shaking my head. "I need to pull myself up by my shoelaces, Rose. I will come with you to your church. I don't know why it matters, I've never been converted by anyone," I stated flatly.

"That's not the point Billy Dan. Just keep an open mind, that's all I am asking. Seek him yourself, he will answer when you're ready to finally listen," she stated.

Chapter 87

When you are lost, the first thing to do is breathe. Slow down, start with what you know. I was alive, in a dark place. The only light is a slight flicker from a scent light spray from the power socket. That illuminated the bathroom enough to tell me that I was still alive, still in the bathroom. My head bleeding a long stream that I felt rushing down half my face. Leaving a warm streak like liquid fire.

I was breathing now, slowly at first. One tinder breath at a time until it was normal. Less erratic. With one hand, I smoothed off any dirt I had on my hand on my pants. With the other, I reached up and started rubbing my face. I winced when I touched the cut; the edges were jagged and shredded to pieces. Pieces of glass poked into my fingers as I rubbed near the cut. The blood was so thick now that one of my eyes was covered. Thankfully, it was only bleeding over my swollen eye from when that giant ape of a man had hit me. I winced again and rubbed my face thoroughly, throwing any caution to the wind.

When it was done, I was breathing hard again, but a part of me felt better. It felt good to do something simple, even if that was rubbing an open wound with dirty hands. It needed to be done, I thought. Next, I started to stand; my thoughts were still sluggish, and I had no idea how long I had been in the bathroom. Long enough, I thought as I came to my feet. The best thing to do now was to get out there. Jacob was gone; the guilty party was not. That was something that needed to be changed. Required to be changed now, with no time to waste.

Anger drifted up my body, sending small shock currents into my arms. I couldn't feed that beast again, though. Not after what had happened last time—my time since entering the church, just a dream now. I needed to stay grounded. I needed to ask for help. I could no longer do this on my own, so I started, "Dear Heavenly Father."

Chapter 88

I kicked open the bathroom door, and it slammed into the adjacent wall. I had been in the bathroom for five, maybe ten minutes. Either way, it was too long; I had no way of knowing how long I had been there. I could smell smoke and grease. Where was I, though? Each direction I looked was death and darkness; I was about to take the hallway closest to me when my headpiece squeaked with a loud buzz. I fumbled with the earpiece until the static cleared, and I understood how essential functions with my fingers worked again. Static came through first, followed by Larry's frantic voice.

"Billy Dan!" he screamed over the line, which almost caused me to throw my earpiece out in response. "Calm down, Larry," I muttered, massaging behind one of my ears. I could hear the heavy sigh of relief come into his voice. "Thank God, Billy Dan, are you alright? Never mind that, dude; you need to move out as soon as possible! The place is about to go up in the heat soon. And I don't know how the police haven't shown up yet, but no way no one hasn't called with that much racket going down," he trailed off. I thought about what I saw after Jacob: a few heavily armed tactical types.

They came into the building fast and loud and were doing a lot of damage. The only reason I got them was sheer surprise. And the fact that I had spent nearly every lazy afternoon shooting for years. Though, I wasn't sure if I had gotten them all. At this point, there was almost no reason for me to still be here. I had failed my mission. I knew there was a reason God had me come into this building. Why would he have me here? Can you confirm that this was where the kids were being taken? No, there had to be something more. I was walking fast when Larry cut me mid-step. "Billy Dan, one more thing:

a huge heat signature is coming from inside the building. I don't think it's a fire. Real small and low to the ground at varying sizes," he stated.

I thought that over, "That has to be something—I'm going to go check it out," I replied, looking at my shotgun. It was empty—I tossed it to the ground. Even if this place burned down, judging by the thick smell of smoke drifting through the halls, it was only minutes at the most—it didn't matter. I wasn't going to get away with what happened here; I didn't want to get away with what happened here. I would atone for my mistakes; step one is facing the consequences of those mistakes. I just prayed before following down the hallway and pulling out my pistol—I had fifteen bullets left. That was the fifth-teen chance to do something worthwhile. Whatever that was, I trusted God would see me through. As I walked through the smoke, I feared nothing in the darkness. Without sight or light, I walked by faith.

Chapter 89

After only a few minutes, I found myself near the garage area again. A few loading vans are set in the docks. The lights were off, but flashlights from at least five black-dressed men illumined the place enough. More importantly, as two men worked loading the vans, a group of children huddled near them. They were huddled, their whimpers trailing off in the cold wind. Melanie was standing near the children, and her tailored suit was gone. Instead, she wore a heavy rope that was decorated with strange symbols and bright colors. She was barking into her phone, handling orders at a lightning pace. I looked past her from my vantage point inside the hallway to the opposite adjacent hallway. Several individuals with very large rifles were making their way towards the loading dock. It was the other group of men that had been shooting up the building from the front.

I took a quick breath, ejecting my magazine and then reloading. I had to be faster than all of them, strike them, and not miss a single shot. I had the advantage of being in the shadows with no light, but that was assuming that they didn't come equipped with night vision. I shook my head; maybe they were that well-trained; I had my doubts, though. They were way too loud coming in. Way too slow to just now being out here. Based on their gear, they definitely weren't working with Melanie. That left them as just loud—loud and dangerous. That gave me the element of surprise. The real hiccup in my quick plan, though, was I had moments at best to react before them. From what I could see, it was three shooters coming down the hallway, fast, small lights scrambling all over the place, casting long shadows. The others in the bay somehow hadn't heard them yet.

Four men were around the kids, and Melanie was frantically shouting into her cell phone. One man was now at the wheel of the van, and another was moving something around in the side. The other three looked at everything but the hallways and the kids.

That was a very small window of opportunity, and I couldn't afford to waste any time or make any mistakes. Thankfully, there was a railing at the end of the hallway closest to me with a box of some kind at the perfect height for what I needed to do. "Thank you, Father," I whispered before going forward as quickly and as silently as possible.

I reached the box, braced my elbow as securely as possible, and took in a shallow breath. The first shooter coming down the stairs was about forty yards away. The kids in the bay were around sixty yards at the center of the room. As the shooters came forward, the goons in the middle of the room by the kids finally noticed the lights and noises coming down the hallway; well, one of them did. He needed to be faster. I aimed at the first man I saw coming down the steps in a hurry; he was breathing hard; I fired once. He fell quickly, and the man behind him staggered a step and tripped forward. The man in front of him suddenly stopped.

I fired again, taking that man out; he lurched slowly backward as the third man at the top of the stairs frantically raised his gun. My heart rate shot up, and I fired three shots his way. Two entered his chest, and the other knocked his gun hand, sending the flashlight he held going wild into the bay, casting long shadows in every direction.

The men around the kids panicked, and I stayed glued where I was and fired another round into one of them, hitting him in the shoulder. He got a round-off that went over the children's heads. That caused me to fire more than I needed at the last guy as he managed to get a few rounds heading my way. None hit, but one came uncomfortably close. In all the excitement, I didn't notice the driver of the van start to pull out in a hurry, going so fast he hit the man who was wounded in the shoulder with the front of the van as he staggered to his feet. I aimed and fired—cracking the windshield and seeing a scream as my only acknowledgment of hitting him before the van tore down the street to an unknown destination. The slide of my gun rocked back, and I was surprised to realize I had miscounted. My hands were shaking, and it took a good amount of willpower to lower my pistol. I dropped it into my pocket, not trusting my fingers to unbutton the straps to hold my gun. Every inch of my body was shaking and sweating. Yeah, it wasn't my first gunfight of the night, but all the night's energy was coming back with a vengeance—hard.

My instructor at the firearms course mentioned the need to be able to keep using my body no matter how scared I was. He would shoot rounds off while I was shooting on the course. Nothing could train you for the real thing. Hearing men scream, hearing yourself scream. My response to fight or flight was fight, but there was a small part of me that wanted nothing more than to pee myself and lay down in a tight ball. I looked at the kids as they huddled on the ground, and Melanie slowly got back to her feet.

One of her long heels had fallen off at some point. Her hair jutted out in each direction like it was trying to reach out to some invisible force pulling on the follicles. Her normally well-kept clothes were dirty and torn. Her strange white mask from earlier was loose around her neck, attached with a string. In any other circumstance, she would have seemed just the type that any man would die trying to save.

Only, I knew better as I passed the three men laying on the opposite staircase—their blood pooling in a deep puddle along with other things floating in the thick crimson spray. I shuddered at that. Real gunshot deaths don't leave just blood; it's as if their wounds become living oceans of death. You will see deep browns, some pink, and who knows what else floating in the pit. It was a pit I was thankful for not getting too close to. You never want to see your reflection in someone's blood—that was a surefire way to see into Hell.

That sickened me; I wouldn't let myself stare into the pit again. I knew from experience that the abyss was full of monsters. It doesn't matter how long you stare at it or not—something is coming in.

Instead, I offered a prayer of apology for my actions. I wasn't sure how many souls had been taken tonight, but the truth of what I had done was coming for me. Sin weighs more than anything else, but grace is stronger than darkness. Still, that didn't make me feel any better about it.

I kept my head busy, my eyes scanning everything—the man who had been shot and was hit by the van was groaning on the ground, gripping his shoulder tightly. When I came upon him, his face contorted into a fit of rage that quickly slid into absolute agony of fear. He wasn't going to be doing anything anytime soon, I could see a bone sticking out of his left arm, and his legs didn't look much better. If the man didn't get help, he was going to die.

He was next on my list of concerns. I turned my attention to Melanie. She straightened up towards my gaze. A smooth, small business smile flattered its way across her lips. She had a heart-shaped head, the type of dangerous dark hair, and a powerful look that I was sure won her way into many people's hearts. However, the idea of kids being harmed made that smile worthless to me. I closed the distance between us, my bad leg dragging across the floor. I looked down at the splintered mess of jeans and wood around my prosthetic. It was a jagged mess; even though my leg was gone, the strain of the straps on the remainder of my knee was stinging. I could see blood mixed into my pants. I glanced back up at Melanie, my thoughts only swimming around one option: kill her. I was vaguely aware of kids whimpering around me; that was enough to stall my anger as Larry squeaked over my coms, "Billy Dan! Are you alright? Dude come in, I don't know what's going on, but some van speed out of there—"he started before I cut in on the mike. "Yeah, Larry, come around the corner from where you saw that van go; there's some kids here. Hurry up," I stated before cutting the line. I refocused on Melanie. She still smiled at me, her high cheekbones catching a low light somewhere. If she was afraid, only the devil knew. That made me angry—she should have been afraid of me then. There was nothing that could stop me.

But something stopped me as I stared at her smile, the void in her almost inhuman brown eyes. It wasn't the children trembling in fear around me. Their forms slowly got off the ground, and I wasn't sure if some were hurt or just staying low to the ground in a protective manner. It wasn't Larry who soon came swinging around the corner. He was out of the massive garbage truck instantly, the motor humming louder than my thoughts but unable to drown out the pull.

No, what was stopping me from doing something awful to Melanie was something outside of myself. It was a universal pull that told me deep down that this wasn't right what I wanted to do. She deserved it—at least, I thought in almost every space of my head. Only that wasn't true—who was I to say who deserved to live or die? Roll back the clock a few years ago on my past, and you would have found someone who deserved death. I was a useless slob. At least that's what I thought. Suddenly, that pull from within expanded like a supernova, and all I wanted to do was vomit. The truth was, I knew that all life was precious. Hers. Mine was from the past, even now, as I look at my hands. They were covered in so much blood. I started to tear up at the idea of what I had done. So much awfulness—so much death. I hated how it was; I hated how I felt like just a leaf in the wind of a cruel current.

That wasn't true either, though. Our ability to understand God is so minimal. That there's a reason for everything—it's not always going to make sense, and some people will just never see beyond their pain. What's cruel is our distance from seeing how much darkness can engulf us. Only the light can deliver us right out of it when we make that step. The moment we choose freedom, we become liberated from darkness. So, yeah, I had no idea about the grand reason for many things other than that it's the will. However, my stomach said nothing about my next move. I closed the distance between her and myself. She held me in a steel gaze. I met her gaze rearing back my fists; a rage far greater than any I had ever felt shot into every part of my body. I was seeing red—I was—I couldn't do it. I lowered my hands. She deserved it—justice wasn't mine to give though.

I glared right back at her as Larry ran up to us. " Billy Dan, this is nuts, man. We need to get out of here," he urged. I focused on Melanie for another moment before turning to Larry, "First, we need to keep these kids safe, I gestured to the group of all ages; some could have been as young as four, others at least fifteen. That felt like a noose strangling my heart, all the pumps at that thought. They didn't deserve this; they were just kids. If I survived this—I was going to have to lay in a tight ball for a very long time and just cry.

God gives us the tools to fight through the darkness, though I remained steadfast at that thought. "Larry, get a hold of the cops; we must be gone in three minutes. Do whatever it takes to get them out here. If they're that bought, get a hold of Gen—she will come," I trailed off, thinking about poor Gen once she found out about Jacob. I turned back towards Melanie, "I will deal with her," I stated firmly, moving towards her. She snarled at me before spitting, "Not settling for a cheap shot, huh? What are you going to do, murder me like you did all these men?" she shouted while gesturing to the group of dead men. I sighed; a big part of me had wanted nothing more than to watch the lights leave her eyes. That wasn't an option now. I glanced around at the kids for a moment before speaking to who I thought was the oldest kid. She was a short-haired girl with a small dash of freckles across her face. She flinched a little under my sight, making my heart hurt. The last thing I wanted to do was to scare these children. Who knew how I must have looked to them, though.

"Is this all of you? Do you know where that van was going?" I asked her. She blinked a few times, steadying herself. Her clothes were disheveled, and she seemed almost in a daze. She came back to the world after a moment. Her head shook silently before speaking. I tried my best to seem safe to the poor girl. She had been through a lot; they all had. More than I could ever imagine. "We don't know—that van is only used when we are taken. Most of us never leave here—" she trailed off. I noticed she looked down, trembling as if the building itself was possessed of evil. I curled in my knuckles so hard I felt the skin breaking on one of my hands. Smoke was coming from behind us; if nothing else, out of this whole thing tonight, these children were now safe from the monsters inside this building.

Soon, the building would be a heap of ashes, along with the demons that lurked in its hallways. "Were there any more of you inside? Are you the last ones?" I asked, concerned by the smoke overhead.

She either didn't hear me or was traumatized. All she did was stare at the ever-increasing smoke coming out of the building as if it were some kind of dark lair of a huge dragon. I cleared my throat, and she came back. "No—the last of us, we were pulled out here. The rest went in the van," she replied somberly.

She coughed and started to cry, "They—turn us into things," she stated.

"What things?" I whispered.

She paused for a long time before speaking, "They turn us into TRIP," she said flatly.

I couldn't respond to her momentarily as the pieces tumbled into place. Jacob had found a stronger version of the drug. Must have accidentally ended up with that baby in the dumpster. The rest of the kids—they were— I couldn't finish the thought as I felt my own tears start coming down. Children were kidnapped and turned into drugs but a new age cult. What was even real anymore?

I debated trying to get more out of her. Instead, I did the only thing I could think of doing. I slowly pulled her into a hug. She did nothing at first before slowly wrapping her arms around me and crying. I could feel the front of my shirt getting wet. She was tall for her age. She should have been at home in the safety of her parents' house. There would be more fire soon. These jerks could count on it. I bit my tongue down to stifle my anger. We stayed that way momentarily before I gently broke the hug off. I kept my bad hand at my side, not wanting to scare her. The other is on her shoulder. In the background, I could see the children all starting to come alive again. Their personalities slowly coming back. I prayed they would be alright. The first thing was to get them as far from this place as possible.

I looked at the girl, "Sweetie, are you sure you don't know where that van got off?" I asked, trying to speak as softly as I could. She shook her head no, lowering her eyes to the ground. Her body language told me everything; she probably knew more, but for now, there was no point digging into her about things that she needed safety from first. They all needed to be back to their parents. The police would handle that—but I needed to handle Melanie first.

She glared at me from behind her huge glasses. She had a smirk on her face as if this was all one giant game to her. It probably was knowing her. "So, what now, Billy Boy, going to take me out in front of all them?" she gestured to the kids as if they were some kind of useless life stalk to be raised for slaughter. I remembered the piles of clothes. I remembered the ways these kids were kidnapped. I remembered seeing Jacob's shirt on the stove.

I was a weak man—I wanted to end her right then and there. I wanted to hit her. I never wanted to do such a thing to be more deserving of a person. But that wasn't right—I knew that from my heart. I just shook my head slowly, "Nah, I have a better thing in store for you, Melanie, but first, where did that van go?" I asked soberly.

She scoffed, "Looks like I have all the leverage, Billy Dan, and you were so close to finally being the hero," she stated, letting her head back and genuinely giving the creepiest laugh I had ever heard.

Larry came up behind us and cleared his throat, "Don't worry about the van Billy Dan. I put a flag on them as they were heading out," he stated. I turned, looking at him, "Where did you get a flag, and how?" I asked, dumbfounded. He smiled a sad smile and then shook his head. "Not that kind of flag, man. He pulled out his phone and pulled up a game with a colorful map of the local area on it. Followed by a bunch of creatures on the map at various locations. I still wasn't following—Larry noticed and cleared his throat again. "All you need to know is we have the location of them, and hopefully none of them are fans of "monster mons"," he stated.

Chapter 90

I was still confused at that, but took it in thankful that all the times I caught Larry on his phone on the job, it had turned out to be a good thing. I turned back to Melanie, looking at her. She was clutching the straps on her backpack. A clear look of panic on her face. The fire might consume most of the evidence, but we needed whatever she had in her bag. I stepped forward, my bad leg nearly causing me to trip, and the move wasn't as graceful as I pulled her towards me and swept the back of her legs out from under her. She fell in a heap, a lot harder than I had intended to do. That was fine with me. I pulled her backpack off using a jerking method and soon had it in my hands. I could feel a computer through its layers and knew that there also had to be other things inside the pack.

Her gaze was white-hot fury, and her eyes darted in each direction as if looking for a way out. I handed the bag back to Larry before I yanked off my belt and approached her. She fought for a moment, a lot of scratches and low blows, but I managed to get both her hands tied and sit on top of her chest. Both of us were breathing heavily—not ideal, but it had to do. Larry came up next and put a piece of cold metal on my shoulders. I glanced and saw it was handcuffed. "Where did you get these from?" I asked him, not daring to look away from Melanie any longer than necessary.

He shrugged, "That dead guy over there had them. I smiled, knowing he meant the guy hit by the van. I nodded and then said over my shoulders. Alright, help me take care of her; then we need to get going," I stated, hearing the sirens in the distance. Larry came over, and I tossed Melanie's bag to the girl I had spoken to earlier. "Hold on to that for me, please. Give it only to a detective, Geneses Rodriguez. Alright? No one else. Can you promise me that?" I asked softly. The girl met my gaze and said simply, "I promise."

Chapter 91

We were on the road, far enough away now to see the smoke bleeding into the night sky—sirens passing away from my hearing quickly. I let out a breath I had been holding. It had all happened pretty quickly. We had handcuffed Melanie to a bench that was out in the loading dock area. I told the young girl, her name is Kim, that if Melanie tried anything, hit her. If any of the goons got up or anyone besides the police showed up. Take the rest of the children and run to the nearest house. Start knocking on as many doors as they could. However, a thought occurred to me now, there was almost no way anyone in the surrounding neighborhoods didn't know what was going on. How could you be so close to all that—that darkness inside that building? Surly smoke, chemicals, or someone screaming in the middle of the night. It was hard to know what was going on. Or just how many kids had been taken there? The thought of the pile of clothes—almost reaching to the top of the ceiling like a twisted statue of a demonic god.

That image would be burned into my skull forever. All those shoes, they were so tiny... I shook my head as Larry drove. He had been silent for the most part, glancing at his phone periodically between the screen and the road. I sighed and looked around. "Have a shirt or something I can use to wipe my face?" I asked the dark cabin. "A shirt or something?" he replied. "Yeah, Larry, I need to clean my face," I stated.

"Oh yeah—sure, look in the back of the cab," he gestured behind us. The dump truck was one of the few cabs that had two rows of seats. It's not really a needed function in most trucks like this. Thankfully, our company spent a little extra money on more space. The argument is that longer hours require more time for rest. I shook my head at that one—if any of us dared be late, it wouldn't even be just our bosses who would be mad. Tell someone you aren't getting their trash, and see how fast the fangs start coming out.

Sure enough, I found a bag in the back. I opened it up and saw a shirt in the dark. I pressed my face into the fabric. Rubbing hard at what was now feeling like a second layer of skin on my face. I breathed hard and could smell the blood on the shirt. I had no idea how much was mine and the people back in the church. I didn't want to think about that, but I knew I would need to answer it sooner or later. I was thankful Larry hadn't asked questions; sometimes, the best way to help someone is to know when to give space.

I dropped the soiled shirt onto the floor as I slid back into the passenger seat. I was utterly drained and still had miles to go before it was over. I thought, at least. Over was subjective, I thought; I knew there was no way I wasn't paying for my sins. I could clean my face and wipe away endless amounts of dirt and grime. It doesn't wipe away what I've done. Can't hide anything from God—you can't lie to him. Could I ever be forgiven—by God, yes. I just didn't want to forgive myself.

One thing at a time, man. The first thing I thought was to find those kids. Speaking of which, "Larry, are you still following them on your game thing?" I pointed at his cell phone comically. Larry snorted at that. "Billy Dan, you're only a few years older than me. Yet you act like a little old man sometimes," he said, staring at me.

I just stayed quiet, looking blankly back at him. He sighed, "Yeah, man, I am still following them. Basically—I made the van an encounter spot. Meaning that it will be there forever until I decide to move it. I can follow him, even stream of the area easily enough," he stated.

I thought over for a moment, "Were you playing that while I was inside that Hell hole?" I asked. Even in the darkness of the cabin, I could tell Larry was blushing. "Sorry, Billy Dan, I get nervous, you know?" he replied shyly. I let out a breath. "Dude, don't even be sorry—you saved my butt back there. You also gave those kids a chance. God bless you for that," I replied soberly.

Larry sucked in a noticeable breath, "I just don't get it, Billy Dan, you know? Why would God allow all of this to happen? Like what happened to

Jacob... and all the other kids," he trailed off, growing silent.

After I found Jacobs's shirt, I had apparently screamed about it nonstop during the rest of my journey inside the inferno; Larry and Rosemary had heard nearly everything that had happened on the inside. I regretted that they—they didn't need to be exposed to my madness, my loss of, I guess, what it meant to even be human. I wasn't human anymore; beast; beast was more accurate—that was probably too mean to beasts, though. Before I could dive deeper into my depression—I felt—I didn't know how else to describe it. Almost like I was being soothed. The darkness flew away. Not gone, but was no longer leading my thoughts.

I was quiet for a moment. I knew what the old me would have said to that many years ago. I knew what I would have said even just a few moments ago. That wasn't an option now—it's best to just go with scripture when in doubt. "Ever hear the story of Job?" I asked Larry.

I waited for his response and after a moment went on when none came. "Well, Larry Job was a man that God held in high esteem. One day, the devil came to God. Saying the only reason Job was so great was because of what God kept him from—all the bad of life. He only loved God because of his blessings. Well, God, knowing exactly what would happen and knowing what was best, allowed the devil to go after Job. Job lost his wife, kids, and everything for a while. Job couldn't make sense of it—could understand why all this was happening to him. He had done everything right. Said his prayers and made his sacrifices every day. Yet, in the end—he was suffering. Job questioned everything. His friends thought it was something he had done and came up with all sorts of reasons to try and describe his troubles. Finally, God came down and showed Job how wrong he was. See, God doesn't see things the way we do, Larry. He doesn't think as men do. What happened to the boy—Jacob. That was monstrous," I growled lowly, gripping the side of my seat hard enough to dig my fingers into the cushion. "I don't know why all that happened to the children. I don't have a clue. All I know is God had us stop them. And he had you help me with that. The demons that did this—there will be a punishment for them, that I can say for sure," I replied, releasing the anger slowly with my fingers into the chair.

Larry was silent for a moment longer before speaking. "What happened to Job in the end?" he asked.

Without looking forward, I stayed steady on the road before us. The image of Jacobs's shirt was replaced by one clear vision as I glanced at Larry's phone. The bright creatures showed along the moving van that was stopping in a newly developing housing district. We were a few miles out—but we could see the lights on the houses. It all made sense now. This was the Mayor's grand project for our small town. Thousands of new homes are being developed—huge money. Loads of contractors from out of state. No one would ask any questions. Brings in more cash for the town. How bad could it be if they had the lights on in abandoned houses in the middle of the night? "The Mayor," was all I could mutter.

"Excuse me?" Larry asked.

I paused again before answering Larry finally. "God had a plan, Larry, that is what happened. There was justice,".

Chapter 92

We were idling on a hill overlooking the housing district on the outskirts of the neighboring city—a long silence between the both of us. I sat overlooking the houses below us, the moon getting lower—the early signs of morning coming. What were we doing now? This whole plan had somehow carried us to this point. Putting aside everything that happened, I wasn't entirely sure what I intended to accomplish.

So, I had some evidence that kids were being kidnapped by a strange cult. Being turned into drugs—how and why was that even a thing? A huge group of multiple people doing crime at all levels across state lines. This was huge, and I couldn't stop it. I also had over a dozen dead bodies and lots of blood left all over the town. If I wasn't in trouble for everything else that had happened—I suspected anything less than life behind bars would be considered a mercy, assuming I lived through the night. There was also what I hadn't told Larry about another small matter. Through my shirt, I could feel it—a constant dull ache—a small hole that was spitting the fire out of the side of my stomach just below my left rib cage. From what I could tell, the bullet had come out the other side, but I had no real way of knowing that. Each time I breathed, I felt my life tick away just a little bit faster.

I just had to finish this—I was getting closer. My race had been so long—I was so exhausted. I hoped that any pain I felt wasn't showing on my face. Larry had yet to notice, or maybe he was in shock. We hadn't spoken much since getting to the housing area. Larry had taken up the sword, laying down his life for a friend without even looking back. He was a good man for that. Both of us would fry for all of this. And I had dragged him into it without a second thought. I wouldn't have been able to make it this far. I knew that still didn't make me feel better. I pressed my hand into my side, fleeing a heavy dampness on my fingers.

"To be honest—I don't know Larry. I am at the end of my rope on this one man; give me a moment—honestly, I just want to go home," I stated dryly.

I could see Larry nod to that statement. "Man, this has been nuts, huh?" he joked.

I blew out my lips, "Tell me about it."

"Can I ask you another question?"

I shrugged, "Sure, man."

"Why didn't you kill Melanie? I get the handcuffing her and having the evidence—but that's a big gamble if it's even on that laptop. Not to mention—if things have been this corrupt this whole time—what can Gen even do about this stuff?" Larry asked, and I could hear the doubt in his voice.

"We just have to have faith, Larry," I stated.

Larry looked out the driver's window, "Yeah, well—I suppose you're right, but you didn't answer the first question, Billy Dan," he said.

I sighed, and he continued, "Don't tell me it would have been too hard to do it—those people—what they did to children. They're demons—I—I don't know any other words for it, man. I never believed any of this God stuff until—I don't know, this sort of shit changes you. You know what I mean..." he trailed off.

I did know what he meant. I knew all too well just how quickly a person's world can be completely switched. Like an invisible rug being torn out from under them while they're walking on what they thought was secure ground. One moment, you will understand your whole life; up was up, and down was down. Now, someone was telling you that not only is everything a spiritual war but that you probably and were likely fighting on the wrong side even if you didn't know it. That there are bigger things out there—that a universal force was binding all things and above all things. When confronted with rock bottom, I guess the biggest question is when you see firsthand that miracles are real. That demons are all around us all the time—what are you going to do about it?

"It's not that it would be too hard," I sighed. My fingers curled into my hands, the metal on my hand prosthetic cutting a deep grove into my palm. I looked down for a moment. It was barely holding together—it looked like a hole was shot clean through on the side of one of the latches. If I had a thumb, it would have been gone. It was just a jagged blade now—covered in gore. Just another reminder—just another reminder.

"I wanted nothing more than to end her—do the same things she had done to those kids. To make her suffer—and only then, after as long as I could make it last—end her. That—that wouldn't solve anything. I have to believe; I have to obey what God commands us to do. I have enough blood on my hands. Taking her life—that wouldn't be what the Father wants. It's hard to describe; I just had a feeling so deep down in my stomach when I looked at her. She is pure evil. And her time here on earth needs to be Hell for her. However, taking someone's life—that denies them a chance to be redeemed," I stated, casting my eyes downward.

He blinked at that, the quick movement casting long shadows on the dashboard that looked exactly like wings. "You really think someone like her, someone like them, can be redeemed?" he asked.

I smiled back, "With all my heart and soul, yes. God will sort it all out," I stated.

"People like them—need to die, man. I don't think I can understand you. I don't get it—does it not make you mad?" he asked.

I thought for a moment and replied, "It did for a time. To tell you the truth, I am weak. I would have done exactly that. Ended her. Killed her like all the rest. That is not what we are told to do. You either believe it or you don't. I choose to believe and have faith," I said entirely.

"I don't know, man, I just don't know," Larry replied, trailing off; he had a loose grip now on the wheel. They still shook—but fishing is knowing when to pull—and when to let God do the work.

"The good news, Larry—we don't have to figure that out. God will do the rest," I stated.

Larry laughed at that before turning to me in the seat, "Well, think God could give us a plan? Tell us what to do now?" he replied back.

"Sure can, let's just ask," I stated.

Chapter 93

"I don't know, man—no offense, but how the Hell are you even still standing, Billy Dan? You look like road-kill having been run over by every car on a holiday weekend," Larry said.

I shrugged, "have any better ideas?"

"No—just dang man, where are the police? Why is it just us having to do this?" he asked.

He turned, whizzing, "We could just walk away. Jump on a plane—find some beach somewhere—get one of those coconut drinks with the little umbrellas," he replied.

I smiled, "yeah, that doesn't sound so bad right now; it will just have to do," I stated flatly. Feeling the gravity of the situation flood into the bottom of my stomach.

Larry gazed out the window again before turning sharply and pulling out his laptop. He booted it up, and his hands moved like lightning across the keyboard. I was awestruck by that. "Seriously, man, why did you settle on being a garbage man?" I stated.

"Why did you?" he challenged.

"You got me there," I replied.

He shrugged while typing with a fury that I didn't think was possible for another human being. I gave up looking at his screen as he glanced between that and his cell phone. Which was now showing a feed of the surrounding area of the van. The doors were open, and there were no signs of anyone inside of them. The only lights are inside the house. That was very amateurish or just cocky. Even in a private neighborhood like this, someone could see the lights in the distance, and a creepy van with its doors wide open in an area supposedly uninhabited surely would send off red flags. That was something to work with, though. I smiled at the small hope.

I leaned over as his screen flashed through several programs at lightning speed, "What are you doing?" I asked, trying to make heads or tails of what he was doing. He pushed my head away from his screen. "Well, I decided I needed to give us some sort of fighting chance. These newer neighborhoods have drones all over them to help with construction. I hacked into one, and that's how you see what's on my cellphone. "You can do that?" I asked, dumbstruck. "Sure, most things are pretty easy once you realize nothing is built these days to keep people out of them. Understand that the internet was never built with security in mind. So, once you know a few certain things—it's not that hard to get what you need done," he said calmly.

I nodded at that, "So—hey, my printer..." I started before he cut me off, "I'm not your Gen Z nephew or tech support. Call someone else, man," he replied, not taking his eyes off the screen. "Sure sounds like a tech support dude. Even smell like one," I mumbled.

He glanced up at me on that one. I looked down, sniffing my shirt, and about gagged from the smell of iron and who knows what else from the last day or so. He had me there, that was for sure. "So what are you going to do with that drone? I am pretty sure they will see it coming, and unless you have the idea to put a bomb on it or something, I don't see how much eyes in the sky will help us," I stated.

"Seriously? You don't see the use of an army of flying cameras?" he asked incredulously.

I shrugged my shoulders at that one—"Yeah, okay, but we don't have an army—you have what one?"

He looked up from the computer and smiled wide. "Oh no, man, I have loads more," he said, flipping his computer around. On his screen were dozens of small video feeds showing all over the house that had its lights on.

"Those are all for construction?" I asked, not believing that he could have done this so quickly. "Yup, modern buildings, man. Supersites like this probably have even more—and in fact, they do. Just that most of them were actually put away. Most of them were left right inside the empty buildings here. Speaking of that, these houses aren't empty. If I was a betting man, this being the Mayor's properties—he probably has all sorts of crap tucked away in these houses," he said flatly.

I took that in, "So we have eyes in the skies now. Can you get me eyes on the inside?" I asked him. "Let me see what I can do; I only need to get a picture of the router. They most likely didn't change their default passwords," he said.

"Wait, you change yours?" I asked, feeling embarrassed. He glanced up at me with a sideways look, and I stopped talking. "I hate computer people," I mumbled. "Yeah, well, get locked out of your email, and I am your guy. Trying to explain the art of password security to the average Joe—well, it might be easier to teach a monkey," he said.

"Hey now," we both laughed for a moment. It hurt to laugh, and I gripped my side. Larry hadn't noticed. I felt guilty for that. I wouldn't have made it this far without his help. "Say, man, just so you know—I wouldn't have been able to do this without you. For whatever it's worth, I am glad you're my friend in all of this," I stated, moving my hand toward him.

He eyed it for only a second before taking it into his grip. "Man, you're impressed by my computer skills? I'm blown away by yours—this is crazy, Billy Dan. But, if we are friends, when were you going to tell me about you being shot?" he asked, taking his hands off the keys.

I winced at that, feeling guilty for not telling my friend. "I'm sorry, man, this was my—"I started, and he waved me off. "Look, dude, we've worked together for a while now. I've never met someone who tried so hard to keep his word, even on small things like promising to help some old lady take her bags to the curve. Or weird little boys that kept playing in dumpsters," he stated, trailing off for a moment as we both thought of Jacob.

"But honestly, man, you aren't a machine. As insane as you are, you can't save the world on your own. None of us can do anything on our own, dude; I used my computer skills for bad. I ended up working the morning shift on a dump truck with an undercover Superman. As amazing of a ride as this has been—if you told me you could kill a crocodile with one arm, I might believe you. Seriously, though, Superman needed help from time to time. We need to get Rosemary out here again; she will know what to do with that. Is it that bad? Let me see it," he stated, moving his hand towards me. I shot him a look, and he dropped his hand.

I regarded him for a moment and sighed, "Neither one of us can do too much about it anyways," I mumbled, lifting my shirt to show the wound. It was bleeding nearly nonstop. The back of my shirt was stuck to the exit wound. It seemed to bleed more as I uncovered the wound, showing about a dime-sized entry hole. It was festering red and poured out blood as if it were a water faucet. Larry hissed at the sight. "That—looks awful, man," he stated. I nodded. He paused momentarily before continuing and leaning back into his seat. He gripped the bridge of his nose for a long moment, pushing up his square-shaped glasses.

"I suppose you don't want to call Rosemary? You know she's been texting nonstop since the church raid," he stated, looking at me.

I nodded, "Think you can find something to help me with this though?" I asked, feeling guilty. I had yet to find out where my phone was. Rosemary had always been there for me. Here, I was bringing her into this all again. She had been there at my lowest; she would be here now if I allowed her.

Larry was working fast as I sat in the seat, suddenly feeling lightheaded as the excitement wore down. He was digging around in the back seat when he came out with a pack. He unzipped it and pulled out a medical kit. I arched an eyebrow at him, "Next, you're going to tell me you were a failed doctor before a porn addict," I said flatly.

"Nope, just really good at looking things up, and I play a lot of video games." He pulled apart a big group of bandages and a packet with the words "quick cloth" written across it. "You do know how to use that, right?" I asked urgently as he had a bottle of isoporthin alcohol in the other hand. "I read the instructions," he said calmly. "When did you—"I started and screamed in surprise as he dosed the wound with the alcohol. I set forward, and he did the same to my back. Next, he tore the quick cloth apart and poured it into my front wound. Shoving bandages into my hands and telling me to hold over my wound. I did as he said, wincing as he repeated the process to the back. He went back to his bag and fished around until he came out with a roll of duct tape.

He shrugged, "It's better than nothing," I nodded as I helped him wrap it around my body. "This should hopefully get us through the next part. Hopefully, you don't bleed out before we get you to a hospital," He said, fishing a thick wrap of tape around my side. I winced and fought the urge not to groan from it.

"Thanks, Larry—for everything," I stated. He nodded, "I'm not done yet—Rosemary said there's a town hall meeting going on with a lot of the parents," he started.

"Larry, don't."

He held up a hand, cutting me off, "Dude, she's going to help. She's on her way now. She got the kids to Gen. In fact, I think we need to tell Gen what's going on now. You can't do this on your own; hell, you don't even have a loaded gun," he stated calmly, fingers flying across his keys.

"When did you text them?" I asked. "Dude, you know email is a thing, right? Everyone uses it these days," he said.

I nodded along, feeling very old and really in need of a break from all this electronic crap. A minute or so later, he shouted, "Done!" he gleamed from over his computer. Exasperated, I asked, "What is done, Larry? Find the password to your online messaging club about nerds and nerdy computer things?" I joked. He didn't even dignify me with a response to that one.

"What did you do, man? Come on, we don't have all night—well, morning now, "I looked out the window, seeing the slow signs of dusk peeping out over the clouds. It would be a beautiful sunrise; under the thick blankets of the dark was a bright orange rising like a fire lifting the night sky. I suddenly wanted to be home, watching the sunset with Zodi. Just being with her— watching this sunrise wherever she was. I hoped she was at peace; I hoped she was happy. That would be far better than here. Not bleeding to death in a garbage truck, about to take down a corrupt Mayor and possible pedos at this point. Not people, I corrected myself. They were monsters—demons. Any other words were not adept enough to describe them.

The fire inside me roared once more. I had to keep that anger inside for just a little bit longer. I only needed it to save the kids—after that, I could let it go. I kept my thoughts on the sunrises with her for a bit longer. They were the happiest moments of my life. Whatever mistakes I had made with her, made in life—I had paid for those. Now I was about the works, planting the seeds that would grow into fruits. "And those kids were going to be able to plant some seeds of their own," I stated.

"What?" Larry asked, looking flabbergasted. I shrugged, "Show me what you have done," I stated as he hesitated for a second, nodded, and then flipped his computer around. There was a live feed of a crowded gym, the local high school where town hall meetings were held. I recognized a lot of the faces. Most were on our route; most were the parents whose kids had been taken. I could see the young girl who had helped us in the crowd. Her mother was holding her so guarded that I think she could have taken down a bear. Her father looked rougher than me, his hair tinged as if he had stuck a fork in a light socket. The only police I saw were Gen and a few other officers. I recognized them, her friends. Probably the only ones she could trust. I trusted that. Like I trusted the father from his look.

His domineering screamed for anyone to challenge him. Good, I believed he hadn't been the one that had taken his daughter. A part of me hated to even wonder what had led to her being taken; family is more commonly to be blamed than is talked about. I let out a breath on that one. I didn't know what had led to her being taken. Or any of the other kids in this town. I shuddered to think how many, considering the mound of clothes at the church. However, I knew who had done it. And I knew it was my job to stop them.

Larry turned up the volume; the parents were yelling at the cops who were at the front of the crowd. The police chief was nowhere to be found. I only hoped that Gen had gotten something from the laptop—that maybe some of the evidence hadn't been destroyed by the fire at the church. That most likely was just ashes, ashes over all the dead. The parents deserved to know that they deserved to fight for their children. I thought, "Larry, is any of this going out to the internet?" I asked him.

He smiled mischievously, "Oh yeah, and then some. I have it going out to everyone—especially police in the state. I'm not sure how far this goes, but I had to have faith that this had been stopped. Or at least slowed down. That justice would be served,".

I nodded, "Good, make sure none of it can be taken down. Promise me that you will help any of these parents get that evidence out there and to the world. There's no telling who's a good cop now and who isn't. I suspect most are—it only takes one person to destroy evidence, though," I declared.

"Yeah, you're right, Billy Dan. I imagine we will have our hands filled once this is over, but I've been thinking a lot about what you said. I think we will have to face the consequences of our actions. We have to—I don't know how we will get out of this, though—this is wild," he brushed his hands through his hair and blew out his lips.

I nodded, "One step at a time, we need to get the kids first. Keep all of this electronically stored. Can you do all your drone stuff without your laptop?" I asked him, gesturing towards his equipment.

He looked around, "Yeah—I'm using my cell phone as a hotspot, I just need that and my laptop, and we are good to go. Once we get inside—I can get set up somewhere—not sure what's going to happen in there..." he trailed off nervously.

"Just stick behind me, man. We will be fine," I stated. "Hey, switch seats with me—I can drive; you need to get your computer stuff going," I said.

"Oh yeah, good, point," Larry said, sliding his laptop into his bag. I picked up his cell phone and placed it in his hands. He started to try and move past me—I gestured towards my side. "Right—my bad. One sec, man," he stated, opening the driver's door and exiting the truck. In a quick motion, I moved toward the driver's seat and popped the driver's door, hitting Larry and knocking him to the ground. He landed in a heap. I felt awful about this, but I started the truck and kicked it into drive, heading down the hill.

Chapter 94

In the rear view, I could see Larry getting up with his pack and running after the truck but failing to keep up with the massive machine. A moment later, my earpiece squeaked to life, "What the ever living heck, Billy Dan! Get back here, man, what are you doing?" he screamed into my earpiece. "Stop screaming into the mic, Larry!" I yelled back.

"Turn that around, Billy Dan; what are you doing—"I stopped him quickly.

"Larry, you're a good man. I'm proud to have had you on my team during all this—don't waste your life. You get everything to the right people. I believe in you; blame it all on me—tell them I am the one that came up with stealing the truck. I doubt it will even be reported, the cops will have other problems. It doesn't matter; blame it on me. Tell them you tried to stop me, whatever you have to do. You can do more good outside of a cell. I have to finish this—Larry. I have no choice—that's what I am; I will not be stopped until my race is finished. I have to fight the good fight; I have to finish my race," I stated calmly, tearing out my earpiece. Larry could do this; the kid had done above and beyond anything I could have imagined. The right people are in the right place at the right time. I smiled as I floated down the hill, snapping on my seat belt. I headed to the overlook above the one house with its lights on.

The ledge was coming up over the hill. I wasn't sure how far the drop-down was, as I felt the thousands of pounds of dump trucks fly off a hill towards the nice house below. "This is really going to hurt," I screamed right before the car smashed into the walls of the house with the force of a rock slide.

Chapter 95

I sat staring at the cross tucked away in the center pulpit area. It was a simple thing, heavy and laden with many 2x4s. Yet, it seemed like a sturdy piece of wood, if nothing else. What was the point of it all? Why did I even care about some empty-shaped pieces of wood? What Rosemary and I discussed these days could have made more sense. It had taken two years of us being together before I finally went with her to a Church. Just saying it felt weird. I leaned back in the pew, blowing out my lips as Rosemary stopped next to me, "Wanna come downstairs—they have pizza. Come say hey to everyone," she gestured behind her to the hallway. I could hear cheery voices carrying out from somewhere unseen.

I sighed, "Nah, I think I will stay up here for a little while," I stated.

"Shoot," she replied before stopping, turning, and reaching into her bag. She pulled out a black leather Bible and pressed it into my hands before I could protest.

I looked at it, and the words "William Daniel" were edged on the front. "What's this for? You didn't have to get me anything," I said, perplexed by the whole thing. "I didn't get you anything, Billy Dan. That was all God's doing," she said matter-of-factly.

She started to leave before I touched one of her hands. "Wait, Rosemary, quick question,"

She nodded, and I asked, "What's the point? What's the point of that cross?" I asked her.

She stiffened and became suddenly sober, "Read it and find out—it will all make sense one day. Read it cover to cover," she replied, walking out of the room. I turned back to the empty room. Just me and the cross—so many pews. None of it made any sense to me. "I guess it can't hurt to read a few pages," I mumbled, opening the Bible to the first line, "In the beginning..."

Chapter 96

I heard once that courage is contagious, but virtue is bold. Right now—I think I was just crazy. And my head hurt. Everything hurt. Dust was flying everywhere—I had just enough time in my daze to see several figures appear out of the fog and raise their pistols. I dropped long ways in the floorboard of the truck as quickly as I could in the front seat as bullets screamed towards me. The racket was ear-piercing, and metal screeched, sending gas and steam from every direction. Sparks shot out like shooting stars racing across the night sky. I prayed—bullets kept coming. I felt the becoming all too familiar puncture of a bullet hole in my good leg. Another in my shoulder and my bad arm. I muffled a scream of pain; explosions of agony rocked my body.

I was dying—there was no changing that now. I gritted my teeth. I had a job to do, and I would see it through. I was going to keep my word. Jacob may have been gone, but I would rescue these kids for him. For all the children. I was going to do this, Father, give me strength. I spitted up blood—and I bit my tongue in fear. My teeth chattered so much that I was worried I might have chipped a tooth.

Magazines fell to the ground, and the unmistakable click of fresh ones loading into the guns seemed to multiply. A moment later, the door at my feet was yanked open. Strong hands yanked me out hard onto the ground. I landed in a heap, the pain causing me to lose focus as I saw stars. "Give—me—strength—Father," I gasped as pain racked my body. Another strong pair of hands yanked me to my feet—my prosthetic leg finally gave out and fell to the ground uselessly as they pulled me around to the front of the truck.

The crash into the house had pushed the front in entirely—the engine block was utterly exposed. Somehow still in place. There were more bullet holes than I could count.

Not that it could do me any good—I couldn't count my fingers if I tried. Stay focused, Billy Dan, stay focused. I cried out from the pain, and I stifled it back in—grunting. A man had one of my arms on each side. They pulled me to the center of the destroyed room. Pieces of debris littered every inch of the room. Drywall, steel, nails, and even part of a gutter jolted at odd angles as one of the smoking tires from the dump truck lay nearby. Farewell, brave truck; you served very well. I lamented for a moment. I was going to go the same way—wasn't I? Yeah, I was going to die. This was it—I was going to die... A wave of cold permeated throughout my whole body. Oh please—"No". That was all I heard—all I felt, the storm stopped. The fear vanished.

I was back in the game; these clowns had no idea what was coming.

Chapter 97

"What the ever living—" sneered the Mayor. "Is that the garbage man again?" The Mayor joked, gesturing to the other two men flanked opposite him. Their body language was tense, but they lowered their guns. Good. "He looks like garbage now—must take his job seriously—you're supposed to throw it away, man, not become it," he stated, spitting at me.

I looked at the man, sizing him up. His watery blue-green eyes are the color of washed dollar bills. His hair was slicked back, a well-kept row of gray and black sprinkled throughout. He held himself high and straight. Along with a long, hooked nose. Angled cheeks that could have cut a loaf of bread in half. Capped off by a perfect white smile that did not stretch to his eyes. Hair-gel Nazi, if there ever was one.

Why Melanie was the true believer of the operation—a predator that deluded herself into thinking she was somehow doing this for some greater good—the Mayor was a more traditional bad guy. He was in it for the money and the power. I didn't doubt if it was also for other more nefarious motives. Why would either of them do this? I would never understand or want to know.

As if he read my mind, his fake smile was replaced with a snare of pure carnage. "it's your fault again. Again and again. I am tired of running into you, garbage man," he growled. One of his goons chimed in, "Boss, what do you want us to do with him?" the goon to his right asked. The Mayor seemed to think for a moment, then spoke with a toothy grin, "Burn him just like he did to all our money," he snarled. The four men laughed; I could also feel their anger towards me. It must have been their money as well. It makes sense; even thugs have a payroll.

One of the thugs spoke at that moment, "I have an idea, boss." He chimed in. The Mayor tore his glance away from me just for a moment, "You have an idea?" he laughed. "Sure—what's your idea, you block?" he joked.

The goon cleared his throat and—for someone so massive that he must have been rented from a bodybuilder goon gym with the express understanding that he could only work between his good duties actually averted his gaze and looked down. Each of the four men, I realized, was thicker than the Mayor and myself combined muscle-wise. I realized that it keeps them in line by putting them down. So much for the nice guy acting in all his awful commercials. He was the type to kiss a baby in his campaign aids; the thought made me sick. Monsters didn't need strength to be monsters—they just needed to know how to use their fangs and claws.

"Let's inject him with the TRIP. Burn him in front of the kid. Who knows what he will see in front of him during all of it" The goon looked up with a genuine smile. His expression froze me to the core. He looked far too happy with himself. He got off in pain.

That's when some of his words hit me like a ton of bricks; he didn't say kids—he said," kid." I panicked around the room as one of his goons left the room. The Mayor stared daggers into me; he licked his lips like I was a piece of meat for the sharks. Which was fair enough at the moment, I thought. Still, though, what did he mean, kid?

My question was soon answered a moment or two later, along with how they planned to burn me. They pulled Jacob out from an unknown part of the house. His jet-black hair was whipped in crazy directions, and he had a far too thin face for any child to have. My heart skipped several beats—Jacob was alive. I mustered up a smile and started to cry. Thank you, Father, for what you have done here. Thank you.

Then I noticed as the goon dragged the boy by his shoulders, his loose shirt constricted tight under the iron grip of an ape-man that his other hand had a red gasoline jog. Well, that explains why they said burned, I thought.

Chapter 98

One problem at a time, I thought. I was in good hands. Seeing Jacob, though— that surged something back in me—I was going to get that boy out. "Jacob," I gasped, along with some blood coming out of my mouth. I wiped the blood on my shirt sleeve, the two goons almost virtually ignoring me as they looked amused. You could have six arms or be the fastest and strongest man in the world. But, if you weren't watching your surroundings—you were going to die. I noted as I glanced at the two bigger men holding me. Searching for a weakness, searching for something.

The Mayor wasn't underestimating me, though—he had made that mistake already tonight. He glared with an even deeper frown, and I was sure his eyebrows were soon going to reach his mouth. "Watch him, boys—he's a scrappy one. Don't let him fool you," he stated towards me as his grin returned a moment later. "Though, he's not going anywhere this time. This isn't a stupid movie—I will just watch you die this time. And in front of the kid, no less," He gestured as the big man moved Jacob in front of the Mayor. Jacob fought, swinging his fists and kicking hard. The big man holding the reared back hit him, sending him to the floor. The Mayor just smiled, "Pick the boy up. That's no way to treat the son of a police officer," he stated.

I opened my mouth in horror to that one—he knew about Gen. "That's right, he smirked; you didn't think I would find out everything there was to know about the officer dumb enough to look into my insurance company— by proxy me. Find out what made her tick. Find out about her many kids and one dumb garbage man who just couldn't take out the trash," he sneered.

I shoot back, "That's waste manager, to you. And you're wrong again; I

340

am here to take out the trash. And from the look of things, not a moment too soon," I roared, puffing out my chest. Instantly, everything hurt. It was worth it; that was my best line all night.

The Mayor curled his lips, showing a lot of teeth. That a boy Billy Dan, rattle the shark right before he eats you, I thought as the man's glare was like looking into a green void. It was as if I was walking in an old forest, and then a massive hole opened up to a bottomless pit—full of darkness and with no light. I feared if I kept looking into the Mayor's eyes, I would fall into that hole, but seeing Jacob again—meant my prayers had been answered. There was no stopping now. I wasn't strong enough on my own to fight against such darkness. I wasn't on my own, though.

Instead of digging for what would be a great comeback, I waited. The goons holding me still weren't paying enough attention. The Mayor responded after staring me down for a moment later. "Get him ready," he snapped to the other man behind him. That man took the gasoline can from the man holding Jacob. He was having a lot of trouble with the kid. I was admiring the way he fought. The big man hit him again. I was going to make it my mission to beat that man once I was free.

The Mayor went on, "This is going to be a good night, boys. We got that officer's kid. We also get the son of a gun that burned our money. Burned your money and stole my product. Where is it, garbage man? I know you were working with Melanie. You had to be working with that crazy cult freak. Where is my product? I might spare your life—I might even give you back this kid. It's harder to take care of the little hoodlums. Don't worry, though; there's a never-ending amount of clientele. Never-ending number of kids in this world," he tilted his head and laughed. The man was losing his mind.

He had snapped under the pressure. I wonder if he was at the top of the food chain or not. There was no telling with these kinds of things. Monsters exist in the shadows—the dumber ones come out in the light from time to time. It was simple, really—there would always be a bigger fish. I had my doubts that the Mayor was the big fish. Perhaps there was someone above him—someone that was pressuring him. If nothing else, everything I had done would cause problems for the Mayor and would hurt whoever was pulling his strings. That was the truth of the matter.

One man can't defeat all the darkness. Only one man was ever able to do that—instead, what the average man could do was carry the fire. Carry the fire—to fight no matter what happens. Do the right thing—making sure that the fire stays lit. I needed to get Jacob out of here.

I glanced around me again; there wasn't much I could do in my state. I was running out of steam, and it would be five-on-one. I just needed to keep thinking. There had to be another way; if I could sacrifice myself, maybe Jacob could get a run on it. Where he would go—I wasn't sure of that. That would give him a chance, at least, to get away. That was more than enough for me. I gritted my teeth and spoke as delicately as I could to Jacob, "Hey buddy, are you doing alright?"

He regarded me for a long moment as if I had spoken to him in a foreign language. His eyes started to water, and mine also started to tear up. "Billy Dan... help me," he stated simply. He was always smart for his age. A tough kid ever since I had met him. That was heartbreaking to witness. No child deserved to go through such awfulness. Getting him out of here would be a start to correcting that. The scars from this weren't going to go away any time soon for him. Some healthy distance and time from this place was a start.

Without trusting my voice to speak, I nodded. God, please get him out of here. A big goon appeared in front of me, pulling out the big canister of gasoline. He tilted the contents of the can over me. The smell was strong, and I gagged, trying to keep my mouth closed as a couple of gallons of gas poured over me. One of the men holding me let go of my left shoulder, shouting, "Hey, watch where you're pouring that, man," he shook his leg out, spilling drops of the gas onto the ground. The big man with the gas can just shrugged his shoulders. The other man holding my other shoulder now switched to holding both my shoulders. I spit up some gas, frowning at the taste. It seemed to be getting into every inch of my body, and the fumes were causing my eyes to burn. The man who had poured the gas can switched to his other pocket, producing a syringe of neon-glowing TRIP. I shuddered at the thought of that stuff again. If it had been anything like last time, this was going to be Hell. Time had slowed down when that first hit had broken my skin. I still felt the after-effects—this would be an awful way to go.

This was it, really; the clock had run out. The man with the gas can put down the gas can and produced a zippo—his sadistic smile stretching across a pair of broken and chapped lips—the fire from his zippo showing gleams of sweat on a shaved head. Looking every bit like the monster he was. I wondered what drove a man to become something like that. I suppose it all came down to our choices at the end of the day—the choices time and time again to never look back. To never admit one's bad behavior. A complete and total love of self. At that moment, I felt sorry for him. I felt sorry for the man who was about to kill me and did who knows what else. He was a monster—that was for sure. But a beast who would never realize the extent of his failings will take that with him to the grave.

I glanced over at Jacob as he struggled against the man holding him. His eyes completely tearing up. "Look away, Jacob," I said calmly. Accepting on some level what was about to happen. Oddly calm—this was it. In the end, I failed him. That's when I felt the voice from within. It didn't speak this time; I knew there was always a way. Even in the darkest of storms, there was always a chance to turn it around. To fight against the darkness and do something more for others. That calm made me focus as the needle came near my face, the zippo in his other hand. The flame moved towards my face as he brought the zippo closer, licking the air towards me like some kind of tongue of a hungry pig. I stayed focused as it came closer when one of the goons spoke, "Hey, don't forget to stick him with the TR—"he started before I slapped the lighter out of the man with the needle hands; it flew onto the leg of the goon that had gas on his leg. While gasoline doesn't go up as quickly as people would think, it does when aided by the material in the man's pants. It shot up his legs as if it was directed by the fire. Quickly going to his waist in a moment. The man with the zippo was stunned; I twisted the needle out of his hands as the goon behind me completely let me go to help his counterpart.

I followed the needle down as my strength faded fast—I stuck the needle into the man's groin—pushing the plunger to the end of the tube. The man screamed out in pain as the TRIP took effect quickly. I fell to the ground. The man with the needle in his groin twitched on the ground, screaming a moment later. Behind me, I could feel the heat as one man tried putting out the fire on the other man. Completely forgetting that the gas was spilled everywhere. Soon, they were both screaming.

The Mayor and the last goon stood dumbfounded. I wasted no time and screamed at Jacob on the ground, "Run, Jacob!" I cried as my voice broke. The boy hesitated for a moment before running out behind me. I wasn't sure where he was going. I stayed focused on the Mayor and his goon, who shook off the moment before returning his attention to me. He snarled; there was no confidence or joyful malice. He just was ready to kill. He pulled out his pistol when a blue light showed on his face.

He winced as white, red, and blue lights flashed inside the house, overtaking nearly every wall. "Boss!" screamed one of the goons. The Mayor stood there staring daggers into me. I was done, though; the last of my strength was spent keeping my head on the floor.

I could tell he debated shooting me, but the police lights brought him back to reality. He turned, and both ran out the back of the house. "The rats flee the sinking ship," I muttered, laying my head back down.

A moment later, Larry came jogging into the house out of breath. "Billy Dan!" he screamed, sliding behind me and picking my head up. I blinked as he pulled me up, "Larry—what are you doing here? You need to go, man—the cops," I started. He shook his head laughing, but it looked painful, "That's the drones, man—they have all sorts of lights on them. I told you— why did you have to go by yourself? I got the whole thing filmed to the parents. There won't be any hiding this now," he said.

I sat with that for a moment. I was feeling so lightheaded now. "That's good..."

I still had a mission; I still needed to finish. Still waiting. "Larry-Jacob," I said through chattering teeth. He nodded his head, his glasses fogging up as smoke was around us, "He's good, Billy Dan. He's going to be safe,".

I nodded my head again. "Good—Larry, get the rest of the kids. Jacob will know where they are. They can't get away with this," I wanted to gesture, but I couldn't. Larry nodded his head. "Sure, Billy Dan. I can do that," his eyes started to water, spilling over.

I looked past my friend—on the roof, as the smoke rose, there was a spot in the corner of the room that remained smoke-free—the flames staying away as if an invisible force kept it that way.

"That makes sense," I stated.

Larry looked around, "What makes sense? What do you mean, Billy Dan?" he almost begged.

I turned, looking at him, "Never mind that, Larry. Just get the kids safe,". He nodded.

"I want to go home," I said gently.

"We will get you home. Hold on, Billy Dan," he said as he started to pick me up.

I shook my head at him—not able to see Larry anymore—all the pain going away. The worry was gone. I have fought the good fight, finished the race, and kept the faith.

"I am going home,".

About the Author

Jonathan Blazer lives in the Upstate of SC, writing and taking care of animals on a small homestead. He can be reached for any inquiries at jblazerwriter@ yahoo.com

Also by Jonathan C. Blazer

Out of the Night

Like a fair flower that wilts in the winter, we all dream of the bliss of spring. "My name is James, and I was a computer guy all my life. I was the best in the world at solving problems. I had a loving wife and a beautiful daughter in every sense of the word. They were mine, and I was theirs. My name is James. I don't want to remember anymore. I am a ghost of the man I used to be. I—we—are the ghosts of what we used to be." James is your average everyday father; he loves his wife, he loves his daughter, he's happy with his lot in life. All of that will change in an instant, thrusting James into a never-ending battle for his sanity—a war for his soul. "A father protects his family; he will lose it all for his family." That's what James tells himself as his city falls apart and ghosts become the new population in his once proud home. To live in a world that is quickly fading into shades of apparitions; while cradling the lines of what it means to be alive: in a world that has become a ghost, will he either stop at nothing to save his family or become a memory along with the rest of the world.

Beyond These Fences

BEFORE YOU CAN DEFEAT THE WORLD'S EVIL, YOU MUST CONFRONT THE BEAST WITHIN.

Brothers Avi and Zevi agree that the Nazis must be stopped, but they disagree on the methods they should use to achieve victory. Both men still struggle with the trauma from their experiences in the camps, but must also protect their new family. In addition to the conflict on the best way to fight the evil of the Nazis, Avi deals with a monster inside; the wolf. Can he find the strength to confront both his brother and the beast, to keep the light of hope burning in the most tumultuous of storms? If you enjoy a compelling and thrilling story of those who fight monsters and their past, then you'll love this novel that is filled with a combination of wounds that will not heal, hope that will not die, and wounded people trying not to hurt each other on the path to redemption. This novel, which can be enjoyed as a stand alone story, is Book 2 in The Longest Night series.

Made in the USA
Middletown, DE
13 November 2024

64146060R00213